SO-BNU-353

ROBIN McKINLEY

DRAGONHAVEN

ACE BOOKS, NEW YORK

THE BERKLEY PUBLISHING GROUP
Published by the Penguin Group
Penguin Group (USA) Inc.
375 Hudson Street, New York, New York 10014, USA
Penguin Group (Canada), 90 Eglinton Avenue East, Suite 700, Toronto, Ontario M4P 2Y3, Canada
(a division of Pearson Penguin Canada Inc.)
Penguin Books Ltd., 80 Strand, London WC2R 0RL, England
Penguin Group Ireland, 25 St. Stephen's Green, Dublin 2, Ireland (a division of Penguin Books Ltd.)
Penguin Group (Australia), 250 Camberwell Road, Camberwell, Victoria 3124, Australia
(a division of Pearson Australia Group Pty. Ltd.)
Penguin Books India Pvt. Ltd., 11 Community Centre, Panchsheel Park, New Delhi—110 017, India
Penguin Group (NZ), 67 Apollo Drive, Rosedale, North Shore 0632, New Zealand
(a division of Pearson New Zealand Ltd.)
Penguin Books (South Africa) (Pty.) Ltd., 24 Sturdee Avenue, Rosebank, Johannesburg 2196,
South Africa

Penguin Books Ltd., Registered Offices: 80 Strand, London WC2R 0RL, England

This is a work of fiction. Names, characters, places, and incidents either are the product of the author's imagination or are used fictitiously, and any resemblance to actual persons, living or dead, business establishments, events, or locales is entirely coincidental. The publisher does not have any control over and does not assume any responsibility for author or third-party websites or their content.

DRAGONHAVEN

An Ace Book / published by arrangement with the author

PRINTING HISTORY
G. P. Putnam's Sons hardcover edition / September 2007
Ace mass-market edition / October 2008

ISBN: 978-0-441-01643-3

ACE
Ace Books are published by The Berkley Publishing Group,
a division of Penguin Group (USA) Inc.,
375 Hudson Street, New York, New York 10014.
ACE and the "A" design are trademarks belonging to Penguin Group (USA) Inc.

PRINTED IN THE UNITED STATES OF AMERICA

10 9 8 7 6 5 4 3 2 1

"An exercise in fantasy subjected to the rigors of science, a close psychological portrait of human and alien minds, and a helluva good read." —*Locus*

"McKinley offers a seamless, believable world, a self-deprecating narrator whose voice never hits a false note, and a poignant message." —*VOYA*

"Robin McKinley has built an admirable career on taking familiar fairy-tale tropes, or long-loved stories, and skillfully combining the architecture of wonder with convincing, realistic detail so that the reader feels she can live inside the story. McKinley has never settled for doing the same thing over and over, but with each new book has experimented with voice, form, and tone, as well as character and plot . . . [*Dragonhaven*] is powerful, absorbing, and exquisitely rendered. McKinley makes those dragons real." —*SF Site*

"Compelling." —*Booklist*

Praise for Robin McKinley

ROSE DAUGHTER

"[A] heady mix of fairy tale, magic, and romance . . . dazzling . . . has the power to exhilarate." —*Publishers Weekly*

"This luxuriant retelling of the story of the Beauty and the Beast . . . is full of asides and surprises, and is suffused with obsession for the rose and thorn as flora, metaphor, and symbol . . . The story is full of silvery images." —*Kirkus Reviews*

"Every sentence and every occurrence seems infused by magic. I will keep this book. I will reread it time and again; it has earned its place as one of my odd coterie of bedside companions." —*Fantasy & Science Fiction*

continued . . .

"An enormously powerful novel . . . dreamlike, urgent, inexplicable . . . Robin McKinley has created a world where nightmare and hope exist side by side."—Patricia A. McKillip

"I did so much enjoy Robin McKinley's *Deerskin*."
—Anne McCaffrey

THE OUTLAWS OF SHERWOOD

"Takes us back to those wonderful first meetings between Robin and his followers. So strong is the power of this story that it catches us all over again."   —*The New York Times*

"Praiseworthy . . . McKinley has done the hard work of reimagining a Sherwood without nostalgia, and she's nothing if not thorough."   —*The Washington Post*

"A great read."   —*Chicago Tribune*

"Enriched with entrancing details of life in the forest, graced with a neat pair of satisfying love stories, and culminating in a couple of rousing battles, McKinley's Robin should be delighting readers for years to come."
—*Kirkus Reviews* (starred review)

SUNSHINE

"*Sunshine* is a gripping, funny, page-turning, pretty much perfect work of magical literature that exists more or less at the unlikely crossroads of *Chocolat*, *Interview with the Vampire*, *Misery*, and the tale of Beauty and the Beast."
—Neil Gaiman

"A smart, funny tale of suspense and romance."
—*San Francisco Chronicle*

"*Sunshine* takes everything we have always known about the menacing eroticism of pale men with sharp teeth, and throws it up into the air."   —*Time Out*

To Holly, Hazel and Rowan

CHAPTER ONE

I keep having these conversations with Dad.

I'm at my computer. He says, "What are you doing?" I mutter something, because the screen has a lot of squiggles on it so he already knows what I'm doing.

"Have you started on it yet, Jake?"

"No," I say, probably more belligerently than I mean to. But we've had this conversation so *often*.

Dad sighs. "Jake, I know I'm nagging you. But it's important."

"So is the dictionary important!"

"It's not important to anyone but you if only you can read it," says Dad. I glare at him, because he knows that I know that he knows it *is* important. But that also it's an excuse.

"I don't know *how* to write it," I mutter. Like, just by the way, I *do* know how to write my dictionary. Which I don't either. In spite of the fancy graphics package.

"That doesn't matter. Just write it." He tries to make a joke. "Your spelling is pretty good."

"I don't know how—I can't make it a *story*!" I shout, or rather, I don't shout, I sort of hiss it through clenched teeth. I *want* to shout. "It's not . . . It doesn't have . . . There's no . . ." I can't think how to finish. I can't think how to *begin*.

"It doesn't have to be a story. It doesn't have to be anything. Just put down what happened. Don't call it anything."

Yeah, right. Make pizza without tomato sauce and mozzarella, just don't call it pizza and you'll be fine. What's the use of pizza without tomato sauce and mozzarella? Like

Alice said before she saw the White Rabbit: "What is the use of a book without pictures or conversations?" Although the pictures are covered really well elsewhere, and the new coffee-table, drop-it-on-your-foot-and-spend-the-rest-of-your-life-on-crutches art-book version is coming out soon. Text, I have to say, by some chucklehead *sensitive* type. Yuck. The thought of it is one of the things that's getting me going here finally. The sensitive version will probably be way too *much* like a story. A fairy tale.

But who *lives* a story, you know? With chapters and things. And as a fairy-tale hero if someone gave me a vorpal blade I'd probably stick it in my foot. Or get lost in the mimsy borogroves. Life is just one day after another, even when the days are really, really strange.

Dad looks at me. I look at him. We both know what we're both thinking. I prod a couple of keys and make the squiggles go squigglier.

"Just do the best you can," Dad says, really gently. "You're the only one who can tell it at all."

Yes. That's the awful thundering can't-get-around-it thing. I'm the only one who can tell you about Lois. And the only way I can tell Lois' story is through me. I feel like starting by saying, I'm not a crazed egomaniac! Really I'm not! I am a crazed Lois-iac. Joke. Sort of. But it's not only the freaking hard work of trying to write it all out coherently that is stopping me now. I don't want to go back there. I've got used to . . . like being able to look out windows again and not worry about what I might see.

Also a lot of the stuff that's about me is stuff I don't want to tell *anyone*. It's also a lot about *Dad* and me, and I don't want to tell those parts either, down on paper and everything, where he can read them. Which he will.

I may not know how to write my dictionary, but at least it's not *embarrassing*.

There's another problem (I should make a list): I don't remember every day as every day, as different from the day before and the day after. Sure, I kept notes—I kept lots and *lots* of notes—but I seem to have left a lot of stuff out. All the connecting bits. All the conversations. All the *sane* bits, if there were any sane bits. I was just trying to stay alive, those days, keep Lois and me alive. And I wasn't thinking in terms of needing to make a story out of it later on.

And I sure don't remember every conversation I've had in the last four years. I remember a few of them—the ones that really got to me for one reason or another—but mostly, who remembers? Not me. And I bet not you either.

I don't mean the ordinary, everyday ones you have a lot, like "How are you?" and "What's for dinner?" (and "I thought it was *your* turn to cook"). Those are easy. I mean the one-off ones. The ones why you're trying to write something someone else is going to read at all. So that why-you're-writing stuff is a lot of stuff you can't remember well enough to write.

There weren't many conversations anyway. Not a lot of he-saids and she-saids, or at least not till the end, and then they're *peculiar.*

But I'm going to try to tell the truth. Except for the parts I'm leaving out, because there's still stuff I'm just not going to tell you. Get used to it.

And then, okay, I've got this far, I'm not staring out the window, my fingers are on the keyboard, the first finger is wiggling over the first key for the first letter of the first word (whatever that is) . . . and then I stop all over again, because how do I get your attention? Not your newspaper-headline attention—your *real* attention. How do I tell you the stuff you need to know if you're going to understand what happened? Because there's really no point if I'm not trying to make you *understand* a little.

And, just by the way, who are *you*?

Dad and Martha say that there are a lot of people—a lot of you (is it going to be easier to think of you as *you*? Or is that going to weird me out even more?)—who don't know anything and will only be picking this up because the headlines have made you curious about the whole show and if I want to rave on a little as background that's probably okay and maybe even a good idea. I guess they figure if they get me raving they've won. They're probably right. So blame them. Although they did say rave *a little*.

It would be easier to start now and go backwards, but then you'd never understand. I'm going to have to start all those years ago, and I don't know how to feel like I felt before Lois, or how to get back there to tell the story the way it happened, so maybe you'll understand. At all. A little.

Mom should be here, reading this, and saying things like, "'Lois and I,' dear, not 'me and Lois.'" And telling me when it's "whom" and not "who." But she isn't. Mom is one of the reasons I don't want to write *any* of this. I keep wondering, would it have happened at all—would Lois have happened—if Mom was still here? If I hadn't been the right kind of nutcase? Was being a nutcase necessary?

Eventually I thought about Eleanor. She never worries about getting anybody's attention (and that "eventually" would really annoy her), or whether they're going to be interested, if she wants something. And there are always he-saids and she-saids when Eleanor is around. She-saids, anyway. Eleanor doesn't have the hugest sense of humor in the world about herself, but I think she'll get this one. That I'm going to start four and a half years ago, with her shouting at me. Also Eleanor shouting is very *rememberable*.

"JAKE!"

That's Eleanor. She has a great future as an alarm system. She's only seven, but she has precocious lungs.

"JAAAAAKE!"

I threw my window open. "I'm *coming*! Keep your hair on!"

She glared up at me. "You're *late*."

I looked at my watch. "I won't be late for another . . . two minutes."

"We'll be late by the time we get there!"

I closed my window, sighed, put my shoes on, and ran downstairs. Our apartment is at one end of the Institute, but nothing is very far from anything else. I flew by a group of tourists gaping at the *Draco* family charts that stand at the way into the diorama and the tiny movie theater, past the ticket booth and the door to the gift shop and café, waved at Peggy in the ticket booth as she said, "Jake, don't run," and was standing beside Eleanor in forty-five seconds. She hadn't finished glaring yet, and stomped off down the path that led to the zoo, barreling through the thickets of tourists like a cavalry charge. I followed.

Offer to hold Eleanor's hand? Not if you don't want it bitten off. Of course there are no highways for her to run across without looking both ways inside the park gates. The only vehicles that come in and out through the gates are our Rangers' jeeps, which were bought more for endurance than for speed, and from age and the effects of the surfaces they run on, tend to kind of lurch along. Our park tour buses crawl even slower so everyone has a chance to take lots of photos and go "oooh." They're solar powered and *can't* go any faster. Tourist cars and coaches stay in the parking lot outside. Even the garage for the staff's private vehicles is outside the gates. (This is not a major issue. If you work here, you probably can't afford a private vehicle.) And the nearest highway, with like more than two lanes, is fifty miles away, on the far side of Wilsonville.

This was Eleanor's first week being allowed to help out at the zoo, and she was a little crazed. *I* was a little crazed, because the grown-ups had decided that Martha was too young to mentor her but I was old enough. I'm not sure the Incredible Hulk is old enough to mentor Eleanor, and Martha is actually pretty good at it. I'm not. It would be okay once we got there, and in another week or two Eleanor should have calmed down a little (I hoped) but meanwhile at 1:55 every afternoon there was a small two-legged elephant trumpeting under my window.

A normal seven-year-old would be happy helping feed baby raccoons at the orphanage. Not Eleanor. Nobody comes to Smokehill for the raccoons, and she wants to be where more of the action is.

I don't really mind Eleanor though. In some ways she's

restful. She's too young to remember my mom very well, or Snark. If you think that sounds really sicko, you try being twelve years old when your mother dies and having everyone around you looking at you and thinking of her and feeling sorry for you. It doesn't help that I look like her. Right after she died—right after we knew she was dead—and people started looking at me like that, I started spending a lot of time in front of the mirror, rubbing my cheeks with my fingers. Well, maybe it was more like scratching my cheeks with my fingers, because I started leaving marks. Dad asked me why. I said I was hoping my beard would come in early. I didn't say, Because then people won't look at me like I'm my mother.

Dad was almost the only person who didn't look at me in that new way, but then he was the only other person who was missing her as much as I was. Dad said, "Oh." He didn't ask me why I wanted my beard to come in early. Maybe he guessed. Dad has a beard which he keeps short and tidy so he can make a good impression on the tourists, and the grant administrators. He scratched his own hairy cheeks for a minute and added, "You may not if it does." I stopped scratching my cheeks. And now it was two and a half years later and my beard still hadn't started coming in, but people didn't look at me so much like that any more so I could wait.

Okay, Eleanor and I usually were about a minute late, and Martha was usually there first, lining out the buckets and checking that the labels were all still legible. If anybody got the wrong grub there'd be trouble, from Eric if nothing else. Trouble from Eric is *way* more than enough however.

"Hiya," she'd say.

"Huh," Eleanor'd say, really offhand and casual. "What've we got?"

It's quieter inside the big shed where the food lives—no tourists. That's another of the big draws for Eleanor, of course, being seen by a lot of *grown-ups* to be going somewhere they can't. I no longer cared about that aspect of it (but if nagged I would admit that I remembered when I did) but just getting away from them—the tourists—was always good. It's a weird life, living at Smokehill, where there's all that gorgeous, amazing, wonderful *empty* (I mean *human* empty) space just behind you, so to speak, but you live in like this tiny permanently besieged encampment where you have to kind of take a deep breath and bolt for it when you go from one cranny of no-tourists to the next.

I don't particularly want to because it makes me feel more of a mutant than ever but I suppose I should emphasize that life at Smokehill *is* kind of bizarre. Certainly us kids were always being told (or asked) that wasn't the way we lived *peculiar*. Uh, pardon me, but I was born here. So I didn't like being asked (or told). Other kids were the worst. They said things like, No *pizza*? Like you might say, No *oxygen*? Of course we have pizza. But no, we couldn't call up the local Super Pizza to deliver, that's true.

Eleanor wouldn't touch the bugs and beetles, and the bigger live (or soon-to-be-knocked-on-the-head) stuff Eric or Katie would deal with, but she'd put the vegetables and fruit in the buckets after Martha or I cut it up if it needed cutting. (*Madagascariensis* is such a lazy slob it won't eat its carrots unless they are chopped up first.) She wasn't really that much help since we had to keep a sharp eye on her; she felt that fairness meant that everybody got the same thing, but most of the fun food is whatever the Wilsonville and Cheyenne supermarkets feel like sending us of the stuff that's still around after its sell-by date and, for example, citrus gives *russo* diarrhea. But Eleanor will get older, and living at Smokehill is weird enough (okay, okay, I admit it) so it's good if you feel involved. But how many kids get to help out at a zoo? Who needs normal?

Although Martha and I both put our hours in at the orphanage. But then the orphanage is pretty good too. I *like* little furry baby things, which there aren't any of at the zoo. Maybe I'm more normal than Eleanor. After the lot at the zoo, something warm and furry or feathery is a nice change too, even if it may throw up all over you. And then there's warm and furry like a Yukon wolf cub. If Eleanor's lucky

...ie day she'll get to hold the broom for it to tear the throat
...at of while the guy with the sedative gun gets into position.

We'd only just started by the time Katie arrived. Katie
makes everyone feel nicer and calmer just by being there,
even her daughters. I mean, even Eleanor. Martha is a lot
like Katie herself. But after Katie got there Eleanor stopped
arguing that since she didn't like celery nobody else was going to like celery either. (*Madagascariensis*, I swear, likes
celery because the sound it makes slowly crunching it up
reminds it of the crack of small bones, without any of the
effort of hunting something. You'd think carrots would be
even better, but no. Maybe it only hunts things with osteopo-
rosis.)

Then Eric showed up and things went into a decline
again—even Katie can't do much with Eric—but Dad says
he's a good keeper and not everyone wants to live a hundred
miles from the nearest real restaurant, work twelve or fourteen hours a day, sometimes seven days a week, *and* get paid
badly, and we're lucky to have him. That's Dad's way of saying "shut up." It's a lot better than saying "shut up" but nothing is ever going to make me like Eric.

We got the buckets sorted and started carrying them out.
Eleanor is not only only seven and the youngest but she's not
exactly large even for seven (Martha's small for her age too
but she's twelve) and only an Eleanor-type seven-year-old
would insist on carrying a bucket too big and heavy for her,
but of course she does. "I'll take *russo*," she says every day.
Russo's her favorite. *Russo* is also at the far end of the row of
cages and Martha and I have to dawdle getting the others set
out to give her time, and then she and Martha have this little
ritual of Eleanor pretending not to notice that Martha has to
lift and dump the food through the chute, because Eleanor
can't.

"She's going to wear that bucket out, dragging it like
that," snapped Eric.

"*You* tell her," I said. Eric glared at me, but I was doing
him a favor, giving him an excuse for a good glare.

Once Eric was there to deal with the serious food Katie and I could get started on the cages. Here's a good example of what passes in Eric's case for a sense of humor. When I turned thirteen the grown-ups decided it was time I had some real chores, not just fun-food detail at the zoo or helping unpack and stack stuff for the gift shop. Especially given my talent for leaving drifts of Styrofoam munchies and stomp-popped bubblewrap in my wake. It had kind of seemed to me that my time at the orphanage should have counted, but maybe it didn't because I never had night duty (a growing boy needs his sleep, etc.) and because there was always an adult there with me. Or maybe because I'd been getting underfoot at the orphanage since I was a baby and Mom used to bring me along while she put in *her* time, and it was like I was too regular and nobody noticed.

Anyway I volunteered for cage cleaning because I knew *odoratus* doesn't make me sick the way it does a lot of people, and by doing it I knew I'd get extra slack for when I screwed up elsewhere, which was definitely an issue. Eric accepted my offer fast enough, but he couldn't let it go without telling everyone that the reason I didn't mind *odoratus* was because I was a teenage boy. Very funny, Eric. That doesn't explain Katie, who also volunteered for *odoratus*, who is not only a girl—I mean a woman—herself but has two daughters. And her slob of a husband isn't around any more if the idea is you have to live with slobbishness to be able to deal. Katie's husband isn't dead but he might as well be since nobody ever sees him, including his daughters. That may be another reason I kind of like Eleanor really. I don't think feeling sorry for people is ever going to come easily to Eleanor, but it wouldn't occur to her to feel sorry for me because my mom's dead. As far as she's concerned we're even, because her dad's dead. Eleanor has a very black-and-white view of the world. That's restful too sometimes, except when you're on her hit list.

She didn't get it from Katie. Katie has no hit list. Katie volunteered for *odoratus* so no one else had to do it. That's what she's like. (And between her, me, and Eric, no one else

does have to do it. Aren't we just the three stooges of won-
derfulness.) And she tried really hard to be careful after my
mom died and not look at me funny or anything but it's like
she got it too well instead so when other people started forgetting she didn't. I mean . . . well, I'll give you an example.
This happened only a few weeks before Eleanor got the
okay to start "helping" at the zoo.

You clean any of the *Draco* cages by halves, with you in
one half and the *Draco* safely imprisoned in the other half,
but *odoratus* is unique in that he and his harem and the juv-
vie males are not only behind bars but behind a glass parti-
tion as well: We say it's for the tourists, but even us tough
guys can only take so much. We also usually do *odoratus* in
pairs to get it over faster. But we were doing it really macho
that day, no masks and helmets (nice cool day with no
breeze, you can just about get away with it with the overhead
vent open, and you're going to need a shower afterward anyway), so when this school group led by this thumping big
assho—I mean nincompoop stopped to look at our big male
odoratus who was busy flapping his ears (*odoratus* ears are
huge and frilly, you know, the better to wave *odoratus* odor
around, except, of course, when there's a glass wall in the
way) and showing off, right next door, we could hear exactly
what he was saying to his students.

He had one of those bellowing voices, like he was used to
lecturing to thousands, so I mean we could hear *exactly*. The
kids looked a little older than me, and that made it worse
somehow. It should have been funny, the nincompoop bay-
ing and posturing and *odoratus* flapping and posturing back,
but it wasn't. I probably started to get sort of maroon, which
could have just been the smell, but Katie knows me pretty
well. "Steady, Jake," she said.

"It's all *crap*," I muttered, so he couldn't possibly over-
hear me: it doesn't matter how pissed off any of us Smokehill lifers get, we always think of how something's going to
look to the tourists. "And he's pretending to *teach* those
kids—"

Katie's usually brighter than this. Maybe the smell was

getting to her. She got sympathetic. "Jake," she said gently. "There's a lot of crap out there. It's not worth getting mad all the time, okay? You've got better things to do. Think about the gate money this group brought us, and forget the rest."

I stared at her, feeling as if my whole head was getting redder and redder, like if they turned the lights off you could have seen in the dark by the glow of my head. Why was she saying this to me? Why was it upsetting me so much that she was saying this to me? She was only telling the truth. Crap was crap and there's a lot of it around. But it was probably *crap* that killed my mother—nobody will admit this but what probably happened is that the guide she'd been promised didn't show and didn't show, and she had to sit there watching her six-month sabbatical from Smokehill going for nothing (that much we knew for sure), and she found somebody else to take her and the somebody wasn't good enough and either got her into trouble or let her get herself into trouble and then fled. But we'll never *know*, okay?

After Mom died, and then Snark, my dog, only seven months and twelve days later, everything started getting to me a lot worse than it used to. All the time I'd been growing up we were both the biggest and acre for acre the poorest national park in the country. Because of the Institute we're sitting ducks for all the dragon nuts out there, and lots and *lots* of them come, and while most of them are happy with the diorama and the film clips and the bus tour, and are perfectly normal okay humans with like *manners*, way too many of them want to bother the staff of the Institute and waste our time arguing and complaining about the traveling restrictions inside the park and the information available at the tourist center and the brush-off they get from our Rangers.

The staff of the Institute, what a joke. That's my dad and a short-term graduate student or two. (Sometimes they're only part-time. Their grant pays for them to live here but they spend most of their time writing their PhDs.) Since Mom died they haven't even given him an extra graduate student. But these people don't get it that we *have* to be this way, this strict and cautious, and we're not ripping them off, we need their ticket fees to stay alive. And the government doesn't get it either, which is why they never let us have enough money.

But Mom's the one who had the sense of humor about it and while she was alive I used to think our fruit loops were funny because she did. She's the one who started calling them f.l.s. It was after Mom disappeared that the f.l.s. didn't seem so funny any more and my brain started zoning out and I started playing a lot more Space Marauder or Annihilate than I ever used to, and then when they found her at the bottom of that ravine with her neck broken and only her teeth to tell them who she was and no way of ever knowing what she was doing dead at the bottom of a ravine because she was a very, very careful person but what would *you* do if the only half sabbatical you were going to get that *decade* was being wasted because some pighead administrator had screwed up? And then my dog died and I was kind of a mess for a while. You don't need to know any more about that, except that as almost-fifteen-year-olds go I was maybe a little twitchier than some.

All this and a lot more besides went boiling through my head for about the millionth time when Katie told me not to be so mad about all the crap there was around, while the nincompoop went on scrambling his students' brains (actually he probably wasn't—I don't think many of them were paying attention), and where I stopped thinking was *If I go berserk right now—in public—start hammering the walls with my shovel and screaming—in front of a bunch of sixteen-year-olds—I'll never forgive her.* Which was true, even if it wasn't her fault. There was a lump like a burning basketball in my throat and I didn't dare blink my eyes for fear of what would spill out. But even Eric's eyes water sometimes when he's doing *odoratus.*

The main thing I was thinking was, It's been *two years.* Almost three. And a little thing like Katie being the wrong kind of sympathetic at the wrong moment and I'm going to pieces.

At last I managed to say, "The gate money wasn't much. They'd've got a school discount."

Katie took this as a joke, and laughed, and the danger was over. I went back to scrubbing, although I probably took some of the floor with it.

When I was younger I used to say that I didn't understand why so many nuts had to be crazy over *dragons*. What about Yukon wolves, cougars, grizzly bears, ichthyosauruses, griffins, several kinds of shark, lions, tigers, and Caspian walruses, any of which will eat human when it's available, and every one of which is on the next-step-extinction superendangered list, partly, of course, because of their eating habits? But no. The biggest, fruitiest fruit loops go for dragons. Enter "dragon" at your favorite search site, and stand back. In fact, go make yourself a cup of coffee, because it'll still be churning out hits by the time you get back. None of the rest of the critters comes close. Well, Nessie does pretty well, especially since they found her a couple of boyfriends in one of those Scandinavian lochs. Now everyone's standing around waiting for her to reproduce. She hasn't though. Maybe she's a he after all, or the hes are shes too. It's not only dragons we don't know enough about.

For some reason I used to like to bring this up at breakfast, about dragons and fruit loops. Mom would say, "Yes, dear." Or, "Eat your oatmeal, dear." Or, "Have you done your homework, dear?" This last was a trick question because I'm homeschooled. If I wanted to spend my life on a bus I could've just about made it in to Wilsonville and back every day, to their crummy little primary school, but I'd've had to go to boarding school once I graduated from sixth grade and there was *no way*. And never mind being the freak who would have to have special transportation out to Smokehill. Mom had tried to get me to go to Wilsonville at first but she gave up.

(That made a precedent then, so when it was time for Martha to go to school she said she wanted to stay at Smokehill with me. Katie did some wavering and I know she and Mom talked about it a lot, using phrases like "social development" and "peer group." But Martha in her quiet way can be pretty stubborn, and then it turned out she could already read—of course she could read, I taught her—so they were going to have to jump her a year, and where's your social developmental peer group then? Especially because Martha was small for her age. At six you could like barely see her. So they let her stay home and it was pretty interesting because that's when Katie and Mom came up with the bright idea of getting some of the Smokehill staff to teach us stuff, now there were two of us, so it was a "class." So it wasn't just Mom, Dad, the computer, and the boring out-of-date textbooks from Wilsonville we barely pretended to use.

I suppose we learned more about the geology and ecology of Smokehill than we'd've got at Wilsonville, and we never got to the exports of Brazil and the national debt of Taiwan at all, but we *learned* what our Rangers taught us and how many kids *learn* the exports of Brazil and the national debt of Taiwan? Then it was Eleanor's turn, and as it happens, there were some other kids at Smokehill then, and they were going to Wilsonville, but then they had been going to normal school when they lived in a normal place and they were so freaked out by Smokehill that being on a bus all day didn't bother them, at least not in comparison to staying here all the time. But Eleanor wasn't having any of that. Of course she could read by then too—she wasn't a big reader, like Martha or me, but it was clear to her that one of the ways to be older was to learn to read, so she learned—but that was just a way of making it easier for the grown-ups to cave. I don't think turning Eleanor loose in a regular school would have been good for her social development anyway. I think if she'd got a taste for playground domination at an early age the world wouldn't be safe by the time she was a teenager.)

But at least Mom would answer me, even at 7 A.M. Dad was always buried in his latest conference abstract or the forty thousand pages of fax I'd lain awake the night before

listening to churn through the machine, usually from somebody from some country that Dad only half knew the language of, so the table would be covered with grammars and
dictionaries too. Mom read just as much as Dad did, but she
never forgot there was a world outside Smokehill. Outside
dragons. In some ways I take after my dad. But it was nice to
have someone who'd talk to me at breakfast.

Dad has tried to learn to talk at breakfast. It was pretty
awful till I hit on the brilliant plan of trying to read some of
the stuff he reads. I don't get most of it (even when it's in
English—have *you* ever tried to read a professional mono-
graph from some thumping big scientific conference? You're
lucky if you can get past the *title*) but it gave us something to
pretend to have a conversation about. And I got credit for
trying. (See: extra slack for when I screw up elsewhere.)

But too many of these people who get hung up on dragons don't know what a dragon is. A Yukon wolf is a Yukon
wolf, which is to say two hundred odd pounds of tawny hair
and long teeth, and you're not going to mix it up with a chipmunk. Calling *Draco odoratus* a dragon just because of the
Draco is as stupid as arguing that a chipmunk is a small
striped wolf that eats acorns.

But you can't say that, and there's only so many ways to
say "that's a very interesting theory" before even an f.l.
catches on that you're blowing 'em off. And when a fruit
loop decides he or she hasn't been treated with due respect
and consideration by the staff of the Makepeace Institute of
Integrated Dragon Studies, the f.l. writes to his or her con-
gressperson and says our weeny miserable funding should
be cut because we're not doing what we're paid to do with
their, the taxpayers', money, which is study dragons, and
they can prove this because we don't agree with *them*.

And we *live* here, Dad and me, right here in the Institute,
like I told you—the rest of the staff are either in the Rangers' barracks or they have their own little houses, there's a
sort of little compound set back behind a lot of spruce and
aspen, away from the tourist sprawl. (A few commute from
Wilsonville but mostly only part-timers.) Sometimes I go

hide out with Martha and Eleanor—at least Eleanor has some sense, even if she's not real open to negotiation with alternative points of view about things she doesn't agree with, like bedtime for seven-year-olds. (I'm a useless babysitter, but that doesn't stop Katie using me when she's got an evening meeting. Admin usually has evening meetings because during the day everyone is chasing tourists.) Actually I can't wait till she gets old enough to tackle the f.l.s on their own ground but that's still a little in the future. No matter how good at arguing you are it's easier if you're taller than the other guy's belt buckle.

Most of the f.l. crap lands on Dad now—a few of 'em talk to the Rangers, but most of 'em want someone they can call "Doctor"—and Dad tries to keep me out of the way because since I'm a kid I have to be even more polite to them. When Mom was around it was different—at our best we'd had Dad, Mom, and three graduate students, two of whom already had their first PhDs and therefore also answered to "Doctor"—but that was a long time ago. Dad's the only real scientist we've got now and he *shouldn't have to waste his time.*

The ones who think that the peculiarities of dragon biology and natural history can be explained by the fact that dragons are an alien species dropped off by a passing spaceship a few million years ago are so far out there themselves that sometimes they're kind of interesting. I've had good conversations with some of them. I've had a lot of good conversations with ordinary tourists, people who just think dragons are really cool and get a bit gabbly when they're actually here at Smokehill and want to talk to *somebody,* which I perfectly understand. The f.l.s that are a pain are the ones who want to drone on about all the *Draco*s that AREN'T DRAGONS. You could say it's our own fault because of the "Integrated" in our name, but that's nothing to do with us. The director before Dad and Mom almost went under, taking Smokehill with him, and the only way he'd managed to dig himself out was by agreeing to have a sort of zoo of all the other *Draco*s, and call the Institute *Integrated.*

But there *is* only one real dragon; there's nothing to integrate, not really.

The Institute is near the front gate of Smokehill, of course, the front gate having been put there at the spot nearest to a road and a town, although the road is only two lanes and the town is only Wilsonville. Since Mom and Dad came and the zoo was built we've got popular enough that there are eight motels, two of them like shopping malls all by themselves, and four gas stations between us and Wilsonville, and the track in from the main road is paved and wide enough for buses and trucks. Having them breathing down our necks like this (in the summer the first coachloads are already there waiting when we open at 8 A.M.) is a drag but it does mean we get regular deliveries of gas to run our generators. I admit I wouldn't like living without computers and even hot baths (occasionally). We're *festooned* with solar panels but they aren't enough. Too many trees and too many clouds, and solar panels don't seem to like the dragon fence much either. (Our solar-powered tourist buses do most of their tanking up in the parking lot outside the fence.) There's the barracks and the staff houses and a few permanent camps farther in, but that's about all in terms of human stuff. It's enough in terms of upkeep to get through our winters.

So I'm going to give you a rundown on the zoo, and then we're out of there, okay? So pay attention. The whole *Draco* mess started with some eighteenth-century British explorer guy calling that Russian lizard *Draco russo*. We have three nice *russo* in the zoo, and the female's pregnant, finally. She's Eleanor's favorite because they're going to be the first babies since Eleanor's been old enough to pay attention to what goes on at the zoo. *Russo*'s pretty mellow too so nobody stops Eleanor from (strictly out of tourist hours) poking rhubarb through the bars at the expectant mom, since only the males are poisonous. And Eleanor does know to call them lizards. I told you she has some sense.

After that we have the Chinese dragon, *Draco chinensis*, which usually goes about eight foot long and mostly eats snails. Sure, if it stepped on your foot you'd go "ow" and it has a scary face, but those fangs are just tufts of hair on the jaw. We have six of them, but they all poop in the same corner most of the time, which makes me like them, as much as I'm going to like any lizard, but sweeping up the snail shells is a pain, because we have to do it really carefully—they won't eat anything they haven't peeled themselves so that limits the options. One of them still managed to get an infected foot once from a broken snail shell and wasn't *that* a big hassle. There's a vet in Cheyenne that knew a lot about lizards before she moved to Cheyenne and has learned a lot more since, but it's expensive to get her here. We don't have our own regular vet, of course—we can't afford it. I have to give Eric credit, much as it goes against the grain, he invented his own correspondence course in reptile veterinary, and mostly he copes.

Then there's the Madagascar dragon, *Draco madagascariensis*, with its vestigial wings, but if you were up on your paleontology you would know that it spent a few million years being a bird and then changed its mind and went back into Reptilia, and it hisses because it hisses, not because it used to breathe fire. It eats anything and everything, including very small children and very tottery old people, but it's no threat to the rest of us and no threat at all as long as it's got plenty of other stuff to eat—it doesn't actually like to go to the effort to catch anything.

My favorite f.l. arguments though are for *Draco sylvestris*. This is just a big chameleon, and the point is it lives in *trees*. The thicker the trees the better it likes it. Sounds like a real short evolutionary dead end to me, evolving flame-throwing when you live in a forest. Duh. Because it all comes back to fire, you know. Never mind the size, or even the wings. Dragons are the only animals (besides humans) who habitually eat their food cooked. They don't like it cooked through, but they like a nice char-broiled effect.

By the way, *sylvestris* is the least popular of the zoo exhibits—they're really hard to see. You don't believe they can be, because they run up to twenty feet long, but you'd be surprised. They look like branches of trees. Really. Us cage cleaners have to count them to make sure we got them all before we lock them up on the other side and clean their empty cage, or we may find one of the tree branches getting startled and trying to run away. I awfully nearly lost one out the door once, where I'd parked my wheelbarrow, but fortunately it didn't like the look of the wheelbarrow either and veered away at the last minute. Kit was next door cleaning out *madagascariensis* that day so he saw what happened, but he didn't tell Eric.

I've already told you about *odoratus*, who is at the very end of the other row of *Draco* houses. It doesn't usually get much more than six feet long, but it has these huge smelly sulfurous belches that the f.l.s say mean that it used to breathe fire like a real dragon, and that it's just evolved in the wrong direction for the last million or so years. Please. It evolved *into* huge smelly sulfurous belches because no one would want to eat anything that smells like that. Which is why our *odoratus* house costs more than all the rest of the zoo put together, because it's all glass, to protect the tourists. We need the tourists to keep coming. We need the money. I know I already said that. We say it to each other all the time. It's the truth. And, okay, I admit it, the zoo is a draw, since you're not going to see our real dragons, except in the tourist center theater.

Listen to me now because there will be a test later. *There is only one real dragon*, and that's *Draco australiensis*. They're extinct in the wild, but there's a place not far from the Grampians outside Melbourne that's been made a sanctuary that has quite a few of them—maybe as many as five hundred—although rumor has it the numbers are dropping and it hasn't been as many as even four hundred in years, but it's not a rumor I want to believe, so I don't. Australia's nearly the only place that has enough space left to give some to dragons. I suppose they also have guilty consciences because it's mostly their own poachers that killed them off, although when dragon endocrine extract became *the* fashionable aphrodisiac about a hundred years ago a lot of foreign poachers came to help, aided and abetted by the local sheep farmers because dragons *love* toasted sheep.

The only other two places with dragons now are the park in Kenya where Mom died, and us, Smokehill. We think we have maybe two hundred here, and nobody knows why; the weather should've killed 'em off long ago. We've actually got more acres than the Australian place, but dragons are native to Australia so it's not surprising they can live there okay if nobody *murders* them.

Smokehill as a dragon preserve is an accident. Almost ninety years ago Peter Makepeace brought four dragons here because the Cleveland Zoo couldn't cope any more and nobody else would have them. That was during the era when most people thought the sooner *Draco australiensis* went extinct the better, although no one said it out loud because there were environmentalists even in those days. Old Pete knocked together a few cages (dragons hate cages, which is why zoos had such trouble with them—nobody ever built a cage that didn't feel like a cage to a dragon, and, of course, dragons are *large*, and experiments in dragon keeping are very expensive), and prepared to try to nurse them through their first winter. He always said later he didn't expect to succeed but somebody had to give it a try and he didn't see anybody else with a few thousand acres to spare in a better climate making an offer.

Smokehill was *really* wild then. It's like suburbia now in comparison. A few of the old cages are still sort of standing, and they're part of the bus tour. They are not in themselves very interesting, maybe, but they are *huge* which kind of reminds you about how big dragons are, and it also gives you a clue about how really *creative* Old Pete had had to be, to do what he did, to do it at all. I'm sorry his old cabin isn't still around. We've got some grainy old photos but that's all. It was where the Center is now. (Think, if you dare, about using an outhouse in our winters, where a bad January never gets *above* twenty below, and where a blizzard can arrive in less time than it takes to pee.)

Well, they didn't die. In fact they thrived, in spite of the cages, and the weather. Maybe they just liked Old Pete. From his journals, he didn't have a clue what he was doing, but he found them really interesting and although they had to live in cages they didn't have a lot of gawkers gawking which would sure be enough to put me off my toasted sheep. Whereupon he found himself the latest unwanted-dragon dumping ground. By the next winter he had twenty dragons and was running out of plausible places to put cages— besides how expensive building dragon pens was. And Pete didn't like gawkers either, so kept delaying turning his charity rescue project into a business. But he had to do it finally and eventually it became Smokehill National Park.

Old Pete's dad had bought up the Smokehill territory because he got the whiff of "gold" slightly before the government did, so when a few people started finding gold, the gov had to deal with old Mr. Makepeace. Old Mr. Makepeace senior was more devious than his son and a lot more aggressive, so the gov found itself between a rock and a hard place, the Native Americans on one hand who believed that the little piece of paper they'd got from the gov a while back meant that they owned the territory, and Mr. Makepeace, who had another little piece of paper that said *he* owned the territory, and he knew how to fight dirty in ways the Native Americans didn't. So the gov went on flapping and fudging, and old Mr. Makepeace died, and his son Pete grew up to have a social conscience ahead of its time. And then Pete found himself with twenty dragons on his hands and a lot of land that nobody was using for anything much.

So Pete got together with the Sioux and Cheyenne and Arkholas and they talked and talked, and Pete fell in love with someone's daughter and then he married an Arkhola (and then none of his dad's fancy town friends would speak to him which in his journals he calls "a serendipitous concomitant"), and maybe that's what tipped the balance, because the Native Americans weren't really in a mood to go along with anything a white man said at that point. But Pete got an agreement out of them that they'd stop being a pain in the ass if the federal government would make Smokehill a national park. And by that time the gov was tired of the struggle, said the hell with it, and folded.

Pete spent the rest of his dad's money first hiring a lot of inventors to create a dragonproof fence, and I can't tell you anything about that because the math and stuff is *waaaay* beyond me, but I can tell you that the inventors only succeeded because some of them got interested in the problem, or interested in dragons, and stayed on when Pete couldn't pay them any more—because once they managed to invent it he still had to pay to put it up—which cost like the national debt of Europe. But they did it. Old Pete spent the *last* of his dad's money creating the Makepeace Institute, and died broke but (I hope) a happy man. And our best Rangers are Native American or part Native American, mostly Arkholas. Billy, he's Head Ranger and a brilliant guy, he's the great-great-grandson of Old Pete and his Arkhola wife.

What I can tell you about the dragon fence is that most of it is sort of invisible, except for these fancy cement pillars every half mile or so where all the gizmos and stuff live, with little metal plates set in and big red DANGER signs. If you try to walk through it it's like walking into a wall but worse. It's like the wall zooms out to punch you. (And no, the science guys say it is *not* strong enough for any kind of serious like war use. I hate it that people keep asking this. So, listen, *no*, one little tiny half-hearted bomb and the fence melts, like holding a match to a balloon, big noisy messy *POP*. When the Borg or the Klingons land, we've still had it, okay?) But when you look through it everything looks kind of runny, and the colors are all wrong, and watching anything moving, a tourist coach or even a bird, will make you seasick so fast you won't know what hit you.

This last effect is so bad that the front part of the park, where the Institute and the tourist center are, and the beginning and the end of the bus tour route (the middle stays away from the fence), has ordinary boring solid walls twelve feet high. The funny thing is that some people think that *is* the dragon fence, and they're disappointed. Like twelve feet of anything would keep in something that *flies*. Yo, left your brain at home, did you?

Anyway. Pete ended up with about fifty dragons before the worldwide crash of *Draco australiensis*, when the few that were left in zoos all died, and they were confirmed as extinct in the wild. There were five parks or preserves to begin with that still had any, but the Louisiana and Patagonia preserves both folded in the first couple of decades, partly because of fencing problems. Which means keeping bad guys *out* a lot more than it means keeping dragons *in*. Dragons don't actually move around that much once they're settled. (They hung around in the middle of Australia for millions of years.) So the poachers just changed their airplane tickets or their donkey cart coupons or whatever and started going to Louisiana and Patagonia because their fences weren't very good. Ours is way far the best, but no one wants to pay for the specs and no one has successfully stolen them. And everybody pretends that we need the fence because dragons are the biggest of all the big dangerous wild animals and they would eat humans if they got out. Sure, they could. But they don't. They never have.

(One of the theories about Mom's death has to do with maybe her finding out that someone in Kenya had managed to steal our fence specs but couldn't get them to work. Kenya has the worst poacher problems and everyone knows their dragon population is going down and they never had more than about three hundred dragons to start with. The worst idea is how maybe she was pushed off that cliff because something was done to her before she was pushed—that someone was trying to get it out of her, about our fence— and she *wouldn't have known*, okay? She wouldn't know any more about the fence than I do. She wouldn't have known *anything*—and then they had to push her to hide what they'd done. You're sitting there thinking, You poor sad paranoid schmuck, it's too bad about your mom but you keep hammering on about Smokehill being so poor and all; you can't have it both ways. True. But we're dead poor because we're trying to *protect* our dragons. There are still guys out there who think there's a fortune to be made off dragon hormones or dragon blood or powdered dragon bone or something—and that the only reason we're not breeding them for this is because we're all wimps.)

So Old Pete took the padlocks off his cages and the dragons ambled out, sniffed the air, and wandered off. You can tell from his journal that he can't decide if it was a huge anticlimax or not. It was, he said, almost as if they were *expecting* him to open the doors.

Dragons have some peculiarities if they really are reptiles, because they aren't, properly speaking, cold-blooded: but that's because they have an extra stomach full of fire, right? Which you'd think might be pretty hard to keep going in the kind of winters we have but they do it somehow. Everybody's first idea was that dragons must have learned to hibernate, but Pete kept saying that they didn't hibernate, that when he had them in cages they just ate more when it got cold and when he let them out of the cages, after the wall went up, he continued to find fresh tracks and shed scales and banged-up trees from dragons passing too close or scratching their backs, all winter long—as well as a lot of disappearing wildlife.

One of the most important things our Rangers do is keep an eye on the numbers of the dragon dinners, partly because bison and sheep and deer and antelope are so much easier to count than dragons. Dragons are incredibly hard to count. Australia and Kenya say the same, it's not just us. The usual sorts of field surveys just don't work with dragons. Uh-huh, you say, thirty to eighty feet long (plus tail), flies, breathes fire, and you can't *find them to count*? Yup. That's right. You can't. After Old Pete opened the cages, they didn't just wander off, they disappeared. That's one of the reasons that a few people—Old Pete included—started wondering if dragons were, you know, intelligent.

Well, the mainstream scientists weren't having any of *that*, of course, humans are humans and animals are animals and anyone who says it's not that simple is a sentimental fool and a Bad Scientist. There is nothing you can say to a scientist that's worse than accusing them of being a Bad Scientist. They'd rather be arrested for bank robbery than for sentimentality. But when somebody found out that all the lichen on Mars get together occasionally and suddenly go from a lot of mindless little symbiotic thingies that eat and excrete and exchange gases and not much else and become a THINKING MACHINE, all kinds of ideas back on Earth blew up into smithereens, including some scientific definitions of sentimentality.

Most of the money has gone into studying lichen—there are getting to be so many information-collecting satellites around Mars it's going to have rings soon, like Saturn—and there's a fair number of new studies of Earth lichen going on too, just in case any of it is getting ideas. But *Draco australiensis* has come in for a little of it, because of the old question of their intelligence, and we can use all the money-dribbles we can get, even if they come attached to obnoxious, know-it-all-already scientists who have to be told no seventy-nine times in a row before they begin to believe that if they want to study our dragons they have to follow our rules.

That's one of the reasons dragons attract so many tourists—and so many fruit loops—the creepy pull of dragon intelligence. It's a thrill, so long as dragons are safely on the endangered list and only exist behind walls in a few parks, to have something that could not only eat you, but *think* about it. Although the fact that dragons have never seemed very interested in eating humans means that we have the slack to be cute about it.

But it's interesting that the f.l.s mostly only ever wanted to argue about what dragons *are*. Not many want to argue about whether *australiensis* is intelligent. They come here because they're fascinated but they get here and they kind of back off. Too scary maybe. I shied away from thinking about it much myself although as a kind of cool distant concept I always liked the idea—dragons are intelligent—right, okay, got it, now *stop*.

It's a big thing with tree-huggers that dolphins might be

intelligent, but you can go have mystic experiences dancing with phosphorescent dolphins in the eternal sea at dawn and come back transmuted into your higher self. Not an option with dragons. The guys with sixty-seven PhDs who submit study projects to investigate dragon intelligence—or rather the very, very occasional ones who actually pass Dad's thermonuclear screening and assessment process—usually give up and go home early. If our dragons were hard even to *count* were they going to come out and play mind games with academic chuckleheads? I kept thinking there ought to be a good cartoon in it somewhere—something like Wile E. Coyote and the Roadrunner. I leave it to you who plays what.

Dorks and villains have been trying to get in here without permission since before Pete got national park status. It just got a little harder after that, not that many of them care about laws, but they have to care about the fence. That fence, which is the single biggest reason why we're so poor. Most of what to Congress probably does look like a multi-whale-pod-supporting ocean of money goes to maintaining that fence. But it does keep our dragons in, in the popular imagination—I told you that dragons don't move around much, but try to convince Mr. Normal of that. The fence would also keep the fruit loops out, except—damn!—there's a *gate*.

I learned to read so I could read Pete's memoirs. Mom used to worry that I was growing up strange because I wasn't interested in the usual kids' books. *Goodnight Moon*, baaaaarf. I didn't even like *Where the Wild Things Are* because none of them looked enough like dragons. But I still remember the first time Dad read me "Jabberwocky." It's probably my earliest memory; I think I was three. Mom—who was busy worrying that *The Cat in the Hat* didn't move me—said, "Oh, Frank, you'll only confuse him. It's not even in English," but Dad was having one of his manic fits. He'd done amateur theater when he was younger, and he could still turn that crazy public thing on when he wanted to. He doesn't do it much any more—except for congressional subcommittees—but he still did it when I was little. I don't know whether I was confused by "Jabberwocky" or not, but I was riveted by it, as my dad shouted and danced and snickersnacked across my bedroom. I'd've named Snark Jabberwock if it hadn't been too hard to say ("Jabberwock, *sit*! Jabberwock, *stay*!") so I settled for Snark.

It was shortly after that Dad started reading parts of Pete's memoirs to me—while Mom shook her head. But it made me want to learn the alphabet. Once I could read there was no stopping me. Dad said once, "Mad, do you really think any child of ours *wouldn't* be spellbound by dragons?" It was always Dad's little joke to call her Mad; her name was Madeline. Mom laughed a sort of grim nonlaugh and said, "I suppose it's either that or he couldn't stand them." I couldn't imagine what she meant.

So I grew up on Lewis Carroll—and Old Pete—and Saint George, and Fafnir and Nidhogg, and Smaug and Yofune-Nushi, and all the others, famous, infamous, and totally obscure. Mom in particular has—had—well Dad and I still have it—this amazing collection of literary dragons and the myths pretending to be science about the evolutionary forebears of the Chinese dragon and the smelly dragon and all of the other fake dragons, trying to justify that *Draco* label.

Because the real problem with *Draco australiensis* is that it raises its kids in a pouch, like a kangaroo or a koala. Things with pouches just aren't romantic. Saint George or Siegfried slaying a critter with a *pouch*? No way. Even the Australians have never quite taken their *Draco* seriously as a real live dragon—even if it is the biggest of the land animals on this planet—*and* still manages to fly—*and* breathes fire—and, you know, looks like a dragon. It's not like the pouch shows. Humans are perverse. You may have noticed. But here we've got thousands of years of pretty much every culture on the planet coming up with stories about big scaly things that breathe fire . . . and then, hey presto, *we've got them*. They freaking exist. You'd think we've have been dancing in the streets and slinging daisy chains across the borders from Ulan Bator to Minsk. But noooo.

Maybe if dragons had eaten more people when they had the chance humans wouldn't have been so offhand. (Although if they had they might have been made extinct before anybody thought to preserve them.) You're looking to design the real, true, only dragon, and what more can you want than big and flying and breathing fire? *No pouch nonsense* is what you want. Hence the attraction of all the silly little lizards like *russo* and *chinensis.*

Because, I hear you say, not only is there the pouch problem, but kangaroos and koalas are mammals. True. But nobody ever told reptiles they couldn't evolve a pouch to carry their babies in, did they? You've heard the phrase "parallel evolution"? And mammals and reptiles are cousins anyway, if you go back far enough, like maybe 250 million years or so, which gives you a lot of room to mutate in. The biology of dragons—and from here on let's get it straight that when I say dragon, I mean our one and only real dragon, *Draco australiensis*—is still pretty much one big blank space in the biology books.

And dragon corpses disintegrate really fast—so there goes that standard research route—including the bones—which is something to do with the fire-stomach too, or the body chemistry that supports the fire-stomach, or maybe the bones are built out of something we don't know about that weighs less than the rest of the planet's bones, which is why dragons can fly. Hitch over one of those rows of the periodic table, there's a missing dragon bone element to get in somewhere. One of the results is that no natural history museum in the world has a dragon skeleton on display, which in a weird way means that a lot of people assume they don't really exist. And there are some unhappy paleontologists and animal osteologists who would like to specialize in dragons and can't.

They *think* that baby dragons are born with some kind of embery gum or mucilage in their tiny fetal fire-stomachs—their *igniventatores.* They think that Mom somehow shoves 'em out—she usually has several at a go—and lights 'em up, that that's when they're born, that maybe the fire-lighting business is where the marsupial business started, that you have to get the fire lit while the baby is still kind of an embryo, for some reason or other, so maybe it makes sense to transfer them to a different holding container while you're at it. So she gets 'em lit and into her pouch where they stay for the next year or so.

So a long time ago the species must have figured out it couldn't go the several-hundred-eggs tortoise route if it wanted to work on this great new fire-breathing racket, so it went for pouch incubators instead. But the lab coats still haven't really decided whether dragons are reptiles. Maybe they're mammals. Or something else. I like the something else idea myself, what else has an *igniventator*? But apparently having some big new thing as high up in the hierarchy as the division between reptiles and mammals upsets everybody too much. Science under Threat by Unclassifiable Critter: film at eleven. I keep telling you lab coats are drones. Although I sometimes think the label guys went for reptiles only because *Draco* was already stuck on a lot of lizards, and it would be just too stupid to have something that finally obviously *is* a dragon called *Thingamajiggium*. Which maybe means lab coats have some imagination after all.

There's other weird stuff, like their scales are made out of something a lot more like mutant hair than like adapted skin. (They seem to shed more here at Smokehill than anywhere else. Something to do with the weather, presumably. But we sell shed dragon scales in the gift shop—as many as the Rangers can pack in—and they go really well. Have I mentioned recently that we're always *desperate* for money?) And they fly, which makes them the only nonbat nonbird that can take off and land and flap and soar like a bird, with none of that cheating stuff that "flying" squirrels or "flying" fish do. So maybe they're birds. (They're sure not bats.) Although the third pair of limbs is still problematic.

All of this bothers a lot of the fruit loops too. Dragons are supposed to be reptiles. Everybody knows that. All the fake dragons are real reptiles. They also behave in nice lower-order ways that scientists who want to study them like. They don't disappear. You can watch 'em having and raising their babies. Their corpses rot the way corpses are supposed to rot, and natural history museums can have as many skeletons as they like. That kind of thing. It's funny what everybody knows.

But the trouble with dragon public relations is pretty well permanent. First, they're too marsupialy and not lizardy enough, and then they're hard to find, to gawk at or to study (which is only a snobby form of gawking really), and then they might even be (do-do-do-do, do-do-do-do) *intelligent*. Why didn't we know about them till about two hundred and fifty years ago? Something that size? Even if they did hang out in the middle of a big empty continent? It's not like no one ever went there. The Europeans thought it was just another quaint aboriginal myth for a long time. I guess sheep are like chocolate or heroin to dragons, they just couldn't help themselves when the ranchers moved in. But they lost the war with the sheep ranchers because they never really fought it. The ranchers and the mercenaries and big game hunters they hired or pitched in with—and the poachers—killed a lot of dragons, and the rest of them pretty much disappeared. Again.

But there was about half a century of the *australiensis* golden age when everybody was fascinated by them, and you could study them all right, so long as the poachers didn't get there first. Well, you still didn't see them get born. But you could see them flying, for example. Something the size of a dragon is pretty damn *visible*, flying. And there are lots and lots of records of all those sober scientists streaming out to Australia to see for themselves. I was really jealous of the guys who could write about seeing dragons flying nearby, the hot smell of them—like fire but not like fire—the way their underparts tend to be paler and mottled—but you can't see a lot of their bellies because of the way they tuck their tails back under their bodies, like a dog tucking its tail between its legs. Birds use their tails as rudders. Dragons have some other system . . . but that's only one of a thousand things we don't know about dragons. We started killing them too soon.

When it was too late some of the politer scientists went round to the aborigines and said, Hey, can we talk to you about your dragon stories? It was those stories that first told the rest of us that *australiensis* had pouches. Maybe by then we were looking for a reason not to like them, since we were busy making them extinct. The really interesting thing about all the old aboriginal tales though is that there isn't a single one about a dragon eating a human. Oh well those are just *tales*, said the guys with the guns. And it's true that a few ranchers got fried in the nonwar, but a rattlesnake won't bite you unless you worry it, and the ranchers were going *after* the dragons—there was no live-and-let-live policy or acceptable sheep loss rate.

I'd never seen a dragon flying—not up close. And I live here. And five million acres isn't big enough to hide (maybe) two hundred flying dragons. So, I hear you say, maybe our figures are wrong? Maybe we don't have two hundred dragons? Then what's eating the deer, the sheep, and the bison? We can count our bears and our cougars and our bobcats and our coyotes and our wolves well enough, and they aren't doing it by themselves. And our Rangers really do cover most of the park slowly, over a period of years. They said there were quite a few dragons out there, and Dad and I believed them.

Billy knows what goes on in this park better than any other human alive, and he'd only seen flying dragons a few times. There's a big valley sort of northwest of the center of Smokehill, one of the friendlier edges of the Bonelands, where he'd seen most of 'em, and he'd say he'd take me there when I was older—which was to say when Dad would let me. I didn't know when that was going to happen, because he'd been a little crazy about keeping me safe since Mom died. He'd barely let me out of the Institute, and the summer before the one I'm talking about we never did take our summer hike, which is three or four weeks backpacking through the park, having left Billy in charge of dealing with the f.l.s. It's true that it wouldn't have been the same without Mom and Snark, but I still wanted to go. The summer before that—no. But that summer—yes. I wanted to go. I wanted to find out what it would be like. Like after a major accident and months in the hospital and six operations and all that physical therapy—so, does the leg work again, or doesn't it? But Dad wouldn't even discuss it, so we didn't go.

That's not to say I'd never seen any dragons at all. I did, lots of times, maybe as often as twice a year—or I did in the few years I was old enough to do a lot of walking before Mom died—but only at a distance, like across one of Smokehill's rock plains, when one of the rocks is flying. They don't come near the Institute (another sign of their intelligence, *I* say), so you only are going to see them if you're one of the lucky ones who ever gets farther into the park. And I've smelled 'em more often than that—smelled 'em close, I mean. There's a dragon smell that isn't like anything else. It's a fire smell, and a wild-animal smell—pungent but not rotten or foul like some kinds of musk or a sloppy carnivore's leftovers that can turn your stomach—but it's something else too. Billy says it's because their fire isn't like the fire you make with wood; they burn some sort of weird resinous stuff they secrete for the purpose. Organic fire. And even way damped down, that fire gives off a little invisible smoke, and we can smell it.

The Institute smells of dragon. The tourists here pick it up immediately, as soon as they come through the gate. (I suppose the wall kind of keeps it in too.) You can see them sort of straighten up and get all sparkly-eyed. And it makes them feel that the dragons are *close*—it makes them feel better about not actually seeing any. And of course they are close, comparatively speaking. I don't notice the smell much at the Institute—I don't really notice it till I get out into the park.

Oh, and every human who walks in the park either carries a squirtgun or has a Ranger with them carrying a squirtgun. This is supposed to be the dragon equivalent of what most animals think about skunks, but I don't know how they think they know. None of our Rangers has ever shot theirs at anything. But the checker-uppers for the squirtguns come round every six months like the other checker-uppers come round to test your fire extinguishers. But even if you happened to have a handy backup antitank gun you're sunk if your squirtgun didn't work, since it's a federal offense to harm a dragon. This is pretty funny when it's also a HUGE messy spectacular federal crime to aid in the preservation of the life of a dragon—in fact one of the hugest and messiest—but that's another story, and I'm getting to it, just shut up and listen.

CHAPTER TWO

Billy must have been working on Dad. Billy misses Mom almost as much as Dad and I do, and I think he knew that Dad barely being able to let me out of his sight any more was starting to make me kind of nuts. (No comments on the "starting to" please.) Dad had offered to get me another dog but I just wasn't ready for that yet. I didn't know how to think about having a new dog; I'd had Snark since almost before I could remember anything. It would be like getting a new mom: no. (I spent some time worrying about this too. If there was ever a man who needed a wife to pry him out of his obsession occasionally, it was Dad. Except I couldn't deal with this either—worrying about Dad or worrying about the idea of a new mom. I can worry about anything, but as an idea it never really got very far because Dad didn't notice women. He'd notice people if he had to, but if any of them was occasionally single and female it didn't register.)

Anyway. I was keeping the homeschooling admin happy (speaking of checker-uppers) but I was spending way too much time blowing up aliens with a lot of other people online who apparently didn't have lives either. But my family had been cut down by fifty percent and there was like a cold wind blowing through that freaking great hole. On a computer you don't have to notice who's missing. I was almost beginning to forget Smokehill, in a way. I hadn't changed my mind about dragons, and I was still going through the motions (most of them), it was more like seeing everything through the wrong end of the telescope. The only stuff up close was just me and the hole, and a dad who only noticed scientific abstracts and problems about the Institute that got in his face and screamed at him, except that at the same time I had to be like the lucky charm he kept in his pocket or something and always *there.*

So it seemed like it came out of nowhere—I'd stopped asking—when I finally got permission to hike out overnight alone.

This is maybe the single thing I'd been wanting to do all my life. I'd always planned to grow up and study dragons like Mom and Dad, but that was a ways off yet. Presumably I'd get my butt out of the park for a few years to go to college . . . and then I'd think about living somewhere with a lot of other people around . . . *all the time?* We get to close the gates at night here. So then sometimes I'd think I'd chicken out and just stay here and apprentice to the Rangers. Most of our federal parks make you go to school for that too, but that's one of the things Old Pete set up when he set up Smokehill, our Ranger system. Billy had told me he'd take me if I decided that's what I wanted to do. He's never been away from the park overnight since he was born (both his parents were Rangers). His idea of a holiday is to hike into the park somewhere he hasn't been before, and stay there awhile, beyond the reach of f.l.s. (I admit I'd have to think about it, whether I'd choose hanging around too close to grizzlies and Yukon wolves, or f.l.s. Billy likes the *really* wild places. But maybe if I was his apprentice I'd feel more competent. I'd *rather* rather hang out with grizzlies and Yukon wolves, if you follow me.)

When the f.l. percentages were unusually bad I was sure I wanted to be a Ranger, but the rest of the time I wanted to have some PhDs like my parents because it meant more people would listen to me. I still wanted to be able to protect our dragons as well as study them and the head of the Institute is the head of the Rangers, as dumb as that is. And when the congressional subcommittee guys come here to stick their noses in and make stupid remarks, Billy has always left it up to Dad and goes all Son of the Wilderness silent and inscrutable if he's introduced to them. (It's proof of how much he thought of my parents that he would babysit the Institute when Dad and Mom took me and Snark for one of our summer hikes in the park. One of the higher-strung graduate students actually left with a nervous breakdown after one of those holidays. Apparently Billy didn't let her weep on his shoulder the way Mom had. Dad used to call her Fainting in Coils.)

But my PhDs were a long way off. I read a lot but I'm not so bright that any of the big science universities were begging to have me early. But I was a pretty fair woodsman for almost fifteen. I'd had the best teachers—our Rangers— and I grew up here, which is a big advantage, like you're supposed to be able to learn a second language really easily if you start when you're a baby. My French and German are lousy, but I've learned the language of Smokehill—some of it anyway. Before Mom disappeared I was going to have my first overnight solo after my twelfth birthday. Then she disappeared and we sort of stopped breathing for five months and then they found her. After that, as I say, Dad could barely let me out of his sight and he could never get away from the Institute himself because he's doing both his and Mom's jobs.

And then one day out of the blue Dad calls me into his office (I go in flexing my hands from Joystick Paralysis) and says, "Jake, I'm sorry. I'm not paying the right kind of attention to you and I know it, and I don't know when I'll have time either."

He glanced back at his desk which was a wild tangle of books, notebooks, loose papers, charts, bits of wood and stone and Bonelands fossils, coffee cups and crumbs. The Institute (of course) can't afford a lot of support staff so we do all our own cleaning and cooking. Although we'd shared it when Mom was still around Dad and I stopped doing any about a month after she didn't show up at her checkpoint. We had started to try to do it again but if it weren't for eating with the Rangers sometimes I might have forgotten food ever came in any shape but microwave pouches or that cooking ever involved anything but punching buttons. And cleaning? Forget it. I can run the dishwasher—hey, I can run the washing machine, are you impressed?—but my expertise ends there.

Dad rearranged one of the coffee mugs on the pile of papers it had already left smeary brown rings on. "I've been talking to Billy. You did really well in your last standardized tests, did I tell you?"

He hadn't. I'd thought he should've had the results by now and had begun to worry. I'd been trying to be extra careful since Mom died because I knew social services was just aching to take me out of my weird life at the Institute, but I could have missed something important because since Mom died I just did miss stuff, and sometimes it was important.

"And I know"—he hesitated—"I know you've been keeping up with your woodcraft." The one thing he would let me out of his sight to do without a huge argument was go out for a day with one of the Rangers—as long as we were back the same night. And it was the one thing that would turn the telescope I was looking through around too. For a few hours. "You're fourteen and a half."

Fourteen years, nine months and three days, I wanted to say, but I didn't.

"And—well—Billy says you're more than ready to—uh—"

Tie my shoes without someone supervising? I thought, but I didn't say that either, not only because my shoes have Velcro straps. I knew Dad was doing the best he could. So was I.

"Well, I wondered, would you like to take your overnight solo? I know you were—we were—" He hesitated again. "Your first solo is overdue, I know. And Billy says you'll be fine. And the weather looks like holding. So—"

"Yes," I said. "I'd love to." I tried not to sound sarcastic. I almost forgot to say thanks. Almost. But I did say it.

If I'd been twelve I'd've gone whooping out of the Institute offices to the Ranger offices which are right across the
tourist center lobby and reception area, and probably telling
everyone on the way, Nate in the ticket booth, Amanda in
the gift shop, poor Bob doing detention in the café, Jo and
Nancy answering questions as they shepherded gangs of
tourists to and from the bus stop, and anybody else I recognized, but I was nearer fifteen than fourteen and it had been
a long almost-three years in a lot of ways. I walked slowly
through Nancy's busload (ID-ing the f.l.s among them at
first glance), waved at Nate, and told Dan, at the front Ranger
desk, that whenever Billy had a moment I'd like to talk to
him.

"He's hiding down at the caves," said Dan. "You could go
find him."

I've forgotten to tell you about the caves. As soon as the
first geologist set foot near Smokehill they knew there had
to be caves here. The Native Americans had known for a
long time, but after a bad beginning they'd kind of stopped
telling the European pillagers anything they didn't have to,
so Old Pete may be the first whiteface to have done more
than guess. The caves near the Institute aren't very good
ones compared to what there is farther in, like under the
Bonelands, but these little ones near the front door were
busy being developed for tourists, so they weren't going to
be much use for hiding in much longer.

Getting the work done was a huge nuisance and everybody who lived here hated it, but we are always desperate
for money (I should just make an acronym of it: WAADFM,
like some new weird alternative radio station), so we were
going ahead with it. Of course in the short term this meant
money we badly needed elsewhere was getting spent on
making the caves touristproof . . . and tourists coming to
the caves was going to mean more staff to keep an eye on
them and more upkeep because tourists are incredibly de-
structive even when they're behaving themselves, but the
grown-ups (including a lot of bozo outside consultants—for
cheez sake, what does some pointy head from Baltimore or

Manhattan know about a place like Smokehill?) all seemed to think it was going to be worth it in the end, if we lived that long. Dad had told me that the caves were going to fund him hiring another graduate student, maybe even full-time, because he didn't think he was ever going to get one otherwise. I was sure hiring anybody was a bad idea because it would mean we *could*, and everybody would cut our grants accordingly.

Billy was sitting by one of the little pools near the entrance. As soon as my eyes adjusted to the dark—the construction crews had gone home for the day, and turned off all the lights—I could see both his lantern and its reflection in the water. I went up to him as quietly as I could, but the caves are totally quiet except for the drip of water (and the bats) and on the pebbly path with the inevitable echo I sounded like someone falling through a series of windows CRASH CRUNCH CRASH only without the screaming.

If you'll pardon the expression from someone who wants to grow up to be a scientist, there's something almost magical about our caves, even the little boring ones near the park entrance. Maybe all caves are like this and I just don't know the analytical squashed-flat-and-labeled word for it. But there's a real feeling of another world, another world that needs some other sense or senses to get at it very well, in our caves. I suppose you could say it's something about underground, lack of sunlight, nothing grows here but a few creepy blind things and sometimes even creepier rock formations, but that doesn't explain it. Cellars aren't magical. The old underground bomb shelter that's now a really boring museum in Wilsonville isn't magical. Our caves are magical.

It could have been the weird shadows that lantern light throws but the moment Billy looked up I knew he was worried about something besides more tourists. I was used to Dad worrying. He'd been worried about something since Mom disappeared, and once she died it's like his worry metastasized and now he worried about everything—and *I* worried about the holes it made in *him*, all the gnawing worry. If I lost any more family there wouldn't be any left. As I looked at Billy I wondered what I was missing. Like that the world's total *Draco australiensis* numbers were still falling and there had been only a few hundred left when they died out in the wild. Like that even with the zoo Smokehill was barely surviving. I knew both of these things. But dragons are so hard to count maybe they were wrong about there being fewer of them. Maybe they were just getting even harder to count. And Smokehill had always barely survived, from Old Pete on. But Dad's a worrier. Billy isn't.

"What's wrong?" I said.

Billy shook his head. He was a good grown-up, but he was still a grown-up, and grown-ups rarely talk about grown-up trouble to kids. Eric took the question "What's wrong?" from a kid as a personal attack, even when it was something like a zoo-food shipment not arriving when it should and it was perfectly reasonable to be worried. I'd often wished Dad would talk about missing Mom to me more. Not only because then I could talk to him back. We could barely mention her at all.

At least Billy didn't lie to me. "Nothing you can do anything about. Nothing I can do anything about either. That's what's wrong." He shook his head again and then looked at me, visibly changing the subject. "What's up?"

I thought again of how I'd've felt if this'd happened three years ago. It was almost hard to get the words out. "Dad says I can do my first solo. Hike into the park and stay overnight." I felt as if I needed to apologize for interrupting him for such a lame reason. It could have waited. "Dan told me I could find you here."

Billy nodded. My solo wasn't news to him—Dad would have discussed it with him first. Even though I knew this was logical and responsible and necessary and all that it made me feel about four instead of almost fifteen. I wasn't really tying my shoes by myself. Dad and Billy were both watching me. I wished Snark was there. Snark was *my* responsibility. And furthermore he didn't seem to mind. That's being a dog, I guess, not minding being totally dependent on someone who may talk over your head to someone else about you and not let you in on it till everything's already been decided.

"I'm going to Northcamp, day after tomorrow," said Billy. "If you want to come with me you can hike on from North-camp alone and meet me back there the next day."

Northcamp was one of the permanent camps, and it was five days' hike from the Institute, after the first day in a jeep as far as the jeep track went. I didn't get that far in very of-ten—never in the last almost-three years. This was a really nice offer. "Great," I said, trying to mean it and almost suc-ceeding. "Thanks."

Billy gave me a look that suggested that he knew what I was thinking, and it made me wonder if he felt about his troubles—whatever they were—not so much different from how I felt about mine. Maybe we both needed a dog.

But by the time we were ready to leave, I was up for it, maybe as much as I'd've been if I was only twelve and Mom was there to wave me off. Dad didn't—waving wasn't his style—besides, he was at his desk, like he was always at his desk. I don't mean that as bad as it sounds—we'd had breakfast together and he cross-examined me about what I was going to do in the park by myself and what to do if anything happened. We both knew that if I didn't know it all already he wouldn't be letting me go, but it was a ritual, like waving.

The answer to most of those if-anything-happens ques-tions was "call Billy on the two-way, and stay put," so it wasn't like it was as grisly as Dad's cross-examinations when they were on stuff like algebra and Latin. I suck at languages but Latin's the *worst*. Maybe "call Billy and stay put" should have made me feel more like a kid too, but it didn't. That's how everybody goes into the park, with a two-way, and someone—a Ranger—always there to listen on the other end. Even Billy didn't go anywhere without someone to check in with. Anyway Dad gave me a hug on the way to his desk and told me to come see him the minute I got back, which should be about two weeks from now. Of course Billy would make me call Dad every day while we were gone, but that was okay too.

Our jeeps were as beat-up and held together with string as everything else at the Institute but the best Land Rover in the world wouldn't get far in Smokehill. Katie drove us in with Martha, deeply envious, in the back seat with me (Eleanor didn't come: one of her few weaknesses is getting carsick, although riding in the back of a Smokehill jeep is more like walloped-by-tornado sick) and late afternoon they let us off by the Lightning Tree, which is one of our landmarks, and a lot of walking trails going all over the park start there. Another way to look at it is that it's maybe one of the (few) good things about never having any money—we couldn't afford to put in any more road even if we wanted to.

"Good luck," Martha said quietly. Martha was *born* polite, it's like she knew she was going to have Eleanor as a little sister in less than six years and needed to get practicing being nice immediately. Martha is two and a half years younger than me so she was maybe close to her first solo, if she wanted to. I knew she was envying me right now. Maybe it was just the idea of getting away from Eleanor for two weeks.

Billy and I did about six more miles before we camped for the night, and that's good going, believe me. I slept like a log, and woke up as stiff as one too, from sleeping on the ground. I didn't do it enough. Billy's older than Dad, but he didn't creak out of his sleeping bag. I did.

Four days later I felt about four years older when we made it to Northcamp and I got to sleep in a bed again. The grim little bunk beds at all our permanent camps aren't very welcoming, but they look pretty good after five nights on the ground. So does the hot water after you get the generator

going. Northcamp smelled funny the way any building does
that's been shut up for too long—a little dusty, a little moldy,
a little mousy—but we cranked open the windows and got a
fire going in the woodstove (and the mice living in the kindling box were *not* happy, speaking of mousy) and it was
pretty nice.

I admit I had a few butterflies in my stomach the next
morning—in spite of Billy's cornmeal pancakes, which I
swear must be the best in the world—but five days' camping
with Billy had reminded me that I still knew how to do everything I needed to know how to do, and I was ready to go
by sunup and I went. I wanted to cover some ground. I
wanted to make as much of a thing of my first solo as possible, so they'd let me do it again. Which meant I had to make
the right kind of thing of my first solo or they'd never let me
do *anything* again. I wanted to come out here for weeks and
study dragons. I wanted to come out here for weeks and find
some dragons *to* study.

I had my radio and a compass (and a squirtgun and a
flare), the weather was perfect, and I'd been drilled since I
was tiny to recognize Rangers' marks. And while Northcamp was a long way into the park by my standards, the area
was well used and well designated by the Rangers. There
was no way I could get lost if I even half kept my head.
There were no grizzlies around here, and you only had to
think about wolves later on in bad winters. It was, in the old
Institute joke, a walk in the park.

I really poured it on. I covered twenty miles that day. I
knew it because I got to Pine Tor, which is nineteen and
three-quarters miles from Northcamp, and another Ranger
landmark. (I'd never seen it before except on the charts.)
Yes, it was stupid of me, and even I knew it. Sure, I was
walking on broken trail, but the emphasis is more on the
"broken" than the "trail." Northcamp is a long way from
the Bonelands but it's still all pretty ankle-breaking going.
And if I missed getting back to Northcamp next day because I was too tired and beat up, it would be a *huge* black

mark against me, and all the grown-ups would give me lectures, especially Dad, and they'd all be *disappointed*, which is the worst thing grown-ups do to kids—can't they just yell at you and get it over with?—and it would be a long time till they let me go out alone again. Like maybe next century or when pigs fly, etc. But I *had* to go as fast and as far as I could. I'm not going to try to explain it because I can't. But I had to. I'd get back to Northcamp the next day somehow.

The thing that makes it seem the dumbest is what was I tearing over all that landscape *for*? I was so busy watching where to put my feet and for the next Rangers' mark that I barely looked around. I could have steamed by any number of dragons—or grizzlies—and never noticed. And our park is beautiful. Wild and strange and alien and not very friendly to humans, but very, very beautiful, if you aren't freaked out by it. Lots of people are. Some people find the Institute as much as they can handle—the Institute with its smell of dragon, and shed dragon scales on sale in the gift shop, and the five million acres out back sort of *looming*. Even as wilderness parks go, Smokehill is pretty uncivilized. It's supposed to be, but it can still kind of knock you over with it.

I didn't see anything that day but ordinary eastern-Smokehill landscape, and little stuff like squirrels, and a few deer and wild sheep. But the weirdest thing is that by the time I got to Pine Tor I had this huge harrowing sense of *urgency*, instead of feeling good and tired and pleased with myself—and maybe deciding to go a last leisurely quarter-mile farther to make it twenty miles and then find a nice place to camp didn't register with me at all. I was so wired I couldn't stand still, despite how tired I was. I had to *keep going*. Where? What? Huh?

I have to say I'd made unbelievable time. That sounds like bragging but it's important for what happened. I got to Pine Tor and it was still afternoon. I stood there, panting, looking around, like I was looking for a Rangers' mark, except I'd already found the one that was there. I wasn't even very interested in the fact that Pine Tor itself looked just like Grace's—Billy's wife—drawing of it and so it was like I had seen it before. It was like I was waiting. . . .

Waiting. . . .

I knew what the smell was immediately, even though I'd never smelled it before. The wind was blowing away from me or I'd've smelled it a lot sooner. My head snapped around like a dog's and I set off toward it, like it was pulling me, like it was a rope around my neck being yanked. No, first I stopped and took a very close look at where I was. Pine Tor is big, and I needed to be able to find not just *it* again, but the right side of it. I was about to set off cross country, away from the Rangers' trail and the Rangers' marks—the thing I was above all expressly forbidden to do—and I had to be able to find my way back. Which proves that at least *some* of my brain cells were working.

It wasn't very far, and when I got there I was glad the wind was blowing away from me. The smell was overwhelming. But then everything about it was overwhelming. I can't tell you . . . and I'm not going to try. It'll be hard enough, even now, just telling a little.

It was a dead—or rather a dying—dragon. She lay there, bleeding, dying, nearly as big as Pine Tor. Stinking. And pathetic. And horrible. She wasn't dying for any good reason. She was dying because somebody—some poacher—some poacher in *Smokehill*—had killed her. If everything else hadn't been so overpowering that alone would have stopped me cold.

I was seeing my first dragon up close. And she was mutilated and dying.

She'd got him too, although it was too late for her. When I saw him—what was left of him—I threw up. It was completely automatic, like blinking or sneezing. He was way beyond horrible but he wasn't pathetic. I was glad he was dead. I was just sorry I'd seen it. It.

There were a couple of thoughts trying to go through my head as I stood there, gasping and shaking. (I was shaking so hard I could barely stand up, and suddenly my knapsack weighed so much and hung on my back so clumsily it was going to make me fall down.) *We don't have poachers at Smokehill.* The fence keeps most of them out; even little half-hearted attempts to breach it make a lot of alarms go off back at the Rangers' headquarters and we're allowed to call out a couple of National Guard helicopters if enough of those alarms go off in the same place. (Some other time I'll tell you about getting helicopters through the gate.) It's happened twice in my lifetime. No one has ever made it through or over the fence before a helicopter has got there—no one ever *had*. Occasionally someone manages to get through the gate, but the Rangers always find them before they do any damage—sometimes they're glad to be found. Even big-game-hunter-type major assho—idiots sometimes find Smokehill a little too much. I'd never heard of anyone killing a dragon in Smokehill—ever—and this wasn't the sort of thing Dad *wouldn't* have told me, and it was the sort of thing I'd asked. Nor, of course, would he have let me do my solo if there was any even vague rumor of poachers or big-game idiots planning to have a try.

The other thing that was in my head was how I knew she was female: because of her color. One of the few things we know about dragon births is that Mom turns an all-over red-vermilion-maroon-with-orange-bits during the process, and dragons are green-gold-brown-black mostly, with sometimes a little red or blue or orange but not much. Even the zoos had noticed the color change. Old Pete had taken very careful notes about his mom dragons, and he thought it was something to do with getting the fire lit in the babies' stomachs. It's as good a guess as any.

But that was why the poacher'd been able to get close to her, maybe. Dragons—even dragons—are probably a little more vulnerable when they're giving birth. Apparently this one hadn't had anyone else around to help her. I didn't know why. Old Pete thought a birthing mom always had a few midwives around.

You don't go near a dying dragon. They can fry you *after* they're dead. The reflex that makes chickens run around after their heads are cut off makes dragons cough fire. Quite a few people have died this way, including one zookeeper. I suppose I wasn't thinking about that. I was thinking about the fact that she was dying, and that her babies were going to die because they had no mother, and that she'd know that. I boomeranged into thinking about my own mother again. They wanted to tell us, when they found her, that she must have died instantly. Seems to me, if she really did fall down that cliff, she'd've had time to think about it that Dad and I were going to be really miserable without her.

How do I know what a mother dragon thinks or doesn't think? But it was just so *sad*. I couldn't bear it. I went up to her. Went up to her head, which was like nearly as big as a Ranger's cabin. She watched me coming. She *watched* me. I had to walk up most of the length of her body, so I had to walk past her babies, these little blobs that were baby dragons. They were born and everything. But they were already dead. So she was dying knowing her babies were already dead. I'd started to cry and I didn't even know it.

When I was standing next to her head I didn't know what to do. It was all way too unreal to want to like *pet* her—pet a dragon, *what* a not-good idea—and even though I'd sort of forgotten that she could still do to me what she'd done to the poacher, I didn't try to touch her. I just stood there like a moron. I nearly touched her after all though because I was still shaking so hard I could hardly stay on my feet. Balance yourself by leaning against a *dragon*, right. I crossed my arms over my front and reached under the opposite elbows so I could grab my knapsack straps with my hands like I was holding myself together. Maybe I was.

The eye I could see had moved slowly, following me, and now it stared straight at me. Never mind the fire risk, being stared at by a dragon—by an eye the size of a wheel on a tour bus—is scary. The pupil goes on and on to the end of the universe and then around to the beginning too, and there are *landscapes* in the iris. Or cavescapes. Wild, dreamy, magical caves, full of curlicue mazes where you could get lost and never come out and not mind. And it's *hot*. I was sweating. Maybe with fear (and with being sick), but with the heat of her staring too.

So there I was, finally seeing a dragon up close—really *really* up close—the thing I would have said that I wanted above every other thing in the world or even out of the world that I could even imagine wanting. And it was maybe the worst thing that had ever happened to me. You're saying, wait a minute, you dummy, it's not worse than your *mom* dying. Or even your dog. It kind of was though, because it was somehow all three of them, all together, all at once.

I stared back. What else could I do—for her? I held her gaze. I took a few steps into that labyrinth in her eye. It was sort of reddish and smoky and shadowy and twinkling. And it was like I really was standing there, with Smokehill *behind* me, not Smokehill all around us both as I stood and stared (and shuddered). The heat seemed to sort of all pull together into the center of my skull, and it hung there and *throbbed*. Now I was sweating from having a headache that felt like it would split my head open. So that's my excuse for my next stupid idea: that I saw what she was thinking. Like I can read a dragon's expression when I mostly can't tell what Dad or Billy is thinking. Well, it *felt* like I could read her huge dying eye, although maybe that was just the headache, and what I saw was anger—rage—despair. Easy enough to guess, you say, that she'd be feeling rage and despair, and it didn't take any creepy mind-reading. But I also saw . . . hope.

Hope?

Looking at me, as she was looking at me (*bang bang bang* went my skull), a little hope had crept into the despair. I saw this happen. Looking at me, the same sort of critter, it should have seemed to her, as had killed her.

And then she died.

And I was back in Smokehill again, standing next to a
dead dragon, and the beautiful, dangerous light in her eye
was gone.

And then I did touch her. I forgot about the dead-dragon
fire-reflex, and I crouched down on the stinking, bloody
ground, and rested my forehead against a tiny little sticky-out
knob of her poor ruined head, and cried like a baby. Cried
more than I ever had for Mom—because, you know, we'd
waited so long, and expected—but not really expected—the
worst for so long, that when the worst finally arrived we
couldn't react at all.

Twenty rough miles in a day and crying my head off—
when I staggered to my feet again, feeling like a fool, I was
so exhausted I barely could stand. And while none of this
had taken a lot of time, still, it was late afternoon, and the
sun was sinking, and I needed to get back to Pine Tor tonight if at all possible. I began drearily to drag myself back
the way I had come. I had to walk past all the little dead
dragonlets again. I looked at them not because I wanted to
but to stop myself from looking at the poacher's body.
Which is how I noticed that one of them was still breathing.

A just-born dragon is ridiculously small, not much bigger
than the palm of your hand. Old Pete had guessed they were
little, but even he didn't guess how little. I'm not even sure
why I recognized them, except that I was already half nuts
and they seemed to be kind of smoky and shadowy and
twinkling. The color Mom goes to have them and get their
tummies lit up lasts a few hours or as much as half a day, but
no one—not even Old Pete—had ever seen the babies or the
fire-lighting actually happening and maybe that's not really
when they're born or lit at all, and it's just Mom's color that
makes humans think "fire."

But I did recognize them. And I could see that the
smokiest, twinklingest of the five of them was breathing:
that its tiny sides were moving in and out. And because no
one knows enough about dragons one of the things I'd read
a lot about, so I could make educated guesses just like real

scientists, was marsupials. If I hadn't known that dragons were marsupial-ish I think I probably still wouldn't have recognized them, nuts or not.

They look kind of lizardy, to the extent they look anything, because mostly what they look is soft and squidgy—just-born things often look like that, one way or another, but dragons look a lot worse than puppies or kittens or even Boneland ground squirrels or just-hatched birds. New dragonlets are pretty well still fetuses after all; once they get into their mom's pouch they won't come out again for yonks.

This baby was still wet from being born. It was breathing, and making occasional feeble, hopeless little swimming gestures with its tiny stumpy legs, like it was still blindly trying to crawl up its mom's belly to her pouch, like a kangaroo's joey. I couldn't bear that either, watching it trying, and without thinking about it, I picked it up and stuffed it down my shirt. I felt its little legs scrabble faintly a minute or two longer, and then sort of brace themselves, and then it collapsed, or curled up, and didn't move any more, although there was a sort of gummy feeling as I moved and its skin rubbed against mine. And I thought, Oh, great, it's dead now too, I've got a sticky, gross, dead dragonlet down my shirt, and then I couldn't think about it any more because I had to watch for the way to Pine Tor. The moon was already rising as the day grayed to sunset, and it was a big round bright one that shed a lot of light. I could use all the breaks I could get.

I made it back to Pine Tor and unloaded my pack but I didn't dare sit down because I knew once I did I wouldn't get up again till morning at least. I was lucky; Pine Tor is called that for a reason and in a countryside where there isn't exactly a lot of heavy forest (pity you can't burn rock) I was really grateful that I didn't have to go far to collect enough firewood. The moonlight helped too. I hauled a lot of wood back to my campsite, being careful not to knock my stomach, because even if the dragonlet was dead I didn't want *squished* dead dragonlet in my shirt. I hauled and

hauled partly because I was so tired by then I couldn't remember to stop, and partly because if the dragonlet was
still alive I had a dim idea that I needed to be able to keep it
warmer than my own body temperature, and partly because
if it was dead I didn't want to know and hauling wood put
off finding out. There'd been too much death today already.

I got a fire going and started heating some water for dinner. There's plenty of water in most of Smokehill (except
where there isn't any at all), and pretty much anywhere
within a few days' hike of the Institute has streams all over
it running through the rocks and tough scrub so it's less a
matter of finding it than of trying not to find it at the wrong
moment and get soaked (or break something in our famous
fall-down-and-break-something streambeds). I pulled out a
packet of dried meat and threw the meat in the water. We
don't buy freeze-dried campers' supplies in shiny airtight
envelopes from the nearest outdoor-sports shop—there isn't
one nearer than Cheyenne, and the outdoors isn't a sport to
us. We live here. Besides, we couldn't afford it. We dry our
own stuff. One of the suggestions for the gift shop was that
we sell some of our own dried meat but the Rangers already
have enough to do, although the pointy-head tourist consul-
tant guy seemed to think that tourists would go for wild
sheep and wild goat and bison and stuff as exotic. Exotic. I
ate at a McDonald's once, and I thought their hamburgers
tasted pretty exotic.

But what I was thinking as the water got hot and I could
smell the meat cooking is that we've always shared the dragons' dinners. Old Pete had figured out what dragons liked
best of what he could offer them while he still had them in
cages and fortunately there was enough of it that could live
here. This wouldn't be a dragon haven if dragons only
thrived on rhino and Galapagos tortoise, neither of which
would do well at Smokehill. And Old Pete ate what the dragons ate because the dragons were the important thing. We
still do and they still are.

This smelled like deer, but would sheep be any better? I'd just picked up the first couple of packets. *I* didn't care.

So I sat there and looked at my supper and thought, Even if it's still alive, how am I going to feed it? We don't know anything about dragon milk, or dragon juice, or whatever, even if Mom makes it from eating wild sheep and so on.

I put my hand into my shirt and the dragonlet woke up at once, if it had been asleep, wriggled around like crazy, and managed to attach itself to one of my fingers, sucking so hard it hurt. So it was still alive and it was hungry. If I'd been thinking clearly I'd've known it was alive, though, because it was so hot. It was hot enough that when I unbuttoned my shirt to get it out there was a red mark on my stomach. It didn't like being out of my shirt; it let go of my finger and started, I don't know, mewing, kind of, a tiny, harsh sort of noise that I didn't want to think sounded like a scream of absolute terror, and trying to burrow back where it came from.

I was tired, and hungry myself, and my head really *hurt*, and I was all wound up about what had happened, and about the fact that I had landed myself with an orphan dragonlet that I hadn't a clue how to take care of, and how it was all going to be my fault when it died and I *already* felt as if everything that had happened was my fault—even though I knew that was stupid—and when it died too I'd never forgive myself and go crazy or something. I was way out of my depth. I wasn't a mother dragon and *I didn't have a* **clue.** Oh yes and what I was doing was totally illegal. Don't ask me who makes the laws or why they don't like get together sometimes and notice if the laws make any *sense.* But while it's illegal to hurt or kill a dragon it's *more* illegal to try and save a dragon's life.

Dad tried to explain it to me once, that it's about *non-interference*—like the way big parks (including this one) let lightning-started fires go ahead and burn everything up because it's part of the natural cycle. Okay. Maybe. But people get bent about dragons in ways they don't get bent about other natural cycle stuff. Apparently the witless won-

der who was pushing for the dragon legislation got so bent
about the anti-harming-a-dragon part of the bill that he
pulled all the stops out getting really vicious language into
the anti-preserving-a-dragon's-life part of the bill. The result is that trying to raise a baby dragon would be like the
most illegal thing you could possibly do, next to assassinat-
ing the president maybe, and is probably one of the extra
reasons the Institute has to beg for money, because we
might do something illegal with it, like learn how to save
dragons.

Well it would all be over soon and it would be dead and
I would be crazy and Dad would have to put my gross
baby-dragon-yucky clothes through the washing machine
because I would be in a padded cell and couldn't do it myself.

I rebuttoned my shirt except for one button over the belt,
muttering to myself, or to it, and tucked the dragonlet back
in, tail first and belly up, with its head near the opening. It
stopped struggling and lay there like it was peering out
through the gap and looking at me. Its eyes were open—
unlike a puppy or a kitten's—but they were blurry like they
didn't see much, like a baby bird's. They were also a funny
purplish color. It was really ugly all over, not just the eyes,
sort of bruise colored, not just purplish but also yellowish
and greenish, as well as smushed-looking and crusty with
dried whatever.

"You are the ugliest damn thing I have ever seen in my
entire life," I said to it, clearly, like I wanted it on the record
what I thought, and I swear its blurry purple eyes tried to
track where the sound was coming from and it made a little
grunt like an acknowledgment.

Have you ever tried to raise a baby bird or a raccoon or
something? Something, you know, easy. They die a lot. We're
way too good at raccoons—that's Eric again—since our suc-
cesses are now bringing their great-great-great-grandkids for
evening handouts behind the Institute—but we all still sweat
when the Rangers bring in new orphans. And even with Eric's voodoo and all the info every bird society or raccoon

society or beetle society (that's a *joke*) can give us (actually we wrote some of it), so you know exactly what to do and you do it . . . they still die. A lot. And it hurts. And that's when you even know what they eat and for stuff that is at least already, you know, born. Which a new dragonlet isn't, not really.

I locked open my camping spoon and dipped up some of the meat broth, gave the dragonlet my finger to suck again, which it was happy to do, and poured some broth in the gap between its mouth and my finger. You'd think I'd know better, but remember I was pretty deranged.

Of course most of the broth went all over me and the dragonlet, but some of it must have gone down its throat because it choked and gargled and then I knew I *had* killed it. I whipped it out of my shirt again and held it up head down in the air and it gacked and gagged and then started mewing again and trying to get back in my shirt. Poor awful little monster. I'd be crying here again in a minute. This time I unbuttoned my sleeve and stuck it in tail first (against the thin skin on the underside of my forearm and let me tell you its body heat *hurt*) till only its face was showing, and I cupped my hand around its head and it subsided, and I swear it looked traumatized, ugly and weird as it was.

I was still muttering. Now I was saying things like "it's okay, stupid, relax." I'm not sure if I was talking to myself this time, or the dragonlet. I stuck a finger from my cupping hand in sort of the side of its mouth to give it something to suck on and tipped just a drop or two of broth into its mouth. (This was way more awkward than I'm telling you.) It went *gulp* and went on sucking. Oh hurrah. A lot of your orphans just won't try to eat and that's that. So the dragonlet wasn't going to die of starvation, it was going to die of being poisoned or of not getting enough of some kind of vitamin because deer broth isn't anything like close enough to dragon milk. As I say, no one knows what goes on in those pouches.

I fed it broth till its belly was stretching my sleeve. It was almost beginning to look kind of cute to me. I was in a bad way. But you do get like this with your orphans. If they eat you feel all . . . mothery. (Mom had been really good with the orphans—maybe almost as good as Eric. I remember getting old enough to ask her, kind of anxiously, if taking care of me had been as bad as the stuff at Eric's orphanage. She'd laughed and said oh no, I was much, *much* worse.) I slid the dragonlet out of my sleeve again and it was either falling asleep because it was full and happy or slipping into its final coma, but it didn't struggle so much this time. I pulled my shirt off and wrapped it up in that because I had a clean shirt in my backpack, and if one of us was going to have the clean shirt I'd rather it was me, and then I put it as near the fire as I thought I could without making dragonlet toast, or anyway setting my shirt on fire.

I looked at the inside of my wrist where it had been lying. The skin there is even thinner than on your stomach, and it was actually burned. Jeez. So I got the wound salve out that is part of the basic kit Billy makes you carry, like waterproof matches and a hatchet to make kindling and a pot to boil water, and put some on, and then I had dinner, which took about three minutes because I was so hungry and tired and shaky.

But by the time I'd finished eating, make that bolting, the wretched dragonlet was mewing again, and trying to get out of the shirt. "Oh, give me a *break*," I said. I thought maybe I'd put it too close to the fire, so I picked it up, and it went floppy instantly, but then the moment I put it down again it was mewing and thrashing, to the extent that something the size of your hand and with legs an inch and a half long and is maybe three or six hours old can thrash. "You're ugly and you *smell*," I said.

So fatalistically I put it back inside my clean shirt and it scuffled a little like you might thump your pillow with your fist, and then went to sleep. Which made one of us. It had managed to relieve itself on my old shirt, so *that* was really delightful, and I got my jackknife out and hacked off the dirtiest bits and then sort of tucked the rest of the old shirt around its rear end where it was asleep inside my new shirt and leaving fresh red marks on my stomach. I lay down gingerly on my side clutching it with my other hand so that the old shirt around its rear end wouldn't fall off and wondering if I'd get any sleep at all because what if I rolled *over* on it? Not merely squished dragonlet but squished full-of-deer-broth dragonlet. By then I was probably a little hysterical.

I did sleep but I didn't sleep much. Every time it moved I woke up, and I suppose my brain had been working in my sleep or something because by the first time it woke me up I'd figured that a dragonlet probably had to be fed every ten minutes or something because if it was in its mom's pouch it would probably be permanently stuck on a nipple for the first six months or so, which is what happens with the ordinary true-mammal marsupials we know about and makes sense. And a lot of ordinary orphans you do have to feed round the clock. (Maybe Eric's personality was just the result of chronic sleep shortage, although all of the—human—adults took turns for the middle of the night, and Mom and Katie and Jane never got anything like Eric gets, even on no sleep. Although Dad got a little scratchy.) I was trying to remember how long they think the full-time pouch span is for a dragon, but if I'd ever known I'd forgotten and it didn't really matter at the moment since this was only the first *night*.

Every time it wiggled I woke up, groggily—now I was definitely talking out loud to keep myself awake—and the first time I had to pour the rest of the broth back into the pot and heat it in the embers because it's not a good idea to leave food around even in summer when there's plenty of other stuff to eat for anything wandering by. But after the first time I thought the hell with it and just put the top on the pot and left it in the fire, and I know this completely destroys your respect for me as someone who should be allowed to go on his first solo, and you're right, but you weren't there. And it was still a horrible night (even though nobody tried to eat our broth and then have us for dessert), and I used almost all of the firewood I'd collected after all, keeping the fire going.

And to the extent I did sleep, it was like I was afraid to move at all, so I woke up every time in exactly the same position because it suited trying to hold the damn dragonlet in the position *it* liked, and by morning when I stopped even pretending to sleep my whole right side was like paralyzed and I had a headache like you wouldn't believe, although really I'd had the headache since everything happened yesterday afternoon. And to think a few days ago I'd been feeling that just relearning to sleep on the ground was tough. I may have slept as much as an hour that last spell before dawn. When I tried to sit up I yelped like a dog when you've stepped on its tail. But I felt the dragonlet stir. My stomach felt scalded so I already knew it was still alive. It was probably hungry again too. I hurt too much to be hungry. "You still there, Ugly?" I said.

I got the fire going properly again (nice hot embers, I thought resentfully, regularly blown on and fed sticks—the dragonlet would have been *fine* lying next to the fire all night) and put some more water on to heat and threw another chunk of meat in. At home Dad makes me eat vegetables but when I'm in the park I turn carnivore. Billy never makes me eat vegetables even though most of the year he can usually find green stuff to eat wherever he is. Even I know about waterweed. I just don't eat it. And I bet dragons don't either. I wasn't going to endanger the dragonlet's fragile welfare by threatening it with vegetable matter.

It had done some more on my old shirt, so I cut those bits out. I needed to get back to the Institute soon because I was running out of shirt. Then we did the broth thing again and while in one way it was easier because I was getting in practice it didn't seem to want to open its mouth any wider than it absolutely had to and now in daylight again the corners of its mouth looked sort of, well, chapped, maybe. So I put some wound salve on it and wondered if maybe *that* would poison it, and some more on the inside of my wrist, and then

I cruelly let it lie near the fire in a nice warm pile of ashes (I checked) while I cleaned up in the hope that it would do some of its business before I had to wrap it up in what remained of my old shirt again and put it next to my stomach, and it did. So that was something.

But it had also mewed and thrashed while I left it—it had added a sort of high-pitched peep to its repertoire on its second day of life—so by the time I finally did put it back inside my shirt it was exhausted and went to sleep instantly. At least I assume that's what it was doing when it did its pillow-punching trick and didn't move for a while. By now I could feel it breathing—I don't know if it was breathing better or I was learning the mom marsupial drill—and, of course, it was burning holes in the skin of my stomach.

I can't begin to tell you what a long day that was. I was aching all over, particularly my head, and tired into my bones. I don't think I'd ever realized what that phrase meant before. It's a good thing I've been trained since I was a toddler to follow Rangers' marks because I was doing it mindlessly, not thinking because I couldn't think. There was no thinking left in me. And it's ridiculous to say that something the size of a day-and-a-half-old dragonlet *weighed*, but it did. It weighed more than my backpack did somehow. I suppose it was just that I couldn't stop worrying about it. I worried about whether or not it could breathe, because I had to tuck my sweatshirt in over my shirt to make sure it didn't fall out while we were moving, but mostly it wasn't anything so logical. It was just worry worry worry about everything. Worry on legs. Worry walking. Worry staggering and lurching.

I didn't anything like cover twenty miles that day. I think I did about ten, which under the circumstances is amazing. I decided after the first stop to feed my new responsibility that if it could live with human body heat it could probably live with human-body-heat food, so I put the pot of broth under my shirt too. The idea that I had to stop and make a fire every half hour was a whole lot too much. And I was sure I should be feeding it more often than every half hour anyway, I just couldn't. Fortunately the broth pot was small. Mind you my shirt had not been made to hold both a dragonlet and even a small pot of broth so I had to tuck the pot sort of down my pants which made walking harder, and cradle the dragonlet with one hand so it didn't fall down the hole, and the pot leaked. Well, so did the dragonlet. After a while I stopped paying attention. Ordinarily I don't think I'd've been able to ignore getting increasingly covered with runny infant dragon poop but there was nothing ordinary about that day. If I hadn't kept telling myself "Billy will know what to do" I'd never have been able to make myself keep moving at all.

When sunset came I pulled myself together enough to look for the next Ranger mark so I'd know exactly which way to go in the morning. Besides, camping near one was almost like company. Human company. I knew that tomorrow was going to be even worse than today had been. I mopped myself up as well as I could out of the nearby rill while a new pot of water was heating over the fire. I didn't even try to put the dragonlet down this time. Sometimes I think personal hygiene is kind of overdone but I would have *loved* a hot bath. And lots of soap.

I had to clean up carefully, moving the dragonlet around so it didn't get any nasty cold water on it, and it wasn't thrilled with the operation anyway, from the amount of scrabbling and peeping, but when it was broth time again it settled right down and started to suck and swallow. I felt kind of funny about that. I mean, it was already learning the system. It was a *dragon* for pity's sake. But at two days old it was already learning what to do, and I was pretty sure a finger and a camping spoon wasn't the system it was born to expect. I'd tried using a piece of shirt (more shirt gone) as a nipple, but that didn't work so well, or it couldn't suck the broth out of the cloth, or something; the cloth just got soggier and soggier and it kept letting go to try and grab one of my fingers again. So we went back to the old system. My finger was getting almost as sore as my stomach.

But when I thought about how much worse tomorrow was going to be, it never crossed my mind to hope the thing would die and let me off.

CHAPTER THREE

I was so tired I fell asleep leaning against a tree with the dragonlet belly up in one sleeve and a potful of broth propped between my legs. A weird sort of distant *whoosh* and a sudden splash of light woke both of us. I opened my eyes slowly, for a moment having no idea where I was or what was going on. The dragonlet was trying to turn itself over so it could dive back into my shirt. Absent-mindedly I helped it while I looked at the big orange streak . . . in the sky . . . over the rocks and treetops . . . the old brain was trying to churn out some kind of recognition. . . .

A flare. A Ranger's flare. And it would be Billy, wondering where I was, if I was in trouble. Knowing that I had to be in trouble, because I wasn't back at Northcamp when I should be. And probably even more worried because I hadn't radioed—I should have radioed in last night—I didn't even have mine turned on so I'd hear him trying to call me. I'd forgotten all about my radio—all about "radio Billy and stay put." That's how tired and crazy I was.

Everything is harder when you only have one hand and are using the other to keep a dragonlet in your shirt, even if you're busy talking to yourself and telling yourself how to do stuff. (Some of the time I seemed to be talking to Mom. Sometimes I seemed to be talking to the dead dragon, except she was alive. Sometimes they seemed to be there too, and to be talking back. Like I keep saying: tired and crazy.) Eventually I turned the backpack upside down and shook it hard, and everything fell out, including the two-way and my three flares. The two-way bounced and made a nasty *clank*

when it hit the second time. Oh well. Flares are less break-
able and perhaps easier to use one-handed. I managed to
wedge one between two stones. Then I clutched the empty
backpack over the dragonlet in case the flare freaked it out
through my shirt, and yanked the flare open.

Rangers really are amazing. I guess I was on the right
trail so it wasn't like he had to do a big search, and the
moonlight was blazing bright again tonight in a clear sky,
but even so. Billy was there by midnight. *You* try following
an almost invisible path in bad country in the dark for nine
or ten miles. I didn't even hear him coming, so I didn't
have to worry about what big animal was about to eat me
and the dragonlet, although getting eaten would have let
me off another six months of every-thirty-minute feedings.
Getting eaten was probably the nicer death. Or maybe I
didn't hear him coming because I was talking again. I used
to talk to my orphans at the zoo—most of us do ("Theeeeere
now, isn't that gooooood?" and other inane remarks)—but
not like this. I couldn't shut up. I think talking kept the
whole gruesome situation at a little distance so I didn't
quite finish going crazy. That and keeping myself awake,
of course. Also if the dragonlet peeped why shouldn't I
answer?

Billy was just suddenly at the edge of the firelight like
we'd been together all along and he'd been gone briefly to
have a pee or collect firewood or something. Maybe it's just
I *was* crazy by then, but I looked up between spoon-tipping
and spoon-tipping (and mutter and mutter) and said, "Oh,
hello, Billy," and went back to the dragonlet. It fell asleep
between one spoonful and the next, the way it usually did
now, and although I woke it up when I turned it over to put it
back in my shirt it peeped one burpy peep and instantly
crashed again. Then I looked up at Billy who was still standing there like Cinderella's fairy godmother had turned him
to stone.

Billy slid out of his backpack very, very carefully and set
it down very, very carefully. I don't know if he was trying
not to disturb the dragonlet or whether he thought I'd gone

off my rocker and had to be treated gently. I noticed distantly that he was acting peculiar but couldn't put it together somehow. I'd also forgotten that I was covered in dried blood, birth slime, dragonlet pee and poop, wound salve, and who knows what else. So he may also have thought I was injured.

He squatted down slowly beside me. "Hey, Jake," he said. "What's that?"

I actually didn't know what he meant for a moment. "Uh—oh, you mean the dragonlet. It's a baby dragon. Oh!"—because I was beginning to remember that Billy being here was a kind of reentry into the real world. "There's a dead dragon . . . and a dead, uh, poacher, I guess . . . just beyond Pine Tor. The dragon had just given birth. All her babies were dead." I had to stop and swallow. "Except this one."

I feel a little better about being as crazy as I was, thinking about it now, because Billy didn't really register the poacher or the dead dragon—why I was sitting there with a dragonlet. It's not that he looked surprised or anything—Billy doesn't do surprise—but all he said, slowly and unbelievingly, was, "It's a *dragon*."

"Yeah," I said, coming back a little farther into the real world. "It doesn't look like one, does it? I suppose I only knew because they were—" I had to stop and swallow again. "It eats *all the time*. You can get a better look at it when it wakes up again. Which it will. Soon." I sighed. "I'm sorry I missed getting back tonight. I know I've blown it. But I'm . . . so tired."

Billy was silent for a minute. I can imagine, now, what he must have been thinking. Nobody had ever so much as seen a dragon giving birth. It was Old Pete who figured out, working backwards from seeing dog-sized dragonlets for the first time, why the dragon whose pouch they fled for when *they* saw Old Pete for the first time had changed color for a few hours about a year ago. No one—no human, not even Old Pete—had ever seen just-born dragons—let alone kept one alive for thirty hours and counting. I was some kind of eco-naturalist hero. Except that what I'd done would also get me thrown in jail for the rest of my life if anyone found out about it . . . and get everyone who knew about it thrown in jail for the rest of their lives too. It might even shut down the Institute—or Smokehill itself. There were always a few people rumbling away about dragons being a danger to society, and writing to the money guys in Congress who kept Smokehill alive about child poverty and cures for cancer and other things more important (they think) than dragons.

Smokehill is actually really precarious, although I know that's kind of hard to get your brain around when you're looking at several million acres of rock and dirt—and that fence. The Bonelands—the deserty part—are probably their own best defense, but developers would love to get their hands on the prettier bits of Smokehill, and the government would love to get their hands on the money developers would pay them, if they could find a good excuse to break their promises to us—and there might be gold here after all. And now I might have provided the excuse the government wanted. My not having made it back to Northcamp by nightfall would have been the last thing Billy was thinking about at that moment.

It's no wonder I kept talking to myself. I wasn't keeping myself awake, I was drowning out thoughts like these.

And that's still leaving out the poacher. A dead human *killed* by a dragon.

On the other hand there'd be no way that Billy would ever have told me to let something that had the possibility of living die without a struggle, and he wouldn't care whether it was a dragon or a caterpillar, so that part of it was all right, as far as it went. But I had put everyone in deep *deep* trouble by what I'd done automatically—automatically as a result of having been Billy and the other Rangers' willing slave from the age of two. What I'd done was exactly what every Ranger would have done. And they'd have done it automatically too. Hey, our Rangers bring back orphaned or injured gray squirrels. They'd bring back rats, if we had rats. Well, we do, but our *Rattus* are *Rattus maculatus* and *R. perobscurus*, and endangered.

My point is, we save things. It's what we do.

I was drifting in and out of . . . semiconsciousness, let's not call it sleep. When the dragonlet woke up again Billy watched very carefully while I fed it, and the next time it—and I—woke up Billy had the broth ready and some piece of something he'd cut off something to make a nipple, and *his* nipple worked, and that made things a *lot* easier. The rest of the night was better. I didn't get a lot more sleep, but I didn't have to think about anything else either—Billy did all that. He didn't offer to touch the dragonlet, but he did everything else. By morning I probably had nearly half my brain available again, which was up on the 10 percent I'd had at midnight when Billy arrived.

We made it back to Northcamp that day, don't ask me how. I think Billy was beaming Strength Waves at me or something. If I could keep a baby dragon alive anything was possible, including Strength Waves. It took us all day, and Billy carried my pack as well as his own, and we stopped a lot, and every time I sat down (which I had to, to feed the dragonlet without worrying about dropping it), I thought I'd never get up again. But I did. Also standing up always made my headache worse (*bang bang bang*), and I kept trying to walk so as not to joggle my head, let alone the dragonlet.

At some feeding or other I noticed that the dragonlet was already bigger than it had been two days ago. If I held it upside down in my hand now, it spilled over onto my wrist. It wasn't going to fit up my sleeve much longer. And it was heavier too obviously. I didn't have to come up with any way to measure that. It was a good thing Billy'd brought food. The dragonlet got through a *lot* of broth.

When I staggered into the little clearing in front of Northcamp I almost couldn't believe it. It was like adopting a baby dragon had sent me into some kind of alternate reality where things like buildings and electricity didn't exist. Billy got the generator going while I was still sitting in a chair and staring at the stove in the big central room. Stoves didn't exist in my alternate reality either. Or chairs. When the tea-kettle whistled I jumped a mile and the dragonlet woke up and started peeping. I wasn't sure whether it was a frightened peep or a "hello, who are *you*?" peep but it stopped as soon as the teakettle did and went back to sleep. Feeding it sitting in a chair was weird too. Dragons just don't fit in the human world. Duh.

And then there was taking a bath. . . . In a way that was the first time some of the hairiest implications of what I'd done began to sink in. I'd told Billy, during some night feed or other, that it went nuts any time I tried to lay it down . . . and then we'd found out the hard way the next day that it hated Billy trying to hold it only slightly less than it hated being laid down. This was a blow. Make that a **BLOW.** Until it happened I hadn't thought about having someone to trade off red welts and disgustingness duty and nooo sleep with—but it occurred to me real fast at that point that I *didn't* have it. That I wasn't *going* to have it. And dragonlets stay in their moms' pouches *how long*??? Also I was used to Billy being able to do anything—including get me out of any trouble I was in. But I was too zonked to follow what this really meant very far. And that's a good thing.

Maybe the teakettle and being in a square place lined with planks (called a "cabin") and furniture and plumbing and stuff were the thing too many for the dragonlet (see: dragons do not fit in the human world, and don't forget the "duh") like getting back to human space seemed to be this weird shock to me. My new permanent headache, which I was almost sort of getting used to, was making me feel queasy and dizzy. But the bath was a kind of a watershed (ha ha ha) moment for both of us. The dragonlet had a complete mini Eric-type meltdown. I thought it was going to do itself an injury when we tried to make it a nest with (a) warm ashes, (b) warmed-up blankets, (c) anything else we could think of.

So the way it ended up was, we kept the dragonlet half wrapped in a piece of my by then truly gross shirt and moved it kind of up and down my front while I *got in the bath* that way and tried to wash *around* it, which is to say Billy held it while I tried to wash—this was more embarrassing than I can begin to tell you and it was only being so tired and out of it that made it even possible—and then I got up on my knees and Billy held it against my back while I crouched forward to wash my face and hair. Oh good. New red spots too.

Billy noticed the red spots, both old and new—he'd probably noticed before but maybe he hadn't realized how many of them there were—and did his more-expressionless-than-expressionless wooden-Indian face thing and I noticed, which was interesting, since I wasn't noticing anything, but I suppose it just proves I was fully into my new dragonlet-defending-and-fostering role, because I said, "Oh, they don't *hurt*, they're just *marks*, they're no big deal, they're no *deal*." And I looked at Billy and Billy looked at me and I could see that Billy knew I was lying but I just kept looking at him and . . . he looked away. I didn't get into staring contests with Billy because I knew who won and it wasn't me, and furthermore I'd had this one standing there naked and stinking (and red-spotted). The maternal instinct is sure powerful.

The dragonlet hated all of this. I started getting so worried that it would explode or something that I sort of hurried up. Besides, there's only so much embarrassment you can take at one time.

The dragonlet wasn't crazy about clean clothes either but I guess it was so glad to see its pouch equivalent again it wasn't going to complain. And Billy had come up with some new kind of salve for my stomach (and my back, and my arm) which the dragonlet seemed to like a lot, so we smeared some all over it and then wiped some off again which kind of cleaned it up too, but the salve made it fantastically slippery like a sort of extra-large watermelon seed with legs, and by the end of the process my clean sweatshirt and sweatpants were almost as sticky and disgusting as my shirt had been, although we smelled a lot better than we had. And Billy—which may be the single best thing he's ever done for me in my entire life—had rigged up a kind of diaper for the dragonlet—it didn't have any tail to speak of yet, just a kind of vaguely pointy lump at the back end—so I stayed poopless.

This was so blissful my third night of almost no sleep seemed almost okay. Even if Mom was in a lot of my dreams, when I got near enough to being asleep to have dreams. Although you may have noticed that you can dream even when you're only about half asleep, and know it, like you know you're still lying on a thin little rubbery mattress under mousy-smelling blankets curled up around a pillow supporting a dragonlet against your stomach. I even said to her once, I'm too tired to be dreaming. Even about you. *Bang bang bang* went the headache. The headache never slept.

If you've ever been for a long time without anything like enough sleep you know that you get pretty non compos pretty soon. I was forgetting things the moment Billy said them and couldn't really think of anything but feeding the dragonlet. (And talking to it. I was still doing that. Although I was still calling it Ugly.) It was like my life had become feeding the dragonlet and I hadn't noticed or *minded*. This was just the way it was now. A haze punctuated by feeding the dragonlet. Speaking of the maternal instinct. Maybe the headache was the fourteen-year-old boy with a dragonlet version of postnatal depression.

The haze was also stabbed and ripped up by visions of the dying dragon's eye. The cavescape was still there when I looked into her eye—which is where the dreams about her always started—but I seemed to get farther in now, when I did that weird stepping-forward thing, till there was nothing behind me either except more caves—reddishy purply and shadowy and smoky and twinkling and something else, I don't know what, some *presence*. Sometimes I got so far in I imagined seeing her with a lot of other dragons there, in those magical-looking caves that I'd got into by looking into her eye. Real Arabian Nights stuff. I didn't try saying "open sesame" but I'm not sure I wanted to leave.

I don't know why I thought the caves had to be magical

except that like I've told you that's the way I've always been about caves. And these didn't look anything like the caves near the Institute. These had stalactites and stalagmites that were landscapes and worlds all by themselves, and in colors you can't even really dream. I'd be looking at some stony sculpture Michelangelo would have killed his grandmother to have been able to do, and thinking, I don't know that color, that color doesn't exist, but like *wow*. Those dreams— whatever they were—were another thing that made the headache worse, although it was a weird kind of worse, there was something kind of curvy and rippling about it, like one of the cave sculptures, and it like fitted into my head differently, almost as if it thought it belonged there and couldn't figure out why it couldn't make itself comfortable. And made me *un*comfortable. Sometimes I felt it would have apologized if it could've figured out how. Nuts of course. Of course I had a headache most of the time—it was just from not getting enough sleep.

At least the dreams about Mom didn't make my head hurt more. They made my stomach hurt more instead—on the inside, not the outside where the dragonlet was operating.

I didn't hear Billy's first check-in after he found us—and I really don't know how he got through the one when I should have been back at Northcamp and wasn't—but that meant two check-ins I should have talked to Dad and didn't. This would have made Dad *frantic*, and while probably the only person who could have talked him out of sending for the helicopter was Billy, it's still interesting that Billy managed it somehow, since even on no sleep I would have noticed a helicopter. Ha ha. But even our special two-ways don't work very well in a lot of Smokehill, which is why we always carry flares too. It's something about the charge on the fence, and the permanent campsites were chosen almost as much for good radio transmission as a good water and firewood supply. So maybe Billy did something cute with the two-way during my unscheduled absence and just undid it once I was back again.

Billy made sure I heard this one. I heard it through my haze, but Northcamp is small anyway, and we were both (all three of us, but I doubt the dragonlet got much out of it) in the central room. Also Dad was pretty noisy. The roaring coming out of the radio as soon as contact was made must have just about knocked the thing off the table except that Billy was holding it down.

Even Billy's eyes narrowed a fraction but he flipped the switch as calmly as ever and said, "You can talk to Jake in a minute, Frank, and he's fine."

Flip—*ROAR*—flip.

"Frank, listen to me. I'm afraid I have some bad news. Something Jake discovered. I think you need to hear this first." And Billy went on to make up some true-as-far-as-it-went story about a dead dragon and a dead guy. The sheer bald chutzpah of it almost jerked me into full attention—Billy sounded like he was telling the truth, the whole truth, and nothing but the truth, so help him whatever.

At the same time what he was telling—even without what he wasn't telling—was of course totally *huge*—the **BIGGEST**—scary news for us anyway, and was going to distract everybody very, very effectively from Jake's first solo, even Dad right now in full roar. Dad sounded almost normal as he said head-of-Institute things like "Where?" and "Just the one man?" and "No visible time line, I suppose?" which is to say who killed who first, which was going to be a *big* one. It was all big and deadly anyway, but if she'd killed him first, it was worse. Dad said a couple more times, "Let me talk to Jake," and Billy finally said, "Jake's a bit in shock, you know. You might let it pass for now. You can talk to him about it later."

There was a pause that probably wasn't so long in actual time terms but it sure echoed in Northcamp's little common room. The dragonlet chose this moment to rearrange itself too, so I felt briefly like I was caught in some kind of nowhere between my old life/world and my new one. Sleeplessness makes you dizzy too, in case you don't already know that.

"Okay, Billy," Dad said finally. "Thanks."

Another, shorter pause, and Billy nodded to me, and I put my hand under the settling-down bulge of dragonlet and went over to sit down by the two-way. I flicked the switch. "Hi, Dad."

As awkward father-son conversations go this one was pretty impressive. It was even worse than the one we'd had about sex about a year before. At least this one was over the two-way where we didn't have to be obvious about not being able to look each other in the face. But I agreed that I was fine, just like Billy had said. And I did try to say something about the dragon, just to sort of, I don't know, show I was trying or something, but all I could manage to get out was, "They're so *big*, you know? You know they're big—I walk by that picture every day—" It's one of those artist's representation things, right outside the theater (and not half bad by the way, it does *not* look like someone who is trying to make ends meet because his only job is part-time substitute illustrator for a bad comic book series), and it goes on and on and on and *on* because eighty feet (plus tail) is a lot of wall, or a lot of dragon. But my voice cracked when I said it, and Dad let it go, and I changed the subject to asking if there'd been any interesting new orphans since we'd been gone, which was the best I could do at subject-changing and Dad wouldn't know how bad a try it really was.

Then I gave the two-way back to Billy and he and Dad started discussing immediate ways and means. Billy was going to stay out here a few more days, needed help, and couldn't spare anyone to see me safe home while they investigated because he wanted anyone who could be spared to join the hunting party. Clue-hunting party. He said, And besides, Jake can help. That was the best joke of all. I heard him say it. He lied *amazingly*. I didn't know he had it in him. Billy can just not say things, although I'd never heard him do it on quite such an epic scale before, but I'd never heard him lie.

I'd better make this point now and then I'll make it several more times later on because it's one of the things that makes no sense—or maybe it's the thing that makes the no-sense make sense to you reading this about Crazy Jake and His Dragonlet. If it hadn't been for this sticky, smelly, hot little blodge of dragonlet I'd've been *totally blown away* by the poacher. I should have been totally blown away. This was The End of Life As All of Us Knew It, at Smokehill. Dragons were safe here, that's what Smokehill was *for*—we may save raccoons, rats and squirrels too, and provide cage space (and cleaning) to a lot of lizards, but dragons are what we're *for*. But to everybody outside Smokehill, the really important thing that Smokehill was for was to prove to people, from the other direction, that dragons were safe—that they didn't kill people and nobody ever, ever had to worry that they might, and besides, no one could get through the fence.

I can't BEGIN to tell you how important this was—how important *everyone at Smokehill knew it was*. Except me. I knew the poacher was really bad and everything—but wasn't it time to feed the dragonlet again? Yes. It was always time to feed the dragonlet again. If there were any cracks in my dragonlet obsession, they were full of remembering its mom. The way she'd looked at me. Slightly in my defense, it was a pretty overwhelming experience. It had been overwhelming enough that Billy reminding Dad of it had stopped Dad in midroar, which wasn't something that happened in the world as I had known it. And Dad didn't know the half of it.

That first conversation with Dad I got sort of for free though. I had to pull it together more after that, because of course Dad was expecting me to. That was pretty bad. I had this brilliant idea of telling Dad I'd walked into a tree branch while I was looking the other way and it banged up my throat, so talking kind of hurt. After Billy assured him it was no big deal Dad let me get away with this too. I don't know if he suspected anything right away or not—but he probably couldn't afford to waste time thinking about it. Dad had to figure out what he was going to tell the world about the poacher, and he had to figure it out fast, so I imagine that he was relieved to take Billy's word for it and leave his clumsy, idiot son in Billy's hands for a while longer. He did sound a little distracted, although it made him keep asking me if I was *really* okay, which I suppose meant he cared, although it sounded a lot like he'd just forgotten I'd already said yes thirty seconds ago. Although really it was pretty amazing of him to remember he *had* a son, in the circumstances. I'm not sure I would've in his shoes.

Billy's everyone, when they arrived, turned out to be three more of the oldest Rangers, and he must have told them what they were getting into because I don't remember their acting surprised when they were introduced to me and my new buddy. Or maybe I don't remember because I was so stupid from being that tired. I registered that they'd brought me some more clothes and a couple of old baby bottles from the stash at the orphanage. I didn't ask how they'd got them past Eric. And I wondered when Billy had told them what kind of orphan to expect.

Anyway, Whiteoak took over the Jake-tending duty while Billy, Jane and Kit went on to Pine Tor. They were away for three days. And when they got back something else had happened. The dragonlet had gone from needing to be fed every half hour (or twenty minutes) to needing to be fed every two hours. Suddenly. On the tenth day of its life it had still wanted half-hour feedings. That night it slept two hours . . . and then two hours . . . and then two hours . . . and then two hours.

When it woke up, there was Whiteoak with warm broth. I don't know if he'd been waiting an hour and a half each time or not and I didn't ask him. Only partly because he wouldn't have answered. I was in awe of Whiteoak—he could speak English but he didn't want to, and mostly he talked to the other Arkholas in their own language which I knew about six words of. (Eleanor, for whom it is a principle of life never to be in awe of anyone, said that he did this so he got off tourist duty. I wouldn't want to say absolutely that she's wrong. But that only made me admire him more.)

It was weird enough to have anyone waiting on me, even if it wasn't for my sake but the dragonlet's, but it was particularly weird that it was Whiteoak. I mean, just his name—all the other Arkholas had some kind of Anglo name that they used. I guess Whiteoak thought he was meeting us halfway by translating whatever the Arkhola for "white oak" is into English. So it was kind of all part of the space-cadet quality of everything that it was Whiteoak who got left behind to keep me going. And then I was dazed by getting some sleep, finally. You know how when you finally do get some sleep you're *more* tired? That's how I felt. Three days without sleep didn't seem to faze Whiteoak at all.

But it was still confusingly weird, like I had any room for any more confusingness or weirdness: wham—two hours was okay, for feeding the dragonlet. I know how it sounds to put it this way, but it was like the dragonlet was now saving *my* life, for saving *its*.

Over the next week I began to get pretty good at sleeping for two hours at a stretch, and since the Rangers were doing absolutely everything for me but actually having the dragonlet down their shirts, the fact that this meant I was spending twenty or more hours a day horizontal didn't matter. Although I got bedsores. Yuck. I was a healthy almost-fifteen-year-old boy (or at least I had been). But if you lie in the same position for hour after hour, whether it's because you're old and weak and sick or because you don't want to wake up a dragonlet, and maybe you need all the sleep you can get because your permanent headache means you don't sleep very well *besides* having to wake up again every two hours (and also because you're maybe having a better time in the dream cavescape in your head than you are outside and awake), you get bedsores. They weren't bad, but that's what they were. Whiteoak had some kind of new gummy stuff for this which stank but helped. Although I'd wake up with the dragonlet trying to get its tongue under me to lick it off. It had a surprisingly long tongue. And its tongue was hot too, so along with the blotches I started getting these sort of skinny whiplash red marks.

But I'd been away from the Institute for long enough by then that I think even with everything else that was going on (or maybe because of it) Dad was smelling a rat pretty hard—and this was the first time he'd let me out of his sight since Mom died and *this* is what happened.

I was still talking to Dad on the radio every day and I sounded a little better than I had but I was still so tired I know I must have sounded funny, even on a two-way where you tend to kind of squawk and squeal anyway, and the branch-across-the-throat excuse didn't cover my brain. He always sounded sort of preoccupied and jumpy at the same time when he talked to me, which is a good trick but I wasn't enjoying it. I was too tired to jump after him. Once my throat had supposedly healed he'd wanted to talk to me about finding the dead dragon and the dead guy again, but this time while I got a little farther I got way over the top upset—and nearly called her "she" which would *not* have been a good slip to make—so he let me off again. It's just as well because he was getting me so spooked with his jumping-around-ness and of course I kept thinking about his not knowing about the dragonlet that I might have blurted out something even worse.

So after Billy and the others got back we left for the Institute pretty fast. Again, at the time, I didn't notice it so much, but I remembered later, that Billy and Kit and Jane had come back even quieter and more expressionless than old Arkhola Rangers usually are (at least when there aren't any tourists around). I suppose, at the time, I just thought they were sad about the mother dragon too. What I did notice is that what conversations they had were all in their own language—which is something Billy never does when any of us poor retarded English-only speakers are around. That should have really bothered me. But nothing much bothered me as long as there was hot broth every two hours.

We took it really easy, going home. All I had to carry was the dragonlet, so I didn't have too bad a time, although I started getting pretty short of sleep again because we kept walking (slowly) most of the day. (At least the bedsores went away.) Billy had rigged a sling to keep the dragonlet in my shirt too—we'd tried putting it in the sling itself but that wasn't good enough, it continued to demand SKIN although that may have been that it liked all the gooey salves—cloth just doesn't slither like skin does. Anyway, with the sling I could walk without having to clutch my stomach all the time.

And while my priorities were a bit skewed I did know we were walking into a huge ugly situation—and that I had to pay attention because my dragonlet's future depended on it. Worrying about this was enough to make me lose sleep, and I couldn't afford to lose sleep. Also it made my headache worse, and there wasn't anything interesting about this worse, like there was about the dream-cave worse. The fact that I knew I wouldn't give it—the dragonlet—up, and that Billy would back me up about this didn't anything like mean we were going to win. He also loved Smokehill—actually I don't think the way most of our Rangers, including Billy, feel about Smokehill is covered well enough by the word "love"—and probably, till he'd found me leaning up against a tree at midnight with a baby dragon in my lap, he'd've said that *nothing* could make him risk doing any harm to Smoke-hill. Or maybe he'd thought a lot about what could happen if one of us (almost certainly a Ranger, certainly not a dumb kid who'd never even soloed overnight before) ever found themselves in a position of trying to save a dragon's life. Or maybe (I was light-headed from sleep debt, remember) it had happened several times in the last hundred years—dragon saving I mean—and I just didn't know about it.

But I was pretty sure (in my light-headed way) that even if dragon saving was a regular occurrence no one had ever rescued a hot, squodgy little just-born blob. . . . And if Billy had had any of these thoughts they didn't seem to be helping him now. Billy is never talkative and he does a brilliant poker face, but you never saw anything so silent and so poker-faced as Billy over most of the hike back to the Insti-tute. And none of them were talking by the last day, in any language. Jo, who met us with the jeep, didn't say anything either. Her eyes rested on the bulge at my middle but she didn't ask for show-and-tell.

The dragonlet did *not* like the jeep ride. It didn't like it so much that eventually Billy and I got out and walked back into the trees so it would calm down and stop yelling and kicking. I wasn't entirely sorry since the jeep was making my headache worse again too. We'd've had to get out before we got to the Institute anyway, we just got out a little early.

I had no idea how I was going to handle the next step myself. Dad and I just didn't get along as well as we had when there'd been three or four of us. I was too much like him. "Laid back" wasn't in either of our vocabularies. (It wasn't really in Mom's either, but she had a better sense of humor than either of us did. And petting a dog is good for your blood pressure—they've done studies.) I'd been trying almost from the first night with the dragonlet to think about what I should do and what I should say (and not do or say) when I had to face Dad again, but then it would be time to feed the thing again, and there goes my train of thought.

When we saw the first gleam of the Ranger office wing—which is the first you see of the Institute when you're coming from the park side—Billy said, "Your dad wants to see you first thing. You and I'll go straight up to his office. I'll go in first and tell him what's happened. You wait till I call you." He hadn't said that many words together since he and Kit and Jane got back from Pine Tor.

I—the dragonlet and I—followed him silently.

I was wearing one of Billy's huge sweatshirts over my own clothes to hide the new bulge in my middle, and to disguise the sling. (None of the stuff I'd been wearing when it happened turned out to be salvageable—dragon birth slime is very, uh, intense. We saved my shoes only because I knew Dad couldn't afford to replace them.) I tried to sort of round my shoulders and slouch along—aren't teenage boys expected to slouch?—but Maria, who was in the ticket office, gave me a strange look, and Katie, standing in the door of the Ranger office, looked worried. Maybe they were worried because it wasn't only Dad who'd been smelling a rat.

But everyone at the Institute would have been feeling strange and worried because however Dad had decided to handle it, the news of the dead dragon and the dead poacher would already be out there in the world by now and the reaction started, whatever *that* was. And here finally Billy and I were back again, the vanguard returned to give witness of Armageddon. But I was only thinking about the dragonlet. Maria and Katie looking at me just made me slouch harder.

There's a tiny vestibule with a couple of dented metal chairs outside my father's office. I sat down and Billy went through the moment he knocked, so he just managed to get the door closed behind him before my father tried to get out through it and get at me. I could hear Billy saying, "He's fine. He's not hurt," because of course my dad thought that that's what the Rangers weren't telling him, and after Mom . . . I was pretty impressed that Billy succeeded in keeping the door closed. I was pretty impressed Dad hadn't hiked out to Northcamp two weeks ago to see for himself what was going on. He really trusted Billy. Well that gave us something in common at least.

But Dad had been busy here, dealing with the world outside Smokehill. I kept forgetting.

Billy's voice dropped and I couldn't hear words, just a low murmur, Billy trying, I guess, to make it all sound normal and okay and scientifically interesting and brave and stuff.

It didn't work. I heard my father bellow, "A DRAGON? Jake's brought home A DRAGON?" in a voice they must have been able to hear in Washington, DC, so they could get started on the paperwork to take Smokehill away from us— good going, Dad—and then the door crashed open, banging against the wall so hard that my father, coming through, had to put his hand out so it wouldn't brain him on the rebound. I jumped and the dragonlet jumped, and it *would* pick that moment to start making the noise I've been calling peeping or mewing. I was used to it by then, but it really *really* doesn't sound like any animal noise you've ever heard, and I could see in my father's face that it was all too horribly new to him and also, at that moment, that he knew what Billy had told him was true.

In this struggling-to-be-calm voice Dad said, still too loud, "Billy says—" and stopped, like it was also finally sinking in that there were other people around who might hear him. He stood aside and I stood up, cradling the invisibly peeping dragonlet in my hands, and went in. He closed the door and I sat down in the first chair that I came to, waiting to see if the dragonlet would quiet down or if I was going to have to whip it out immediately and feed it, which was usually the answer to everything in the dragonlet's case, feeding. (I was, of course, carrying a bottle. A bottle, unlike a camping pot, at least fits in your pocket.)

I was glad when it subsided. I thought my father needed a little more time before he saw it.

When I looked up again and saw the expression on my father's face. . . . In hindsight I think he was having a parental crisis moment. Traumatic experience or no traumatic experience I had Broken the Rules—I hadn't radioed Billy and I hadn't got back on time—and I was in *huge* amounts of trouble and should have been totally focused on finding out what kind of punishment my father was going to give me, or whether he was going to force me to go through the "let's discuss this like rational adults" lecture which I would have to go along with to prove that I could be treated like a rational adult although only a parent would ever think that a kid believes that's what's really happening. And instead I'd positively ignored him while I attended to this other responsibility that was not only mine but had nothing to do with him. At least when I used to shut him out by saying I had to take Snark for a walk, Snark was really his fault. My parents had bought and given me Snark. The first time a kid ignores a parent because something else is realio trulio more important, has to be hard on a dad, especially when the kid is only fourteen (and eleven months).

And that doesn't even touch the federal-prison-for-the-rest-of-our-lives, losing-Smokehill aspect of this case, which Dad had only just found out about this minute. And the eyes of the world were already on us, because of the dead guy. And I don't suppose Dad was sleeping too well either.

I didn't understand any of that at the time but I did see the expression on his face. The bits of it I understood were that he was furious and at a loss. I hadn't seen this expression before. I was pretty scared, but I didn't want to scare the dragonlet too, and . . . well, having that kind of responsibility does make a difference. All that crap parents give you about Learning to Take Responsibility . . . it's not crap. And what was happening wasn't even in the same universe as being "responsible" for Snark had been. I was probably having a son crisis to go with my dad's dad crisis. Things you can do without at the age of fourteen and eleven months.

"I've heard it from Billy," said my dad. "Now you tell me what happened."

So I told him. I don't think I told it as well as I'd told it the first time, even on no sleep, and in the first shock of everything. But when I'd told Billy I'd known he'd be sympathetic. Three years ago I'd've known—I think I'd've known—that my dad would be sympathetic too, but I didn't know that any more. The last three years had screwed up a lot of things. So I left out a lot. I didn't tell him about having to feed the dragonlet every half hour or about being so filthy I *wanted* a bath or about being so exhausted I was hallucinating and crazy. I wanted to sound a little bit remotely in control. And I didn't mention the headaches. Or the dreams. I hadn't even told Billy about crying when she died. I stopped when I got to Billy finding me.

My father didn't look at me while I talked. When I was done he sat down, heavily, in his desk chair, and Billy quietly took the remaining third chair.

"You realize that if anyone finds out, we'll all go to jail," was the first thing my father said. I had my mouth all open to reply—and while I don't know exactly what I would have said, I guarantee it would have been the wrong thing—when he raised his hand to stop me, even though he still hadn't looked at me. "No, you don't realize. You haven't thought about the fact that you'd be sent to a reformatory, and when they let you out you'd go to a foster family, they'd have their eyes on you all the time, and so would the media, and about half of them would think you were a hero and the other half would think you shouldn't ever be let out of reform school at all to corrupt the rest of our population with your depraved ideas, and while I'm not going to tell you your life would be ruined, it would certainly be complicated, and I *am* telling you they'd never let you within a mile of studying dragons. They'd probably bar you even from taking natural history or biology or ethology in college.

"Meanwhile, of course, we'd all go to jail too, and my guess is that any parole any of us got would be on the condition that we didn't try to make contact with each other." My father paused. I semi-registered that he hadn't bothered to mention that being sent to jail almost certainly would ruin his life, as well as Billy's and any other adult they decided to crucify.

At the same time I could feel stubbornness breaking out all over me like measles. "I won't give her up," I said, which is how I found out I thought it was a she. "If she dies then she dies, but I won't *let* her die. I'll go away in the park and hide till she gets big enough to fend for herself"—like I knew how to keep either of us alive till then, or that the social workers wouldn't prosecute Dad for making away with me if I disappeared—"but I won't just let her die."

"Yes." My father heaved a deep sigh, still not looking at me.

"Sir," said Billy. Billy only called my father "sir" when it was really serious. "We can do this. It will be difficult, but we can do this."

"You've kept my son hidden at Northcamp till you figured this out," said my father with a bitterness that scared me.

"I was really *really* tired," I said, before I thought whether this was wise or not. "I was spending all my time looking after her. She eats all the time. I couldn't've walked this far any sooner. And she'll only—she only—only I—" There was no way to say this without feeling like a complete jerk. "She thinks I'm her mom."

But I think blurting it out like that helped. My father

looked at me, finally, as if registering the real problem, which was the dragonlet, instead of all the other problems, which were created by the fact that some morons in Washington had decided that a bill against saving dragons was good for their careers—plus the dead guy, which because of all the other moron laws against dragons no one would be able to think about in terms of "self-defense" or "what was he doing in Smokehill after our dragons in the first place because pardon me he *killed* a dragon which is also you know illegal?" But he was dead, and wasn't going anywhere (except into the headlines). Which is what my dad would already have been coping with and been thinking was enough, thank you very much.

But the dragonlet was not only here, she was *alive*. And it was up to us to try to see that she stayed that way. Dad *had* to see that. It was, as I keep saying, what we—us and Smokehill—were *for*.

I tried to make myself get it that part of my dad's bitterness was that he knew he was going to be stuck with all the treacherous political stuff—and Mom again had been the person who poured the most oil on the permanently troubled waters between the Institute and everybody else, chiefly Congress and the Federal Parks Commission, partly because she didn't start off all heavy and scowly and hyper the way Dad did. Which meant we were *already* in worse shape going into our little treason-and-insurrection dance around my adopted daughter because the FPC, goaded by Congress, was already looking for reasons to think the worst of us because Dad couldn't always remember that to a bureaucrat bureaucracy is important. Dad would be all on his own with not only the totally unrewarding admin stuff and the horribly dangerous new stuff about the dead poacher and the dead dragon . . . but hidden in the background there was a secret *live* dragon . . . and the Rangers and I got her.

And he was right. All of our necks would depend on whether or not my dad lied, and kept on lying, convincingly enough, first to the squinty-eyed congressional subcommittee drones, then to the FPC guys, who weren't all morons but tended to be horribly law-abiding, and to everybody else who walked through the gates who thought they had a right to talk about "accountability," which had been hard enough, since Mom died, without the lying part. And now we'd be having a whole new lot of squinty-eyed types who would arrive determined to disbelieve everything but the worst, just when we had the Secret of the Century to keep. Dad had every reason to be bitter. And scared. And I want to point out that he's the *real* hero in this story.

But for the moment he let himself be distracted. After all, he *was* here running the Institute because he was fascinated by dragons. "She would expect to be able to eat all the time, living in her mom's pouch," he said. "Couldn't the Rangers help you?"

"Well," I said uncomfortably, "she seems to have sort of—imprinted on me."

My father nodded, and I saw his eyes flicker to the short shelf of primary sources on dragon contact.

The dragonlet chose this moment to wake up again. I'd already begun to notice that she was a little more active in the daytime, when I was (comparatively) more active—and I was also wondering if she could pick up anxiety. A dog does, and a dog doesn't live pressed up to your stomach all the time. On the other hand, dogs have been living with humans for thirty or forty thousand years and dragons have been *avoiding* humans for a lot longer than thirty or forty thousand years. Maybe it's just that my stomach gurgles more when I'm nervous and the noise would wake her up.

"I think I'm going to have to feed her," I said apologetically.

"Go ahead," said my father. Very drily he added, "I want to meet her."

I pulled up my two layers of sweatshirts and slid her out behind the sling inside my shirt in what were by now very practiced moves, but having my father watching me made me self-conscious in a way the Rangers hadn't. My stomach isn't particularly lovely anyway, but I wanted to be sure my father did *not* notice any strange red scalded patches (although chances are, with a baby dragon in the room, he wasn't going to notice anything else short of a pterodactyl divebombing through the ceiling). Also, while to me the dragonlet looked a whole lot better than she had that first afternoon I'd picked her up still covered with birth slime, she still looked . . . while I balanced her in one hand before smushing her up my (extra-large, extra-stretched) sleeve, and fished for her broth bottle I saw her as my dad must: ugly damn little critter, shapeless pulpy-looking body in that awful bruise color, little spastic legs with half-formed toes (no claws yet, fortunately for me) and a squished-looking head, and glistening all over from the salve.

The diaper made her look like some kind of truly grotesque doll—you know how little kids will diaper their teddy bears or whatever. Eleanor used to put diapers on her purple plush iguana (speaking of tail problems), although the dragonlet's at least hid some of her unloveliness which had to be a good thing. (It hid quite a lot really due to the logistics of keeping it in place.) But the dragonlet looked like one of those gross things you see supposedly pickled in bottles in movies about mad scientists. Not just hairless—or in the dragonlet's case scaleless—but somehow skinless, although she wasn't, and deformed, which I had no idea if she was or not. She was more or less symmetrical, in her squashy, sort of jelly-y way, which was probably good as far as it went. But she looked, well, fetal, which she pretty much was. She wasn't supposed to be out here in the air, needing salve and sweatshirts. And broth bottles. She was supposed to be in her mom's pouch, stuck on a nipple for the next however many months. Or something like that.

I decided not to try to tell my dad how much better she looked than she had a few weeks ago. Or why she was still alive on deer and squirrel broth, which I didn't have a clue about myself.

Or that I dreamed of dragons, big grown-up dragons, almost every night, in those two-hour chunks, and now that I was sleeping for longer the dreams felt like they got *bigger*, and I used to wake up out of those dreams lately with my headache bigger than my skull for a while. There was usually a moment, before I was fully awake again, where I'd think, *that's it, you* stay *out* there, before it fell in on itself like a tent being taken down and jammed itself and all its sharp edges and too-long pointy tent poles back inside my head again.

She drank half a bottle and collapsed, the way she always did, going from some kind of pathetic baby animal with something terribly wrong with it, to something more like a beanbag or a water balloon in the shape of a you don't know what, but whatever it is, you hope they don't make any more. I gathered her up—she was nearly twice as long now as she'd been when I'd found her—shoved her back under my shirt, and wiped my greasy hands on my jeans. I was going to have major trouble if she started jumping around much before she grew thick enough skin not to need to be oiled all the time.

There was silence for a long tense moment.

"And what is it you're suggesting we do?" said my father to Billy.

"Jake will have come back from his first overnight solo in the park knowing that he wants to apprentice as a Ranger," said Billy. "You will believe him, and decide that this is a good thing for him to do. He will have to keep up with his schoolwork—"

"Yes he will," said my father.

"—But so long as he does so I don't think anyone will ask too many questions." I loved Billy at that moment for not taking the opportunity to give me an "are you paying attention to this, I am the grown-up and I'm doing you a biiiig favor so you'd better cooperate" look. I knew what he was doing for me. "Meanwhile we'll have accepted him as an apprentice and therefore he will live in the Rangers' quarters. Since we do not usually accept apprentices so young he will have a special billet; but while we are accepting him this young because we know him, we cannot allow him to go on living with his father. The Ranger apprenticeship is very serious."

It is too. Because of the dragons—and because more than half our staff funding is still from the trust Old Pete set up—we do get to make some of our own decisions, and our Ranger program has like trickled down through everything. You couldn't even work part time in the café or the gift shop without being vetted six ways from Sunday. Twenty-seven ways. This drives the National Park Service crazy because they think *their* rules and regulations are the important ones, but they do a crap job of keeping the congressional drones off our backs so why should we pay any more attention to them than we have to?

There was a longer, even more uncomfortable silence while my father thought this over. My hand had involuntarily gone to my stomach again. Let's say that it's just that I still wasn't quite convinced of the safety of the sling to hold the (greasy) dragonlet where she wanted to be, and that my hand cupped itself around her because my hand was still used to being needed to keep her there. And let's really not get into the way Katie used to put her hand under the bulge that became Eleanor when she was upset or uneasy, which she was a lot, because she had found out she was pregnant right around the time her jerk of a husband said he was leaving because he was tired of living a hundred miles away from the nearest real restaurant, and he wanted her not to have Eleanor because he didn't want to pay child support on another kid.

(Yeah, it's amazing what some grown-ups will say when there's a kid right *there*. Martha told me because she was worrying that *she* was the reason why her father was such a creep. All I want to know is how Katie married the guy in the first place. He must have had a brain transplant after the wedding. I was only eight, but Martha's story made an impression. Also having a five-year-old girl to play with—and Martha loved Snark—was better than having no other children around at all, and the bulge might have turned out to be a boy.)

But I wasn't holding the sling in place, of course, or the dragonlet. I was protecting her from my father. I didn't know that at the time—and fortunately I didn't think about Katie and Eleanor-the-bulge either—but I know now what I was doing. And that some of my feelings (including lower back pain) weren't so different from Katie's.

My father's a very bright guy. He knew what he was seeing at the time. And, of course, a dragon . . . whatever the damn laws were, dragons were why we were here.

After a couple of eons he said, "Okay. Let's do it."

It was the second time in my life I wished I knew how to pray. The first time had been when Mom disappeared. I was going to do better by my dragon.

CHAPTER FOUR

I named her Lois. She looked like a Lois. I know how that sounds: It sounds like the ugliest woman I ever met must have been named Lois. But that wasn't it at all. It was really interesting after having that weird flash when I was seeing her how my father saw her. Maybe when Billy and the three other Rangers saw her for the first time it was still so soon, or I was still so tired, or I hadn't finished realizing that we had, you know, bonded, and I wasn't going to be able to hand her over to someone else, or maybe it was just that I couldn't read Rangers the way I could read my dad—my dad in a passion anyway, which didn't take a lot of reading.

But it was like the Rangers just saw her. My dad looked at her with all this other stuff going on about it. Granted that he was my father and the head of the Institute, and an Institute that was under sudden siege, but even so, it was interesting. And it gave me kind of a shock. And another teeny insight into what I was going to be doing and how hard it was going to be. Teeny because I slammed the door on it, before I saw any more of it, and then tried to forget what I had seen. I'd let myself see a little bit of the bigger picture in Dad's office—but only long enough to understand why Dad was so wired, even for Dad, who is always wired. This was what Dad later named my Footman Period. Remember the Frog-Footman in *Alice*, who, while all hell was breaking loose around him, sat on the doorstep and said, "I shall sit here till tomorrow—or the next day, maybe. I shall sit here, on and off, for days and days."

That was me. Days and days and days and days. While plates whizzed past my head and there was lots of screaming.

I named her Lois because I liked the name. And the reason she seemed like one to me was because after my father had looked at her I realized that I thought she looked like one of those wallflower girls in kids' books that suddenly grow up one summer and then they get a new haircut and contact lenses and go back to school that autumn and wow. (I used to read a lot of books about kids going to school and having normal lives, even ones about girls. You figure out why.) Lois was still in her squatty-with-glasses, wallflower stage, but I knew she was going to get over it. It was just up to me to make sure she lived long enough to do it.

Yes, I did think about calling her Alice—I thought about it a long time—but she just wasn't an Alice. Also, I didn't feel like encouraging any loose karma hanging around to put her through any more of the human wonderland than she absolutely had to go through—which was already more than enough. Also I was seeing the dragon caves nearly every night and they were just nothing like Alice's underground, and this seemed important somehow.

The Rangers' wing of the Institute is really two wings: barracks and offices. If you were on night duty, you had to sleep in the barrack wing, but once you were a real Ranger, which took anywhere from two to six years, you got your own little cabin in the woods beyond the Institute—with the Institute buildings protecting you (somewhat) from all the tourist stuff that went on on the other side. Tourists still managed to gatecrash sometimes, because tourists are like that, but it was supposed to be private. You were pretty much automatically on call all the time if you were in the Institute buildings. I'm not blaming my dad for being a little touchy, you know? He lived there *all the time*. And while I did too—till I adopted Lois—I was still only a kid. And some of how he protected me was that I didn't realize how much he did protect me.

Once you got your Ranger badge and sewed it on your shirt, you got a house. Sometimes you built it, and on the night of the day it was finished, the other Rangers came round as soon as it was dark and sang to you and your house, sang these long songs in Arkhola, and the chills went up your spine, even if you were just a kid hiding in the shadows so you could listen, and it had nothing to do with you. If you didn't build it, they still sang, telling the house that you were its new person (Arkhola doesn't have a lot of words about owning stuff). And once you had a house you could even get married. To another Ranger was a good idea. (People who weren't Rangers tended to leave, taking the children with them. A few tough guys compromised by having their families in Wilsonville, and didn't see much of them.) Billy was married. She wasn't a Ranger, but she was an Arkhola, and she'd grown up in this weeny village the other side of Wilsonville, so she should have had some idea what she was getting into. They were still together thirty-five years later so maybe she did.

As an apprentice I should have been in the barracks wing but (this was the official version) since I was an underage apprentice, I got given to Billy instead. Billy's cabin happened to be a little farther in the woods than most of the rest of them, and farther away from the Institute and the tourist trails, so that was good too, and also just farther away, period. The other Ranger houses, if you went to the front door and shouted, all your neighbors heard you. Except Rangers don't shout much, especially the Arkholas. Billy and Grace's house was a good half mile from the Institute, and what's really interesting is that it was one of the oldest. Old Pete's son, who built it, obviously took after his old man in terms of seriously not wanting a lot of human society.

Lois and I lived in the tiny bedroom Billy's son had grown up in. I was used to little—my bedroom at the Institute was little—but Lois made it smaller in a way Snark never had. (Billy's son was now an investment banker in Boston, but—surprisingly—not a bad guy. He's the one who got me interested in the political side of what Old Pete had done—had made me see he wouldn't have got Smokehill going if he hadn't been able to play the political game. Jamie had obviously learned those lessons well. There aren't exactly a lot of Native Americans who are successful investment bankers in Boston.)

Grace had at least as much to do with Lois' continuing to thrive as I did. She's the one who, once we were installed in the spare bedroom, made the broth, and she kept putting different extra stuff in it, all that vitamin and mineral stuff for babies that are still growing, but how she knew which extra vitamins and minerals a growing dragonlet needed is beyond me. She did all the plant and flower drawings for the various Smokehill guidebooks as well as a lot of stuff for national guidebook publishers about Smokehill's vegetation. (Which is, they say, increasingly uniquely peculiar because of the fence. We've still got big old full-grown elms in eastern Smokehill. Eat your heart out. There are beginning to be botanists out there who are getting on as crazy to do research in Smokehill as the dragon nuts.) When you saw Grace at her drawing board you could believe that *everything* about the plant she was drawing was soaking into her brain, including what was good for making baby dragons go a better color and grow some scales. She'd also always been a fabulous cook—most of us who lived at Smokehill would do anything to get invited to dinner at Billy and Grace's—but I don't know if Lois noticed.

By the time the next lot of school equivalency testers came around to aggravate me, Lois could bear to stay by herself for an hour or two, knotted up in our very-us-smelling bedclothes with a hot water bottle. This only worked if the sheets hadn't been changed in a while. I thought this was very funny, because it meant that when our sheets got so high that Grace insisted that I change them—and this happened pretty fast; baby dragons are smelly little beasts, however often you change their diapers—we couldn't wash them till the new ones had got pretty high too, so that I could go on practicing leaving Lois by herself. We couldn't even keep the door to our smelly bedroom closed, because part of Lois' fragile feeling of security was that it wasn't too quiet, and it was, too quiet I mean, in there by herself. She needed to hear Grace or Billy moving around. Which also meant that one of us had to be home *all* the time. (Occasionally one of the other Rangers who were in on it baby-dragon-sat.) Very labor intensive, raising a dragonlet.

Anyway I aced all my tests so fast the testers didn't know what hit 'em. I'd always been a pretty fair student—I've told you this already, I knew I needed to be—but this was almost ridiculous. I even aced *Latin*. Well, A minus. (But *boy* did I earn it.) But I was *home* all the time, wasn't I? I had a lot of time to study, so I might as well—and because the school-equiv creeps weren't going to go along with this apprenticeship scam if I didn't look like I was blooming and booming on it. (I actually gave up playing Annihilate—I mean completely. Lois didn't like the way I jerked and shouted when I was losing.) I was still having sleep-and-dream-and-headache problems, but I was getting more used to them, and it was actually easier to ignore—no, not ignore, live with—the headache if I was doing something, even schoolwork.

Martha was usually the grind who did the extra work and didn't just get As but hundred percents. I say it that way because I felt really bad about Martha (okay, here's a deep dark secret for you: also I was jealous that she is brighter than me), because she knew there was something up beyond just that I'd had some kind of freaky vision during my first solo and for some reason the grown-ups were taking it seriously. We used to do a lot of our schoolwork together, and we didn't any more, and because of pressure elsewhere the "class" lectures when some Smokehill person talked to the three of us stopped pretty much altogether so we didn't have that either. And that I was supposedly spending more

time on learning Ranger stuff didn't cover it while the social worker and school-equiv gang still owned my ass,
which they did. Even when I was there it was like my mind
wasn't there with me—which it wasn't. It was on Lois, and
whether she was okay. Zombie Jake, the New Not Improved
Model.

Martha was sad because I hadn't told her what it was all
about, but, being Martha, didn't nag me about it. She barely
even asked, just wanted to know if I was okay. "Sure," I
said, and she smiled, that smile you do when you know the
person is lying to you. I felt *lousy*. She knew that I was—
had been—planning to go off and get a few PhDs so I could
study dragons like my parents. She also knew that I peri-
odically packed that one in and swore that I was going to
apprentice to the Rangers—but she also knew I said that
mostly out of funk. Most of the grown-ups might buy it that
I suddenly really knew what I wanted, but Martha knew me
pretty well, and she also knew that Billy wouldn't've accepted me if it was just funk. Martha takes after her mom.
They're both way too sharp to be easy to have around.

Eleanor knew there was something I wasn't telling her
too and she was a total brat about it, but at seven, being a
brat was almost her job and I didn't take it too seriously,
except that Eleanor's force of character did kind of mean
you had to take it seriously. She took it particularly personally from me because I was another kid, and there were
only the three of us. The last family with kids had come
and gone while I was still pretty out of it after Mom and
then Snark, so I didn't remember them much (although I
remembered their dogs), but Martha and Eleanor had been
friendly with them and Eleanor really noticed when they
left and kind of realized that what it was about the three of
us was that we were the only ones who ever stayed. Eleanor
nagged me, all right, but she didn't get any more out of me
than Martha did. The difference was that sometimes I almost told Martha, and I never had to stop myself from telling Eleanor.

The real point was that Lois was, amazingly, still a secret from most of the Institute—usually everybody knows everything about everybody else who lives here. (It's a joke among the grown-ups that either your partner is faithful or gone.) *Somebody* was watching over us. Maybe the Arkhola had a song for it. But even if the Arkholas had a lot of songs for it, Lois' guardian angel was going to need a very, very, *very* long vacation when all of this was over.

This is hindsight again, but you weren't there, so I'm trying to tell you the story as it might have looked to a sane person at the time, if there had been any sane people around, which obviously there weren't. Hindsight tells me that we couldn't POSSIBLY have kept Lois a secret. So we didn't. But I've told you how ginormously difficult it is to get hired to work at Smokehill, and all that vetting does a pretty good job. I think the Rangers who do the hiring, and the senior ones pretty much all have a lot of Arkhola blood, sort of hum over the candidates, and if the humming goes right, you get hired, and if it doesn't, you don't. So what we had at the Institute is a lot of people who were willing to leave a secret alone, because they would guess it must have something dangerous to do with dragons. Maybe Dad suddenly looked twenty years older and Billy stopped making his peculiar bone-dry jokes because of what was going on after the dead dragon and the poacher . . . but in that case why was Billy's house suddenly off limits now that the Rangers' underage apprentice was living there? Not to mention my mysterious semi-disappearance—what was I *doing* all those hours I was holed up at Billy's house? Vision on my first solo, huh? It must have been sooome vision.

Even now it's an effort for me to think about the poacher, even now when that part of it is more or less over and I'm trying just to tell it as a story. I don't even know his first name—I don't even really know what he was doing in Smokehill, except ruining everything. He was—and still is—always just "the poacher" to me like you might say "my worst enemy" or "the devil," if you go for devils, which I don't much since I stopped playing computer games, but it's that kind of feeling, that blasting him through seven levels isn't good enough. He's "the poacher" because I *hated* him so much.

Sometimes I stopped even pretending to have any rational view of anything and called him "the villain" or "the bad guy" like what was happening was a Clint Eastwood film or something. He destroyed Smokehill. He did too. Sure, Smokehill is still around, and everyone (maybe even including me) would say that it's in massively better shape than it was four years ago. But the old Smokehill is gone, and he killed it, when he killed Lois' mom. This is the new Smokehill, and not everything about it is better (like me writing this story), and making anything *better* was certainly not in his plan.

Anyway. The whole big thundering emergency that the poacher created was enough to make Dad look (and feel) twenty years older, and Billy stop telling jokes. So some big cheezing camouflage. And that we *are* here means that anyone who couldn't keep the secret about Jake's solo bought it that the only big stressful thing going on was about the poacher. Which is not the sort of thing you want to have to rely on, but sometimes when there's nothing more you can do and you know it's not enough it works anyway. As I say, maybe the Arkholas have a song for it.

Which isn't to say we didn't sweat *trying* keeping her a secret. We did. So when carrying a spectacularly illegal and mercilessly increasing in size wiggly baby animal under your shirt is your only real alternative, you stay home a lot. I'd—we'd—started working on convincing her to stay by herself as soon as we got her back to the Institute but it was a *struggle*. I was really disgusted that the best cover story anybody could think of, the first two or three months, for why I never seemed to leave the house at all, was that I was having nightmares so bad that I wasn't sleeping, because it made me sound like such a wuss, but it did explain the way I looked if anyone did see me—haggard and haunted. I didn't know it at the time but the people who'd been involved in removing what remained of the poacher said that it had given *them* nightmares—and these were outside guys who did stuff like Official Wilderness Cadaver Removal or whatever, so maybe it wasn't such a bad cover after all—except for the offer of counseling, which Dad helped me to fend off.

But even at four months old an hour without me began to stress Lois—and not too long after that she'd start mewing and scrabbling at the blankets, and once she'd uncovered herself she got panicky, because while being able to hear Grace and Billy was okay for noise, she couldn't bear being handled by anyone but me. We eventually found out that if they buried her again wearing gloves that I'd also worn and Lois and I had also slept with for a while that worked pretty well, but it was still all really *hairy*.

Scrubbing up before I went up to the Institute was a *colossal* bore like I can't begin to tell you too. Especially all the sore hot-baby-dragon bits. But as I say, baby dragons are smelly little beasts—and the scrubbing-up had to be done *fast* because my time was ticking away. (I had had some practice for this part of it though, having perfected the ninety-second shower as soon as we moved into Jamie's old bedroom. I was *not* going to do the Bath with Friends thing even one day longer than I had to. For ninety seconds once a day she could just lie on the bathroom floor in my old clothes by herself and live with the vile and tragic trauma of separation.)

I don't think we'd ever have got away with that part—the smelly part—if it weren't for this sinus-blasting incense Billy started burning, and he used to like *soak* me in it. All the Rangers started using it, burning it at their doorways, even bedrooms at the barracks, and later on they got enough of it made up to sell in the gift shop; tourists will buy anything, and if it's true that smell is our most evocative sense, well, any tourist who lit a wand of the stuff once they were home again would be transported back to Smokehill all right. WHAM.

I don't know how anyone who didn't have a secret baby

dragon around to give them a powerful motive stood the stuff, but the story was that it was to keep off the bad luck/fate/ghosts/spirits/supernatural thingy of choice that were flying around as a result of the death of the dragon and the poacher. Yeah, it was too woo-woo for me too, and then again it kind of wasn't. After all, I was dreaming about caves full of dragons every night, I no longer knew what woo-woo was.

And, you know, I'd try anything for Lois. Too goofy? Fine, bring it on.

I should explain a little more about the dragon smell. The main thing is that there was so much of it. It wasn't a proper stink like *stink*. It was just really *thick*. It didn't make you feel sick or grossed out or anything—it wasn't destroying your life, it was just *there*. It was kind of almost like another person (well, dragon) in the room. There's you, your dragonlet, and the way your dragonlet smells. That makes three. It was kind of the second cousin twice removed of the normal Smokehill dragon smell—not only was it a lot more up close and personal but it just wasn't quite the same thing. Whether this is the difference between baby dragon and grown-up dragon or because Lois was having a seriously nontraditional dragonlethood I don't know.

Smell is kind of underrated generally. Other than how evocative it is and like you don't taste your food right when you've got a head cold, and you open the window if you've made a really bad *stink* stink in the bathroom, we don't really think about or live with smells much. I mean we try not to live with smells much. Except stuff like perfume and aftershave. Rangers—and anybody who helps out at the zoo and orphanage—are forbidden to wear it, but sometimes the front hall at the Institute is so full of tourist perfume and gunk smells—this in spite of the fact that the roof of the dome is thirty feet overhead—that I want to run away. It used to make Snark sneeze. I'll take baby-dragon smell, thanks.

But once we both had our first bath after she was born it wasn't really awful. It was just strong, and it really hung around. It got sort of the edges worn off as she got older, or maybe it was our edges that got worn off instead, because it's also true that Lois was kind of, uh, smeary, for kind of a long time. Some of it was that I had to keep slapping salve on her because she started to crack at the corners if I didn't, but some of it she produced her own self. I helped poor Grace hang plastic sheeting over the bottom half of the walls and doors all over her house, as soon as Lois started climbing out of her sling occasionally—and caroming off things, things besides me. That started really early—at about three months—which is also to say *I'm so glad* because it was not early from my viewpoint, and if I'm going to be honest it's the dragon dreams that had kept me going even that long, they provided a sort of alternate nonreality since the reality I was living in had got pretty non- in other ways.

I slept a lot, those first three months, partly because getting up four times and then three and then twice a night still left me pretty tired and partly because when I did sleep I got to dream about dragons. You don't normally know where you're going to be when you go to sleep, you only know where you're going to be when you wake up. But those first few months, the stronger the panicky sense of being trapped by this little live thing that was *utterly* dependent on me and *only* me got, the stronger the dreams got. And if I slept I dreamed of dragons. In the dreams it was like *they* were responsible for *me*, and this was such a relief it even weirdly carried over a little into being awake and being RESPONSIBLE for Lois.

In the in-between bits, falling asleep and coming awake, I thought/dreamed of Mom, and how much I'd've liked to have her there, making me laugh with her stories of diapers and 2 A.M. feedings—I knew she'd've even been able to make me laugh about that awful scary imprisoning dependency. I could have really used a laugh. I could've asked Grace—and I did later on, about other things—but it didn't occur to me. It was like I was too far away and holding on by too skinny a thread.

I might have been just holding on myself but only three pouch months has to've been way early from dragonlet perspective, it's just that there was a limit to the size of sling you could hang on me, and it's not so much that Lois grew out of it but that she *gyrated* out of it. There was about a week when you kept seeing baby dragon butt or nose or foot sticking out briefly from under my shirt . . . and then not so briefly, and when it was the nose it was more and more nose till it included eyes and . . . I remember Snark as a puppy being a perpetual motion machine but he had nothing on Lois. Fortunately she didn't have the needle puppy teeth and the habit of cruising with her mouth open, looking for things to chomp. She gunked them instead. You know how in someone's house you can tell the furniture that the dog or cat sits on most—either it's completely trashed or there's a blanket or something over it and the blanket's really trashed. (Snark's and my TV sofa was about three layers deep in semi-trashed blankets: we moved 'em around so none of the holes went all the way through to the sofa.) Grace kept their bedroom door closed all the time and everything else in the house was wrapped up in old blankets *and* oilcloth. Even table legs.

For something with no legs to speak of Lois-just-out-of-the-sling sure liked to climb. Maybe it was being short when everything else was so tall (Eleanor liked to stand on chairs). Maybe it was the complicated process of getting in and out of the sling which had kind of a lot of up and down to it. Anyway, Lois climbed. Or tried to climb. At first she was too tottery to do anything *but* totter and then for a while when she'd come to something in her way she'd just stop, like it was the end of the universe. Then later she tried to climb. Going *around* appears to be a very late developing concept in dragonlets.

After a while she stopped trying to climb on anything she'd found out wasn't very dragon-shaped—the kitchen chairs for example—and I sat on the floor a lot to make life easier when she was first starting to explore life outside the sling, since at first she'd go two steps and then run back to

Mom and then she'd take three steps and run back, and the house was small enough that when she got up to four steps she started bumping into things. At first this was just The End, as I said. But then it was like . . . sometimes I imagined she bumped into them almost kind of thoughtfully, because I don't think she ever tried to climb on anything if she hadn't bumped it thoroughly first.

I don't know if her eyes didn't focus right to begin with (which would be my fault for raising her wrong, guilt guilt guilt) or maybe were built to focus in different light (the light in the dragon caves in my dreams was always weird) or on something very different from human house stuff (duh)—or if baby dragons just do bump into things a lot, like instead of having whiskers, which dragons don't, telling them about how much space there is or what the shapes of the solid parts in it are. But she was a big bumper, and she did a lot of bumping into things sidelong; she didn't necessarily lead with her nose, the way something with whiskers does. But it was like she didn't know what it was till she'd bumped into it a few times. Which was harder (or at least gunkier) on the things than whiskers would have been.

I didn't mind sitting on the floor, I'm mostly not big on soft squashy furniture and certainly no cold draft had a chance to bother me with Lois nearby, and also I found watching her so interesting. (Proud Mom. Obsessed Mom. Silly with relief for even a few feet and a few minutes of semi-freedom Mom.) For example, not only did she do a lot of her bumping from a funny angle, bumping into things to learn what they were seemed to depend on the thing rather than where it was. She'd bump into some things no matter where they were and some things after the first few times she never bumped into them again, also no matter where they were either. Go figure.

Even when she was no longer using her sling she still didn't want to be more than a few feet away from me if she could help it, and she preferred some kind of contact. She was hopeless as a lapdog—the wrong shape, and she was too thick-bodied to curl properly—but she'd lie pretty contentedly on my bare feet, or behind my ankles—that's *when* she was willing to stop exploring, and lie down at all. She went on wanting skin, and she still spent the nights lying against my stomach.

Fortunately Ranger cottages don't run to wall-to-wall carpeting—I don't even want to think about wall-to-wall carpeting with a greasy, low-slung dragonlet in residence. Grace rolled up their few little rugs and stashed them, and I helped her mop the floors, except that Lois usually wanted to play with the mop. And if you held it steady for her, in the developmental stage between Too Small and Too Big, she could climb up onto the top of the broomy part of a broom and sway there for a minute, like a high-wire act.

Grace is a *saint*. After all, she was there all the time— Billy mostly wasn't. She'd used to go hiking to find her own plants for her drawings, but once we moved in she stayed home. The Rangers brought her what she asked for, plants and photos, but it wasn't the same—not that she said so. But I knew she was trapped too—that she'd just let herself be trapped. And nobody had asked her. We just showed up, that first day, after my interesting interview with Dad. I was too shell-shocked to notice much after that so I can't tell you about the expression on her face when we arrived. I don't remember what Billy said, or whether he said it in Arkhola or English. I don't remember anything, except I also don't ever remember Grace being anything but Grace, which is to say kind and unfrazzled, all the time Lois and I were infesting her space. (Her Arkhola name translates as Beautiful Dancer. I think I was raving to Kit about the way Grace put up with us and he's the one told me. So "Grace" is a pretty good job.)

And I've said that everyone at Smokehill would sell their grandmothers to be invited for a meal that Grace cooked— she liked cooking for people, and now she couldn't do that either, or only for the few of us official secret Lois society members. *And* she lost her studio because Lois and I took over Jamie's room—she had to set up her drawing board in the kitchen. But the funny thing is that Lois learned not to whang into the drawing board first, when she was still really little and tottery. She was still crashing into the kitchen table occasionally when she was big enough to make a glass standing on it fall over, just from not paying attention. (Maybe she picked it up from me. I've made a few glasses fall over in my time.) But she never did that to the drawing board. And it wasn't that Grace was ever mean to her about that or about anything. Made you wonder just what she was learning by all that bumping.

But the stuff about the poacher and the dead dragon—Lois' mom . . . I mostly didn't know how bad it was till a lot later. Even at the time I knew that everybody was trying their damnedest to make sure I didn't know . . . but I was trying not to know too. I know how much of a jerk this makes me look. But I had really, really, *really* as much as I could handle with just Lois. And the dreams. And the headaches. And the no-way-out. I don't want to get all moany and whiny about this but even if it's a unique scientific opportunity giving up your life to keep someone else alive is kind of hard, and pain is tiring and headaches, you know, hurt, and while the burn marks weren't too bad, they were tender, so if they got clawed or gouged that hurt too.

And the dreams . . . sometimes, after a really vivid one, it was like I never quite woke out of it all day, like if I only went a little bit farther into this trance I was trying to hold off (or maybe I was trying to bring it on), I'd see big bus-wheel eyes shining at me from the trees around the house. I wasn't putting on the Space Cadet thing, I was *there*. And I'm sorry I was a jerk. But Lois pretty much blotted everything else out.

I don't know how everybody else stood it, everybody else who knew about Lois, even if it wasn't them she couldn't be more than three feet away from all the time. Being a Space Cadet was also kind of a help, for me, being so out of it.

Anyway. However boring—and painful—scrubbing up to go to the Institute was, I had to do it. I had to go on leaving Lois by herself so she *could* be left (of course I worried about stressing her till she had a heart attack or whatever dragons have, and died; from my perspective at the time we could have afforded to lose a few staff members, they were only human) and I had to start going to the Institute as soon as I could and keep going because it would have looked even weirder than it did—about my conversion to early Rangerhood I mean—if I never came. And if the "nightmares" hadn't cleared off pretty soon, they'd've had a psychologist in to test me for echoes, and I'd probably've resonated like a cave full of bats. Besides, there were the school testers and I really didn't want to get on their suspicious side. So I went up to the Institute every day and tried to be as conspicuous as possible so it seemed as if I was up there more.

My time at the zoo and the orphanage of course got cut down to almost nothing. Eric was really pissed off (surprise) and tried to make out that I didn't really want to be a Ranger, I was just looking for a way to get out of doing any work, i.e., at his zoo, because I'm a teenage boy and teenage boys are always lazy and dishonest. (Made you wonder what kind of a teenager *he'd* been.) But hindsight even makes Eric being his normal super-avoid-worthy self look different. Eric was the head of the zoo and the orphanage—if anyone would know about an orphan baby dragon, it would be him—and all he was doing was kvetching about that worthless lump Jake . . . like maybe he had a suspicion it would be a good idea to distract anyone from wondering if the worthless lump had a reason for disappearing, besides being a lazy and dishonest teenage boy?

I did start cleaning *odorata*'s cage again. The smell was still awful but it wasn't as overwhelming as when I lived like a human being rather than an *australiensis* mom, and as another sign that I had lost my mind I began to notice how beautiful the damn critters are, no matter how they smelled: The parrot-green and crimson-and-yellow frills on the big male are really amazing, and if you can hold your breath long enough to appreciate it the way he flaps 'em around is almost choreography. And I was used to taking really violent showers these days so the prospect of another one after I took the last radioactive *odorata* barrowload to the pit where we buried the stuff was no big deal.

It's funny though—another thing that's funny—I got all kind of loosened up about all the things in the zoo. They were what they were and they were probably pretty interesting, even if they weren't dragons. I almost missed having some herpetologist around studying the Effect of the Tourist Gaze on *Draco somethingorotherensis.* Hey, you lizards, how's it going? Eaten any nice celery/rhubarb/beetles/snails lately? But the zoo was happening on another planet, which was almost like relaxing—I'm only a visitor and *boy* do I not belong here.

But not belonging here was an advantage, dealing with f.l.s. I'd smile at them and let what they said (because smiling only encourages them) roll over me. I found myself nodding calmly to a major f.l. one day from *sylvestris'* cage, saying "mmm-hmmm" as I kept on with my shovel. He was talking about how something or other, I don't remember which one he liked, is the *real* dragon, and most of that stuff at the tourist center about *australiensis* is just hooey to pull the tourists in, everyone knows *australiensis* is extinct, because when's the last time anyone's ever seen one, and it wasn't like that even when it was alive . . . but then his wife interrupted to say that *something* had killed that poor man and it was *criminal* the way the Institute was flogging the story about his death to draw media attention when any half-intelligent person knew that there'd been some *human* screwup and they just didn't want to admit it and . . .

I was starting to straighten up over my wheelbarrow and reconnect with my surroundings and I don't know what might have happened next but Eric came along and snarled at me to stop standing around wasting time when I was supposed to be *cleaning* that cage and then the f.l. and his wife turned on *him* and said that that poor boy should be taken away from this den of scoundrels and liars and given to good honest folk who would try to reverse the effects of the warped and wicked Smokehill brainwashing . . . but I'd picked up the handles on my wheelbarrow and was trundling as fast as possible out of earshot, and I hope Eric had a good time. Those letters to congresspeople about cutting off our funding never mention Eric, so he must actually know how to weasel. More hidden depths in our Eric.

I might still have gone stir-crazy, trapped in the cabin with increasingly hyperactive Lois and only brief nerve-twangling paroles up at the Institute and the zoo—the dragon dreams, for better or worse, did begin to tail off as Lois started climbing out of the sling more and I started going to the Institute regularly—but then for a while the more active she got the harder it was to leave her because she wouldn't stay buried in her nice smelly sheets any more. For a few days there this looked like it was going to be Jake's Last Straw and one day as I was trying to leave and I'd only just got her buried and (apparently) settled but she'd started to cry before I got to the *door*, and I don't remember what I said but it was in the "aaaaugh" category.

Grace said mildly, "Children are like that sometimes," and I said, "But she's not a child, she's a *dragon*, and what if—" And Grace said, "Every mother says, 'But *my* child. . . .' That's how it works."

"But I'm *not* her mother," I wailed, hearing in my own voice that I sounded like a baby myself, crying for a toy or an ice cream. "That's the *point*."

"You're the only mother she's got," Grace said, smiling, "just like Eric was the only mother Julie had." Julie was the first, and only, Yukon wolf cub any human had ever successfully raised and successfully released into the wild—without getting eaten in the process, that is. Even Yukon wolves thought twice about Eric, although Julie had left a few marks. "Go on, Jake," said Grace. "I'm here. Lois will be fine."

I wanted to say, *How do you know she'll be fine*, but I didn't. I went. And she was fine. Even if that was when I had to start really *working* at wearing her out so she'd actually sleep while I was gone.

So what is the point of living on the edge of five million acres of wilderness if you spend all your time inside four walls? But Billy took me out with him every chance he could invent, and while as Lois got bigger walking around carrying her got harder, Billy was really clever with his sling making and at the point I really wasn't going to be able to carry her in front any more she hoisted herself up another of those developmental stages, and agreed to ride on my back, and even more exciting, *over* the T-shirt. I think this must have been the moment when she would have started looking out of her mom's pouch sometimes, if her life had been normal, because she used to look over my shoulder (and snorkel around in my hair, making it stick together with smelly dragon spit) and (except for the spit) that was kind of fun, although it meant Billy had to be even more careful where he took me. Having a large bulgy restless stomach was bad enough, having an obviously exotic animal riding in your backpack is something else. Although I don't believe anyone could have recognized Lois as a dragon yet (she looked more like the Slug That Ate Schenectady, only lumpier), still, she was obviously something pretty strange, and anyone who caught us would have wanted to know what, and why whatever it was wasn't safely at the zoo in a cage being studied.

So anyway that was my life. Meanwhile . . .

The very very first instant thing that had happened after Billy gave the bad news over the two-way from Northcamp, is that our rules for anyone getting normal permission to enter the park to study something, any farther than the usual short, guided tourist treks, suddenly got impossible—even the zoo lizard note-takers got banned. You have a certificate signed by God that you can come in? Sorry. God's not good enough.

At first since as I've told you, I wasn't into the big picture about anything, I just thought "some good out of a whole cheezing lot of bad" that we weren't going to have nosy prying researcher types around at all. But we'd only ever had a few researcher types around at a time, and their nosying and prying was usually pretty focused—and actually some of them were pretty nice too—and instead we had all these *investigator* people hanging around wanting to, well, investigate, and there were a *lot* of them, and *none* of them were nice, and they wanted to investigate EVERYTHING, so we didn't finish ahead after all.

Almost everything. At least they didn't want to investigate the Chief Ranger's house and even the Institute director's nutcase son was mostly only interesting as a side issue, of how living in the wilderness was bad for children, I guess. Because I was a kid—and because of the nightmares and what the cadaver removal guys had said—and Billy had somehow managed to subtract the "solo" out of it so most people kind of thought he'd been there too—they didn't insist on interviewing me all over the place. Some nice-cop type took my statement once and then they left me alone. Maybe I put over "pathetic idiot" really well too and they decided they weren't going to get any more out of me. Although that meant they immediately wanted to take their high-tech magnifying glasses and deerstalker hats (ha ha ha) and stuff into the park where it happened, but they were going to do that anyway.

A long time later I asked Dad if they hadn't thought of pretending not to know anything about the poacher or the dead dragon—Pine Tor is twenty miles from Northcamp, and Billy had only officially scheduled us as far as Northcamp. Dad said that of course they had but had rejected it. In the first place, we don't *like* lying. You have to work too hard on keeping your story straight if you're lying. (We know.) But the big issue was, as always, PR.

Some of the other big predators bag the occasional human in some of the other wilderness parks, but that's okay or something (except to the bagged guy's friends and family), part of the natural order out in the wild, the risk you take by going there, yatta yatta. Dragons are different. Like those two speleologists who disappeared on their way to the

Bonelands twenty years ago—you know about them, right?—
are still getting brought up pretty much every time Smokehill gets mentioned in the national press, and the point is
they *disappeared*. Nobody knows what happened to them.
Quick—how many people have been taken out by grizzlies—
are *known* to have been taken out by grizzlies—in the last
twenty years? You don't know, do you? But it's more than
two. Maybe it would be easier if more people did deny that
our dragons exist.

We couldn't risk it that the villain hadn't told someone
what he was going to do, and then having to arrange our
faces in the appropriate expressions of surprise and conster-
nation when someone came to ask where he was. Which in
fact he had done—left a record of what he was planning to
do, I mean. ("I'm going to break into Smokehill and ruin
everything because I'm a sick, greedy bastard.") With his
girlfriend. Can you imagine a guy like that having a girlfriend? But our Rangers cover eastern Smokehill pretty
thoroughly, and a dead human might have turned up anyway
(even if the dragon was ash by then), and it would be major
bad press for us if it didn't because nobody but someone
who lives there realizes what "wilderness" really means,
and, as I keep banging on about, everybody's really jumpy
about our wilderness because it has dragons in it.

So anyway we had the investigative police-type people
and the investigative scientist-type people and the investigative tech-type people—and a few investigative spy-
type people, who tried so badly to look like the rest of 'em
that even I noticed: I hadn't realized dragons counted as
intrigue—and of course the investigative journalists who
were a total pain because if it wasn't bad it wasn't good copy.

Especially now that a dragon had killed someone (circumstances irrelevant) there was no way anyone, which is to say
investigative creeps, was going to be allowed into the park
without an escort, and Dad did manage to prevent our being
swamped with the National Guard right away (that came
later), which left the Rangers, and then some high-ranking

jerk insisted that as a condition to not being swamped by the National Guard, all the escorts carry guns. If anyone had stopped to think about it they would have noticed that the grenade launchers and bazookas and things that the poacher had been carrying hadn't done him any good. . . . Anyway this made even our Rangers cranky, and it takes a lot to make our Rangers cranky, but being investigator-minders meant that they weren't doing any of the stuff they felt was their real job, about keeping an eye on the park. And the dragons. And Rangers only carry guns if they want fresh meat for dinner. Not to mention what a big rifle weighs.

But since the fence went up, and Smokehill became Smokehill, we hadn't had any successful burglars, thieves or murderers. At least we didn't know of any—the two guys from twenty years ago still haven't turned up. That's an eighty-six-year clean record. Till now. And the first conclusion everyone had jumped to was that someone must have finally managed to steal the fence specs—that that had to have been how our poacher got in. And if it had happened once presumably it could happen again. The thieves might even be out there flogging them on eBay. Speaking of feeling insecure. We'd *trusted* that fence. The techies were working like blazes to change the waves or fields or the particle flow or some damn thing or things so that if there *were* stolen specs out there they wouldn't work any more, but the fence had been hard enough to invent in the first place. . . .

So why we didn't have staff dropping like hailstones in a spring blizzard with weird stress diseases and panic attacks and stuff I have no idea. But we didn't. We all hung in there. Even Dad. He's a great guy, my dad, even if he tries to hide it sometimes. Sometimes I think about those first months with Lois, before we were like *used* to unbearable strain, and I think Dad and I probably never looked each other in the face that whole time. Although Dad came down and had dinner with Billy and Grace and me (and Lois) almost every night. And started a joke about how he'd let me sign on as an apprentice when he found out I'd be living with Billy so *he* could sponge up more of Grace's cooking. So at least he got something good out of it.

But somewhat strange behavior on the part of the only child of the widowed head of the Institute wasn't too much commented on. I heard one cop investigator say to another one, "You know I think this has addled Dr. Mendoza. He's pretty well turned his only kid over to the Rangers, you heard about that?"

I was sorting postcards on my knees behind the counter in the gift shop. This was the sort of thing I did now, to make myself noticeable, instead of mooching around in tourist-free zones. You wouldn't have caught me dead offering to sort postcards in the gift shop before Lois. And furthermore I'd got there on time. I'd said I'd be in at three, and here it was 3:05, and I was already here with a lapful of boxes.

In this case while postcard-sorting was making me very noticeable to Peggy—and to Dan, who'd almost tripped over me when he came to steal some pens, since tourists are always walking off with the info booth's pens—it was making me invisible to the cops, although I'd seen them come in, through the gap in the counter so the staff can get in and out. I looked out of the corners of my eyes and could see Peggy wearing a very fierce, un-gift-shop-like frown (mustn't scare the customers). But I could imagine her trying to decide whether to tell me to stand up or the cops to shut up. I stopped peering out of the corners of my eyes and looked up at her. She looked down at me and I shook my head. Her frown deepened (any deeper and her face would fold up like a fan), but she didn't say anything.

The other one said, "The kid's apprenticed. Nothing wrong with that."

"The kid's fourteen. Three years too young."

Just by the way, I'd turned fifteen by then. Only two years too young. I sat there staring at the photo of Indigo Ridge. It's one of our best sellers, for good reason. I thought, They could at least find out my name, and use it.

"I think if I were Dr. Mendoza I might think my only child was safer in the Rangers' hands too."

"If I were Dr. Mendoza I'd think my only child was safer outside the park somewhere. Send him to live with relatives and go to a normal school. The fence gives me the heebie-jeebies. Have you noticed what it does to the sunlight? At least we don't have to stay here, and I can get some real daylight with my coffee in the morning before we have to report in."

Oh, good. Some really balanced individual who can get claustrophobia in five million acres. Our fence only does something funny to sunlight if you stand next to it all the time.

"He probably doesn't want to send him away because he'd never see him."

"But the Rangers are *crazy*. They seem to think this park and the damned dragons are some kind of sacred trust or something."

Peggy's head snapped up at that. She's still only an apprentice, and she's black and grew up in Chicago, but in a way that shows how much she wants to be here and a Ranger. She'd survived the vetting to get here and after three years she was still here. I didn't hear the cops apologize, but they did suddenly move out of earshot.

It *is* a sacred trust, I thought fiercely. It *is*. And then the box of Indigo Ridge fell off my lap and two hundred postcards plunged across the floor.

As I said, mostly I was preoccupied. But even I could see all these flaming (I wish) investigator people trying to find more people like Nancy and Evan who weren't even apprentices, trying to get them to dish some dirt, but people who aren't crazy (yeah, okay, *crazy*) about the place don't work here. Eric, who hates everybody who doesn't have fur or feathers or scales, hates everybody outside of Smokehill worse than everybody inside, so even he wasn't any use to them. (In fact he was so nasty that they decided he had something to hide and began to investigate *him*. At the time I was hoping they'd find out he'd escaped from jail for extortion or bigamy or something which was why he was willing to disappear in a place like Smokehill but no such luck.) I complained to Grace about the way they acted like escapees from a bad secret-conspiracy movie but she only laughed. At least she could still laugh. "If you're an investigator, you want there to be things to investigate," she said. Yes. Exactly. They might find out there were.

As it happens Dad was graduate-student-less when Lois arrived and the roof fell in, which all things considered was more good than bad but it meant he couldn't help trying to drag Rangers off the other things they already couldn't keep up with because of all the escort duty to try to bail some of the Institute stuff out. Later on he hit on the idea of asking me to type some of his letters for him. This worked pretty well. It was something I could do back at Billy's house with Lois, especially on those afternoons after she'd definitely outgrown the sling and would *not* just go to sleep and let the humans get on with human stuff, so I was mostly keeping an eye on her. Not paying attention was the best way to try to translate Dad's handwriting—which kind of looked like the White Queen's hair—what the words were would kind of tango out at you if you were looking somewhere else. And it did mean that I had some clue some of the time about some things that were going on outside Billy's house. Outside Lois. Whether I wanted a clue or not.

Billy and some of the other Rangers cremated Lois' mom. They knew they had to let the cops and the scientists measure and test and take millions of photos and so on, but barring a few samples they wouldn't let them move her. Some of the scientists got pretty shirty about the "wouldn't let" part but Smokehill as part of its charter has absolute control over its dragons (within evil little caveats like not saving any of their lives) and while people started spitting phrases like "legal challenge" and "in the public interest" around—and they'd already been using words like "obstructionist" when

Dad had refused to okay their doing a mini rainforest-type raze for a gigantic helicopter pad to fly all these visiting bozos in and out—they couldn't actually do anything.

So after about two weeks Billy said "that's it" and one night they burned her. They burned her and they *sang* while the scientists and cops and journalists stood around with their mouths hanging open. The Arkholas are usually dead private about their singing so I was amazed, but Grace told me and while it's not like I doubted her or anything I still asked Kit too, because he was there. He almost smiled. "Yeah. They thought we were raising demons or something."

"Wow," I said.

Kit knew what I meant. "Yeah. But it stopped them from trying to stop us, you know?"

It's not like we have a lot of practice at it but we knew already that dragon bodies burn a lot easier than human ones. Human ones, they're all water, they don't want to burn. Dragon ones, it's like you just show 'em a matchbox and they go up—*whoop*—bonfire to the stars, no boring ignition necessary. (The guys that went out to Australia two hundred years ago reported on this, over and over again, like they kept not believing it.) You'd've thought that the *smell* of something that size decomposing after a couple of weeks would have made everybody think burning was a good idea, but ironically decomposing dragon doesn't stink as spectacularly as decomposing most-other-things do, although I guess that "as spectacularly" is relative. Forensic morgue guy is a job I've never been interested in.

There might have been more trouble but then all the samples everybody'd collected started turning to ash and some kind of sticky black tar stuff. We were lucky that there was a lot of info on the way dragon stuff does disintegrate really fast—the scientists had been doing their tests in quadruple-time because they knew the clock was ticking but they still didn't get anywhere: Every test said something different, and nothing made any sense. What a good thing scientists would rather die under torture than be accused of

being Bad Scientists or some of them might have been a little tempted to go along with the Arkhola curse thing that the
National Stupid People Press tried to get going.

That was about as much as I knew at the time. What I
didn't know anything about was what happened when they
ID'd the poacher. You've got it that I was what you might
call pathologically *not* interested in the poacher, I hope. So
you get it that for a long time I didn't think about not hearing
about him.

CHAPTER FIVE

The first two years of Lois' life are both really blurry and really clear in my memory. There are all kinds of little sharp clear pieces in it, mostly about watching Lois grow and worrying about keeping her healthy, that are still dead immediate like they happened yesterday. But I have very little sense of the time passing, except for Lois getting bigger, which I really liked seeing, was hooked on seeing, because it was the only clue I had that maybe she was okay and thriving. I'm sure we had lots more close calls than I know about (or want to, even now) but one that I do know about, and scared me to death at the time, was the next time the school-form-filler-outer gang came to test me on the nonacademic stuff.

I think they were suspicious of the apprenticeship, although at that point, with the hoo-ha about the poacher going on, everyone who wasn't one of us was suspicious of everything at Smokehill, and maybe it wasn't only cops who hang around talking loudly in gift shops who thought there was something strange about Dad "handing over his only child" to the Rangers. So what happened was that the usual school pencil pushers brought a doctor along without warning us. Usually I got a complete medical only once a year, and the last one had only been about six weeks before Lois happened, so I should have had a long spell yet to get her used to staying by herself, or at least not needing *skin*, which she kept burning. And here less than six months later was this dweeb telling me to take my shirt off so he could listen to my heart. And he took one look at my stomach, of course, and freaked.

Don't panic, I said to myself. You look guilty when you panic. This is another of those great hindsight things—he must have been thinking about some kind of really kinky child abuse or self-harm (I can't offhand think of anything that would leave marks like a dragonlet's tongue), and if I'd seemed frightened that would have made him think so all the more, and he would have started raking through our business and discovered that we *were* keeping some kind of big horrible secret. Child abuse didn't cross my mind at the time, but the big horrible secret sure did. I don't know where I got the nerve—maybe from spending so much time with Billy, who even told cops where they got off calmly—but I looked at my stomach and said, "Oh, yeah, eczema. My mom started getting it when she was about my age."

The tension level immediately sank about sixty fathoms and although he still wasn't happy—"Why didn't you report it? We could have given you something for it long ago, before it got this bad"—I think he stopped worrying that he had something to report back to headquarters. He muttered about stress levels and preoccupied single parents and looking at my diet and changing our laundry detergent and taking some scrapings to see if it was some kind of weird fungus instead of eczema (he did this, and the results must have been negative for weird funguses, even if Lois did kind of look like a large walking weird fungus), since it was rather unusual eczema (duh), and then he said he'd prescribe some cream for it as it was a pretty painful-looking case (that was true enough; I give him credit—he was very gentle with the scraping taking) and it was peculiar that it was only on my stomach. Here I showed him some other littler Lois marks on my arms and my feet and legs, and this seemed to cheer him up. Doctors are weird.

Then when he found out I was living with Billy and Grace he wanted to talk to Grace about laundry detergent and what I ate which I found pretty insulting but Grace thought was funny. But at least it meant I got back to Lois before she had a heart attack and Grace had to go up to the

Institute and get her instructions how to take care of me. At least the doc didn't insist on coming to see my room.

After that it was always the same doctor, and after a while he wanted to write some kind of paper on my skin complaint, which he wasn't even sure was eczema, he said (bright of him), and he sure tried to get me to come up to some hospital and have some fancy tests done, but I didn't want to go (leave Lois *overnight*?) and Dad wouldn't make me, obviously, and since I was healthy except for the eczema, the doc reluctantly let it go.

The other seriously scary near miss—except that it wasn't a miss at all—was Eleanor's fault. That she and Martha knew something was up in itself wouldn't have been a big deal, necessarily, kids at the Institute were always being not told stuff, and overlooked or got out of the way—or told to *get* out of the way like it isn't *normal* to want to know what's going on. Being a kid is probably like that everywhere. It's maybe worse here in some ways because we all live here—nobody goes home from the office. Martha and I knew this—I've been here since I was born and Martha since she was two—and it was just the way it was. But it's one of the reasons that families with kids old enough to know the way the rest of the world works never stay here long. Even if both parents have jobs they like the kids hate it. They're kept out of the grown-up stuff and there *is* no kid stuff. Since pretty much every kid I've ever talked to (and most grown-ups) say they hated school I don't entirely get this—seems to me not having to go to school might balance not having lots of friends your own age. But I guess it doesn't.

Eleanor was another story. Of course she's the youngest, so that's a big thing right there—she's always trying to be older. But Eleanor has to be out there. Martha and me, if we're told to go away and leave the grown-ups alone, find a book to read or baby orphan to feed (ha ha). Eleanor *hates* being shut out of anything. Which is why, since she got old enough to be usefully and sort of *applied*-ly a brat instead of just a general brat sort of brat, Martha and I knew more stuff about the Institute than we used to, because she's always generous (to the other members of our oppressed race, the children) with her info. And this time whatever they weren't being told bothered Martha too, because I was in on it. I think Martha might have been kind of bracing herself for this to happen—that I would suddenly become one of the grown-ups, or at least not a kid like her and Eleanor any more—and maybe she thought my solo overnight really had been it, the place where I crossed the line. But this was kind of more spectacular than she expected. And it drove Eleanor *insane.*

I've already told you I felt bad about not really being friends any more. Friends with Martha anyway, interactions with Eleanor don't really come under that heading. It's like I'd barely seen Martha and Eleanor except for my fifteenth birthday party which after the first hour I just wanted to be over with because I had to get back to Lois who I knew would be starting to shred the bedclothes. That's not too flattering to the people at your party. It was already a strange party because Grace hadn't come—but someone had to stay home and make not-alone noises for Lois. Billy brought the cake she'd made but it was still strange. And I saw Martha and Eleanor when the school testers came, but none of us was at our best then. That was one thing we had totally in common. All three of us hated the grown-ups who came to prod us and take notes like we were some kind of science project or field survey. I felt like giving them tips. Our Rangers did it so much better.

But while it was Eleanor's idea, I think in this case Martha went along with it. And so one afternoon when Lois was about seven months old and I was home alone doing extra schoolwork so I could sit still longer and let Lois sleep on my (bare) feet for longer, first because any time she was asleep I wanted to keep her that way as long as possible and second because I'd been over three hours at the Institute the day before and she'd been pretty panicked and crazy by the time I got back. (Panicked and crazy was getting bigger and heavier too, she was going to be leaving bruises some day soon, as well as eczema, never mind the grisly idea of her giving the slip to Billy or Grace or whoever her jailer was that day, and galumphing up to the Institute to look for me. Or just getting hopelessly lost in the woods. This really was *not* likely—at least not until she was big enough to keep galumphing with Billy or Grace hanging around her neck—but it was still another thing that worried me.)

Also . . . this is another of those things I don't know how to explain, even in hindsight, although I have a much better idea what was going on now than I did then . . . my stupid permanent headache was sort of better when I was thinking about stuff. I've said it was easier to live with if I was doing something, but that's not quite right. It's like it liked certain kinds of brainwork. It liked educational stuff, not worry stuff. It didn't exactly hurt *less*, but it hurt *better*. Remember I said, about when I first had it, that it sometimes seemed like it was trying to fit inside my head and couldn't figure out why it couldn't make itself comfortable? Well now it was like something in my head that was interested in some of the same things I was interested in. Headline in the National Stupid People Press: Boy Believes He Was Kidnapped by Aliens and Has an Alien Spy Thingy Implanted in His Brain. Photos on page seven. I didn't—didn't think I'd been kidnapped by aliens, I mean—but I did start to sort of half think of my headache as almost another *thing*—like me, Lois, Billy, Grace, the Smell, and the Headache—but without finishing the other half of thinking about it, because it was too weird.

Anyway. So Headache and I were deep in this afternoon when I heard the door bang and I had about five seconds to jerk myself out of what I was doing and think that the bang didn't sound right and that neither Billy nor Grace was due back till later, and then a voice I knew only too well said, "What is that *smell*?" and I was on my feet and would have been out of my bedroom door and closing it behind me in another five seconds but Eleanor was too fast for me.

"Oh, *shit*," I said. If Dad had been there that would have been my allowance for that week. (Sure I have an allowance,

even in Smokehill. How do you think I paid for all those
on-line hours of Annihilate?) But if he'd been there he'd've
stopped it from happening somehow, I don't know how, put
a bag over Eleanor's head and said three magic words or
something. Dad copes. It hasn't been good for his temper but
he *copes.*

Lois poked her nose around the desk leg, not happy at the
abrupt removal of my feet, but generally speaking always
ready to be thrilled at meeting someone else so long as I was
there too. She did one of her peeps. Not that I could ever say
for sure what happy was in Lois terms, but her spine plates,
now that they were big enough to do anything, tended to
erect themselves when she was what I would call happy and
interested. They stiffened now. And her nostrils flared, and
she did a kind of *ooonnngg-peeEEEeep-oooonnngggg.* I
told you about my dad suddenly believing Billy's story was
real when he heard the weird noises coming from under his
son's shirt. Sound and smell are very convincing. Just seeing
something that looks like a low-level goblin out of a bad
computer game isn't so convincing.

"*What* is *that?*" Eleanor said, in that way you do when
you're really surprised: Whaaaaat is thaaaaaat? It takes a lot
to surprise Eleanor. By this time Martha had joined Eleanor
in the doorway, except by then Eleanor was out of the doorway and going toward Lois. I grabbed her arm. "Leave her
alone," I said.

"Her?" said Eleanor. "Ow. You're hurting me."

"Tough eggs," I said. I was so shocked it was taking me a
little while to get angry but I was going to be *spectacularly*
angry when I got there. "What are you doing here?" I looked
at Martha, but she wouldn't meet my eyes. Eleanor wouldn't
meet them either, but that was because she was staring at
Lois. Eleanor has no conscience. And Martha was pretty
fascinated too. Who wouldn't be?

"What is that—she?" said Eleanor. "How do you know
it's a she?"

"She's a dragon, isn't she," said Martha in this spaced-out
voice. She was as shocked as I was, sort of from the opposite

direction. We were both seeing the last thing we expected to see.

"No, she's an aardvark," I said. I couldn't quite come out and say, yes, that's right, this is my baby dragon, Lois. This is the big secret no one has been telling you. "What are you *doing* here?"

Eleanor finally turned away from Lois long enough to look up at me. I still had her by the arm. "I wanted to know what was going on," she said in her shoot-from-the-hip way. She might lie, cheat and steal to get where she wanted to go, but she'd tell you she'd done it once she got there.

"But—" I said. I didn't know where to begin.

"They're all in some meeting about something," she said. "The grown-ups. So there wasn't anyone watching us—for a *change*," she said with scorn, although at eight years old and living in the biggest and wildest wild animal park in the country it was hardly surprising she wasn't allowed to wander around by herself—and Katie did know that Martha couldn't be expected to keep Eleanor from doing something she was determined to do. Where was Katie when I needed her?

"Meeting," I said blankly. I was trying to remember if Billy and Grace had said anything about where they were going. Billy usually didn't. Grace usually did. But Grace wasn't a Smokehill employee; she just sold the admin some of her drawings. She wouldn't be going to a Smokehill meeting. Would she? *All* the grown-ups. And she loved Smokehill as passionately as any of us. "It can't be all the grown-ups," I said.

"It is though," said Eleanor. "They've closed the park for the day and everything. For this big special meeting. We're not supposed to *know* about it. They close the park and the grown-ups all *disappear* but we're not supposed to *notice.*"

"Mom said she'd only be gone a couple of hours and everyone was busy," said Martha mildly.

"Busy going to the *meeting*," muttered Eleanor.

"We're short staffed," Martha continued as if Eleanor hadn't said anything.

"We're *always* short staffed," said Eleanor. "But there's never been a meeting for *all* the grown-ups before."

"About the caves?" I said, completely at a loss. I remembered Dad yesterday saying, really casually, that I could have the day off, stay home, away from the Institute. At the time I thought he just meant, and give Lois a break, because I'd been so long we knew she'd be in a state when I got back. He probably did mean that—but had he arranged for me to be delayed yesterday, to give himself the excuse to tell me not to come up today? *What* damned meeting? But suddenly I knew. And I didn't want to know.

Eleanor gave me one of her famous you-don't-know-anything-you-pathetic-schmuck looks. "No, stupid. About the *dead guy.* Oh!" She looked back at Lois. "You're right, Martha. It's a dragon." That's another thing about Eleanor. She never believes anything anyone tells her until she works it out for herself and it suits her to believe it. "The dragon the dead guy killed was a mom dragon, and this is her baby."

I decided without any difficulty not to say that this was her fifth and only living baby, and how I knew this, but I didn't deny that Eleanor was right. Pretty good thinking for eight.

"She doesn't *look* like a dragon," Eleanor continued. "She looks like . . ."

Eleanor actually paused. I'll tell you for free that most people's imaginations aren't up to describing what a dragonlet looks like, and Eleanor was always so busy trying to figure out how to get in the way out here in the real world she hadn't worked on her imagination much. I was allowed to describe Lois to myself as looking like roadkill or one of the monsters out of the first series of *Star Trek*, but I didn't want anyone else doing it. So I managed to interrupt. "Just *stop* there. I don't want to hear."

Martha knelt down, the way you do with small children and animals to get them to come to you. This works too well with Lois—she peeped delightedly and shot out from under the desk where she'd been keeping the backs of my legs hot.

I dropped Eleanor's arm just in time to fend Lois off. "Don't—she'll burn you." Too late, of course—Martha might have listened but Eleanor instantly reached out to pat her. *"Ow,"* she said, like Lois had hurt her deliberately.

This made me madder than it should've. Not at Lois. At Eleanor. "I told you," I said, trying to be patient. "She'll burn you. She can't help it. She's just hot."

"What do *you*—" Eleanor began accusingly, and then stopped and looked at her hand. She hadn't touched Lois long enough to have left a red mark. "Oh," she said. "Eczema. It's not because your mom had it."

The things that kid picks up. "No," I said.

"If she opens her mouth, can you see the fire inside?" said Eleanor. It was a reasonable question for an eight-year-old.

"No," I said. "It's a special organ, like you have lungs to breathe, dragons have a fire-stomach for fire." Which was about as much as anyone knew: We were all eight-year-olds about dragons. I was down on the floor now too, with my arm around Lois' neck. It was mostly only fresh bits of me that weren't used to it that really burned any more—although my stomach stayed pretty scaly—and I was wearing a long-sleeved shirt. Eleanor sat down in front of me, staring with renewed fascination at Lois, now only a few inches away. I was used to it, but at this distance you could feel her radiating heat, like sitting too close to the stove.

"Your eczema should be a lot worse," said Eleanor.

"You get used to it," I said.

"I've always wanted to see a dragon up close," said Martha.

And suddenly we were on the same side again. Suddenly I realized that while everything, Lois' life, Smokehill's future, everything that mattered, was about to have to rely on whether we could come up with a good reason to make Eleanor keep her big blackmailing mouth shut, it was also a relief to be a kid among kids again, even if I was the oldest and Eleanor was a pain in the butt. When you're the only kid surrounded by grown-ups, even when the grown-ups are busy protecting you, you spend a certain amount of time just holding your own line, just hanging on to being yourself. When you're with other kids you don't have to do this. Well, not so much. Eleanor has always been pushy. She was a pushy *baby*.

"Yeah," I said. "Me too."

"What's her name?" said Martha matter-of-factly, as if naming a dragon is a perfectly ordinary thing to do. As if having a dragon to name was a perfectly ordinary thing.

"Lois," I said.

"Lois?" said Eleanor. "That's a stupid name for a dragon."

This was so typical an Eleanor remark I didn't bother to answer it, and I didn't care either. But Martha said quietly, "I think it's a nice name," and mysteriously this made me feel really good.

We all sat there a little longer, staring at Lois. Lois, who was extremely used to me holding her off from flinging herself on the few people she ever got to see, had given up, and collapsed half onto my lap, grunting and murmuring a little from the awkwardness of her position, but also because she had this funny habit of muttering into silences in conversations. That was how we usually have conversations, right? Someone talks while everyone else is quiet, then someone else talks while the first person shuts up, and so on. I hadn't had a good shouting-over-each-other match with Dad since Lois came. Probably all the conversations she ever heard were polite ones. Snark had known my schedule better than I did, and if I was late to be doing something (like getting on the sofa after dinner to watch TV, so he could join me), he reminded me. Lois didn't seem to have much sense of time, but she had a sense of conversation. If no one else was saying anything, she did. And I'd got in the habit of letting her finish. After Lois had had her mutter, I said, "What is this about the poacher?"

Martha sighed her worried sigh, but Eleanor launched straight in. "His parents are on TV all over the country saying that dragons are too dangerous and they should all be killed!"

I gaped at her. "They'll never make that stick."

Martha said, "They're very, very, very, *very* wealthy."

I don't know how good an idea about money most kids have, but I'd grown up listening to my parents not just trying to figure out how to make the year's budget work and what we could get along without so it would stretch a little farther, which probably most kids listen to in most families, but about the really dazzling mess of getting, keeping, justifying, and accounting for funding for the Institute. I knew about congressional subcommittees and private donors and action groups and lobbyists. And I knew instantly—as Martha, whose mom was a member of the Institute's budgetary council, also knew—that very, very, very, very wealthy people who wanted something and didn't care how they got it were very, very, very, very dangerous. I hadn't thought I *could* worry any more than I was already worrying, all the time, about Lois. I was wrong.

"It's been going on for months," said Martha. "Well, since—since it happened. At first nobody took them seriously. But they just kept at it—"

Kept throwing money at it, I translated silently.

"And they've started the *Human Preservation Society*"—I didn't know Martha knew how to sound that scornful—"and they're really well organized."

Have hired goons to write letters and hang out with members of Congress and other people who like playing with money and power, I translated. And because they have lots of money, they've hired effective goons and send lots of letters.

I hoped Dad's coping mechanism was up to it. My brain was doing a slow, dazed reshuffle of my awareness of the tension level around the Institute. It made me feel silly and self-absorbed (or Lois-absorbed) to be reminded that the world—the world that mattered—didn't actually revolve around us. I wasn't enjoying the reminder. It was also incredibly *stupid* of me to have forgotten about the death of the poacher, even if it had been months ago now, and I didn't want to remember. I remembered the death of Lois' mom all right. I still thought of her every day.

You can't pet a dragonlet. Well, you can, but in the first place you'll probably burn your hand, depending on how sensitive your skin is, and in the second place I figured it couldn't feel like much to the dragon. Even as a squishy baby Lois had noticeably thick skin, and now that she was growing scales, it was more like running your hand over pebbles. But she was certainly an interactive creature and, as I say, noisy. I was having the petting-reflex as I thought about the poacher—I'd half petted the hair off Snark when I was worried about something—but I'd learned to deflect the reflex in Lois' case. Unfortunately I didn't think about this any more—I wasn't used to having people around with me and Lois—so I burbled at her. I could do a half-decent Lois burble. I couldn't peep and I couldn't mew, but I could burble. She turned her funny snout up toward me—she'd been staring at Martha and Eleanor as keenly as they were staring at her—and burbled back.

"You're as goofy about that dragon as you were about your dog," said Eleanor, who was four when he died and shouldn't have been able to remember him at all. He wasn't her dog and she'd never found him interesting. She probably didn't mean to sound as snotty as she did sound, but she sounded pretty snotty.

I stood up. I did *not* have a brilliant coping mechanism. "You shouldn't be here, and if I tell anybody you were here you'll get into more trouble than you've ever imagined getting into," I said to her. This was not what I'd planned a few minutes ago when I'd been thinking about how my first priority was to think of a way to make Eleanor keep her mouth shut, but then I hadn't had *any* plan. If I hadn't been so pissed off at her saying what she'd said, though, I'd have known better than to threaten her, which was always the thing that worked least with her. But Martha surprised me.

"She won't," said Martha. She'd stood up when I did.

Martha wasn't big for thirteen the way I was big for fifteen, but she was still a lot bigger than eight-year-old Eleanor. This is a lot of Eleanor's problem, as I say. She takes on the world because she hates being littlest, and she's a *little* littlest. But although I saw her face pulling into its usual pig-headed brat the-thing-I'm-going-to-do-first-is-the-thing-you-don't-want-me-to-do lines, she looked at me and then at Martha and wavered. This was a first with Eleanor so far as I know. She doesn't know how to waver. Martha and I must have looked pretty fierce. I was feeling like pig-headed brat roast for dinner, but I didn't know Martha knew how to look fierce. I looked at her though and she did.

She didn't sound angry the way I did, but she said, very calmly, "Eleanor, this is about all of our lives. This about you and me and Jake, and Mom and Dr. Mendoza, and Billy and all the Rangers, and everybody you know. And it's about Jake's dragon and all the dragons in Smokehill. You know dragons are why we're here, don't you?"

Eleanor is one of these people who when she comes into the room, whatever is going on becomes all about Eleanor. I didn't think even Smokehill really got through to Eleanor.

I was wrong. I don't know if Martha knew her better than I did—if maybe she was more Martha's sister than I'd realized. But Eleanor looked thoughtfully at Martha for a moment, and she looked smaller for that moment, just an ordinary kid. "Yes," she said, "I do." She added in more her usual manner, "I'm not *stupid*." And then she turned on me and stuck her chin out and clenched her fists and said, "And I'll even keep your secret for you, but first you have to *apologize*, and then you have to ask me *nicely*, and I don't care what you think you can do to me."

I was over my bad temper by then. And besides, Lois was so much more important. (Lois, who I was keeping trapped between my shins so she couldn't go burn Martha and Eleanor and, among other things, maybe give the game away after all.) "I'm sorry," I said, almost sincerely. "Please don't tell anyone about Lois, okay?"

She pulled her chin in a little and crossed her arms. "Okay," she said. And I believed her.

The grown-ups were really preoccupied at dinner that night, so they didn't notice I was really preoccupied too. Kit and Jane were there as well as Dad, and Grace and Billy. I don't know if having more silent grown-ups there was supposed to make the silence less obvious but it didn't. Grace and Lois and I kept the conversation going. Grace did a pretty good burble too, although she always did it the way you make "mmm-hmmm" noises at a four-year-old (human) who wants to tell you a story. It reminded me of being four, when Grace sometimes babysat for me. This didn't actually improve my mood. It seemed to me they were still "mmm-hmmming" me really.

I wanted to ask them how the meeting had gone, but I couldn't, since I wasn't supposed to know about it. It did make me a little angry that they seemed to think Martha and Eleanor wouldn't have noticed, even if they thought they had me safely tucked away (they were right about that, which was part of why I was angry), but I've noticed before the way children are conveniently assumed to be dumb when adults need them to be. You'd think the adults would learn. But who am I to be sarcastic? I didn't want to know about the poacher. The villain. I didn't want the poacher ever to cross my mind for any reason whatsoever. It was bad enough thinking about Lois' mom, every day, which I did, as I told you. I used to try to blot out the memory part of it by deliberately calling up that dragon cave I still dreamed about sometimes, which usually had her in it, because there she was *alive* which is how I knew it was only a stupid childish dream and it meant I really was a wuss.

I mostly could blot the poacher out. But this was the worst yet: that he had parents who could make big trouble for Smokehill. How do I explain this to you though? I did think about it, that evening, with all these preoccupied grown-ups eating Grace's food and pretending really badly that everything was normal, whatever normal was any more. I thought about it and kind of realized—although writing it down like this makes it again a whole lot more rational than it was at the time—that I *couldn't* think about it. It was too much. If there was a line, this was over it. My job was to raise Lois. Somebody else was going to have to deal with the villain.

About the time Lois started riding on my shoulders she also suddenly hey presto housebroke herself. What a major relief *that* was. Dragon diapers are the WORST. (And I should say I didn't do all my own laundry, if you counted Lois. We all did Lois' diapers. And—speaking of needing generators to run stuff—I *can't imagine* doing baby dragon diapers without a washing machine. Or anyway *I don't want to.* Mind you we were probably destroying the local groundwater table or whatever. They took more than one go and you didn't just throw them in without some preliminary detox either.)

But it was weird, how fast it happened, and how little I had to do with it. It makes sense if you figure that this must be the stage when the baby dragon is not merely old enough (and scaly enough) to look out of its mom's pouch but old enough to climb out and do its business outdoors, which must be a major relief to *Mom.* I had noticed that Lois' scales first started really looking like scales on her head, like they grew there first so she could look out and get used to the *idea* of out.

It was a relief in other ways too—her tail was turning into a tail, and the diapers didn't fit so well any more, and even Billy's ingenuity has its limits. Big disgusting yuck. I used to make jokes about Super Glue. Especially when— No, never mind.

The point is that suddenly it wasn't a problem any more. Except that it was because everything about Lois was a problem and the problem got bigger as she got bigger, and while no more dragon diapers was TOTALLY a good thing, dragon dung doesn't disintegrate *that* fast, so I had to get out there and bury the stuff all the time, and dragonlet digestion really puts the stuff through, so while I would have said she was never out of my sight when we were outdoors together (she'd better not be) she still managed to leave piles I didn't notice her leaving.

Then there was the fact that dragonlet pee slowly burns holes in almost everything it touches (it didn't burn right through the diapers, but it wore through fast enough that we had to patch them, and needlework is *not* my thing but Grace let me use pretty much anything in her sewing box, so some of them got kind of artistically interesting over time and repeat mending) and fortunately Billy and Grace's house didn't have any lawn to destroy, but she still almost managed to kill one of Grace's Smokehill-winter-proof, tougher-than-the-French-Foreign-Legion rhododendrons before I figured out how to persuade her—Lois, not Grace—to pee and crap in one sort of general area. Although this still wasn't fool-proof. I swear I was *always* out there with my shovel—to the extent that if a dragon could get neurotic I should have given Lois a complex—and even so half the time when Kit or Jane came round the conversation would begin like this:

Kit or Jane: "Hi, Jake. There's a—"

Me: "Okay." And I go get my shovel. (If it was Whiteoak, he just *looked* at me. And I'd go get my shovel.) And miss whatever they'd come to say, probably, which may have been the idea.

Lois would always come with me. Far from developing a complex she was delighted for an excuse to go outside and play some more, and as far as she was concerned (evidently) my strange compulsion to bury her leavings was as good an excuse as anything else, *and* the house was getting smaller and smaller as she got bigger and bigger. (I wonder what she thought about the toilet. I always used to wonder that about Snark. I don't know how good a dragon's sense of smell is, but it would have to be really bad not to draw the correct conclusions about what the toilet is about. And a dog has to know. So isn't it thinking, Hey, why do you get to use that thing when I have to go outdoors even when the wind chill makes it sixty below and the snow is coming in *sideways*?)

She weighed about thirty pounds when she housebroke

herself, but that's still a pretty fair weight to carry around on your shoulders (if you're only a human), especially when it wiggles. The thing I worried about the most—the most after the possibility of someone taking a wrong turn and wandering into Billy and Grace's back yard some day, especially some day when I hadn't got out there with my shovel, or maybe in fact I *was* out there with my shovel, *and* with Lois herself—was that she was going to start practicing her fire-throwing. The fact that she was alive proved her *igniventator* was working, and the skin on my stomach sure believed it. And as well as getting bigger and noisier she was getting livelier and she wanted more action. How do you teach a dragon to come, sit and stay? Fortunately she still had little short legs and couldn't run as fast as I could. (Snark had been able to run faster than me by the time he was twelve weeks old, although I was still pretty little myself then.) But I was pretty sure this wouldn't be true much longer. I was also keeping a sharp, anxious eye on her wing stubs, but they didn't seem to be doing anything much yet either.

But speaking of training a dragon, it was at this stage, when she was beginning to spend significant amounts of time outside her mom's pouch equivalent that I began to realize . . . this is going to sound really stupid . . . that she was trying to, uh, respond to me, I mean aside from the fact that she still got hysterical if I wasn't around for more than about two hours.

I've raised, or helped raise, baby birds and baby raccoons and baby woodchucks and baby porcupines, and watched the Rangers raise baby bears and baby wolves and baby eagles, and some of them even survived to grow up and fly or run or trundle away. But when a baby robin gets all excited and sticks its neck out and opens its mouth and goes "ak kak kak kak kak" at you it's not exactly responding to *you*. It's responding to the prospect of getting fed. It never thinks about being a robin, and it doesn't care what you are, so long as you're feeding it the right stuff. (Chopped up earthworms rolled in dirt are a favorite. Delicious.) I also know that animals raised by humans tend to grow up funny because they aren't getting socialized by their own kind and don't learn how to do it, but even then I'm not sure that what they're doing is confusing themselves by trying to be human. What they're doing is failing to learn how to be themselves.

And I *was* a little silly about Lois . . . okay, more than a little. But can you blame me? The point is, when she started spending more time at a little distance, so we could like look at each other—that was another thing, her eyes had suddenly gone all sharp and focused at about five months; I'd begun to think that maybe dragons don't use sight much (and then I'd remember her mom's eye, sharp and clear and focused as anything—and dying—and then I'd remember all the impossible stuff I'd seen in that eye about hope and despair—and then I'd *take* my mind off it like peeling Snark as a puppy off the shoe he was disemboweling)—anyway, when Lois could watch me properly, she started trying to do what I was doing. For a while I could ignore it, put it down to why your cat walks on your keyboard when you're trying to use your computer, why your dog suddenly wants to play fetch when it's your turn to get dinner.

But she wasn't just trying to get my attention. It took me a while to figure this out—dragons and humans are shaped so much different. It's not like baby chimps learning to crack coconuts with stones by picking up a stone and banging with it because that's what Mom's doing. Or maybe it is. When I was typing, if she didn't want a nap, Lois used to dance. I should maybe say I'm kind of a dramatic typist. I had had to practice keeping my legs and feet still when Lois first got out of the sling, so she could lie on them while I typed. If they weren't held down, my feet started tapping all by themselves. (Which wasn't actually such a bad thing, because if she didn't want a nap—and she way too often didn't want a nap—she'd dance with my feet. This was a little distracting I admit, but I usually managed to keep typing.) She made great wheezy inhale noises when I was breathing in something especially wonderful that Grace was taking out of the oven, but that may just have been that she agreed with me. When I'd scratch my head or pull my hair and grunt while I was doing schoolwork I didn't like (which tended to make the Headache worse too) she'd scratch and shake *her* head—and grunt.

Sometimes it was more complicated than that—or maybe what I mean is it was harder to decide it didn't mean anything. But when I was doing laundry she began to collect whatever small loose stuff she could around the house, shoes, magazines, dropped pencils, wet rain stuff hanging over the radiators, and including snaffling towels off the rails (which in theory were hung too high for her to reach), snurgle them around a while on the kitchen floor (I tried to rescue the towels in time), leave them while the washer ran, and then bring them outdoors and spread them out on the ground (sometimes this was kind of hard on the magazines) when I hung the stuff up to dry.

This really did catch my attention because it seemed to me to say something about *her* attention span and her, you know, mental processes generally. It was way too complicated, you know? In fact it started making me think scary Dragons Are Intelligent thoughts so I concentrated on trying to prevent her from "washing" anything that would make more work for *me*. I told myself that baby critters are always getting into other things—especially things you don't want them to get into—it's what they *do*. It's part of being a baby critter. It's part of growing up. Half-grown raccoons are *incredibly* creative escape artists and *nosy* and *boy* can they get into trouble. It's hardwired. Nothing to get paranoid about. Nope. Nothing at all.

And I've said she was noisy. Well, I talked to *her* a lot. That went back to that very first day, that awful day when I found her, when we were like both yattering from our different traumas. Well, same trauma, different angle. It's like we'd just never stopped, it's just the frenzy level had dropped some, and most of our yattering now was pretty cheerful. A little overwrought sometimes maybe but pretty cheerful.

I've told you she had learned really quickly to "talk" during pauses in a conversation—the one time she consistently broke this rule was while I was in the shower. (She'd gone on not liking to get wet.) I always left the bathroom door half open so she could follow me in if she wanted to (which she always did, but I kept hoping . . .) and she talked to/with the *shower*. I could hear her—the water going *whoosh whoosh whoosh* and Lois going kind of *woooosh whooch waaaaaaaash wiiiiiiIIIIiiiish*, as if she assumed the shower was either one of my noises or a major monologist, and didn't quite understand why it only made this one sort of splash-and-splatter-punctuated roaring cry.

So if there was no one else at home sometimes I sang. Now there is a noise to drive the birds from the trees and the dragons into the deepest caverns of the Bonelands. Even Lois' mimicry boggled at trying to do the dragonlet version of a shower *and* Jake singing. Although she did do a good hum. In fact her humming was the nearest of all her noises to any of the noises humans make. Sometimes we hummed together.

But I think I played with her more once Martha and Eleanor were in on it. Things just felt a little less harrowing. That being-on-the-same-side thing even made me feel a little more at ease with the child welfare people, and I swear child welfare people pick up the smell of fear like mean dogs do and have no clue that the fear might be of *them*. (Mean dogs know perfectly well that it is. We've—Smokehill I mean—only ever had maybe two mean dogs since I've been old enough to notice, and they don't last past the first snap. One of the families with kids, one of the kids ran away when Dad banned the dog, and then the rest of the family gave up and left too. More of Dad's graduate students. He doesn't have the best luck with his graduate students.)

Eleanor nearly ruined everything though by deciding to be helpful by adding corroborative testimony like in police shows on TV. She asked the doctor if he couldn't do anything else for my eczema (his creams hadn't worked, not surprisingly, but also because I hadn't bothered to use them) because she was sure it hurt more than I admitted. Thanks, Eleanor. Maybe it worked out okay though since the doctor knew that Eleanor was a busybody. So maybe that Eleanor pretended she knew it was eczema *was* corroborative testimony. (I taught her to say "corroborative testimony" and she forgave me for being ticked off that she'd opened her big mouth about it at all.)

Anyway. Lois used to lie on my feet at supper (everybody else carefully and awkwardly keeping their feet out of the way around Billy and Grace's little kitchen table, especially after she started to generalize about people and wanted to be friends with everybody she saw. Even if you were unsympathetically wearing shoes she'd put her hot scratchy nose up your pantleg to be sociable) which was usually the four of us humans plus one dragon. Except when Dad couldn't get away or Billy was on duty or aggravating some investigators or checking what the diggers and builders were (still) doing to the caves after they'd closed down for the day (work on this had slowed down a lot since the scandal started). And then sometimes we had Jane or Kit or Whiteoak—or Nate or Jo, who Billy'd added to the dragonsitting/Jake's Sanity Conservation rota—and people having a meal together talk (except Whiteoak of course. I learned "thank you" and "please pass the whatever" in Arkhola from having Whiteoak for dinner. Even Whiteoak wasn't going to risk being rude to Grace I think). Maybe they talk especially when they aren't completely comfortable with each other, and Dad and I hadn't been completely comfortable with each other in years, and we also weren't seeing as much of each other as we used to, so most of the time we talked a lot to cover up the silence.

(Except of course if there'd just been a big meeting about what to do about the poacher's parents—which nobody ever did tell me anything about, just by the way, until years later, when I asked Dad. He looked at me blankly for a minute and then gave a sort of hollow nonlaugh. "We didn't figure *anything* out, that first meeting," he said—and Dad doesn't talk in italics all the time the way I do. "We didn't figure *anything* out. We just sat around and moaned and shouted and tore our hair." He stared into space for a minute, frowning. "It was pretty goddamn awful.")

It was a joke for a long time when, if a silence did manage to fall, we'd hear Lois doing her peeping and burbling under the table, which got gruffer and rougher as she got older. But I think I'm the only one of us humans who noticed that it wasn't just getting gruffer and rougher, but it was starting to rise and fall in a rhythm—kind of a lot like the sound of people talking.

I thought about this for a while, kind of hoping that someone else would notice too, but if anyone did they didn't say anything to me. But dragon noises, as I say, are *peculiar* so probably only my ears could make anything about Lois' sound effects seem familiar.

It had been Eleanor's remark about my goofiness that had really made me think about it. Between Lois and . . . between Lois and *Lois* it was really easy not to think about anything but getting through every hour as it came. So up till Martha and Eleanor met Lois I suppose I had kind of been thinking about Lois almost like a funny-looking dog with strange habits. Snark imitated all kinds of human things and we all just said oh, what a clown. Eleanor made me realize that while I *was* just as goofy about Lois as I'd been about Snark, I was goofy about her *differently*. Not just because she wasn't a dog. Not just because she was the first addition to my family after fifty percent of it had died. Not just because of the dreams.

So one afternoon when I'd done more schoolwork than I could stand, and it was sunny outdoors, and we were alone at the cabin, I took her out (she waddled and murmured behind me, her scaly feet and the tip of her now steadily lengthening tail making a funny little scuttling noise on the kitchen linoleum like maybe there were several baby dragons following me instead of only one) and sat down on the ground with her and said, "Hey, Lois." I said it very carefully and deliberately. "Heeeeeey" on a falling note and "Lois" as two distinct syllables, "Lo" higher and stronger and "is" dropping off and down.

I didn't sit on the ground with her so much any more because for some reason this got her all excited and she was too inclined to stick her face in my face and give me more eczema (what a good thing she wasn't a face-licker), but it was a good way to get her attention. When she rushed over to touch her nose against mine I fended her off with a hand and said "Hey, Lois" again.

She stopped trying to make face contact and looked at me as if she knew this was important. She didn't have that squashy look of something that had been stepped on any more, and her head was beginning to look almost a little horsey, narrow at the muzzle and wider between the eyes. Her eyes were a little bulgy like an animal's who expects to have a lot of peripheral vision, but they were also protected by some nobbly, bumpy ridges, so who knows. Maybe dragons see the world with a nice scalloped frame around it. Baby dragon eyelashes, by the way, are halfway to being spines, which means that when your baby dragon blinks its eyes when it's falling asleep against your stomach, you feel like you're being peeled. (Some of the spinal plates, the erectile ones, have slightly serrated edges too, which are in effect more like a cheese-grater.) I must have good resistance to pain or something. I never minded the eczema or the peeling nearly as much as I minded the diapers, and the diapers were *over*.

She peeped at me.

"Hey, Lois."

She peeped again, except it was more of a grumble.

"Hey, Lois."

Another rumbly peep. But this one was a three-syllable peep, and the first syllable was longer than the other two.

"Hey," I said, more softly. "Lois."

And she answered a quieter three-syllable peep, and the long syllable fell down the scale and the first short syllable was higher and stronger and the second short syllable was lower and deeper.

I looked at her and she looked at me. Sure, mynah birds can do better, but do they do better while you're both *straining* with alertness at each other? It takes weeks to teach a parakeet to say its first words. The air was nearly humming

around us, and the Headache tried to break out of my skull
again, which it didn't do so much as it used to except when I
woke up from dreaming about big dragons and caves with
weird lighting effects. I suppose I'd noticed before that the
Headache tended to get worse when Lois and I seemed to be
getting, you know, *intense* at each other. But I wasn't thinking about that either. I did wonder occasionally if maybe it
was a brain tumor, but weirdly since I'm so good at worrying about everything I could never really get going worrying
about that.

So I sat there looking at her with her looking at me. I was
excited and thrilled and also . . . frightened and horrified.
Frightened because it was like I was finally facing that I had
this whole *extra* responsibility. I'd only been trying to keep
her alive, which had been more than enough, but now I'd
been reminded, forcefully, that just feeding a wild orphan
isn't enough, and *what do you teach a dragon about being a
dragon?* What was Lois trying to learn from the very
funny-looking dragon she thought was her mom by mimicking the noises she (well, he) made?

I had no idea. And nobody could tell me. And I had read
Old Pete's journals so often I knew them almost by heart
and he couldn't tell me either.

And I *hated* the idea that the best Lois had to look forward to was growing up to live in some kind of cage and
being dumbly fed by humans for the rest of her life because
no one would've taught her how to be a dragon. Okay, Lois
being alive was a miracle.

I wanted more miracles. That's all.

I also perversely suddenly *didn't* want any other humans
to notice that Lois was trying to speak human. Add this to
the long list of things I can't really explain. I was afraid
of . . . how their reactions might make me think about it, I
guess. Just the fact that they'd have reactions (Dad would get
all fascinated and remind me to keep careful notes and Billy
would just nod slowly and go on with whatever he was doing) felt like someone putting a hand on your soap bubble:

pop. (Although as soap bubbles go, Lois didn't make the grade.)

But I was realizing what it really meant that Lois was Lois to me first and a dragon second, however stupid that sounds, like I could forget for half a nanosecond that she was a dragon. But everybody else could *afford* to see her as a dragon. And this meant I saw her as . . . ?

I had a lot of sleepless nights after that afternoon, while Lois snuffled and gurgled under the bedclothes. While I worried I also noticed—especially noticeable in an enclosed space like between your sheets—that her burps and farts smelled more and more like singe and char. I was sure Lois would be brokenhearted if she woke up one morning and discovered she'd fried me in her sleep . . . but what if she did?

CHAPTER SIX

I'm still doing a lousy job of giving you any sense of time passing. Well, time passed, and all of us preadult things kept getting bigger, me, Martha, Eleanor . . . Lois. And the seasons kept changing, the way they do. You don't not notice things like which season it is in Smokehill. (Well. You get confused sometimes, like when it snows in August, or when the February thaw is longer than usual and every critter in the zoo and the orphanage starts shedding, and everything underfoot that isn't rock turns to mud, and that year you have to go through this *twice*.) But weather and seasons are kind of the same even when they're different: It may be spring now, but winter will come round again soon enough. You *know* that. So I was lying awake smelling farts like burned toast and scorched hamburger, and thinking about how Lois was getting on for two years old.

She'd turn two right before I'd turn seventeen. I'd have my high-school equivalency certificate by then easy, and then I could stop pretending to be a fast-track early-acceptance Ranger apprentice and become a real one—out of reach of social workers and bureaucrats at last. And doctors trying to treat me for a unique variety of eczema.

We'd been so lucky so far. (I keep saying that. But it's maybe the most important thing of all.) Martha told me there was a big new Friends of Smokehill movement that was holding the Searles off. The Searles were the parents of the villain. Somehow I didn't manage not to learn their/his last name. They said that while it was true that their son had been in the park when he shouldn't, he only wanted to *see* a

dragon and that this one had turned on him for no reason.
Like they were there and saw it happen. Like that explained
the spare grenades he'd still been wearing when she flamed
him and the big-bore lightning rifle heavy enough to pene-
trate six rhinos standing in a row. Even I'd half-noticed the
heavy artillery at the time. Sure he'd only wanted to *see* a
dragon.

Our Friends had made a biiiig fuss about the lightning
rifle and the grenades, which is why the Searles hadn't
closed us down yet, but the Searles said that he would of
course have taken gear to protect himself in case of an un-
provoked attack . . . blah blah blah. . . . The forensic morgue
guys had even proved that he'd died instantly when she
flamed him, so he had to have shot her first. But . . .

Several eons ago I'd been hanging around the ticket booth
bugging Katie who has always been really good about being
bugged (even before Eleanor was born). Snark was with me
because he always was with me. I had him lying down. My
parents had hammered it into me that if I was going to have
a dog I *had* to train him because of all the tourists (and, of
course, the park itself). This was fine with me. It's not like I
wanted to play football with my pals every afternoon after
school. So I trained Snark to do all kinds of stuff. Lying
down for a few minutes while I gave Katie a hard time was
nothing to Snark.

There were only a few tourists around and I wasn't paying attention. Snark was behind me, and Katie's view was
blocked by the corner of the ticket booth. I turned around in
time to see some kid only a little younger than me trying to
poke Snark in the eye—I don't know, to get a reaction or
something?—because Snark would have been ignoring anybody who was a stranger. Several things happened at once. I
saw Snark jerk his head away from the poking finger, the kid
said, "You're a really *stupid* dog, aren't you?" and poked at
his other eye, I yelled, *"Hey!"* and Snark jerked his head
again . . . and growled.

And the mother of this kid suddenly appeared from
nowhere—where had she been a minute ago?—shrieking

that this was a vicious dog and we were to destroy it at once and it was savaging her only child in a *national park*, and she was going to write to her congressman—I was screaming that her kid had been trying to poke my dog in the eye, and Katie was trying to shut us both up. Katie lied and said that she'd seen the kid—she knew Snark, it wasn't really like lying—the mother said she didn't believe it, I was nearly in tears—I now had Snark standing beside me with my hand around his collar—and it might have been a whole lot worse than it was except the kid tried to sneak around and give Snark a kick while everyone else was busy yelling at each other, and not only Katie but a couple of other Rangers who'd been drawn by the commotion saw it. The mother saw it too although she denied it. She didn't deny it convincingly however and when Katie told her she had better take her freaky kid and leave, she actually went.

People are amazing. They'll do stuff you can't believe anyone would do and not believe stuff that is under their noses. You can't trust them and you certainly can't *reason* with them. The laws are schizophrenic because *people* are schizophrenic. So even if the Friends of Smokehill might win against the Searles about their should-have-been-drowned-at-birth son because dragons are rare and endangered and romantic (so long as you forget they have pouches), you still had to assume we wouldn't survive the discovery of Lois. We'd not survive even worse if it came out about the eczema. It wouldn't matter that it wasn't her fault and that I didn't mind (much). It would make her a bad dragon—and it would make all the grown-ups around me bad grown-ups for letting it happen. And she was a bad dragon anyway—look at her homicidal mom—and we were bad (and crazy and dangerous) for having sided with the dragons against our own kind by trying to save her.

Or maybe when Lois grew up crippled or something I'd be the bad human who raised her wrong. You just don't *know* how other humans are going to react. And there were of course so many ways I could be raising her wrong. It was like even in my own head I couldn't answer all the people who would tell me I was, if they knew I was trying to. ALL ways were ways for me to be raising her wrong.

. . . And at this point my synapses all snap simultaneously and one of the emergency circuits cuts in and diverts me onto a familiar worry loop before I self-destruct.

. . . For example Lois ate *everything* now, at least she did if I didn't stop her, everything from raw spinach (ewwwww) to cream puffs with ice cream and chocolate sauce. Grace made cream puffs to die for, I admit, but you don't necessarily expect a dragon to get the details. The funny thing about Lois is that unlike a dog she never went around nose to ground vacuum-cleaning the floor or the yard or anything. What she did was watch us and eat whatever we ate. She didn't get many vegetables till she started watching Grace and Billy and not just me. But she'd eaten apples and popcorn almost from the beginning which seem even less dragony than vegetables. (You know the business of carnivores getting their greens from what the herbivore they're eating has in its stomach. And a lot of dogs like *graze*. Snark didn't eat grass so much as moss. He loved moss. Given the landscape around the Institute he had plenty of opportunity.) If she'd ever learned to open the refrigerator door we would have been in big trouble. Fortunately she didn't. (I did keep her away from the cream puffs, after the first time, when I hadn't realized how sneaky she could be: Chocolate is poisonous to dogs, for example, and sugar isn't good for *anybody*, and Lois had enough marks against her already.)

And have I mentioned she *snored*?

But the point was that I was losing my nerve. The emergency-worry shunt was beginning to overload too because it was getting used so often. I began to feel like me turning seventeen was some kind of deadline—and the ads the Searles were paying for were so everywhere on TV now that Martha told me even Eleanor didn't want to watch TV any more. (Billy and Grace didn't have a TV. The farther-out Rangers' cabins mostly couldn't pick up the signal that the

Institute's Godzilla-being-attacked-by-a-flying-saucer special unique aerial/dish thingummy somehow squiggled through the fence.)

I was making up the deadline part, of course. Me turning seventeen—so long as the school equivalency went through okay—was going to make the game we were playing a little easier. But it wouldn't change the fact that the game was a deadly one. And you do start going nuts under pressure eventually. Not to mention the increasing difficulty of keeping a perpetually hungry, German-Shepherd-sized, more or less untrained and so far as we knew untrainable, very-high-activity-and-curiosity-level illegal animal, who might start setting fire to things any day now *and* whose wings were finally beginning to sprout, cooped up in a small house.

And it's a lie that Lois was untrainable. It's just that the idea of training usually means that you're supposed to end up where, if you ask someone to do something, they do it. If it's a dog it's like "sit" or "leave it." If it's a kid it's like "do your homework" or "turn the TV down." Or training like teaching a kid to get dressed in the morning, till he does it himself. Or a dog to go outside and not on the floor. I didn't housebreak Lois, she did it herself, which Billy and Dad and I sat around agreeing probably means that dragons have dens where they raise their kids, even after the kids climb out of the pouch.

I forgot to tell you, Lois doing it outdoors began the era of *amazing* numbers of outdoor barbecues, to give some disguise—and some excuse—for the latest eye-wateringly peculiar smells that hung around Billy and Grace's cottage. We were such barbecue freaks we were even out there in the winter and, trust me, at Smokehill, that's *wacko*. We did stop as soon as it got cold enough that even hot dragonlet poop froze pretty much instantly . . . but Billy had to help dig the trench next spring when it all melted—and we dug that trench *fast*.

Lois in the winter was a hoot, by the way. By her first winter she was way active enough that I'd've had to get her outdoors somehow to run some of her energy off anyway, but she was little enough and short-legged enough that without her body temperature acting as a natural snowplow it might have been a problem. As it was I worried about anybody who didn't know about her wondering about the weird snow mazes around the cottage, where Lois had melted some extremely bizarre trails. She didn't run, really, she *cavorted*. And I had to cavort along with her or with my pathetic human heat production I'd've frozen into a Jakecicle.

By her second winter her neck plates gave me enough purchase that I could grab one and be kind of towed along, all bent over of course, and more clumsy than you can imagine. But laughing helps keep you warm too. The only drawback was that she ate even *more* after she'd melted a lot of snow. Just like in Old Pete's diaries about dragons in winter. Also just like Old Pete's diaries she showed *no* inclination to hibernate.

It was also pretty interesting—you do get a little claustrophobic here in the winter. Even being closed to tourists for three months doesn't quite offset this, although, believe me, it helps. And the main Institute building is pretty big, especially when it isn't full of tourists. (Snark and I used to have great games in the empty tourist hall.) But you miss being able to go outdoors easily—or being able to breathe without your nose gluing itself together and your lungs going into shock—or having to *re*shovel the path you just shoveled the *last* time you had to hack your way down to the zoo or whatever—everybody does a lot of shoveling, besides the big plows that fit on the front of some of the jeeps—and although the fence slows some of the wind down, it'll still kill you if it can, and the big winter storms are just *scary. How* much bigger than you are are things like weather? A WHOLE LOT BIGGER. I guess you can ignore this most of the time if you live in a city, but you don't forget it for a minute in a place like Smokehill, and it sort of comes *after* you in winter.

But having an *igniventator*-equipped companion had a really funny effect on me—suddenly I didn't care about winter. If I felt chilly I could just warm myself against Lois

for a moment; leaning over her to breathe would even un-
stick my nose. Except for the eating, and the relative increase of difficulty in cavorting due to whatever quantity of
snow had to be melted first, the cold didn't seem to faze Lois
at all. Although I admit that *not* having up to several thousand visitors a day the way it was in peak season, any one of
whom might manage to be in the wrong place at the wrong
time, might have had something to do with my suddenly
more liberal attitude toward deep winter.

But even Billy's incense and me burying everything I
found wasn't enough, we needed to add charcoal briquettes
to the bouquet. But while Lois getting it that the entire cottage was a no-go area might mean that she was prepro-
grammed by thousands of years of dragons raising their
dragonlets in dens, I wondered if that was all it was. Because Lois *was* so amazing a mimic. When we were out in
the park we all went outdoors so there was a precedent. I'm
just grateful I didn't have to teach her to use the toilet. But
the mimic stuff gave me an idea about training. Which is
how I trained her to fetch sticks—by fetching them myself
first. Getting her to pay attention to me and what I was doing was never a problem. (Pity I couldn't teach her to do
French, or Latin.) I thought of fetching sticks because it was
something I thought would translate—I wasn't sure I could
get "sit" across to something shaped like Lois, and while I
tried to train her to lie down, she didn't seem to think she
had to do this unless I stayed lying down too. That's the
thing—I never felt like Lois' owner, or boss. Mom, maybe.
But how many little kids actually do what their moms tell
them?

So I went to Billy and told him I wanted a project that
would take me into the park and let me—us—stay there for
a few months. As near as to uninterrupted as we could manage.
I'd still be under seventeen, but as I put it to Billy (I'd
thought this out pretty carefully), the reason we were going
to give was that I wanted to be sure that this Ranger thing
was what I really wanted to do before I turned seventeen and
signed the contract. Between having to stay home and keep

Lois company and the rising worry level, I'd gone on acing every test the school guys could throw at me, and they'd been throwing them at me harder *because* of the early-acceptance Ranger thing that I think they suspected was undue influence or something. Which it was, of course, but not from the direction they were looking in. Also because I kept proving I *could*, which seemed really unfair. If the rat can learn to find the food at the end of this maze, let's try a harder maze. Like just for laughs. I think school-equivalency bozos have too much time on their hands.

Why I still wanted to take all these stupid languages I was so bad at if I was going to be a Ranger no one ever asked me (if I'd wanted to make myself useful as a foreign tourist guide I should have been choosing Swahili or Catalan, the Rangers've already got most of the big languages covered)—but then I never let on how much I sweated those tests. And I guess it was a way for me (and maybe Dad) to pretend I still might get a PhD some day.

We cooked it up that Lois and I would stay at Westcamp, which was the smallest and the least used of the permanent camps, and study the incidence and patterning of found dragon scales, and any other signs of dragons, in that area. There'd already been dragon tracking studies at South, Limestone and High camps—North and East were too close to the Institute to bother—but nobody had bothered at Westcamp either even though it should have been the right general area. But there were too few dragon sightings there and grant writers had to go for numbers because the money givers tend to understand numbers.

But Dad had actually wanted a dragon survey done at Westcamp for years because what signs and sightings there were were odd, even for dragons, and that was why Westcamp had been built, and Dad might have done the study himself if Mom hadn't died. Maybe that was why he let Billy and me talk him into letting me go. Maybe he'd been trying to get used to the fact that I really wasn't going to be totally answerable to him any more soon enough anyway—and while Dad's a control freak he tries to be a *fair* control freak, and he *would* have been thinking about this. And not letting me out of his sight just wasn't an issue after Lois, it no longer existed in the new universe with Lois in it.

Maybe he'd been braced for my asking to do something much worse. I'd thought of worse things, certainly. I'd thought of trying to go to Silver Valley where we all knew there were dragons, and trying to introduce Lois there, like taking your kid to the local playground to meet other kids. I doubted that would work, and I also—selfishly if you like— didn't want to die, which seemed to me a possible side effect. I know I keep saying dragons don't kill people, but don't forget *we'd* just killed not just any old few dragons but a mom and her babies, and even if this didn't piss them off it could certainly have made them *twitchy*.

Because the dragons seemed to have noticed the poacher too, or the death of Lois' mother, after all. They're only animals, right? What really would they notice? Everybody dies, even dragons. I might keep telling myself that the dragon dreams were only dreams and what I remembered about Lois' mom was just some side effect of how awful that had been . . . but I kept remembering and I kept having the dreams and they had an effect. So I didn't seem to have the luxury of the old they're-only-animals thing much any more. What I kept thinking instead was stuff like if there'd been any other dragons on the spot, presumably they'd've taken Lois with them before I got there—perhaps if they'd got there soon enough they'd have rescued some of her brothers and sisters too—and all these thoughts brought me back to the pissed-off place. The weird thing, it seemed to me, was that it seemed to have taken almost two years for them *to* notice.

But the dragon movements that the Rangers could read had changed . . . and then a busload of tourists had been thrilled, almost into seizures, by the sight of a real live dragon flying by. It was so far away it was only just recognizable— but there really isn't anything that looks like a dragon except a dragon, if it's big enough to be even a speck with wings.

A weirdly long and humpy speck with fantastically long wings, even as a speck.

And no ordinary tour-bus tourists had ever seen a live dragon before in the history of Smokehill.

It was a headline in our local papers and it made the national wire service. (Martha told me that the Searles tried to insist that we'd faked it somehow to get the public on our side, but this time the public definitely liked our version better.) As a result we got even more tourists, and we were already getting more tourists because of the Searles and their vendetta. But while a bunch of tourists seeing a dragon *really* made our numbers soar, which we were just about able to deal with and the money was nice, that made it even more urgent that Lois and I get as far away from the tourist area of Smokehill as possible.

I said we were just about able to deal with the latest increase in numbers. Usually we have like one person a year who manages to get away from their guide and start poking around where they're not wanted. In the two months after the tourists saw the dragon we had *three* escapees, and one of them (from where Nate had found him) must have gone right past our cottage. What if it had been one of the afternoons that Lois and I were outdoors training each other to fetch sticks and roll over and play dead? And talk. It wasn't. But it might have been. It was right after that that I asked Billy to help us think up a project to take us deep into the park.

The last week at the Institute I was jumping at shadows and I had to control myself really hard when I went down to the zoo because Eric knew I was leaving and while I suppose the idea that *you're* going to be stuck cleaning *odorata*'s cage more often—I was cleaning it twice a week again by then—is enough to put anyone in a bad mood, Eric on a tear makes Krakatoa look like a hibachi. I was having a lot of trouble not giving him any kind of reaction that would please him. At least I could scowl because since I was a teenage boy my face was expected to be paralyzed in a sullen adult-defying expression till my twentieth birthday. But I really wanted to tell him to get the hell off me and *then* what to do with himself, only he would have enjoyed that. He got on my nerves so much I nearly put a pitchfork through my foot, which would have been really *great*, since it would have stopped me from taking Lois to Westcamp, and that made me even madder.

"It's just that he's worried about Smokehill too," Martha said in an undertone, as we were cleaning out one of the raccoon cages at the orphanage the next day. I blinked at her. I hadn't realized she'd gotten over being afraid of him in the last two years. I wanted to say that what Eric worried about was *Eric* but I was two years older too and I finally knew what Dad had been talking about when he'd told me that we were lucky to have him. Although why it was like he had to make up for all the good stuff and hard work he did by being sheer torture to be around is one of those mysteries of life.

"He got worse right after the poacher got killed," Martha went on. Well, I knew that, but at the time I was too Lois-possessed to recognize any subtleties about worseness, beyond the part about him cleaning *odorata*'s cage more often because I wasn't available. And since then while I still put my away-from-Lois hours in as evenly around the Institute as I could I really dreaded the time within hoarse-bellow range of Eric, which I hadn't before, and lately, when I'd started taking three or even four hours away from Lois, one and a half in the morning and maybe two and a half in the afternoon, depending on how mellow she seemed to be feeling about it, that meant I had to show up at the zoo every day and I felt like Eric was leaving worse marks on me than Lois ever did.

"And he's got worse again lately," she added. "I'm quite worried about him really." She looked over her shoulder—toward the noise of Eric's voice roaring about something or other—with a tiny frown and she looked all grown-up and wise.

"Only you—or your mother—would waste time worrying about Eric," I said, probably rather bitterly.

Martha was silent for a minute while we lifted the

raccoons back into their nice clean cage and gave them a few peanuts to make them think the process was worthwhile. Raccoons are pretty easy if you're nice to them. It doesn't have to be a hugely complicated niceness with raccoons. When I'd first had Lois some of the orphans didn't like me for a while; I suppose I must have smelled like the enemy although I can't really see a dragon bothering with little stuff like chipmunks and sparrows. It was the raccoons that were willing to overlook my kinky new smell first and then in one of those weird ripple effect things everybody else decided that I was still okay too, as much as any human (any human bearing food) was okay and I'd never had any trouble since and occasionally something seemed to like me better. I'd had my first hands-on experience with a Yukon wolf cub about ten months before. (Because of Julie when San Diego's nursing bitch died they sent her one surviving cub to Eric.) It still hadn't started biting me—I don't mean puppy bites, I mean *biting*—weeks after everybody else was wearing heavy gloves and boots, including Eric. Curiosity probably killed the raccoon about the same time it killed the cat though.

Finally Martha said, "I know he picks on you. But he has to pick on someone and you're—you're really the most *Smokehilly* of all of us, you know? You've got that same okay-maybe-there's-a-world-out-there-but-I'm-not-interested thing that he does. You were like that before—before." Even out of earshot of anyone else, away from Lois you didn't say her name. "Even your dad and my mom have more of a clue."

I looked at her and felt my look turning into a glare. The idea that I was even more clueless than my dad wasn't going over too well either. "Are you trying to tell me that Eric hates me because I'm *like* him?"

Martha laughed. (She wasn't afraid of me at all.) "No. I think he picks on you because you're what he'd've liked to have been. Do you know he grew up in the city? Washington, DC. Twelve stories up. He started out with goldfish and turtles because they were small and cheap and they didn't make a lot of noise, and he could get them past his parents, who were some kind of lawyers for the government." Which only goes to prove that Martha can get *anyone* to tell her their life story. "And you know I think he's horrible to the investigators deliberately. Let them waste their time on him."

It kind of made me thoughtful, especially since Martha had the same idea about Eric and the investigators as I'd had. I might've come up with the idea out of perversity as much as anything, but Martha was coming at it straight on and still thought so. So on the last day—I'd be leaving before dawn the next morning, the better to smuggle Lois past anyone who might be looking blearily out their kitchen window waiting for the kettle to boil—I actually tracked him down in his office. I admit I wavered on the threshold, before he'd seen me.

He was crouched over his computer (very unhealthy posture: someone should tell him: not me) where he was surrounded by piles of papers even scarier-looking than my dad's—this was partly because the window was always open in there (any time the temperature was above freezing) and not only wind and rain came through but also Eric's crow and this summer's crow offspring. A lot of crows croaking and creaking together actually sound a lot like Eric (in a *good* mood). But it was only Eric (muttering to himself) this afternoon.

I stepped firmly over the doorsill and as Eric whirled around in his chair with a scowl no mere teenage boy could hope to compete with, I said, "I just wanted to say thanks for everything you've taught me about—about animals. And stuff. It's going to be really useful when I'm out at Westcamp."

He'd stood up when he recognized who it was, which didn't help his mood any because in the last year I'd got seriously taller than he was, and with him glaring at me I forgot the rest of what I was going to say. So I stuck my hand out instead. This was *not* planned. There is *no way* I would have *planned* such a great opportunity for Eric to make a jerk out

of me, when he refused to shake it. But he did. Shake it, I
mean. It felt like a perfectly normal hand too. A little more
callused than some, maybe—like a Ranger's hand. And then
I turned and fled. Trying not to look like I was fleeing, of
course, but I was. But Eric must have been as spooked as I
was because he didn't shout anything after me.

So I got back to Billy and Grace's house—my house for
the last almost two years—actually feeling kind of good,
like I'd achieved something. I was in a bad way.

I was already as much packed up as I was going to be
before tomorrow morning and adding the toothbrush and
so on so I didn't have anything much to do—except play
with Lois, of course. There was always playing with Lois.
I'd often wished she slept more, like dogs do, and we'd
never found a way to pen her up effectively. As she'd got
bigger and friskier we'd tried. But she had a habit of simply walking *through* anything she didn't think should be
there, and I didn't want her to hurt herself. Or to get any
ideas about like house walls. In her mutant armadillo way
she was pretty tough and strong. When she'd first been doing her I Am Master of All I Survey thing she'd managed
to get herself stuck between two rungs of one of the
kitchen chairs and she'd cracked the chair frame before I
got her out—and she'd still been pretty little then. Although some of how the chair frame had got cracked was
because she'd rushed screaming to Mom, and Mom took
some collateral damage while as you might say fighting
for the off switch.

But I was glad of the distraction that afternoon because
while there is no way I'd've admitted it I was feeling kind of
strange about this trip. It could have been only the grind-
ingly ongoing thing of Lois as this increasing problem—
plus I'd never done anything like this study I was supposed
to be doing—because I really was going to try to do it, as
well as hide Lois where no one could find her—plus I'd
never been away from the Institute that long either—plus I
had no idea how long that was going to be. The longest I'd
ever been away was when I'd found Lois, and that wasn't

exactly a reassuring memory. Did I just say "it could have been *only*"?

But it wasn't going to be that big a deal really (I told myself). It wasn't like I was ever going to be alone. There'd be a Ranger with me all the time, although only one—whoever they could spare—who knew about Lois. It wouldn't be Billy very often. He actually had national profile these days, did Billy. Martha and Eleanor told me that he was one of Smokehill's best counteroffensives against the Searles. A lot of people are still willing to get all soggy over any Native American with a cause, and Billy really looks the part. He didn't do a lot of talking (of course) but he'd stand there and look solemn and chiseled while Dad or someone did the moving-mouth thing.

Which meant we kept having camera people at Smokehill, and didn't *they* hate what our fence did to their equipment. At least this dampened their enthusiasm for trying to wheedle themselves into filming more of Smokehill, not that they would have succeeded. Sometimes they had the interviews at Wilsonville's weeny TV station instead. Wilsonville's weeny TV station, which looked like somebody's garage, possibly because it *was* somebody's garage, didn't know what hit it. The only live interviews they were used to getting were things like with the eight-year-old who got a kitten for her birthday but the kitten was so freaked by the party that it went straight up a tree and the fire brigade had to get it down. (They interviewed both the kid and the fireman.)

And I'd miss Dad and Martha and Grace and everybody else. Partly because I know what wilderness really is I had the sense to be in awe of it. And to know that living at the Institute is nothing like living in the park. And then there was Lois. (All trains of thought lead to Lois.) What would *she* think of living in the park? To the extent that there was ANY long-term plan about all this, because even I knew I couldn't just spend the rest of my life marooned at Westcamp with Lois (. . . could I?), the plan was that the dragon study I was supposed to be starting was going to get so interesting (were we going to have to *make up readings*? That was a really depressing thought. That really is the worst thing in the world to a scientist—being accused of making stuff up, of falsifying data—worse even than being a Bad Scientist or a bank robber) that we'd decide to make it permanent. Which would mean somebody could always be out here keeping it running.

Ultimately this was supposedly going to mean that we got Lois used to having some other human stooge than me, so I got to cycle back to the Institute again and see everyone, while Jo or Whiteoak or somebody kept Lois company for a while. Martha was old enough, she could hike out with some change of the guard some time and come see *me*. Us. The idea of leaving Lois behind was way scary—being away from her for like weeks, which is what it would take. I'd— we'd—got her from ninety-second showers by herself to four-hour stretches a day by herself . . . and dragons *do* grow up . . . it ought to be possible. The idea wasn't entirely new, you know? It was just an extension of what we were already doing. But . . .

But it wasn't that, or maybe that was the beginning of what it really was. Which was that everything was changing. Whatever happened now—even if some big-deal fairy waved her magic wand and suddenly Lois was okay and we didn't have to hide her any more—this was the end of something. And the beginning of something too, but I knew what it used to be, and I had no idea what it was going to be. It might be *worse*.

While I was whizzing around this stupid little circle of useless thought and only half paying attention to Lois, who seemed to be trying to teach me to balance a stick on the end of my nose (very evolutionarily important in dragons I'm sure), Martha turned up. Occasionally she—very occasionally Eleanor—managed to sneak over to see Lois. I kind of suspect that Billy and Grace knew about this, but they weren't making any trouble for us about knowing it officially, so it had gone on happening.

Martha didn't have much to say, but she wasn't a big

chatter, and besides, if she was going to mess with my head like she did about Eric, I was glad she didn't do it any more often. I wanted to tell her about talking to Eric that afternoon, but I was too embarrassed. So I just stood there leaning against the kitchen door and having idiotically nostalgic thoughts about the claw marks on the sill, and watching her petting Lois—with gloves on. It had turned out Lois liked this, despite my attempts to be rational and assume she wouldn't because her skin was too thick (a Warning against Rationality) and would roll over and offer her tummy almost like a dog, although since her tummy is even hotter than the rest of her, the gloves are really necessary, and the spinal plates prevent her from really rolling onto her back either. I had been a little bit jealous of this at first. It was the first time anyone but me had ever figured anything out about Lois, I mean anything interesting, not like Grace putting vegetables into baby Lois' broth.

There was a funny noise and I realized Martha was crying. I started to say, "Oh, shi—" but I stopped, because I really do try not to say shi—, unless Eleanor is driving me nuts, even when Dad isn't around to make a scene about it. I went over to them and patted her on the shoulder and she stood up and turned around and put her *arms* around me and sobbed into my shirt. Two years ago this would have horrified me so much I probably would have said "oh, shi—" while I shook her off and jumped back about a mile, but that was before Lois, and a salty wet spot and maybe a little snot down my shirt is nothing to me now. And nor is—er—someone leaning on me, you know? But I was still pretty embarrassed. For one thing she was almost fifteen and had breasts. The only breasts I was used to being hugged up against were Grace's. Grace was a good hugger. And this was Martha. Martha had always been special (breasts or no breasts).

But mainly I was just surprised. It was that extra empathy, or whatever it was, that Martha had. The kind that could get someone like Eric to tell her about his childhood. (That he'd had a childhood was revelation enough.) Her record keeping orphans alive was better than mine. I was never much good with the ones that wanted to give up, I just got really upset and frustrated. Martha could sometimes like make the ones who didn't want to live want to live after all. It was the same empathy that made her try petting Lois with gloves.

I did wonder, wistfully, if maybe Martha was worrying a little about *me*. And maybe even going to miss me. I mean, she had to like me, it was just her and me and Eleanor, like I keep saying. But there's missing and missing.

"Sorry," muttered Martha, letting go. I was relieved (except maybe about the breasts).

"We can talk on the two-way," I said. "I'll let you know how she gets on."

Martha tried to smile. "We'll have to make up a code."

"We'll need a lot of words. We'll need a lot of words just for Lois."

"We can pretend she's a crow and her family, like Eric's Zelda." Martha looked thoughtful. "If her wings start growing you can tell me about your fledgling." Lois had lately started flapping her wing-nubs when she got excited. If she was still doing this and her wings started growing properly I'd probably be talking about my scars.

"If she breathes any fire I'll tell you about the lightning strike," I said, hoping I wasn't being too literal there either.

"If she's being a pest you can tell me to say hi to Eleanor for you," Martha said, and now she was smiling.

"What if I just want to say hi to Eleanor?"

"It's the same thing. Lois is always a pest. Like Eleanor. We love her anyway."

The next morning Billy and Jane and Lois and I set off for Westcamp. I didn't really start to breathe easier till about the fourth night out. We weren't going very fast because twenty-three-month-old dragons are not built for walking but they're way too heavy to carry very far. *You* try carrying a big German Shepherd, even in a tailor-made backpack, for more than a mile or two, on top of all your gear. I still carried her a little, but that was more for comfort than covering ground. We had thought about making a litter for her, but she would have hated that; she'd been pretty much into everything since she first started climbing out of her sling, but she was in some kind of extreme toddler stage lately of wanting to poke her nose into EVERYTHING (fortunately if there were any skunks around they saw us before we saw them) although she was better natured about keeping up (so long as you never went much faster than an amble) and not having tantrums than most of the human toddlers I saw at the Institute tourist center.

But with about fifty miles between us and the gate, that fourth evening, I actually felt myself relaxing. It was such a strange feeling at first I didn't know what it was. I felt light-headed and sort of floppy or sloppy and my first thought was, "Oh no—I can't get sick *now*"—and then it occurred to me that I was just unwinding for like the first time in almost two years. (Or maybe four years. Since Mom died.)

It was true I always felt a little easier about things, which is to say about Lois, when I was out in the park with her, on our little field trips with Billy or Kit or Whiteoak, although even then it took about a day to sink in. So on the fourth evening of our *not* little but Big No Going Back trip, when Lois indicated that her working day was at an end by galloping up to me (she had a very strange gallop, diagonal, with her unwieldy tail held awkwardly to one side, and while her little legs were nearly a blur she didn't actually go very fast), cannoning into my feet, and starting to snore, I sat down, slipped my backpack off, and started trying to unknot my muscles, both from General Permanent Life at the Institute Maximum Stress and also not-familiar-enough walking-and-packing-through-the-park sheer physical weariness.

We were at the top of a little dell, with a stream at the bottom (there was always a stream at the bottom of dells in eastern Smokehill) going *chucklechucklechucklehahahaha* over the stones, the way running water does, and spruce and a few white birch raggedly climbing the slope among the rock and scree and scrub. I'd managed to slither into an al-most chairlike series of small hummocks padded with dead leaves and pine needles (which were probably wet, but I didn't have to know that till I got up again) and wasn't sorry to be sitting still for a few minutes, guiltily aware that I should be helping gather firewood and set up camp, but if nobody called me. . . . I was half asleep myself when a bare browny-gray branch near the top of the nearest spruce spread its wings and turned into a great horned owl. I swear it came swooping down in our direction for no other reason than to get a closer look at Lois. That woke me up. But even awake (well: call it fuzzily half awake) I felt different. Lighter. Sil-lier. Tell me a bad joke and I'll laugh. I just lay there enjoy-ing the sensation (and feeling my backside getting soggy).

In about half an hour I had to wake Lois up and coax her toward the fire Billy by then had got going at the nearest plausible campsite, flickeringly visible from where we sat, or lay. Once Lois had crashed, she tended to stay crashed, and if I tried to move her mostly she ignored me, but if I performed the ultimate betrayal and went off and *left* her she would peep heartbreakingly (although as her chest deep-ened so did her peeping, and she had to work at it to sound as pathetic as she had when she was littler) and scrabble feebly with her claws like she just couldn't move another *inch*, and since this was, after all, an orphan baby animal of a rare and endangered species no human had ever success-fully raised before, I was always worried that she meant it. Fortunately she could be lured by the prospect of a nap be-side a fire. She did love fires. It was one of the things that made me, poor flimsy 98.6-degree-Fahrenheit wuss that I am, feel really guilty. (I fortified myself by remembering the first night twenty-three months ago, trying to convince the repulsive little globby thing I'd picked up that it didn't *have* to live in my shirt, that it'd be *fine* by the fire.)

She groaned like she was being tortured but she came. In her defense she wasn't used to spending all day walking any more than I was (she also didn't know how to walk—she was either zigzagging full tilt from Interesting Thing to

Interesting Thing or keeled over) and I was built better for it, but I'd unfolded kind of slowly when I got up too, and I was really glad she agreed to do her own staggering, so I didn't have to carry her.

I already had a new mantra, from about the afternoon of the first day: We're farther *in* than we've ever *been*. It repeats really nicely when you're walking: da da da *thump* da da da (well, da again, but you can run "we've ever" into two) *thump*. We weren't really, not yet, but that's where we were going, and also it put a good spin on all the No Going Back. We were going farther in than we'd been since I first brought her home as a blob, when she was still small enough to fit under my shirt. The fourth night it was like I was beginning to believe it, or believe that we were going to get away with it somehow. At least for a while longer.

I couldn't think about it that I'd probably never be able to bring Lois back to the Institute, because she'd've got too big, and would have wings and a flamethrower . . . couldn't think about the fact that no doubt Billy and Dad knew this just as well as I did and they hadn't said anything about it either, at least not to me. I mean, sure, we'd talked about our long-range plan-substitute, about Lois getting to the point that she didn't have to have me around all the time, but we'd only talked about it sort of sidelong and half casual, like it was obvious and irrelevant and didn't really need discussing.

Lois and I were both stiff the second morning and worse the third (although this may have been aggravated by the power struggle over how *close* we slept to the fire every night). I know this is a fitness thing and proves that we weren't, but it's funny how you get one day like free of charge. The second day starts to count (especially after that first night on the cold hard ground). And then it's the day after the second night when it all catches up with you. In my defense I *was* carrying a lot more gear than I would've been if this was just a few days of an ordinary field trip.

That third morning Lois was so slow starting off that nobody had to notice I would have been slow. Although maybe this wasn't so useful (I mean worth it to my vanity) because I had to carry her more. Finally Billy and Jane split my gear between them and I concentrated on carrying Lois for a while. I was a little worried about her because there was no drama about her collapses. She just collapsed. And if I didn't notice right away and kept shuffling on she didn't even sound like an opera heroine when she cried after me. She just sounded exhausted. But I thought about how tired *I* felt and decided this was just what happens to you when you're still pretty little and you go for a real walk in our park. She may have been picking up on our motivation or something too—I wouldn't put it past her to notice that this wasn't a field trip like our other field trips. We weren't really going any faster than we ever went when she and I were part of the convoy, but we were more *determined*. And then of course I had to have one of my Guilt Attacks because she was a dragon and she shouldn't have spent the last twenty-three months in a *house*.

She fell asleep with her head on my shoulder and her (prickly) brow ridge wedged under my left ear. I hadn't had a burned ear before; on other, less intense trips she was too busy looking around. Always new experiences with Lois around. Oh well.

But like all the rest of us (humans) who'd gone for walks in our park and had to learn how, she brightened up again slowly over the next few days. She was already better that fourth day, when I had my unexpected insight into the concept of "relaxation." And a good thing too, since the farther we got from the Institute the rougher the tracks got. I was also starting to notice that while we went up and down and back and forth and sideways and other-sideways the trend was definitely uphill. The Bonelands were several thousand feet higher than the Institute, they were just far enough away to make the slope gradual. Sort of. You rarely went *up* anything: You were busy tacking for the best footing, and sometimes you snaked up the same bit of slope several times before it like *stayed* up and stopped sending you back down into another streambed.

We had lots of prairie farther in, mainly north and south; the Bonelands sucked up most of the west, although beyond them it began to get a little friendlier again; where we were the landscape was still mostly a mixture of patchy forest and meadow with the occasional sudden startling burst of hill and rockface. You wouldn't think it possible that something a couple hundred feet tall and *vertical* could jump at you from nowhere, but sometimes it did, and you'd have to swerve aside, like not walking into a wall, with it *looming* over you. But the moments when you had the best view and might have wanted to stand still a minute looking around and saying "gosh wow" I was mostly looking around for Lois and her Interesting Things; the farther we got in too the more wildlife, and I couldn't guarantee that everything was going to get out of Lois' way. And ours of course.

Most things will give humans a wide berth if they have the chance, and I assume they feel the same about dragons. And Lois made a lot of noise. She talked to herself—and to me—*and* she crashed and lolloped through everything. Going *around* was mostly not in her vocabulary. (I was reminded of how late she figured out "going around" in Grace's kitchen, when she was first experimenting with leaving the sling.) I did occasionally see her doing her sideways investigative bumping-into trick, but not very often. Mostly it was just plunge and thunder. As we got into more open territory I told myself that any self-respecting rattlesnake would have got out of the way long before she arrived—and I'm not sure a rattlesnake's fangs would get through even a twenty-three-month-old dragonlet's skin, which is already pretty horny. Fortunately I never had to find out. (Or whether skunk musk will stick ditto.) But there was so much birdsong (and bird warning-screech) sometimes I couldn't hear Lois burbling and crashing and then I *really* had to look round for her. I had reason to be tired by the time we stopped for the night: Nobody else was twisting themselves into pretzels keeping an eye on their hyperactive dragonlet.

By the seventh day I was carrying all my own gear

again—and I'd noticed, when Lois scrabbled around at night, that the bottoms of her feet had got rougher and grittier, like when you take your shoes off for the first time that year, when you're (probably) not going to get frostbite from going barefoot. First few days you wonder if it's worth it and then suddenly you're okay, except the noise your feet make on the kitchen lino is suddenly less of a slap and more of a scritch. I was used to sleeping with an overheated self-maintaining turbine going nowhere fast so this comparatively minor alteration for the worse didn't really wake me up . . . but then I was awake already.

The dreams about the dragons' cave were getting worse, or more vivid, again, out here deeper and deeper in the park, and about a week in the Headache seemed to be trying to change shape again, and it pissed me off in this fretty, oh-go-*away* useless way. The dragon dreams were *enough*— and the way they had too many moms in them, Lois' and mine. Can't stick reality, and this time imagination is no comfort either. Well, damn. So much for relaxation. It had been a nice idea. Although also in a strange, freaky, not-going-to-admit-it-even-to-myself way I was kind of glad to see the caves again, it was like going back to somewhere you used to know really well and haven't been in a long time. Oh, yeah, remember that tunnel, with the long pink streak in the rock overhead, it always used to catch my eye like it might turn out to be a sort of monster Cthulhu earthworm, and it still does . . . I even recognized several of the *dragons*, not just Lois' mom.

But last time I was seeing the caves this clearly and graphically I was spending up to twenty hours a day asleep, wrapped around a small sticky dragonlet. There wasn't enough of me to have *two* lives, you know? The sleeping and the waking. And I had a life (of sorts) when I was awake, now.

But I must have been sleeping pretty okay in spite of Lois' feet and the dreams and the Headache. Because I really enjoyed the last few days of the hike in a way I couldn't remember enjoying anything. The nearest I could think of was from when I was like ten and Snark and Mom were still alive. Pretty sad really. (But it made me think of one of Martha's and my favorite jokes: *You need to get out more!* It applied to almost anything about life at Smokehill. And then we'd laugh like we were going to break a rib. So that cheered me up again.) But it was like time out, in a way. We weren't *there*, wherever there was. We were leaving one there and going to another one. (We're farther in than we've ever been.) But at the moment we were suspended in between. Footloose and carefree, except for the thousand pounds of backpack and the baby dragon.

The other thing that messed me up sometimes was in the evenings when we called in to the Institute. We called in every day just like everyone who walks in our park has to. I always talked to Dad and since we couldn't talk about Lois over the air we had a nice fresh valid reason not to have anything to say to each other. He found different ways to make jokes about not talking about her though, which was brighter than I was. He'd say things like "Hope your pack isn't too heavy" or "Hope you aren't sleeping too close to the fire and waking up toasted." And then I'd laugh and then we'd agree that he and I were both fine and then I'd give him back to Billy for the grown-up debriefing.

No grown-up had still ever mentioned the Searles to me, or the Human Preservation Society. Sometimes it was hard to remember I didn't know anything. Occasionally Billy actually had the chutzpah to send me off to collect firewood while he was talking to Dad. Oh come on. Second time he did it I said, afterward, after I'd brought some more firewood and Billy was off the two-way, as blandly as I could, "What's going on?"

Billy never looked sheepish. He knew well enough what I meant. He gave me one of his almost-smiles and said, "Nothing you have to worry about." From Billy this isn't the put-down it would have been from almost anyone else. When Billy said it he meant, "You've got the dragon. It's up to us to do the rest of it." He'd been totally like this from the beginning, you know? Billy was big on focus. He'd understood a lot more a lot sooner than I had—from when we'd had that first awful bath at Northcamp and Lois hadn't wanted to be put down *his* shirt. But I still couldn't help wanting to know something.

Martha and I had figured out a code about some of it. I got to talk to her a couple of times on the hike in, and I'd say, "Anything good on TV?" And if she said, "No, just stupid science fiction," it was okay. But if she said, "There's a new cop show, and it's kind of scary," then it was *not* okay. The second time I got to talk to her was after Billy had sent me to pick up firewood the second night in a row while he talked to Dad, and when I asked her about TV she hesitated and said, "There's supposed to be a new cop show starting soon and it sounds pretty scary." Oh great. "Well, try not to lose any sleep over it," I said.

"I'll try," said Martha. "But I'll probably watch it anyway, you know?" I knew.

CHAPTER SEVEN

Westcamp was in a bit more of a mess than the permanent camps usually are. And I actually helped with some of the clean- and patch-up. It was weirdly exhilarating. It was because we were out in the middle of nowhere and I didn't have to watch Lois every minute. And also because I was doing something that both was not about Lois and was about helping somebody else out for a change. Even my time at the Institute, the last couple of years, had been about Lois really—about pretending everything was normal, to try and keep her safe and secret—even if most of the work I did was also useful that had been almost beside the point.

Of course like a good parent I quickly learned to shift my worries to the present situation so now that we'd got here and weren't immediately leaving again I was afraid she'd eat something that would poison her the third or fourth time she went by it because it had got familiar (or that she'd been snatching mouthfuls right along and the third or fourth time the toxic accumulation would finally get her) or get lost because she hadn't learned where the new edges of her new territory were or blunder into something like a herd of no-nonsense Bighorn that would recognize her as a predator even though she didn't know it yet herself, and stomp her to death. But she stuck pretty close to me just like she usually did (. . . so I started wondering how long *that* would last before she got used to the idea that I wasn't watching her every minute, and how her next developmental stage would be exploring beyond Mom, and *then* she would blunder into the Bighorn, etc.), and then after a while it wasn't so exhilarating but we had to do it anyway. Also I couldn't stop myself jumping every time the two-way yammered at us.

A tree had fallen on the roof and poked a window out on its way, in spite of the heavy shutters. Jane climbed up onto the roof to lop branches till we could get the rest of it off without doing any more damage (waste not, want not, I would be cutting it up and stacking it for firewood, but I like chopping wood, so that's okay . . . just so long as a baby dragon doesn't get in the way. Worry worry) while Billy looked to see if there was any spare glass in the store (there was) and if it could be made to fit (yes) and if there was a glass cutter and sealer (yes). And made notes to replace what we were using. Fortunately the tree hadn't taken out the solar panels for the generator—*that* would have been a disaster. Then all over again for the door frame, where some kind of Arnold-Schwarzenegger-wannabe sapling had managed to crack the door away from the sill. (That was a bit of a mind boggler to me since I believe that the Rangers, you know, *rule*, and that no mere sapling would *dare*.)

And the hole that sapling had made, with the window, meant that the indoors had been pretty well colonized, which is why the Rangers are so anal retentive about keeping the permanent camps as invader-proof as poss. It's a lot of remedial work when things go wrong. I did way more than my fair share of the blanket-mending because I was so cheezing good at it from all those months of patching diapers. I did a lot of muttering when I had a needle in my hands. Lois really did pick up that mood—she'd come and mutter too, winding around my legs like a cat except for the fact she wasn't built for winding, and she was tall enough now that my legs would go *bumpbumpbumpbump* down her spinal plates which did *not* help, and the blanket would fall or get pulled off my lap when she'd get tangled up in it, and. . . . Billy managed not to laugh at this. Jane didn't. Manage *not* to laugh.

So anyway both Jane and Billy stayed longer than they'd originally meant to because there was all this work to do. Billy also went out hunting one afternoon. I'd noticed he'd bothered to pack in a rifle, which I was kind of surprised about, since we didn't have any *investigators* with us, ha ha ha. Maybe it was just a Ranger thing for longer hikes, although generally speaking a Ranger would rather sit up a tree for a week than kill something that had a perfect right to be there, and to keep themselves fed on long trips they mostly used snares or bows and arrows—no, I'm serious. I keep telling you our Rangers are good. Jane had her bow with her.

I suppose I must have noticed when Billy left Jane and me replacing shingles with his rifle cracked over his arm, but I didn't think about that either. He came back later and told me to come with him. He'd shot a deer and needed someone to carry the other end of the pole, to get it back to camp.

Lois came too and was very surprised by the deer. She was used to her food coming to her in small pieces in a bowl of soup, or flicked at her. (I'd managed to teach her "Yours!" without having to demonstrate grabbing stuff tossed to me in my mouth, but food is a great motivator to learning.) Dragons don't chew—they have pointy, widely separated teeth, for stabbing, tearing, and holding on—but along with all the other things nobody knows about dragons we didn't know when Lois' infant digestive juices might be up to bigger chunks, so she wasn't getting any yet. (Lois' teeth were one of her trouble-free zones. They just appeared. She never went through a chewing-everything-she-could-get-her-jaws-around-but-particularly-the-things-you-most-mind-being-transformed-to-gloppy-shreds phase the way puppies do. This was actually sort of off-balancing. It's one of the ways you know a puppy is growing up. There were *no* familiar markers with Lois, except that she kept getting bigger.)

She had a lick at the spilled blood where Billy had gutted it but didn't seem to think much of it. She was a little subdued on the way back like maybe she was thinking about it. I was a little subdued on the way back because why was Billy already laying in a whole *deer*? I'd seen the store cupboard, which was still about half stocked with usual stuff, plus everything Billy and Jane had brought, which seemed to me enough even for several Loises, or if one Lois put on a tremendous growth spurt, and it wasn't like they were going off and leaving me. Oh well. Maybe he just wanted a break from cabin repair.

The smoker was already there, but I'm the one who kept the fire going. However smoking is smoking so you might as well do more than less so I told myself the deer was fine. Billy made me practice some of the cutting-up too but you could sure see which he'd done and which I had. You'd think all you'd need is a sharp knife and a steady hand. Wrong.

He also tried to make me practice a little with his rifle, but Lois hated the noise so he let it go. He'd taught me to shoot a few years ago and I had been a demon with old beer and soda cans (they recycle just as well with holes in them) pretty much up till Lois arrived, so I still knew the, you know, theory, and my hands still knew the motions, but I was way out of practice and Lois hating it meant I was freezing before I pulled the trigger which ruined my aim *and* my shoulder. I might not have been able to hit what I was aiming at anyway for thinking about why Billy was suddenly taking it into his head to have me brush up on my gun non-expertise.

But then Billy merely shifted survival-skill gears and got me brushing up on snare-setting instead. (I'm not exactly hopeless with a bow, but . . . close.) But rabbits are smaller. I could've coped with the idea of the occasional fresh rabbit. Supposing I could set a snare properly. We'd eaten rabbit and pheasant on the hike in. But it *didn't really matter* because I was never going to be here alone, of course. There was always going to be a Ranger with me, and Rangers can set snares in their sleep (I mean snares that catch something).

We'd just about got everything fixed up so Jane was finally getting ready to go back. There'd been a lot of radio contact including about stuff Kit could bring when he came to take Billy's place. After this there was only going to be one Ranger at a time here with me. So Jane left and then

Billy waited for Kit, and Kit turned up on schedule with various small crucial bits and pieces—including one to make the radio work better; it had been dropping in and out a lot in a pretty uncomfortable way and everyone on it sounded like they were being strangled while breathing laughing gas. We'd had a lot more problems with the two-ways since the techies had monkeyed with the fence, so we all hoped the monkeying was *working*—there was no real way to know except backwards, by people *not* breaking in.

So Billy left (leaving me the rifle, just by the way, and spare ammo and reload stuff), but Kit finished making everything as everything-proof as you can ever make anything everything-proof out in the middle of a nowhere that didn't care if you were human, dragon, or squidgy tentacled blob from Alpha Centauri. Which was the good news.

Because the bad news was they had an outbreak back at the Institute. Nothing to do with dragons—*flu*. I'd been worrying about everybody's stress levels and why nobody had a heart attack or a nervous breakdown yet, right? Well they got summer flu instead. (Maybe it was because *they* all relaxed as soon as Lois and I were out of bus-tour radius.) First flu epidemic we'd had since I'd been alive, and believe me, tourists on holiday come and sneeze and cough all over you rather than miss their chance by keeping their germs at home. (No, you're right, I don't really blame them. I'd come to Smokehill with terminal body-parts-dropping-off-itis if it was my only chance.)

By the time Billy got back to the Institute there were seven Rangers down and with it being summer which is high season anyway, the extra tourist load (and lingering investigative drones, although there were mostly only a symbolic crab and grumble of these left) meant everyone still standing was going crazy. Kit sort of hung around being twitchy for several days and then he asked me if I thought I could stay at Westcamp alone for a little while. The alternative was going back with him to the Institute. No way.

There's maybe a drawback to suddenly looking like a

grown-up, which is what I had started to do the second half
of the year I was fifteen. By now—and yeah, no doubt partly
as a result of all that good-student crap first so they wouldn't
take me away after Mom died and then later to protect
Lois—I could put over maturity-beyond-his-years like you
wouldn't believe. I'd also had my own growth spurt and was
six-foot-something and bulky too—*you* try hauling a baby
dragon around and see if it doesn't grow you muscles like a
furniture mover. So I knew what I had to do with Kit—I'd
also guessed it was coming so I'd been like secretly practicing my role. I just about packed his gear for him and shoved
him out. There was no question about risking Lois back at
the Institute. That tourist who had bumbled past our cottage
had gone missing when we had a full complement of Rangers watching out.

So I had to stay, and I had to convince Kit it was okay if
he left me. Us. I did. And I'm afraid Billy's rifle helped—
helped convince Kit. (He hadn't seen me try and shoot it.)
But then I had to convince Dad. That really challenged my
competent-maturity program, and it was only a beta really.
Turned out that he'd just *told* Kit to bring me (us) back.
When he mentioned that—almost in passing—like it was no
big deal—then I mainly had to not lose my temper and yell.
If I'd yelled Dad would've just yelled louder and ordered me
back to the Institute, and the main thing about handling Dad
is preventing him from giving an order, because then it's an
order and that's the end of the discussion.

The problem was that I *was* scared. But it wasn't a scared
that anybody else could do anything about. When I was
younger sometimes being ordered to do something was secretly kind of okay because then it was Dad's (or Mom's)
fault, I couldn't do anything about it. I kept telling myself it
would actually be easier if there wasn't anybody else around;
Lois' and my training-each-other-to-do-things sessions were
getting more and more complicated, and if it was just me
and Lois I could concentrate more on her, and not worry
about explaining anything to anybody who caught us at it,
and who knew how far we would get how fast.

But, you know, look at what had happened to me the last time I'd been in the park alone, which I know I've said before, but are you surprised it kept kind of running through my mind? Okay, maybe it had been a *good* disaster. But it was still a disaster and it had changed all our lives tremendously in a stretch-till-you-snap way and there was no stretch left for even a little tiny disaster-ette. This flu was pushing it. And I was also not absolutely sure I *wanted* to find out how far Lois and I could get how fast—or why didn't I want anyone around to notice?

There's another little tiny factoid about all this. Sure, I'd been Billy's willing slave since I was two. And I knew a lot more about Life in the Wild than your average seventeen-year-old. But that's not the same thing as knowing what you're doing out here. To the extent that you ever know what you're doing. And then I also had to work way too hard not to wonder what, exactly, Billy had been anticipating when he left me his rifle (even if I couldn't hit anything with it, except maybe stomping beetles with the stock end. The beetles in the cabin were kind of a plague).

But I smiled and did my *responsible* trick, and Kit was satisfied, and maybe Dad was so impressed that I *hadn't* lost my temper that he believed my beta program after all and said okay. Or maybe it was worse back at the Institute than I realized and what Dad really hadn't ordered me to do was *not* come back, but stay at Westcamp, and he'd told Kit to bring me to piss me off, so I'd be sure to do the opposite. (Although this is a little devious for Dad.) Martha sounded really worried when I talked to her, and she was obviously trying to figure out a way to tell me something we hadn't got into our code. There weren't any cop shows, she said, but there was new thriller that everybody was talking about but she hadn't seen yet.

"Maybe you should stick to science fiction," I said.

"Maybe I should," Martha said. "The problem with science fiction is . . . that it's just all *made up*, you know?"

Uh-oh. I knew. "Anybody else come down with the flu?"

"No, but Mom's driving one of the buses and *I'm* cleaning *odorata*'s cage."

"Oh, yuck for you. You know about using lemon juice on your hair after?"

Martha giggled. It was good to hear her giggling. "Yes. I have to use so much it's making me *blond*."

Which proves Martha has superior hair too. All lemon juice ever did for mine was make it go kind of rusty in streaks, like there'd been a terrible chemical accident on my head.

And then we had to stop because the two-way went into one of its snits, which it was still doing, even with the new gizmo. Kit was out of earshot so I didn't tell him about the radio. It did *not* bear thinking about if the radio went seriously gazooey, but I was not going back to the Institute, so everything else was just going to have to be whatever it was, grotty radios included.

Kit took off the morning after I had that conversation with Martha. I checked in on the two-way as soon as he'd gone. I now had to check in twice a day, Dad said. He would've liked to make it three times but I said I was still going to go on with the dragon study even though there was no one to help me, which meant I'd be out a lot of the day. I could hear Dad thinking about ordering me to take the radio with me but fortunately he didn't. Reporting in even twice a day I was wondering if my crummy sense of time was going to be cover enough if the radio had too many hissy fits and I checked in at the wrong time too often. But I'd worry about that when it started happening . . . and then, before I had to think about staying here alone, where the nearest other human being would soon be a light-year or two away . . . Lois and I went for a walk.

Lois was thrilled. Usually we were doing chores in the morning. I know, she thrilled easily, but she totally loved the greater freedom of the camp almost as much as she loved fires. She was either on a constant adrenaline high (insert Unknown Dragon Equivalent here) or two-year-old

dragonlets are like that. She galloped and rootled and scrabbled and poked . . . and peeped and chortled and gurgled
and burbled and purred and hummed and cheeped and chir-
ruped and hooted and . . . her amazing range had only got
amazinger as she got older, and her qualifications as a chat-
terbox had been established long ago.

And it was like she was in her element once she had the
conversation all to herself and didn't have to wait for anybody but me. I was also kind of broody so I left her to it.
And boy did she go for the opportunity. I couldn't help
thinking about it some more. I'd never heard that dragons
talked (all right, "talked") to each other. Old Pete had never
mentioned it in any of his journals. And if his dragons had
been anything like Lois he would have. In fact he'd've spent
his life wearing earplugs. Also usually one of the limitations
on animal "speech" is that animal vocal cords and larynxes
aren't set up for a lot of variation. Lois had lots of variation.
She could do anything *but* human words. She probably could
have done the tentacled blobs from Alpha Centauri, but she
was stuck with me.

Her humming had like expanded. At first it was just kind
of a bumpy mutant purring—what I've been calling purring, although if any cat made that noise I'd recommend you
call the vet fast—and then after a lot of time practicing with
the shower it got pretty, well, hummy. Almost, like I said,
like a human might hum. (Emphasis on the *almost*.) But
after she caught on it wasn't only with the shower any more.
And whatever it was, it went more up and more down, jig-
gedy jaggedy, more like a, well, musical scale than her
other noises.

I had brought my old player from the Institute when I
moved in with Billy and Grace, but I decided pretty much
all by myself that arena rock probably wasn't a good thing
for your infant dragon, and besides, I'd been reading up (a
little wildly) on parenting and about how Mozart is soothing
to fidgety kids, so mostly I played Mozart, and even got to
kind of like it myself. (Except the operas.) And I sang to her
sometimes the way all of us (even Eric) sang to our zoo

orphans; once you've been caught saying the standard "Theeeeeere, isn't that gooooood?" a few times you have no shame left. Shamelessness is required if you sing like me. But humans are just so *voice* oriented, you want to *say* things, and you get bored with "Theeeeeere, isn't that gooooood?" after a while. Singing is the obvious alternative to moronic monologue. You think you're being soothing, but does a raccoon or a robin think "Barbara Allen" or "The Ash Grove" is soothing? I think we're soothing ourselves. But there wasn't any music, soothing or otherwise, at Westcamp so maybe Lois was reinventing it for us.

We went for a lot of walks after Kit left. Away from Westcamp I didn't feel quite so alone. Or rather, it was okay to feel alone away from the camp—away from the human place. And I took my notebook with me, and my marker sticks, and sometimes I brought a few scales back to the camp and labeled them and bagged them up like I was getting ready to take them back to the Institute, like this "project" was real.

The project was one more legitimate reason to keep me outdoors as much as possible—indoors at the camp my voice echoed. Of course the main thing keeping me outdoors as much as possible was Lois—but the dragon-scale-counting project suggested that I was still a part of the Institute. That I still had something like a normal place—and future—at the Institute. My security blanket. I don't think moms are supposed to need security blankets. Two or three nights after Kit left I dreamed that I was wrapped up in the holey old blankets Snark and I had watched TV on a few centuries ago, leaning up against Lois' mom's side in one of those flickery red caves, and my own mom was singing to me. At least it was her voice, although I couldn't see her. When she sang "Barbara Allen" you knew what it was.

It was a gorgeous summer that year. That helped. I'd brought rain gear of course as well as long underwear and a goosedown vest and wool socks and stuff. Even in August you can get a frost in Smokehill, and Westcamp wasn't in one of the milder bits of Smokehill either, and the Bonelands started just over the Glittering Hills to the north. (They're called hills, but they're mountains really. You'd know this if you tried to climb one.) But I didn't need any of it. The skies stayed blue and it was hot enough at noon to lie down in a meadow and soak it up and warm enough even early and late that if you kept moving you didn't get cold.

Lois had got a lot fitter since we'd left the Institute (well so had I) so if I wanted to walk really fast for a while she managed to keep up with me, though she still did it in spurts. She'd walk—she'd finally learned to walk, I think because she discovered that you can be more thorough about prying into stuff at a slower speed—till she got far enough behind to make her (and me) nervous and then buzz past me at her funny gallop and then maybe walk again, although sometimes the enthusiasm level was just so high and the world was just so big and exciting she *had* to have an extensive hurtle. You know those cartoons where animals run by all four legs going forward at once and then all four legs going backward at once. I know no real animal runs like that but Lois sure looked like she was.

I ambled sometimes too so we could walk together. Her walk was one foot at a time, like a normal walk, although looked down at from above . . . you know the way a dog looks surprisingly sinuous, almost snaky—explains why they can curl up in a *circle*—well, maybe it was just the way the spinal plates waggled along her humpy back that made Lois look like she was coming unhinged.

She never offered to chase—or flame at—any of the wildlife we saw, and despite the amount of noise Lois made, both with her mouth and her feet—and I couldn't walk nearly as quietly as Billy even when I was concentrating, but there was no point trying with Lois around—we saw a lot. They'd stand there and stare at us like they couldn't believe their eyes. Is that a dragon? Is that a human? Are they *together*? Some things like raccoons do that anyway—but our four-legged dragon suppers couldn't seem to decide if they had to bother about us or not, and mostly they didn't, although I sometimes expected their eyes to pop out from staring. Once we even saw a lynx and lynx are usually really shy. The times the deer or the sheep or whatever would scatter they didn't seem to be paying attention to us at all. Which was kind of nervous-making in a different way. If those tales about cougar curiosity are true probably the local puma was following us around and maybe sometimes the suppers got wind of him. Or her.

But we still had to go back to camp eventually. I found out the hard way that I wanted to get back in daylight. I wanted to be indoors with the fire lit and one of the lamps burning before it got dark. There were bears around here—as well as the cougar—but that wasn't why. Nor was the fear of getting lost. It was that coming back to a silent dark cabin was too creepy. First time we did it, coming back in twilight, even Lois shut up, and that made it worse. You'd think the sky would get bigger in daytime, when you can see more of it. It doesn't. It gets *way* bigger at night. And the forest and prairie and desert don't go on for five million acres after dark, they go on *forever.* I pretty much turned my dragon-scale-counting project into a real project after all, sweating over my charts and graphs in the evenings, studying and noting down the differences from one scale to another to another (long, short, cleanly shed or ragged, color, texture, blah blah), marking where I found them (and the map this made *was* different from the readings from the other camps) to be doing something. Something that made me pay attention to it, instead of sitting there trying to count up to eternity.

And the rifle helped again, about that, about being alone. Just hanging there in its rack, it made me feel a little less helpless. And in spite of the deer all beautifully smoked and wrapped up in the store I did start setting rabbit snares—the pile of deer parts was going down, and that deer had been nearly the first thing Billy had done, and I (almost) always believe what Billy tells me, even when he doesn't say anything. Also once you get in the habit of counting up to eternity it seems to stretch in a lot of different directions. And after about a week—hey presto—my snares even started catching the occasional rabbit. Weird. Maybe I could learn to hit what I aimed at with the rifle if I had to. (Besides beetles.)

Maybe because of Lois, but somehow the noises didn't bother me so much, even knowing that I was in the middle of five million acres of them. A lot of what I heard I knew from Billy's teaching me to recognize, say, the crunching noises a pheasant makes when it crashes through the undergrowth (pheasants are *amazingly* noisy) compared to the noise a deer makes compared to what a cougar makes. (That last is an easy one. A stalking cougar doesn't make noise. I saw the scat a few times, but I never saw our cougar. I knew there was one. Every neighborhood in Smokehill has a cougar.) That was pretty much my limit though.

But most of what I can do by myself is daylight ID. Sometimes I didn't know what the moving-around noises were at night and then I poked the fire to make it crackle or turned up the two-way, or rattled my graph paper. Or all of the above. I did hear bears occasionally nearby, but I buried our garbage a *long* way from camp and locked up the meat store every night like it was the crown jewels of the supreme commander of the universe, and they never tried to get in. They just snuffled around for a while and went away. Then there are the vocals. Coyotes and wolves are easy, and it's actually kind of reassuring to hear them *far away*. They never got very close. Since I can only tell a Yukon wolf if I've heard an ordinary gray wolf recently to compare it to I don't know which one I was hearing, and if it was Yukon I'm *very* glad it was far away.

The fact that I was never sure the radio was working—or, if it was, that it wouldn't suddenly stop working—didn't help me feel comfy and secure and in touch either. Fortunately it mostly was working. I'd only missed one check in by about half an hour while I shook the thing and called it weekly-allowance-eliminating names before it decided I had fulfilled my entertainment function for the day and coughed and hiccupped and *kkkkkkahed* and *glahed* into action.

There was a lot of squawking that I couldn't always make out but I kept it on all the time I was indoors after Kit left, partly because I really wanted some remote clue about what was going on, and partly because listening to human voices even if they weren't talking to me or saying anything I wanted to hear was kind of soothing. This made its sudden dramatic dropouts all the more dramatic—the silence would land on you in a deafening *wham*. Keeping it on like that wasn't good for the batteries, but the generator was working and except for recharge (and maybe a little hot water) I wasn't using it much. (I hadn't brought my laptop—camp solar generator power is a little spasmodic for laptops— although sometimes, those evenings rattling my well-smudged graph paper, I wished I had.) Even the static when the radio was in a semi-bad mood, or the stand-by when no one was using it, was better than nothing.

In the old days, before the poacher proved our fence could be broken through, we'd also believed that no one could hear our two-ways outside the fence. That was maybe still true but it wasn't just Lois we couldn't talk about be-cause (in theory anyway) not all of Smokehill knew about her. Nobody trusted any of the damned hanging-on-and-on investigators—make that *priers* and *nosiers*—any farther than they could throw a full-grown dragon, and (Martha said) the grown-ups assumed that the Searles had bought some of the investigators anyway—that the bought ones would find reasons to stick around, and have pieces of legal paper that told Dad he had to let them. So everybody was talking in secret code speak, and sometimes it was so frus-trating I stopped listening and pretended it was just white noise—that plus what the radio did to human voices some-times I felt even more isolated when I *was* talking to some-one.

When I did talk to anybody myself—at least anybody but Martha—we were pretending that everything was still all business as usual except for the flu. They probably didn't want to think about me being out here alone with Lois since it was still our best option, so they didn't, and I didn't tell them I left the two-way on all the time for the sound (well, sort of) of human voices and looked at Billy's rifle a lot. I can tell you I was hair-trigger on the "talk" button though. I didn't want Lois audibly adding anything to the conversation just in case anybody at the Institute end heard something that didn't sound like random static.

My birthday happened while Lois and I were in our Westcamp exile, and only Martha remembered. No, that's not an example of poor neglected Jake, all by his feeble self (aside from the dragonlet) and no one cares. It is an example of just how stressed out of their minds they were back at the Institute. Oh, and I didn't remember it either, till Martha told me happy birthday. I knew it was around there somewhere but I'd stopped trying to keep track of the days, and I wasn't going to bake myself a cake either.

I wasn't allowed to talk to anyone for more than a few minutes, because of needing to keep our teeny bandwidth clear for something more important. We had like no width left, I guess, after the practical-sorcery guys had done their worst on the dragon fence some more. One of the things Martha told me was that airplanes didn't fly over Smokehill any more—whatever the solder-and-sparks (ha ha ha) guys had done made aeronautic radar go berserk, even from thirty thousand feet up. This meant a surprising number of flight paths or what-you-call-'ems had to be changed, which caused some more uproar which was our dragons' fault again and there was too much stuff that was already our dragons' fault. Our conversations usually ended with Martha asking me if I'd seen any lightning.

"Nope," I always said.

After the first few times she asked this she added, "Not even at a distance? There are some *big* thunderstorms out there—especially over the Bonelands, you know, Billy says."

I translated this without difficulty. "No. Not even a— a shooting star."

Martha said, "I can't decide what to hope for, you know?

I—you don't really want lightning close up, of course, but it would be—exciting, to see it, like over the Glittering Hills, wouldn't it?"

Exciting. That's one word for it. Since I was out here supposedly counting dragons, if Martha just meant had I seen any dragons, she could've said that. But I had a dragon with me. If I saw any dragons I'd have to wonder if they'd notice Lois. We didn't know diddlysquat about interdragon communication—what it might do and how far it might stretch—whether baby dragons smell like that so big dragons can find them—or if that unmistakable flying-dragon shape would mean anything to Lois if she saw it. That was the sort of thing that Martha was thinking about. So was I.

What I called a meadow, that's kind of a euphemism. As the scraggy, stony forest of eastern Smokehill starts breaking up into the Boneland desert and the prairies around it there's some weird in-between stuff. Westcamp was in a weird in-between area. The camp itself was on the edge of some semi-forest, and there was a semi-clearing on two sides of it, partly Ranger- (and lately Jake-) maintained. Then there was a big pile of stones—say twenty feet high— like a thoughtless giant had left them there for no better reason than he didn't want to carry them any farther, and some tough little saplings had colonized one side of it where a little soil had somehow accumulated, and were trying to turn it into a hillock. Beyond that there was more mixed-clearing-scrub-and-the-occasional-obstinate-tree.

The clearer bits wiggled like some kind of game of follow-the-leader, and there was something nearly like a real clearing not too far from the camp, that Lois and I had found the first week with Billy. It was almost like having our own private playground. There was a series of small heaps of boulders with sand at the bottom as well as the usual local striated stone pocked by scrub underfoot, and several of the standard little eastern-Smokehill rivulets cutting up the stone and going nowhere but making nice noises while they did it, and reminding you what you were going to be missing if you kept going west.

Amazingly though there was also a pretty good mead-owy sort of meadow, mostly at the southeastern end but kind of snaking through the stony bits too, and surprisingly large—well, I'm an eastern-Smokehill boy, it was surpris-ing to me—which meant we saw a lot of sheep and deer there. They'd leave if we got too close, but usually a few of them just kept an eye on us while the rest grazed and did deer and sheep things. After the first week or so we even saw some of this year's babies, which were old enough to be getting serious about grazing too but still had to have regu-lar outbreaks of rushing around and jumping over things that didn't exist. I suppose the old ones couldn't afford to ignore the grazing but they weren't entirely happy about us. Lois used to watch them watching us, and when she did her cheeps and burbles they sounded more tentative, like she was trying for a definition of what she was looking at. (Is it a bird? Is it a plane? Would it leap tall buildings at a single bound if there were buildings?)

After we'd been at Westcamp a while and fallen into some kind of schedule, going to the meadow and just kind of hanging out there became part of it. And I guess she was getting enough exercise elsewhere because sometimes she'd actually be quiet and still for a while without being asleep. (Although as I've said she was neither a quiet nor a still sleeper either.) And she was now watching the grazing crit-ters *silently*, which in something (or someone) who was never silent and was always in motion (even when asleep), was interesting.

I started thinking again about what could happen when something of her size found out that she had a fire-stomach with fire in it. I doubted a dragon had perfect aim without practice. But Smokehill had no more fires than any other big park, so presumably there was an answer to baby-dragon target practice. Maybe dragon moms had a fire-extinguisher organ, tucked away like under the spleen (if dragons have spleens). . . . Westcamp had a fire extinguisher, of course, but I wasn't going to lug it around with us. Also you have to be conscious and have your arms working to use it. . . . But once we were alone at Westcamp, Lois *really* started growing—like if you stared at her long enough you could see the next scale spring into being to cover the stretching-out skin. Six weeks after we left the Institute she wouldn't've fit into her baby-dragon backpack any more even with all the straps let out, and I probably wouldn't have been able to lift her even if she did. And the deer meat was going down fast, even supplemented by snared rabbits.

I've already said we were training each other to do tricks. I haven't told you a lot about this because . . . well, because. I'm not a Good Scientist who knows that animals are animals and humans are humans, and I think the situation on Mars is really funny and anyone that is freaked out by it needs to calm down and get a grip, but there are limits. Particularly when something with a face like a small rockpile and little bulgy, beady eyes is staring at you and going, Weeeeeeeerrrrrrup? And you know she's not just doing the large scaly version of the parakeet thing. How do you know it? There are little old ladies who swear their parakeets know what they're saying. I'm not going to say they're wrong either. But the little old ladies probably aren't getting any other weird signals at the same time as their parakeet is saying "Give me a peanut or I'll peck you to death." Although this may be because the parakeet is clearly saying "peanut" and I needed help understanding Lois', uh, words.

So we were training each other to do tricks. It seemed the obvious way to . . . well, create a language. I don't want to get into exactly what I mean by *a language*. About three years before this when I was looking for more creative reasons to get out of doing Latin I read a lot about the history of language and how us humans are hardwired to learn it blah blah blah and also a lot about whether or not animals have it. I had a kind of crisis of faith there about wanting to grow up to be a scientist because while I knew my parents made jokes about Good Scientists and Bad Scientists I thought they were *jokes*. I couldn't get my head around these bozos who were so dead set against believing that animals have anything but like an autonomic nervous system to keep their hearts beating and so on and a lot of instincts saying things like "eat grass" or "bite that rabbit." Okay, a boy loves his dog, but I couldn't see this *at all*. Of course animals think and feel. Any moron who's ever *met* a dog or a cat should know that, and how many people have never met a dog or a cat? Even scientists were little kids growing up once even if they haven't come out of their labs for the last sixty years.

Anyway. Getting pissed off had made me think more about how Snark and I talked to each other, and I'm not even going to put quote marks around *talked*, although I never did construct a good argument against Latin. So maybe I was a little more set up for talking to Lois than some people might have been. So let's say that when you teach your dog to come and sit and not pee in the house, that's part of a language.

But when you get a dog you have some clue about dogs. About what they're good at, about how they respond to people. And the stuff you don't know, or get wrong, you can order a book from the library that will tell you. And if you don't live some place like Smokehill you can go to a dog-training class. Lois and I only had each other. Sometimes I felt like Helen Keller and Annie Sullivan, and I was afraid that Lois was playing Annie.

She seemed to like it that I talked to her. Well, that's not strange, dogs like to be talked to, although they don't talk back so much usually. So I kept talking, although even my decision that she "liked" it seemed to me dubious when I was in a gloomy mood. Maybe frolicking around and thwumping her tail and flapping her wing nubs and cheeping was an expression of frustration and despair, not pleasure. I tried to keep an open mind. She couldn't be too miserable, could she? How could I tell? She was still eating and still growing. And curiosity about her world had to be a good sign, didn't it? It was also hard to be in a bad mood myself when she was dancing around *apparently*, by irrelevant human standards, being as happy as a kid on the first day of school vacation (even us homeschooled exiles know about this), which she usually was, so why fight it?

Gestures are a huge amount of language. Aren't they? But most gestures out of context are silly. I had started out trying to "teach" her to wave—this was back a long time ago at the Institute, after I'd had my uncomfortable little jolt about her trying to say "Hey, Lois" back at me—but she didn't get it with me sitting on a chair, I guess, and as soon as I sat on the floor or ground she got too excited, and I sort of lost conviction about the idea anyway because why did I want a dragon that waved? That's when I hit on teaching her to fetch sticks. Like a dog. And the good reason for that would be that it would help use some of her endless energy. That was the first time I'd tried to *train* her to do anything, as opposed to just hovering over her in a universally paranoid 100 percent way and worrying about keeping her alive. Except that I taught her by throwing the stick, going after it, and bringing it back to where I'd been when I threw it. I told you she was always more interested in me than she was in anything else, so keeping her attention was easy.

This had been a while back, as I say, really when Lois was only just getting big enough to like experiment with, including that she'd be willing to go far enough away from Mom *to* fetch a stick. So I got a stick, waved it at her a moment so she'd notice it instead of me, said, "Fetch!" in a firm, no-nonsense manner, and then I threw it. First time I went after it she went after me because that's what she always did. Second time you could see her thinking about it. Please feel free to insert a verb you like better than "thinking." Third time I threw it and yelled "Fetch!" she came with me when I went after it like she was still xxxxxxing about it but hadn't reached any conclusions. Fourth time I hesitated a little bit at the end so she got there first. She sort of pawed at the stick for a moment and looked at me inquiringly. So far so dog really. The fifth time I went after it a little more slowly yet, just to see what would happen, and this time she positively shot in front of me (those legs a blur and her panting a little harsh grunting noise with breathless I'm-sure-explanatory peeps in it), and started to pick it up. . . .

She tried to pick it up with one of her forelegs.

Fourteen-month-old dragons don't have much grasping strength, and they're also still effectively four-legged. According to Old Pete they start using their front legs more like arms when their wings get big enough to provide a different balance, before they can fly. In Lois' case that started happening when she was about three, although that may be early because, of course, she was still trying to be me, in spite of . . . no, I'm getting ahead of myself: believe me, it's getting harder and harder not to . . . *she was trying to be me* and I'm two-legged and two-handed. And so she tried to pick up a stick with a front claw, and she couldn't do it.

And the joy *instantly* drained out of her. It was awful. She flopped down on the ground beside the horrible stick and started to cry. No, there weren't any tears, but I didn't have any trouble translating what the noise she was making was, any more than you don't know what a dog's wails mean when you've locked him up and are leaving him behind. And the sound she was making went right through me and aggravated the Headache till I was seeing her through this twinkly red haze and that did *not* help the situation.

I raced up to her, threw myself down beside her—swearing at myself for a fool—and picked the stick up in my mouth. (This was not easy. Human faces are too flat, and your nose gets in the way.) And then began waddling back the way we'd come, on my hands and knees.

She stopped crying and followed me. It was a measure of how demoralized she was that she wasn't instantly thrilled that I was down on her level. But she'd never seen me go any distance on my hands and knees before (ow ow ow ow ow, just by the way: also yuck yuck yuck yuck about the taste of the stick) and she got, I think, so interested, she forgot to be her usual kind of excited. And I *swear* she suddenly got it about how helpless *I* was on all fours. It was like this aspect of my strange reluctance to get down on the ground with her finally made sense to her (so far as I know she never understood about my eczema. For which I am very grateful. Awful sort of thing to know, that you burn your mom every time you touch her). I went *all* the way back on my hands and knees, and very tired and cramped and chafed I was when I got there too. But I wanted to be sure that if she was getting the lesson at all this time she was going to get it RIGHT. Then I threw the stick again.

We both started after it. I didn't hurry and she got there first. She picked it up in her mouth. She carried it back to where I'd thrown it from, and then danced around peeping and burbling (through the stick in her mouth. A sort of *urrrrrglrrrrrr* noise). "Hot stuff, Lois," I said (there was no way I was going to say, "Good *dragon*, Lois!" and "hot stuff" seemed kind of a relevant praise-phrase for a dragon), and gave her a hard rub between the eyes, which she liked. (Rubbing her between the eyes would actually make her sit still for a few minutes, while you did it, which was useful, till your fingers started getting tired, because you had to do it *hard*.)

Okay. This is pretty cool. Training stage accomplished. She was happy, I was happy, it worked, we're back on track, trauma averted (I hoped). So it's time for rationalization. Dogs aren't trying to be you, they automatically do stuff with their mouths because that's what their instincts tell them to do. (Although I don't think a dog ever brings a stick back first time. They've got it that it's a game, but they have other ideas about the rules.) So dragons imprint on their moms more individually than puppies do. No big deal.

Except that there's one other thing. *She took the last three steps back to me on her hind legs,* or she tried to. She fell over between each step, mind you, but she got up again, half-swayed and half squunched on her butt forward, and fell over, three times.

I could have got round the picking-it-up-in-her-hand, I think, but this was a, ahem, step too far, ha ha. I don't know about yours but my okay-maybe-they-sort-of-have-a-kind-of-language-sometimes-but-animals-are-only-animals-really rationalization faculty goes *screeeeeeeeeek* at this point and then breaks down entirely, and like suddenly it's a whole new world and anything is possible.

Maybe it won't seem like that big a deal to you, because you already know what happened later. But it was a big deal to me. The Headache was so bad at that moment that I'd had to sit down, so Lois pranced over and sat on me, complete with victory stick. The red haze began to clear, but my vision was still kind of distorted, and I had a stronger than usual feeling that if I looked really carefully into the trees I'd see some of those big deep shiny dragon eyes that I saw in my dreams looking back at me. It's hard to think clearly when your skull is trying to explode, but this is the idea that I suddenly couldn't get rid of: That the reason why I'd got away with this Scam of Scams, this Swindle of Swindles, this Flimflam of Flimflams, this human raising a dragonlet, was because Lois' mom was hanging around keeping an eye on me. Plus Grace's cooking of course.

But it's way too late for you to send for the small white van with the smiling men holding out the jacket with the sleeves that tie round the back, so you might as well relax.

And Lois did occasionally remind me of Snark. This was one of those times. Possibly because this was a very *special* stick she was compromising her principles and chewing on it, and drooling lovely gooey wood fragments all over my jeans.

Anyway. It wasn't some kind of geometric progression of insanity after that. I don't think. It was like only a small gradual worsening in the mental terrain (with about as many switchbacks as hiking across Smokehill). I still missed having someone who spoke good English to talk to about it, but because of stuff like this, I mostly hadn't told anyone else about it. So once we were alone at Westcamp I didn't feel so much trapped-with-Lois-the-baby-dragon-my-unique-and-dangerous-responsibility as the people back at the Institute might have thought I did. Although I was and she was. And I did have the two-way on all the time I was indoors.

And this was when the Headache changed *again*. It had sort of given warning on the trip out to Westcamp but had then subsided when we arrived and started dragging the trees off the roof and killing deer and so on. Maybe it had been regrouping. I know you're bored with me and my Headache. My fairy tale about Lois' mother keeping an eye on us is *creative* but unconvincing, right? A headache is a headache. No it isn't. Lois headaches had always been different, had always had a slight sense of the Alien Spy Thingy in Your Brain. This latest model was definitely several rungs higher on the ladder of weirdness.

Usually a headache just sits there and throbs, right? It may get bigger or smaller and it may be in one place rather than another and it may spread, but it doesn't feel like it's shouldering aside your gray matter and putting up signposts like for other travelers. (Note: *eeeeek.*) When I'd had them when she was a baby they'd been . . . smaller, although in a weird way they hurt more, like I wasn't used to them yet, like my brain muscles weren't up to it, like a couch potato trying to get into hiking. Except the ones that came with the dreams about her mom. They had always felt like they were going to crack me open somehow, and maybe as if they'd *been* slowly cracking me open over the last two years, so that other stuff could get in. . . .

I did remember faithfully to check in morning and evening with the Institute (and the two-way continued to cooperate, with a few sniggers and the occasional firecracker noise). And I still talked to Martha every chance I got. The second week we were out at Westcamp by ourselves, when Dad told me they were now fifteen down with the flu and had had to take on some temp help as well as a full-time nurse who was staying in my old bedroom at the Institute, and in spite of everything I've told you about missing everybody and counting to eternity a lot, I found I had to be careful not to sound a little bit *happy* about the fact that they still couldn't send anyone out to keep me company (Crazy Nature Boy: film at eleven).

Of course I was worried about everybody, and I was also missing the human bond to balance the growing dragon bond, like I was getting too *dragony* myself (Lois

hammering away at me during the day and the dreams hammering away at me at night and the Headache hammering
away all the time). But it was also impossible not to be a little bit pleased—just to let the dragon bond happen without
having to second-guess it or you or us all the time because
some other human would be coming back soon. Soon I'd
have to figure out what to tell (or show) the people who did
know about her, because someone would *eventually* come
back out here and see what we were up to . . . but not yet.
People had stopped getting the flu and the first ones who'd
had it were getting over it and Dad was beginning to say
things like "We should be able to think about sending someone out there soon" . . . but not *yet*.

It was the end of the fifth week Lois and I were at Westcamp alone that I almost died.

CHAPTER EIGHT

Lois and I were sitting facing each other in one of the little sandpits in our meadow. I'd been trying to teach her to count. What we were really good at is what I called mirror-dancing, which was using Lois' fantastic mimic ability in three dimensions—and my idea for it had begun with the stick-fetching. But Lois was actually better at it than I was—she could remember a longer series of steps/hops/rolls forward and back and sideways and around trees and so on than I could—which was pretty embarrassing, and I was looking for a way to reestablish my superiority. Parents can be like that with uppity children. So I'd thought of counting—nice low numbers you can handle in pebbles, it's just another little easy three-dimensional sport, no big deal. At least that's how I was explaining it to myself. I have no idea what she thought we were doing, but she was always up for a game.

I had an especially big buzzy headache growing that morning too, but maybe that was just because I was proving to be such a useless teacher. Maybe my basic attitude toward arithmetic ("yecch") was breaking through. Lois was certainly trying to pay attention, but she kept wanting to rearrange the pebbles. I'm not sure that her heaps weren't more interesting than mine anyway. When things got discouraging we reverted to stick throwing. Since we'd had that big breakthrough about being-the-same-but-different over fetching sticks, it always seemed to cheer us up—and when I had a useless-teacher headache (this wasn't the first time) sometimes it eased off a little too.

Out here she'd learned to throw sticks for me by dragging one—her special favorite for this activity was one she was barely big enough to drag, but she insisted *I* carry it properly when I fetched it, but then once I wrestled the thing up I could put it over my shoulder, which wasn't an option for sloping, low-slung Lois—but mostly I threw and we both fetched. Usually she took off the moment it left my hand—and she never, ever got fooled by a fake throw the way Snark used to, but then she didn't love running just to run the way Snark did either. And I was a little tired that morning too—she'd kicked in her sleep more than usual the night before—so she was well ahead of me after I threw the first one. But we both noticed the sudden black shadow over the meadow. And the noise. And the smell.

Lois saved my life, although I don't think that was what was in her mind. She was *terrified*, and she spun around and hurtled back toward me, shrieking, and knocked me down, trying to get back into the sling I hadn't worn in more than a year, trying to hide in her mom's pouch from the gigantic greeny-black demon out of nowhere that had landed on the far side of the meadow . . .

. . . And shot a long musky-spicy-smelling stream of fire over us, where my head had been two seconds before, before Lois knocked me down. My skull felt like it was bursting, but that was probably just that I was terrified too, and it may have been the terror rather than having had the breath knocked out of me that was why my lungs felt paralyzed. The heat of the fire that had almost killed me seemed to sort of hang around and stick to my skin, like mist drops when you walk in heavy fog. It *dripped* off my hair. I shuddered. More like a convulsion. With that film on me I wasn't quite me; I belonged to the dragon.

You don't always react sensibly in an emergency, especially when it's an emergency there is no sensible reaction *to*. There was a fifty-foot dragon sitting on its haunches on the far side of the meadow and I didn't have a grenade launcher at hand. I yanked my T-shirt up and stretched it down over as much of Lois as it could reach, crossed my

legs, tucked her tail into the circle of my legs to the extent
that it would go, wrapped my arms around her, and waited
for the second blast.

It didn't come. Oh. The dragon probably didn't want to
kill Lois too. I tried to peel my T-shirt back up over her
again—if I was going to die I wanted it over *soon*, so I
didn't have to keep *thinking* about it—but she shrieked
again, and started trying to *claw* her way into my stomach, which made me do some shrieking too, and then the
dragon raised its head and let out another blast of fire, but
straight up this time, and the roar that went with it *really*
made my head want to burst, and I could *feel* the dragon's
rage and confusion, as well as the throbbing scratches on
my stomach.

Lois went strangely still when the dragon roared. Then it
stopped, and there was a dreadful pause, and then Lois
jerked herself out from under my shirt, scrambled over my
legs, and set off toward the dragon. I just sat there. Stupidly,
I suppose, but intelligently wasn't going to save me either.
I'd never seen Lois like this. She stomped along, her tail
trailing and her neck stuck stiffly out in front of her, and her
spinal plates like *straining* with erectness . . . for a moment
I half saw the dragon she was going to become.

She gave a gag or cough, stopped, opened her mouth, and
produced a thin but unmistakable thread of fire. At the
dragon.

The tumult in my head changed, like changing gear, like
putting one book back on the shelf and taking another one
down—or more like having one of the muggers stop kicking
you and another one start. It's impossible to describe, but it
was so definite a sensation that I rocked where I sat, as if I
really was being kicked. I put my hands to my head as if I
literally trying to keep it from exploding. Sometimes if you
squeeze in the right place it does help a headache. I
squeezed.

The dragon dropped down to all fours. (Good thing it
was a big meadow.) It stretched its own neck till its enormous snout was way too close to Lois, but Lois stood her

ground. Indeed she danced up and down a few times—and while I'd never seen her have a tantrum, she somehow looked like someone getting ready to have a tantrum—then spread all four legs out like she was bracing herself, *snapped* her neck down and her head out, and . . . shot out some more fire.

This second go was pretty impressive for something that looked like a short-legged overweight wolfhound with really bizarre mange. The big dragon actually drew its head back a few feet to avoid getting—burned? Maybe the nose is a sensitive area. I somehow hadn't thought to look if the dragon pulled its lips back carefully before it fired. I know there's supposed to be a gland that produces fireproof mucus that lines the throat, blah blah blah, which is why a dragon coughs before the fire comes out. There are stories from what the humans have the nerve to call the "dragon war" in Australia, about guys who survived by throwing themselves down *immediately* or diving to one side or something when they heard that dragon cough. But you need *really* good reflexes. I have to say I hadn't noticed the warning cough when the big dragon tried to kill me.

I didn't piss myself when the dragon raised its head and looked at me again, but I don't know why. Beyond fear, I suppose, but I couldn't have stood up or walked away if that had been what my life depended on, so it's a good thing it didn't. Lois, having made her point, turned her back on the big dragon and flounced back to me. The pressure in my head moved *again*, and this time it seemed to me there were two different pressures sort of emerging from a general background of thumping and whanging—like Nessie and one of her boyfriends rising out of the stormy water of the loch to swallow your boat, oh well at least you can stop bailing— the great big one that was trying to make my head explode, and the little one that was the tiny jerky knot that had been there before. (I hadn't thought of it as *tiny* before though.) The great big one was ANGER ANGER ANGER but it was turning, changing, now more like a prism turning in bright light, but *blinding* bright light, so it hurt to look at it, and becoming SORROW SORROW SORROW. The little one was more like, *oh help eek eek eek oh help* which I understood completely.

Uh-huh. I understood *completely*.

I'd never read anywhere that dragons are telepathic. Maybe anything the size of a dragon that has a good brain can put out big unmissable vibes, if you hang around one long enough, which most people don't. Old Pete's journals never mentioned headaches particularly though—I didn't think? If I got out of this alive I'd have to check. But Old Pete might not have mentioned it even if he had skull busters; mere human foibles didn't interest him. . . . And I knew Lois awfully well, in my clueless human way, even if it was good scientific practice not to make too many assumptions. Don't we read each other's human emotions all the time? Don't you often know what your dog is thinking? ("I wonder if I could pinch that chicken off the counter in the kitchen before he noticed?")

So I knew that Lois' flouncing was phony. She was still terrified—as was I—but she was making a much better show of it than I was. I tried to look back at the big dragon as it looked at me, but it wasn't *only* terror that made me prefer to look at Lois. Her last few steps were not flouncy at all, and she dragged herself over the ridge of my crossed legs as if they were a mountain, and collapsed exhausted in their circle. I didn't try to pull my shirt over her again (one of the seams had parted the last time, so it would have been easier), but I did put my arms around her, and then I did look back at the dragon. *Hey, big dragon, yeah, we're a family. You can like it, or you can fry me.* I wasn't sending the message in words. But I was putting out vibes as hard as *I* could.

The dragon looked at us for a while—with big shiny dragon eyes, only from where I was sitting, underneath the surface gleam these eyes were bottomless blackness. It felt like a very long while, but I don't think it was. And then, very slowly and carefully, it settled down, and farther down, butt end first, then front end, till its body was flat on the

ground, curling its front legs under it rather like a cat, with
its enormous snaky neck arched, and its nose (and fire-
spouting mouth) still aimed at us. Finally it stretched its
neck out on the ground too, but then at the very last minute
it turned its head so the nose (and mouth) was aimed a little
to one side of us, and tipped up slightly on the cheek. It
rolled its only visible eye back toward us to check that we
were paying proper attention (I at least was totally riveted),
opened its mouth a crack, and gave a long, long, *long* sigh.
There wasn't even any smoke. The vast gentle backdraft of
its breath smelled rather like chili powder.

I had to name the big dragon too, because she kept coming
back. Also because I was sure she was a she too, and you
can't go on calling something that isn't an it, it. I had no better excuse for believing that she was a she than I did Lois,
mind you. I never saw her pouch, any more than there were
any findable slits, sacs, or bulges on Lois' rapidly expanding
anatomy, which, since Lois went on liking having her tummy
rubbed, I went on getting a good look at. (Every time I did
this I thought of Martha.) But she just *was* a she, and the
next step was that she had to have a name. So I named her
Gulp, because that's how she made me feel, no matter how
many times I saw her. Uh-oh. Big dragon's back. Gulp. The
fact that I was stiff as a plank for most of a week after Lois
knocked me down—I had *not* fallen well—didn't help my
attitude any. Neither did the claw marks on my poor much-
abused stomach.

A full-grown dragon can't sneak up on you gracefully but
I think she was trying to be tactful. She landed at a
distance—and no, the earth did not shake; pheasants make
almost more of a thump, but the wind her wings made was
pretty spectacular—and then sort of *ambled* toward us, and
as soon as she got to the edge of our meadow—the more
meadowy part of our meadow, I mean, as opposed to the
boulder-field end—she went down on her belly, as small as
she could make herself, which wasn't nearly small enough if

you're asking me, but she gets points for trying. Rattly things, big dragons. Folding up her wings was a sort of loud rustle, *clitterclatterclitter*, even from the far end of the clearing, and folding *her* up made a soft slightly clanky thunking noise, although again she hit the ground with no more noise than a sheep lying down.

And for all I know the apparent attempt to be slow and gentle was as much for her benefit as ours—trying to relate to something like me, whose proportions are all wrong from a dragon perspective, maybe made her feel queasy, aside from what she might think of humans in general, which, at a guess, wasn't too positive either. And it made sense if you're something the size of a young hill hanging out with something the size of a fat wolfhound (skin problems, short bowlegs and peculiar skull development optional) you need to try and find some kind of compromise. Since her *neck* was half as long as the entire meadow (well nearly) she still had a lot of negotiating room.

And she was *hot*. Zowie, was she ever hot. But it's funny though, it wasn't as overwhelming as you might think. You know how the closer you get to a fire the hotter it gets and if you're cold and you're longing for the heat you're like always trying to decide how close you can get before your eyelashes singe and your cheeks flake off? She was more like an electric blanket turned on high. So grown-up dragons develop temperature control maybe—although I wasn't offering to rub her tummy. She was almost *attractively* hot, like a hot water bottle that never cooled off. Except that she was the size of 1,000,000,000,000 electric blankets and had teeth as long as my legs. Not to mention my graphic memory of her flamethrower.

The way she smelled was kind of the same. It was a monster smell to go with the monster critter but it wasn't a bad smell, exactly, even if you slightly felt that if you peeled it off the dragon somehow and then it like fell on you it would probably crush you just as thoroughly as if the dragon itself sat on you. It was intense. Of course the famous Smokehill dragon smell was always a lot stronger once you got into the park away from the Institute—but here was living fire-breathing proof that the famous Smokehill smell was definitely *dragon*.

I tried not to run to the other end of the meadow from wherever she was as soon as she arrived, but I somehow always found myself at the point farthest from her kind of soon after. It gave Lois lots of exercise galumphing between us. Ha. She didn't always come at the same time and she didn't always stay for very long, but she came every day after the first. *Every day.* Every day I got out of bed with a knot in my stomach and wondered if she'd be back. Gulp. And she always was. *Gulp.* We weren't always in the meadow when she arrived either but like being called into your dad's office to get yelled at—I mean when you know that's why you're going—I used to turn around from wherever we were and trudge back there, if we weren't there, to get it over with.

I never didn't see her flying in, although I never really got used to not feeling the ground shake when she landed or as she was walking around. I don't know if we—I—got points for going to meet her or not. First time we weren't there she was sitting up looking around when we arrived. (A sitting-up dragon looks a lot bigger than any two-hundred-foot cliff, just by the way. Dragons have a *corner* on the whole looming thing.) After that first time she was always lying down when we arrived. Like she knew we'd come and she might as well get comfortable. If lying flat *is* comfortable for a dragon, which actually I wonder. But she lay down like I came to the meadow, I think. We were both trying hard.

She never fired at us—well, me—again. Although some days when she showed up she smelled smokier than other days and I wondered if she'd been hunting and if so, what. Oh, Jake, *stop* it. Dragons don't eat people. They never have. As far as we know. They just *could*. What Lois' mom did to that guy was self-defense—she wasn't trying to eat him. And it didn't even work.

But Gulp's first act on seeing me and Lois had been to try

and toast me. That was almost as hard to forget as what the dead poacher had looked like.

Lois and I went on with our games, or our lessons, or whatever they were, although my concentration was a tiny bit shot somehow. I was getting used to the pressure, that is pressures, now, in my head, having something more particular to do with Lois than I'd recognized back at the Institute, where I thought it was all just some kind of hangover from the shock of Lois' mom after my mom, plus my la-la dream sense that Lois' mom's ghost or spirit or something was hanging around giving me a hand with things. But now Gulp. There'd been nothing like Gulp at the Institute.

"Getting used to" is a joke though. There was no "getting used to" about it. I was so far out of control in this situation it wasn't worth even *pretending* anything else. If life with Lois the last two years had been sort of day-to-day, I was down to minute-to-minute now, with Gulp around. Maybe second-to-second. But, I don't know, it was also maybe like the dragon had fried my worry list instead of me. I was still here. New world. New Jake, maybe.

Telepathy in books is always sort of *misty*. All woo-woo and staring earnestly into the middle distance and delicate and sensitive and stuff. This was like having rocks in your head. Ha ha. A whole freaking boulder field, but two of them—one big, one little—were especially active. Having two of them like that was what finally made me begin to pay attention to them as, uh, communication, even if they didn't communicate much besides "ow."

I don't know how long it might have taken me if it was just Lois and me, but thinking about it, I was pretty sure the real *rock* feeling had only started after Kit left—when Lois and I were alone together. I'd had Lois-related head-aches since I'd had Lois, bad headaches, some of them, and kind of *self-motivated*. But they were still all maybe understandable—just—in terms of stress and worry and the boy lost his mother when he was twelve and was a little peculiar after that wasn't he? (Humans always want stuff to be understandable the way they already *do* understand it.) So why *wouldn't* I have visions of old mom dragon? When I was still dreaming about my own mom, and sometimes I'd woken up from those dreams with headaches too.

It's kind of embarrassing now to remember me assuming that since I was the human I was the only one of us who had anything to teach the other one. But Lois was a *baby* . . . it wasn't only species arrogance. I hope. I came around pretty quickly after Gulp arrived. I want to believe it's not only because I was too scared to be arrogant.

When Gulp was there she moved her head around to be as near to Lois as she could be, according to some rule of her own (I guessed) about not getting too close. At first Lois ignored her, but I've already said that Lois was curious about everything, and Gulp was far too big and strange not to be interesting. And didn't it occur to Lois that there was something, you know, *familiar* about Gulp? It had been her roar that had jolted Lois out of terror and into defiance. Maybe Lois had just decided that she was going to go down fighting (while her pathetic mom remained glued to the spot, draped in his ripped T-shirt). But she'd reacted to that roar almost as if it meant something to her.

I was really torn, watching Lois begin to pay attention to Gulp, and Gulp trying to respond—I was sure—in a way that would make Lois, well, *like* her. I was torn because this was what saving Lois was supposed to be about: raising her till she could go back and live with dragons and *be a dragon*. Not have to spend the rest of her life at Westcamp or some other human place. If we could figure out how to socialize her first so the dragons would take her. But I hadn't expected to have to think about it so soon (speaking of my reigning tendency to want not to think about things). It would be a huge, HUGE load off if Gulp was going to take Lois away from me . . . it should be the most WONDERFUL thing, that ultimate miracle I desperately *wanted* for Lois. Why wasn't I leaping for joy? But . . . I would miss her. A lot. (Duh.) Like I'd maybe adapted too far or something, headache-blasted dragon-mom Jake. Could I *remember* how to be an undragoned human any more?

And even in the middle of worrying about losing Lois and/or being made into humanburger it occurred to me pretty strongly that Gulp was acting, well, weirdly. Isn't it this whole big thing when you try and return a human-reared animal to the wild? It doesn't know how to be what it is, and its real relatives won't have anything to do with it because it stinks of human and doesn't know how to behave. And here was Gulp trying hard to win Lois over—*and* letting me hang around. The first successful reentry of two half-grown Yukon wolf pups to a wild pack had involved the gruesome death of one of the human minders, and they'd given up trying to reintroduce griffins and Caspian walruses and brought them back to their nice cages before they died. Which has to have been really depressing for the humans. (Although less depressing than being eaten by your fosterling's relatives.) I could maybe guess how they felt. (I don't know what they'd've done if they ever found an orphan baby Nessie. Sat down and cried, probably.)

But that's supposed to be at least part of the excuse why saving a dragon's life is against the law. A great big fire-snorting *flying* thing that got a taste, even accidentally, for human was *way* too dangerous. We weren't going to *hand* them any ops. And a smelly hot palm-sized slimy grub that was going to grow into a great big fire-snorting flying thing that couldn't be sent back to live with its relatives was going to be even *more* dangerous. I couldn't bear to think about Lois growing up to be dangerous but . . . Maybe the lawmakers weren't quite as stupid as I thought. They probably had in the backs of their tiny mean minds too that humans who do stuff like half kill themselves and/or get paid crap wages and/or live a hundred miles from a decent restaurant and/or have never seen a movie in a real theater, are crazy, or they wouldn't do it, but the reason they do it (besides being crazy) is that they get kind of *fond* of the animals they rescue. Which is maybe the most dangerous thing of all.

The first time I saw Lois climb up Gulp's shoulder and hang over her neck like a two-year-old dragon would do with its own real mom, there was a big lump in my throat that had nothing to do with the prospect of what might happen to me the next time Gulp lost her temper.

But Lois always came back to me—so far. And I didn't know whether I should be trying to persuade her to stay with Gulp, or whether that would just mess her up further. Who knew what she'd had to learn to survive her weird upbringing. I sometimes felt I was "overhearing" conversations between the big rock and the little rock, but if you're going to ask me, I'm going to say that they weren't speaking the same language. Like if a German parent was suddenly reunited with his kid who'd been being raised by a French family. They wouldn't talk to each other very well. And Gulp was always silent, and Lois, having spent her first two years hanging out with yacketing, nontelepathic humans, was always, well, chattering. I wonder if Gulp got this. I hope so.

I didn't talk to Lois anywhere near as much when Gulp was around as when she wasn't, but I still talked to her. For one thing, if Gulp was watching over our shoulders (*br-rrrr*) while we played one of our learning games, I needed to hear myself talk about what we were doing to steady myself down. I just didn't chat. It also occurred to me, rather uncomfortably, that if I talked, Gulp might get the idea that Lois didn't talk because she was defective, but because *I* talked. This probably wouldn't make Gulp like me any better, but . . . well, like what if the German-speaking parent found out that the French family that had been raising his kid were all drug addicts or serial murderers or something? How do you balance the fact that your kid's alive at all because of them with the fact that they're really *bad* for her?

And the little rock in my head got all sort of warm and soft and glowy and gooey every time Lois left Gulp and came galumphing back toward me. I wasn't making it up. I *wasn't*.

* * *

So, this non-idyll had to end, one way or another, right? It ended a lot sooner and more dramatically than I might have guessed, although if I hadn't been so preoccupied with Gulp I would have picked up that something was going on back at the Institute. Among other things it should have occurred to me that there was no way I was keeping my own interesting new preoccupation to myself. Anyone who had any spare brain for noticing anything except that I was still signing in like I should, should have noticed that I sounded funny. Distracted. Okay, *more* distracted. And they didn't.

I wasted some time trying to figure out some kind of code to get the idea of Gulp across to Martha, but I couldn't think of any. It wasn't anything we'd set up code for. "Hey, guess what, there's this big dragon who comes to visit Lois every day." We had a phrase ("good sunrise this morning") for having *seen* dragons, but I was afraid if I said that every day she'd get frightened, so I didn't. I didn't even say it once. It didn't occur to me to say it after Gulp's first visit, because there's a big difference between seeing a dragon or dragons flying gloriously silhouetted against the sky at a nice distance and having a close encounter of an almost fatal kind with a dragon.

I tried to remember if Billy had ever mentioned any close sightings of dragons on the ground—coming around an outcropping or out of a narrow pass or something "gee what's the funny smell, smells like dragon only stronger . . . oh"—and I couldn't remember any. I personally had never even seen one of the trees they used as scratching posts although Billy had—not till Gulp I mean: and watching her make a big pine tree shake like a sapling in a gale is another of those little awe-inspiring details of time spent in the company of a full-grown dragon. Mostly dragon sign like that is way far in (the scales blow in the wind, so you get them everywhere), farther than I've ever gone. Westcamp's on the edge. It wouldn't have been surprising if I'd, uh, had a good sunrise at Westcamp, but Gulp was cruising out of normal dragon range.

So I should have been worried when I didn't hear from

Martha for three days. Martha checked in most days. But all I was was disappointed—and a little worried that maybe she'd tried some time when my radio was pretending to be ornamental art. (Pretending *badly*. Our radios are not beautiful objects.) But since I hadn't figured out how to tell her about Gulp, I wasn't missing talking to her as much, if you follow me. I just wanted to hear her voice. Even radio-squeaky.

You can't really tell much from the voices over our two-ways; when they're clear they're clear enough but too clacky and mechanical to guess much about tone. One morning about twenty days after we saw Gulp for the first time, Dad said, "How are you doing for food?"

"Fine," I said, more or less truthfully. "Getting a little tired of beans, maybe."

"You need the meat for—" said Dad in one of those weird sentences that if anyone had been listening they should have thought suspicious. Maybe Dad just sounded like your usual nutty professor type, never finishing his sentences. Martha and I had a much better system.

"Well, I'm careful," I said, which was to say that Lois was getting the meat, and I was getting the beans. I didn't mind all that much because I was pretty tired of venison too and I didn't seem to have time to set rabbit snares any more. Not that I think they'd have caught anything. *Everything* cleared out once Gulp started visiting. We didn't even get as many noises at night.

Unfortunately during a slack moment (mine) Lois had made a dive for my plate and got a mouthful of ketchup and fallen instantly in love. So now she tried to climb in my lap and eat my beans once I put ketchup on them. Obviously I wasn't going to tell Dad this over the two-way. Or about what I was going to do if she got mad and squirted some fire at me the next time I pushed her away. (Do dragons have a Teenager from Hell phase? And if so, when? Before or after they get so big you *can't* push them away?) Or about wondering what ketchup would do to dragon physiology. I spent most of my life wondering what something or other was doing to dragon physiology. I hadn't realized till we got out here how much I'd left all the nutrition stuff up to Grace. But in theory I didn't let her eat anything with sugar in it, just like a good mom. Ketchup has sugar in it. (Do dragons get ADHD?)

"I'm okay," I said. "Really." Westcamp could hold six (humans) and was automatically kept provisioned for a siege. Weather around here can be pretty dramatic and it doesn't pay to take chances. Although Billy's deer was mostly gone by now, which is why I'd stopped eating it, even the way Lois ate we weren't going to get through all the rest in a hurry. And if we got desperate enough I suppose I'd get Billy's rifle down from the wall and put some shells in it. But with Gulp scaring the neighbors I'd have to go a long way to find anything to shoot (at). If Lois looked hungry, would Gulp bring her something?

There was silence on the two-way. A *crackle-crackle-crackle* silence, but Dad wasn't saying anything.

"Dad?"

"We have a . . . situation here," he said at last. "There appears to be some . . . question, in certain people's minds, whether we are . . . fulfilling . . . our trust."

Oh help. Has someone guessed about Lois???

"I—"

"Not you. Exactly," Dad's voice continued, slowly, with its painful pauses. He sounded funny, even allowing for radio whimsy. If the pauses were to give me a chance to think about he was trying to tell me . . . they weren't working. They hadn't guessed about Lois but—?

"They feel you might be in danger," said Dad.

So they might try to come after me. Us.

"I'm not," I said, too quickly and for once not thinking about Gulp at all. "I call in twice a day like I'm supposed to and I'm always fine. You know that. The—er—dragon study is really interesting and I don't want to leave. And you're still short from the flu."

"I believe you," said Dad. "We all believe you. But there have been some . . . incongruities, which some . . . other . . . people have found . . . alarming."

Other people meant not Smokehill people. That was easy. Nothing else was easy. Did he mean more dragon sightings? Westcamp was well beyond visibility from the Institute; even if you had a telescope you'd have to be able to see through rock with it. So it can't have been Gulp herself that was making anyone (else) jumpy, and there wasn't anybody else in the park now. We were still turning everyone from outside away; and any stubborn investigators would have a Ranger on them. (Until this minute I'd forgotten all about my "study" since Gulp came, but what I said to Dad was, ahem, still true.) But I'd already worried about the fact that the reason Gulp found us was because she was flying where dragons didn't fly. If one dragon was going where they shouldn't . . . Was whatever it was so bad Dad couldn't even say the word "dragon"?

"They"—and furthermore who the hell *was* they?—"feel that we who . . . live here, or who have been at Smokehill a long time, may have grown negligent through familiarity."

I didn't dare say what I was thinking: *Do they think I might need rescuing?* Because it had occurred to me that Dad didn't merely sound like he was assuming there *might* be someone monitoring our two-ways. He sounded like there was someone in the room with him, listening intently to every word.

"Your . . . youth has also been a source of concern."

"Oh," I said. It probably wasn't the moment to remind him that I had turned seventeen, which probably wasn't that much protection anyway.

After another pause Dad said, "Jake. Be careful. Be as careful as you possibly can."

I almost laughed but I was too scared. Be careful about *what.* "I will."

"I'll talk to you tonight," said Dad, and the two-way went dead.

I'd spent the last two years so paranoid that my brain

went into killer overdrive like Dr. Frankenstein closing the circuit when the lightning storm struck his tower. And I was probably moving like Boris Karloff when I walked away from the table where the two-way sat. And that was exactly the problem: I was freaked, all right, but I couldn't think of anything intelligent to do about it. Sure, I could round Lois up and make a dash for it, but a dash *where*?

Even in the middle of summer you don't want to pack into Smokehill without knowing where you're going and what you're going to do when you get there. Even supposing I took the rifle with me on the assumption I could use it to feed us. You can get sudden, savage, dangerous storms any time of year in Smokehill, including midsummer—we'd had a Ranger concussed by a fist-sized hailstone once when I was a kid, and another one nearly drowned in a flash flood only a few years ago, and as I keep saying our Rangers are *good*—and Westcamp was the last, the farthest into nowhere, of the human-built-and-maintained full-service generator-op shelters in Smokehill. Although the cave network all over Smokehill would probably make any number of Neanderthal tribes delirious with joy I was a spoiled modern human and while a cave was better than nothing—especially, say, with lightning stabbing around looking for Boris Karloff—I liked the four walls, roof, and closing *door* system. Cougars and bears lived in caves, and I didn't want to disturb any tenants either.

And what happened if Gulp followed us? Or if she decided I was running away from *her*? Trying to take Lois away from her?

Also I didn't think there was any way to wipe out the signs that I had been here at Westcamp with some, um, large animal. Even if it took them a while to figure out that if it was this big hairy secret it just had to be a baby dragon—and they'd have to be great creative thinkers to get that far, and I don't think they'd have been helped much by what there was to look at. Lois wasn't shedding yet and baby dragon dung doesn't look like anything we're trained to look for when we're trying (or pretending) to track dragon movements (especially a baby dragon fed on canned hash, rabbit soup, and venison stew). Still, whatever it was was pretty good-sized and strange, and if they came looking for me and I wasn't there, and there were signs of a large strange animal having been here with me. . . .

No. It was worse than that. A lot worse. Because there were clear signs of Gulp's having visited the meadow—repeatedly, if they had any idea how to read signs—and while she was actually amazingly discreet about bodily functions there's no way to disguise that something the size of a dragon has been around a lot over a short space of time and in a restricted area—for example sure dragon dung disintegrates fast, but the ash sticks around a while longer, and dragon-dung ash is identifiable from other kinds. Dragons also scrape their big selves across the ground in open areas and scratch themselves on boulders as well as trees and take the occasional munch of leaves very high up too. (Do top leaves taste better? Or do dragons do it because they can?) Not to mention standard scale-shedding. Gulp did all these things. It was pretty amazing actually watching, instead of reading about it in a book, like checking off stuff on a list or something. I kept wanting someone to talk to about it. (And I had some imaginary conversations with Old Pete. And Mom of course. And Martha.) *And* Gulp spent probably more than the usual amount of time scraping along on her belly, to make herself small for us.

The only thing I could think of to do that might work had the drawback of being deranged and impossible. I had to convince Gulp to take Lois away with her—and convince Lois to go. I felt my heart break—*crack! snap!*—but I was now so preoccupied with Lois' safety I barely noticed. Or maybe if my plan had seemed more plausible I would have been more miserable about it.

The small rock in my head was rolling around thudding into things, which is to say that Lois was worried because she knew I was worried. I looked down at her. The rock stopped, got hollow on top, and began to teeter back and forth, which meant that she was suggesting that I sit down and let her get in my lap (oof) for a while, for mutual comfort and support. I sat down, on the floor beside the table where the two-way stood (suddenly it looked like some malign alien thing glaring at us), with the door still open from where we'd been playing outside while I waited for morning check-in time. It was a beautiful day, with the sky going on forever in all directions but in a friendly way, and the trees with Smokehill's signature spires and accordions of stone sticking up through them, stretching almost as far as the sky.

I put my arms around Lois (this was getting harder and harder) and she started to hum one of her soothing hums. It sounded like a lullaby. To be more precise it sounded a lot like one of the Arkhola lullabies I sang to her when I first noticed that she was trying to mimic human speech. I sang that one because the melody only had about four notes in it which is about the limit of my capability. Or Lois', although she was probably mimicking my singing *ability* too.

I sat there listening to her and thinking how Gulp had been almost completely silent around us, after that more-than-terrifying initial roar, and I wondered all over again if that's because dragons, or grown-up dragons, usually are silent, or whether she was still trying not to scare us (after that more-than-terrifying roar). Even at a whisper, the voice out of something that size was probably pretty extreme. Or was it that living with humans had taught Lois to make mouth noise which was now so totally ingrained a habit that like all the other ways she was growing up wrong, it was going to be one of the reasons Lois never fit in with other dragons, despite Gulp's best efforts (maybe Gulp was as dragons go soppy and sentimental and any other dragon would know better than to try) and maybe dragon culture or dragon safety or something *required* silence and . . .

It took several minutes for it to occur to me that Lois had asked me to sit down and let her get in my lap, and that I'd done it and hadn't thought twice about it. Or that she was humming a recognizable human melody (in fact she carried the tune a lot better than I did)—and I *had* recognized it.

A lot had happened in the last month.

So maybe my plan wasn't totally impossible and deranged.

Gently I dumped Lois back out of my lap again, and for some reason picked up the two-way too and clipped it on my belt. Usually I left it at the cabin, but it was some kind of token that morning—or my only source of breaking news. Then I led her to the meadow. Dad hadn't said that anyone *was* coming to rescue me. Would he know? Would they tell him? Would they let him tell—warn—me? What kind of warning would he have? How would they come? If they hiked in and they started now and they were in a hurry, I had maybe six days. But if they thought I needed rescuing, they might choose something else. The meadow would serve perfectly well as an emergency set-down for a helicopter.

Smokehill was *supposed* to have dragons. And I checked in every day! *Leave me alone!*

That morning, while we waited for Gulp to show up (I'd never waited for Gulp before, merely steeled myself for her arrival), I tried to teach Lois the idea of *stay* or *go with* or *go that way*. She already knew a kind of *stay* because we used it to make our races after the stick more interesting. She found my jogging along beside or behind her kind of a snore, if we started even, and I'm sure she knew I was faster than she was. So she'd learned to wait—stay—somewhere while I went a little distance from her and threw so that the stick was nearer her than me, and then we could both tear after it. It was more fun for me too. It only occurred to me that morning that maybe the reason it was more fun was because I was putting out *more fun* vibes as I hurtled after her trying to catch up.

I wasn't putting out any kind of fun vibes that morning, which is probably why my attempt to teach her something new was a total disaster. It was a great big drooling object lesson in "I'm not going to do what you say when what you're doing is way big-time something else." Also to the extent that anything I taught her—or she taught me—*was* based on vibes, it was doomed. Any kind of teaching, you have to keep your mind on business, and maybe she could even pick it up that I was worrying about her safety, and her safety had always and only ever meant one thing to her: me. She wouldn't stay in one place at all but glued herself to my leg and wouldn't listen to anything I was saying and that began to make me angry, except it wasn't her fault.

When Gulp showed up I was lying on the ground with Lois draped over my legs, humming. This time it was one of her own hums. (Very Winnie-the-Pooh-ish. Similar waist-lines too, although Lois was built that way. She was also growing too fast to have any slack to get fat.) Lois would have been sitting on my chest while she hummed only I couldn't breathe if she sat on my chest for more than a min-ute any more, so I'd shoved her farther down.

I had an arm flung over my eyes so I didn't see Gulp land but I felt her. I felt—and smelled—the wind of her coming, and the faint—tinily faint—tremor of her landing. Maybe it was because I was lying down that I felt it this time. And I felt the shadow—and the wash of heat—when she . . .

My eyes shot open and I moved my arm. She was stand-ing right *over* us. She'd never done that before. An adult dragon is big enough that when you're lying down you might as well be a beetle. My first instinct was to get up and run like hell . . . but if she'd been going to eat me, she'd've done it weeks ago. I didn't think my lying down was likely to be some kind of irresistible come-on. Dragons aren't carrion eaters if they have a choice.

And then she lay down *beside* us, like she had that first day, when she was apologizing, if that was what she was do-ing, and seeming to make an even greater effort to make her-self as small (yowzah) as she could. She'd never put *all* of herself down next to us before, if you follow me, she'd like tried to leave most of herself at the other end of the meadow. But then we'd never been lying down when she landed either.

She curved her ridiculously long neck in an arc, so that

while her body was already really close to us (*really* close), her head was too. (Well, comparatively. There was still fifty-feet-plus of her relative to six-feet-plus of me.) Once she got herself settled, Lois and I were the center of a spiral, *and the spiral was all dragon.* Maybe it was just as well I was preoccupied with Dad's check-in because if I'd panicked and tried to run, there wasn't anywhere to run *to*, except into the dragon. The hump of her body, especially with the spinal ridge plates, pretty well shut out the sun. It had started to get chilly lying on the ground (except where Lois was on my legs), but being that close to her body heat was something else—although adrenaline surges kind of warm you up too. I had noticed her being hot before, of course, but this was another something or other. Degree. Dimension. I noticed Lois' body heat because she was usually pressed up against me. I know, why would dragons waste their fire heating their surroundings? But Gulp was *close*. I could hear her breathing. It sounded like wind in a cave, and one in-and-out breath took several *minutes*.

On a whim—a whim I didn't dare even recognize as a whim—I stretched out an arm. I did it quickly so I wouldn't lose my nerve, which is never a good idea with a wild animal—doing something quickly I mean—but I did it anyway. Besides, what was she going to be afraid of? It would be like having a toothpick attack you. I wasn't quite close enough, so I hitched myself over a little closer to her, trying not to dislodge Lois (still humming). I put my hand on Gulp's jaw. I could touch my baby dragon without gloves (except on her belly), as long as I was careful that only the palm stayed in contact. I assumed I could keep my hand against Gulp's greater heat—and probably her thicker skin helped.

The hot part went okay. The hot part and the Gulp not moving her head with a dragon equivalent of "ugh" part. It was still a sensationally stupid thing to do. Like maybe telepathy works better with a conductor, like those tin-can telephones you maybe made (if you were poor, or lived out in the middle of nowhere, or both) when you were a kid.

They don't really work very well, but that they work at all is weirdly exciting (if you're pathetic enough to have made them, then you'll probably find them exciting, okay?). I started *thinking* at her. I guess I started out thinking words, as if I was talking to her, but words aren't really all that good, you know, one picture is worth a thousand, etc., and especially if you don't speak the same language, and while maybe dragons had been keeping up their English since they spent all that time with Old Pete (and he says in his journals he used to talk to his dragons, although his never talked back), there's a limit, I guess, to what an insane whim will stretch to.

And there are so many times when words are nowhere near enough even when you're talking to an ordinary human person who speaks the same language. And *that's* even when you're talking to someone who knows you well and knows almost everything about you, like Dad or Billy or Kit or Katie or Martha knows me. I didn't deliberately shift over to pictures, talking (or whatever) to Gulp, but I did, since I was in my head anyway and could do what I liked and it was all either crazy or imaginary so who cared.

And then it *really* started getting weird. The pictures started like going through my head faster than I was thinking them, like they were getting sucked out of me; but as they went they were getting all distorted. Not like Dad suddenly had six legs or Billy was eight feet tall and green, just . . . I don't know. But you know how sometimes when two of you who were there start to tell a story to a third person who wasn't, and you keep laughing because it's like you're telling two different stories and one of you is crazy? It was a little like that. And if I *wasn't* imagining it, well, a dragon's point of view and attitude would be a lot different from a human's, wouldn't it?

But what was the dragon perspective doing to my story?

By the time I got to the guys in black with the machine guns and the helicopter—and why I was imagining guys in black with machine guns I don't know, too many TV shows at too young an age I suppose—I had a headache so bad I could hardly bear to keep thinking at all, and the pictures I was making seemed to *rip* at me as they were pulled away—a little like skinning a sunburned arm, only worse—and with every picture the Headache got even worse and worse and *worse*. I suppose that's why I didn't hear the two-way immediately. I might not have heard it at all except that I noticed that Lois had stopped humming. My brain (or my Headache) was thundering in my ears so hard I couldn't hear her either, but my legs had stopped vibrating—and my hip had *started* (vibrating). Even Gulp shifted her head very slightly—not enough to shake my tentative hand though. And there was the hiccupping *brrrr* that was the two-way asking for me to answer it.

I seemed to be paralyzed. My brain was doing or having done to it things it didn't understand, and it didn't have any neurons left over for telling my not-on-Gulp's-nose hand to reach down and flip the switch. There's an emergency override for talking when the other person doesn't pick up, if the two-way is at least turned on. I'd left mine turned on. But you'll never believe the voice that screamed out of it though.

Eric.

"Jake, can you hear me? Your dad's been pretty well taken hostage, and I'm pretty sure they're monitoring unscheduled use of any two-way which means they'll be coming for me in a minute. They're on their way, and they know you're at Westcamp. I don't know when they left, so you may not have much time. *Hell.* I didn't expect them . . . I've still got to . . . *Do what you have to do, Jake.* Can you—" And there was a clatter and thump and that was all.

But there was something else too, which I could hear more clearly now that the two-way had gone silent—and after what it had said had sharpened my ears for anything that wasn't wind or dragons. Another sort of buzz or *brrrrrr.* Distant but coming closer. A sort of heavy, rapid *whomp-whompwhomp.* Unless I was imagining that.

And I *would* have thought I was imagining it, if it wasn't for Eric. I would have thought I was just being paranoid. I was so used to being paranoid it wasn't even doing its job any more.

No. I wasn't imagining it.

The paralysis splintered like stomped ice and fell away. I shot to my feet, tumbling poor Lois off very roughly. I heard the two-way lose its grip on my belt and *clunk* to the ground. (The second two-way I'd killed in the business of saving Lois.) I stooped down and picked her up—heaved her up—I could only barely lift her any more, let alone hold her. She gave an anxious, protesting little grunt, but she didn't struggle. Gulp was sitting up by then too, her head stretched up at the end of her long neck—she'd rolled up away from us, so she was now like far away by being the distance of the length of her body, although she'd left most of her tail behind—looking as tall as the Devil's Tower, as if the hard blue of the Smokehill sky was something you could touch, and she was touching it. She was looking—or listening—hard.

When she looked down at me again, from twenty or so feet of neck, I took a step forward, and tried to hold Lois out to her, although my arms were shaking—maybe not only with Lois' weight.

Gulp didn't take Lois away from me though. She took us both.

This is pretty embarrassing, but the first thing I remember about that journey is throwing up. I guess Gulp didn't want to hang around for explanations—or maybe she'd seen helicopters before. We do have the occasional dramatic air rescue at Smokehill, and dragons live a long time. Or maybe my panic vibes were impressive. She scooped us up in her front claws, spread her wings, and *left*. Dragons are not graceful takers-off—or maybe that was just our weight. And my not being used to flying. Mostly a dragon carrying something as big as us would be carrying a kill, and kills don't care. Also since she didn't have her front feet she kind of bounced along on her hind ones till her wings took over, and her wings took over by going *WHAM, WHAM, WHAM,* which meant the dragon and any passengers were going *JOLT, JOLT, JOLT,* with her entire body doing a massive recoil jerk with every wingbeat. Riding in the back seat of a Smokehill jeep has *nothing* on flying with a dragon. And by the time we were thirty feet in the air I lost it. Breakfast all over the meadow. I wonder what the guys looking for us made of that, if they were doing the on-your-knees forensic-shuffle-for-evidence thing. They were probably looking for blood.

Between my head—which was still throbbing, make that **THROBBING**—and my stomach I was pretty miserable, but I closed my eyes for a while and the cold air began to help. Like her flying style wasn't ghastly enough, Gulp was corkscrewing around *through* the landscape— we, I mean us at the Institute, had always assumed that dragons must fly as low as possible sometimes or we'd have had sightings more often. Or more evidence of them walking. But guesses varied about whether this was about energy expenditure or desire to be as inconspicuous as possible for something that runs thirty to eighty feet long, and at the moment it sure felt like she was trying not to be seen. Also her twisting and jinking felt pretty high octane to me and the bigger the predator usually the more energy-conscious it is. (Bleeeeeaaauugh. It was a good thing I didn't have anything left to throw up after the first time or I'd've been leaving a trail.)

She ducked behind stone pillars and outcroppings and took sideslips down little canyons and valleys (often where her wingspan was I swear *unquestionably* too wide for clearance) even when they weren't going in what seemed to be her direction, like she knew there were bad guys following her. And where did she get that idea? There'd never been bad guys at Smokehill, till the poacher. And he didn't fly, or go *whompwhompwhomp.*

She didn't hold us painfully or anything but I was pretty horribly uncomfortable all the same, and scared that somehow Lois would slip out of either my hands or Gulp's. This didn't seem to be bothering Lois at all. Lois was like a kid having her first roller coaster ride. I kept expecting her to say *Wheeeeee*, although with the wind of Gulp's wings I couldn't've heard her. I hadn't trained her what to say for her first roller coaster ride anyway. Joke.

We stopped once, by a stream at the bottom of one of the little canyons. Gulp came down almost as awkwardly as she'd taken off—holding her, well, her hands stiffly and as if anxiously out in front of her, like someone carrying a birthday cake while walking downstairs in the dark. Phew. I was glad for a drink. We all had a drink. I had a drink and a *wash*.

Even that was peculiar—doing something *with* Gulp for the first time. Like we had something in common. Besides Lois. But Gulp got down on her belly again afterward. Lois knew exactly what was wanted—this was a game they'd played back in the meadow (although I'd never think of the concept of "game" in quite the same way again) and she climbed up to the top of Gulp's neck and settled down what looked like pretty contentedly, while I watched and reminded myself about how I should *want* to lose Lois . . . but not necessarily get stranded who the hell knew where in the middle of Smokehill alone with no survival gear. . . .

Gulp raised her head just enough to give me a very pointed stare and then laid it down again. So I could *step* on it, I suppose. That's how Lois climbed up there. I didn't want to, but what are you going to do when a dragon stares at you? *And* I was lost.

I hope I didn't hurt her. I was only wearing sneakers, but I'm not a baby dragon and all my weight's in two feet not four and you don't *step* on people. And I didn't step on her head. I found a way to crawl up her shoulder and then up that infinity of neck. Dragon scales are slippier than you think *and* the jagged bits aren't nearly as jagged as they look, nor do they give you much purchase. I settled down pretty gingerly with a leg on either side of the top of her spine, Lois right in front of me, where there's a little hollow where the skull meets the neck. But maybe it's the thickness of dragon skin there, she was never more than hot. In fact pleasantly hot, when you're flying in an open cockpit.

I didn't fall off. Neither did Lois. Even without the cage of Gulp's claws. Among other things the head and neck don't kick in the wingbeat-recoil the way the body does, so you can afford to kind of relax. Kind of. The dragon still looks *around* and you may not be looking at/for what the dragon is looking at/for, so you will find yourself very unnervingly looking one way while the head you're on suddenly swivels around some other way while you're still flying some other way yet. This is worse when your dragon is actually changing direction, when head and neck become part of the banking and balancing tackle. I also don't recommend looking down, however good you are about heights.

Lois was having the most fun she'd ever had in her life, if the blasting-bright-hot little sun in my skull was anything to go by. Maybe it was the comparison with the little sun, plus my own fears, that made the big rock in my head seem even bigger and knobbier and heavier and more headachy than usual and the boulder field squallier. At least up on top here the Headache eased a little but that internal storm-mauled feeling kept me dizzy and nauseated. I spent most of that flight with my cheek pressed against the base of Gulp's skull, because it was like I didn't have the strength to hold my head up. (Also that meant more of me stayed warm. And flying was a lot less confusing when my eyes were shut.) Lois had managed to wedge herself between these sort of horny plates a little higher up and farther forward, and every now and then I got hit in the head by her wildly flailing tail—which was now long and heavy enough for some pretty impressive wild flailing. Ow. Not among my best moments however you look at it.

We stopped several times, but that could have been because Gulp needed a breather, carrying passengers, or a chance to get her normal balance back. And yes, she did stretch and shake her neck every time we got off. I know that horses can carry something like ten percent of their own weight in tack and rider over big jumps, but Gulp was flying. And flying and flying. *Very* energy intensive, flying, and worse when you've got like a very heavy hat tipping you forward all the time. But there wasn't any place else we could have stayed on, not bareback anyway.

I'm pretty sure Gulp went the long way around. The angle of the daylight kept changing direction from more than the sun rising and going back down again. (At one point I wondered faintly and queasily if even Billy could keep his sense of direction, flying dragonback.) Was she deliberately confusing our trail, or did dragons always leave a confusing trail? Something as big as a dragon you wouldn't think they'd've learned to bother—that they'd think they needed to. Unless, of course, this was all part of the Smokehill dragons trying not to be watched or studied. Or maybe they never had the faith in our fence that us stupid humans had had, before the poacher.

We arrived where we were going a little after sunset, although I think that was deliberate too. We'd had kind of a long pause, the last time Gulp came down, and the last flight was more of a hop. The Lois-sun in my head began to fade and it wasn't round any more. As the bright light died the shape of the thing began to soften like the light did, and by the time it was no more than a faint glow it was also a sort of collapsed blob, like jam let out of its jar. Lois was tired. So was I. The big Gulp-rock had sunk down so it was lower than it was high too, but it hadn't got softer, it had got harder. Just having it in my head hurt. It wasn't so much a headachy feeling any more though, it was more like by sheer literal weight it was grinding its way down through the bottom of my skull. If I'd had to give it a definition I'd've called it stubbornness. I didn't want to think about what Gulp might have to feel stubborn about but I couldn't help being pretty sure I could guess.

After we climbed back up her neck the last time and settled in, she shook herself a couple of times, sharply, and the big rock in my head developed spikes and sank them into my brain. *Ow*. I felt like a mountainside with pitons being banged into it. Lois gave a little squeak or mew, so I put my arm around her and tried to brace my feet and hands. I was tired and *starving*, and it wasn't easy—the waning daylight felt like the waning *me* and nothing to do with the sun setting like it does every evening—but Gulp was obviously saying "hang on."

Because my head was so sore and heavy anyway and the wind made my eyes water—and yeah, I was scared, but try and tell me you wouldn't be—I put my face down against one of the thick plates on Gulp's neck again, although I could peer a little. Lois, who'd been pretty much playing Gallant Figurehead Breasting the Airy Ocean all day like something out of a blue-yonder version of Hornblower, was subdued enough now to let me pull her down too. Also as soon as the sun disappeared it started getting cold and plastering myself along Gulp's hot neck felt good.

We were at the bottom of another, bigger canyon with a lot of tumbled rock and scree everywhere and a few little patches of dull greenery. The remains of daylight couldn't show much down here though. The shadows got pretty spooky pretty fast but I was *on* the scariest shadow of them all . . . and my sense that she was nerving herself for what happened next was scarier yet. Gulp went round a pillar and between two boulder falls with this amazing snakelike (passenger-cracking) writhe she could do . . . and suddenly went *down* and it was suddenly *very* dark, and then it wasn't dark any more but the light was red and flickery, like firelight, only not like normal firelight either. The light kind of made me remember something, it was way too familiar. . . .

. . . And then there was an **incredible** roaring in my head *and* my ears, and Gulp was standing up on her hind legs and roaring back—the vibration felt like sitting on the biggest engine in the world at the moment when the biggest engine in the world is about to fly into smithereens—and twice she turned herself sharply one way or another and the arrow of fire that had no doubt been meant to wipe me off her back went wide, and I only *barely* stayed on, still hanging on to Lois, who was howling with terror and trying to look for her mom's pouch again which wasn't making my life any easier.

After the first two flame-spears there weren't any more, maybe because whoever was doing it had noticed that there was a little dragon up there with me (are all dragons this trigger-happy?), but the roaring still seemed to go on for a very long time. . . . I *have* to be imagining this, but at the time I would have sworn that Gulp's spinal plates rattled like castanets from the reverb of her roaring . . . although maybe not as long as it seemed because even after I stopped hearing it in my ears I was still hearing it my head. It felt like an avalanche of boulders and I couldn't see or hear through it. I wasn't sure I wasn't in a *real* avalanche of boulders, and if I was, presumably I was about to die.

Gulp may have tried to let us climb down the way we'd been doing all day and I didn't notice or couldn't do it. Which is how I found out that she could reach around to the back of her neck with her forelegs when one of her front claws closed—gently—around me. I think I may have yelled—okay, screamed—but then I recognized what she was doing, and tried to let go of the way I had myself wedged in but I was so stiff with terror and confusion that it was pretty impossible, it was like I'd lost track of my own legs and arms, and I couldn't let go of Lois who was petrified and clinging to me. Mom instinct had kicked in again: I was off my head, but I was *holding on to my daughter.* Even Gulp had some trouble peeling us out of there and we had a very jerky and stomach-turning ride down to ground level.

My legs just folded up like wet string, although I was also carrying the hysterical Lois. We collapsed together, and then had the *insane*-making sensation of Gulp coming down to four legs over us, with us directly under her belly, and her heat *poured* over us like one of Yellowstone's boiling geysers. A tiny little portion of my mind, still trying to make rational thoughts against stupendous odds, which was pretty heroic of it in the circumstances, was saying, She's *protecting* you! I could hear it, and it made sense and everything, to the extent that anything was making sense, but I was way beyond my deal-with-it boundary. Also the Headache was doing what felt like the cranial version of the John Hurt scene in *Alien*. I'm afraid I passed out.

CHAPTER NINE

When I came to, my head still hurt, but not quite as much, and I had Lois' head jammed under my chin, humming. It wasn't a very good hum, it kept breaking up and then starting to rise as if it was going to turn into a shriek, and then she'd catch herself and yank it back down into a hum. But she was trying to hum. And she was only a *baby*. Time I started dragging myself back together. If I could still find all the pieces.

So I tried to sit up. The moment I moved, the avalanche in my skull started again and I put my hands to my head and squeezed. The avalanche stopped. It wasn't the squeezing though, it was another roar from Gulp: I moved, the avalanche started, Gulp roared, the avalanche stopped. Well, it didn't stop exactly. All the boulders got smaller and they did stop rolling around, as if they'd been flash-frozen by the noise. Or glued. But if the glue wasn't strong enough they'd fall over and start crashing around again. And I doubted the glue was that good. The ones that had stopped rolling were only the up-close ones anyway. There was still a lot of crashing going on at a little more of a distance. It was very, very weird. Almost weird enough not to be horrible. But not quite. And very, very painful. There was a softish, as rocks go, rather quivery, bristly glowing blob from Lois . . . and a great big sort of angular looming thing, like she was still standing over us except she wasn't, from Gulp.

And outside my skull there were a lot of big looming things. *Big* looming things. Big *looming* things.

Yes. You knew this already, reading it here, but I was having *a lot of* trouble with reality. We were in a cavern full of dragons.

I'll let that sink in for a minute. It takes a lot of sinking in. Think yourself *out* of your comfy chair and your nice house with the roads and the streetlights outside—and the ceiling overhead low enough that a fifty-foot dragon can't stand on her hind legs and not bump her head—and think yourself *into* a cavern full of dragons. Go on. Try.

There was an actual fire in a big hearth-space (big = Wilsonville would probably fit into it) not too far away from where Lois and I skulked in a little half niche in the uneven stony wall, although I couldn't see what it was burning, and it didn't smell like wood, and the red light it cast seemed to me more purple than wood firelight. (It didn't smell like meat or blood or dead things either, which was just as well. Although I was weak and shaky probably from lack of food too I was not up to the concept of eating from any direction, eater or eatee, and I was particularly not up to thinking reassuring thoughts about how dragons don't eat humans.) There was a very strong smell of dragon over the strong smell of the smoke, which was almost as overwhelming as the sight of them was—and the echoes, when Gulp roared, must have been making old Earth totter on her axis.

It was like there was some kind of geometric progression-explosion for every sense I was forced to use: sight, hearing, smell . . . the smell was strong enough that I was tasting it too, which only left touch, and Lois and the nobbly rock at my back were not much comfort. If you wake up and find yourself chained to a wall in a dungeon and there are a lot of spiky-looking iron things hanging by the fire, you're relieved there isn't anyone looking at you thoughtfully while he's holding the spikiest *in* the fire, but that you're alone isn't much *comfort*.

I say the nobbly rock wasn't much comfort, and you have to remember I was aching in everything I had to ache in, but we were also in some kind of nest. I was so sore and tired and rattled that it took me a little while—what with the cavern-full-of-dragons thing kind of taking my attention—to realize this. I was lying on the ground, but I was really well padded with—I picked up a handful of the stuff and let it slip through my fingers and patter back into the heap. Dragon scales. They're a little prickly I admit, but in heaps they're surprisingly soft. And warm. Even a cavern which is full of dragons *and* a small-town-sized fireplace going a blast has drafts, particularly when you figure the ceiling is over sixty feet up.

Gulp sat or crouched near us, with the end of her tail flung out in front of us, so we were barricaded in, by the fire, by the wall, and by Gulp's tail. Here Gulp was a dark but streaky iridescent green; it was some weird light, because she looked darker by ordinary daylight, and it was like thick red twilight in the cavern. Remember I said that when we'd first come down here last night (if it had been last night) there'd been something almost familiar about the weird light? Yeah. It was just like in my dreams. I couldn't decide if I recognized the smell from my dreams too. And I was often frightened in my dreams. But the damn crushing *terror* was new and like *complicated* in this Toto-I-have-the-feeling-we're-not-in-Kansas-any-more way, like maybe I had a whole five horrible *new* senses to experience it with or something, thanks a lot.

The dragons around us were different sizes and different colors; there were a dozen of them, maybe fifteen—that I could see—that I thought I could see. No, I didn't recognize any of them—which was a relief: I know, I'm spending a lot of time here redefining "limit" and "edge" (and "crazy" and "impossible") but recognizing one of these dragons from my dreams of dragons would have been *waaay* over any definition of any edge you like—even if in my dreams they were, well, friendlier. Or at least they were okay with my being there, which these guys were *not*.

It was hard to tell dragons from rocks and shadows, and while I was never sure about this either it seemed to me that it wasn't always the same dozen or fifteen dragons—although I thought Gulp was nearly as big as most of them. The one I could see most clearly, however, was a *lot* bigger than Gulp, facing us from the other side of the hearth. He was black, with no iridescence at all, although on some of him—eye ridges and nose, spine, elbows—the scales were outlined in red. I had thought Gulp was scary—*he* was scary. He made Gulp look like a cuddly toy dragon. A fifty-foot cuddly toy dragon. Looking at the size of his head and the one front claw that were reasonably illuminated by the firelight I figured he probably went on forever. His tail probably came out at the caves by the Institute, near where I'd seen Billy that time I'd gone to find him, to tell him Dad had okayed my overnight solo. What a long time ago that was. Sort of the time version of the length of this dragon. And I wondered, suddenly, if dragons were what Billy had been worrying about, down there in the cave. He hadn't *really* seen a dragon tail, had he? Sitting in a cavern full of dragons, anything was possible. I might as well just get rid of "impossible" as a concept and stop wasting time trying to redefine it.

Monster Dragon's eye slowly blinked. It was like watching an eclipse. I had the feeling I didn't want to look into that eye, as if it might blind me, like you're not supposed to look at the sun, even during an eclipse. The leader, maybe? Alpha male and all that? In that case he might be Lois' dad too, if Old Pete was right and it's only the alphas that breed. I wondered who had inherited Lois' mom's position.

Cautiously I checked the inside of my skull to see if I could tell which boulder Monster Dragon's was. I expected him to be the largest and the hurtingest, but he wasn't. He was large, all right, but he was almost not a boulder at all, more like a . . . a big lump of clay the potter hasn't decided what to do with yet. A bit, you know, malleable. Or poised. Balanced. Almost peaceful, which was pretty damned dramatic under the circumstances. How did I know it was him? I don't know. And to the extent that I could wonder about anything in the old, comparatively-normal-human-Jake way, I wondered just what the last three weeks of hanging out with Gulp had done to me.

Had she meant to teach me to—talk to her? Or was that an accident of having to spend too much time with me—because of Lois? Having decided not to fry me, that is. Then why hadn't it happened with Old Pete? Because if he'd started having dragon-shaped, dragon-identified headaches, he'd have mentioned it—because it wouldn't be just boring human weakness any more, it would be about *dragons.*

Was it Lois again—the *emergency* of Lois? First the extended emergency begun by having stuck her down my shirt front right after she was born. And then . . . you know those stories of moms lifting the front ends of trucks off their children the trucks have just run over? Maybe it was like that. In the stress of those last moments back at Westcamp, I managed to get through to Gulp. I mean, just having a headache . . . *Eric* gives me a headache, and we've never gone in for mind-reading. (Automatically the thought followed: Now *there's* a *really* horrible idea.) And then I thought of his voice over the two-way, and I wondered how he was doing. How everyone at the Institute was doing. My father was *hostage . . . ?*

And I'm sitting around, trapped and helpless and hallucinating, in a cave full of dragons. I know dragons don't eat humans . . . but if we're playing the Walrus and the Carpenter here, I'm definitely an oyster.

So there I was—out of time, out of humanity, out of *life,* certainly life as I knew it, with an aching, echoing head full of . . . waiting. Oh great. What do I do now?

I can't tell you how bad this was, how lost I was, how mind-smithereeningly *alone* I was, in this flickery shadowy red-purply nowhere, full of **huge** breathing shadowy *things* with huge shining eyes. And there I was, scared silly, scared beyond silly. And one of the things I came out of that experience with is a total inability to use the word "telepathy." It just doesn't fit, okay? And also . . . telepathic dragons.

Pleeeease. That is so last century. I've got like shelves of Mom's old story books with telepathic (if pouchless) dragons in them.

But the problem remains that us mouth-flapping talking-crazy humans don't have any words for any kind of silent stuff, which is maybe why we overuse "telepathy" so hard. Like a color-blind species making everything red because it's the only color they've heard of, even though they can't see it either, but it makes them feel clever, like they can *imagine* color. We can deal with radio waves, that they exist I mean, and even stuff like our dragon fence, but communication that isn't through our standard five senses is as taboo as the idea that any animals but us have real intelligence. So I've called it "telepathy" a few times already because I haven't got anything else *to* call it, but I'm stopping now. You can just make up your own word. "Ummgmmgmm" or something, because it occurred to me eventually that the nearest thing us humans do have to some of what dragons do is a kind of inaudible hum. Which is maybe how Lois and I groped toward a common wavelength at the beginning. Mouth talking isn't completely on a different planet from an audible hum, and once you've got to the vocal-cord-jiggling humming part.... That's still not right, okay? But it's a piece of some of it. Maybe.

I'm sitting here now, a long time after I woke up in the cave full of dragons for the first time, thinking, *It's nothing like that.* But what is it like? If it's like anything—and it's *not* like anything or I wouldn't be making such a drooling idiot of myself trying to explain—it's maybe more like sign language, except that it's going on in your head, with a little audible harmonic background some of the time. Like you might wave your hands (or you do if you're me) while you're talking. Part of where my Headache came from was just trying to grab on to something that almost makes sense, but not really—like the brain strain version of your eyes struggling to see through somebody else's glasses.

I remembered that thinking words at Gulp hadn't done much good, and while I wasn't sure what Gulp had understood, she'd got us away before the helicopter had arrived, and while she might have had a big avoid thing for helicopters the way all our dragons seemed to about all human stuff . . . she'd got *us* away. Maybe only because Lois was too young to leave her mutant freak serial murderer mom, but I couldn't quite believe that. I may have been her worst nightmare but I just didn't feel Gulp was defending us both now only for Lois' sake. Which is also to say that I freaking-mutant well was picking stuff up from the Gulp rock in my head. Emergency may be a hell of a way to make contact, but by golly it works.

So one way or another here I was in a cavern full of dragons, and still alive to tell about it. Supposing I got out of the cavern full of dragons again, alive, and there was anyone I dared tell. . . . I was going to tell them *what*? I squeezed my skull with my hands again, till my wrists ached. Sometimes it's just your thoughts you can't deal with, and I couldn't deal with mine.

Slowly I tried to organize a picture in my head of Lois and me playing in the meadow where Gulp had first found us. Sort of out in the front of my head, away from my private thoughts.

This was *sucked* away—the same dizzy, queasy no-longer-entirely-me-doing-it feeling as I'd had when I'd been trying to "talk" to Gulp—and almost immediately there was a picture in my head of . . . well, in hindsight, it was a cavern full of dragons, but I didn't know that at the time. It was way too bizarre. The only reason I even knew I was receiving something was that it was way too bizarre for me to have made it up. I've learned a little more now about how dragons see things, or at least how they make their head-picture-communications of what they see, which I guess is also some kind of shorthand like an alphabet is for us. I know the this-group-of-dragons, uh, thingummy. It isn't even really a picture. But it's an image, or a symbol of an image, or a *gesture* of an image.

But it's not only an image. This is the really hard part. You have to do something too—like if one person puts out a hand the other person is supposed to put out their hand too and shake it. It's the handshake that makes it—a handshake. Or like the famous stability model of the three-legged stool. If there was a dragon-alphabet version, it would have one of its legs missing: You'd hold it up—you'd make it stable—by thinking about it, or by thinking, "This is a three-legged stool. Never mind one of its legs is missing." The dragon alphabet mostly doesn't just lie there like ours does. Mostly you have to connect with it somehow, with what you're seeing or receiving, you have to hold something up or plug something in, to make it really work. This makes "reading" it a lot harder. If your two-legged stool falls over, you aren't getting the message "stability." More likely you're thinking it's something about falling over, which it is, kind of, only backwards.

This was the first time I'd *received* something *sent* from a dragon. At least that I knew about. Well, any dragon but Lois. That I'd started maybe picking stuff up from Gulp was new and uncertain—and I hadn't learned about having to plug in yet either. This time at least I was sort of expecting it—expecting something—probably because I'd "known" that the big lump of peaceful clay in my head was actually Big Goes-on-Forever Dragon. It was a little like—a little tiny microscopic like—looking through one of those cheesy 3D viewer things, that you put a wheel of pictures in and click them around, and what you see is really nothing like what you see in the world—it's sort of too flat and too jumping-out-at-you simultaneously. (Okay, how retro are we at the Institute? We still sell the glasses, and half a dozen wheels of 3D photos of Smokehill. The funny thing is that people still buy them.) It was a bit like that, only worse. At least when you're looking through the viewfinder at several rows of mountains that don't line up in any direction, including with the horizon or with each other, you know what they're trying to do—what the picture is *trying* to be. And you can take the viewer away from your eyes and your normal, ordinary life is still there.

But this—this was—gah, I've run out of words again.

"Amazing"—boring. "Incredible"—too vague. "Stunning"—my least favorite adjective even *before* the Headache because it always sounds to me like being hit on the head with a hammer.

So sending-and-receiving, so, proving that COMMUNICATION was going on, or at least that was what both sides were trying to make happen, didn't make my poor fractured head hurt any less, but it made having a headache sort of make some sense: my brain was being coerced—like a window being jimmied—into behaving in a way that it was never built for. Cue sound of splintering. Gulp hadn't done anything like this—although "talking" to her had briefly paralyzed me to the point that I couldn't flick the switch on the two-way. Maybe this was the next stage. Because I had the strangest feeling that Monster Dragon was actually *helping* me somehow. That he was really trying to teach me . . . maybe even trying *to be taught by me* . . . poor freaking dragon.

The mess in my head seemed to be saying, *Yes, we know about that. Go on.* Although I want to emphasize that there wasn't any impatience or rudeness about it—even in the state I was in I could feel that. Could feel that gentleness. It just *was*, like being in the cave of dragons (hungry, shaking, bewildered, and terrified thrown in free) was.

Okay. Right. Go on with what? And like *how*?

I could tell you a lot about those first days I spent in the cavern full of dragons, trying to learn to talk to them, and they to me, but most of it is about not succeeding, which pretty much any scientist will tell you is 99 percent of what you do, finding out what does *not* work. A scientist, though, puts his notes down and goes away and has a cup of coffee or reads a newspaper or something. Even a field biologist counting scales or scat has a campsite, somewhere that is *away* from the specimens he thinks he's studying, something that's his not theirs (whoever they are). A good field biologist *wants* to be able to go away, because one of the things you're always supposed to be worrying about is affecting your object of study's behavior by your presence. The Institute had been worrying about that ever since Old Pete opened the cage doors, because it's always been so hard to learn anything about our dragons, beyond that they apparently were still out there somewhere. And if our best attempts at being tactful had already driven them underground, *before* what happened to Lois' mother. . . .

We hadn't known it was literally underground, although that was always a good guess, in a landscape like this one, with a lot of underground caves. So maybe that *was* what Billy had been worrying about. But I doubted that if I wandered down one of the tunnels out of the fire-cave I'd find myself coming out beside the Institute, at least not before I starved to death. And besides, I wasn't going anywhere. I was sitting in a cave surrounded by dragons and far from being a discreet note-taker I was the object of study—the lab rat, in fact. And I didn't get to go away. Lab rats don't. I was there and they were all looking at me, with their huge sheeny bottomless eyes. And climbing around inside my head and making my skull sore. When Gulliver got stuck in Brobdingnag, the giants didn't climb around *inside* his head.

I told you way back at the beginning that I've always found caves magical. I'm not sure this tendency was helpful under these conditions. If things get too surreal you haven't got anywhere to, you know, *stand* any more, to say "okay this is *real* real," so you can maybe measure some of the rest of it, so that "up" and "down" and "breathing" are no longer dangerously alien concepts that you have to keep checking up on. And that's hard. But these caves . . . even now that I'm used to them, and used to sharing them with a lot of dragons . . . it's like the caves themselves are part of the, uh, conversation, part of the *something's-here* prickle down your spine, part of the watchingness—the *consciousness*. Part of the communication process—the connecting, the plugging in. The up and the down and the breathing.

I still have no idea how far the caves extend, nor in how many directions. But they're big enough to hold quite a few dragons. And while I never have found anything down there that shares the space the dragons use, except some beetles and spiders and a few tiny flying things to get caught in the webs, all the shadows are populated. Which is what I mean about the consciousness. And the breathing.

And there are a lot of shadows. The rock itself is beautiful, mostly red and black with some dark green and gold, and there's silver veining that runs through a lot of it with no pattern I can see, although it also has a sort of wrinkly gleam almost like scales. As if the rock is dragon colored, dragon adapted—almost like it's part dragon itself.

In daylight I've never seen any silver-veined dragons, but down here in the shifting, shadowy darkness a lot of their scale patterns suddenly seem silver-edged, or seem so for a while, and then they move or stretch or half-turn and it goes away again and you wonder if you imagined it. Except that if you're imagining it you're imagining it a *lot*. I've stopped thinking I'm imagining it, because I see it so much, and this place no longer freaks me out the way it did in the beginning. But it does make me wonder about the caves. And how the dragons make somewhere a home. And the stone water-sculptures—stalactites and stalagmites and the other heaps and coils and masses and spines I don't know the names for—some of them are beyond even what I saw in my dreams. And why do so many of the heaps and coils look like sleeping dragons?

They kept me well fed, if a steady diet of grilled mutton and venison counts as well fed. There was a pool next to the hearth where we were, which was filled up by a trickle that ran down the wall. It was weirdly greasy and ickily warm and tasted of sulfur, but it was water, and I crept that step or two out of our niche when I needed to, so I wasn't thirsty, but food. . . . Lois tucked in at once and it obviously helped her, eating, but it was like, yeah, well, she's a *dragon* and it's not really me they're trying to feed anyway, I just happen to be here too—and I couldn't face it. If I could have curled up into a lumpy little ball of self-pity and stayed that way I probably would have.

But there was always Lois. I started eating finally because it obviously bothered her that I didn't. After she finished hers she'd come look at mine and look at me and look at the food again and look at me again . . . and it wasn't because she was still hungry. It was so obvious . . . and I was so stressed out it seemed okay that my baby dragon was doing something so easily translatable in human terms. It seemed sort of *restful*, in the middle of everything else that was going on. And eventually it was like "well you know if you ate something it might make the nausea go away, think of it as a scientific experiment" and hunger won.

And it did make me feel better—food—like I was still recognizably (duh) alive in all this totally impossible (no wait, "impossible" has been banished from the vocab) stuff, that it wasn't just all some really messed-up dream—that it wasn't just my dragon dreams had taken a really tyrannical (one might even say *draconian*, ha ha ha) turn for the worse. Which was kind of a mixed blessing really—if it was a messed-up dream eventually I'd wake up. Persephone eating those pomegranate seeds didn't mean she had to stay, it meant that she was finally waking up to the fact that she already *was* there and she could either cope or die. I think Alice was trying to wake up, grabbing all those EAT MEs and DRINK MEs. Maybe it was those first days in the dragons' cavern when I parted company with Alice at last.

Big dragons don't eat very often. So I suppose I should be grateful that they fed me as often as they did. A baby dragon my size eats a lot, but then it's busy growing up to be a dragon. And they must know that humans don't actually get a lot bigger than what I am. Maybe they just kept offering me food because, once I got started, I kept eating it. Maybe they noticed that Lois worried if I didn't eat as often as she did.

I missed carbs and fruit immediately and after about

three days—I think it was probably three days—I even found myself thinking a little wistfully about vegetables. After a week I might have eaten a green bean or two with pleasure, which would have been a first. I discovered the sulfur pool outlet, so I managed to have a bit of a wash now and then too without polluting everyone's drinking water, but it didn't work awfully well, and there was nothing I could do about my clothes except keep wearing them. Lois saved me from certain embarrassments. After her first meal she did her I-have-to-go-outdoors-*now* thing of scuttling in little circles making her distressed-peep noise, and the little Lois-rock in my head . . . well, it's not true that you can't imagine a smell. You can if it's a dragonlet who's trying to put across her immediate need for latrine space.

I don't know if running in circles and peeping is a common baby-dragon thing, or whether she was making smells in some of the big dragons' heads too, but Gulp reached her long neck out, touched her (enormous) nose to Lois' (tiny) nose—me busy trying to *sieve* myself through the rock at the back of our niche as Gulp's more-than-niche-sized nose got closer and closer—and then, well, pointed.

I followed, because I was going to need to make some smells too, pretty soon, and discovered this . . . *brimstone* chamber, I don't know what else to call it. It didn't smell like what humans did nor like what Lois did—it smelled like burning rock—like what I'd imagine you'd smell if you were standing somewhere near a volcano. It wasn't disgusting. If anything it was scary—I know, I keep droning on about how *everything* was so scary, but it's not as stupid as it sounds, maybe, giant poop *is* kind of scary—and it did make your eyes water.

I got in and out as fast as I could, although over time and use I noticed that the reason the chamber wasn't dark wasn't only that what the dragons left, uh, glowed slightly, but also because there was a very tall rock chimney that opened into the outer world and during the daytime a little light came down it. I wondered what the smell was like at the top—whether there was a blasted patch around the opening from the fumes. Also, the trench we used lay, or had been dug, at an angle, and everything tumbled or was washed down (there's a lot of inertial force to Giant Poop, and a big dragon takes a *long* time to have a pee) a big hole at the bottom end. It took me quite a while longer to figure out that the reason the fire that burned in the big central chamber smelled the way it did was because it was burning dried dragon dung. How did they dry it? And where? How did they figure out it burned? That last is probably a no-brainer to a dragon.

You're probably going off in six directions at once now, wanting to know if this means that dragons are *civilized*, or maybe you're busy shouting about how stupid I am for not Addressing This Very Important Subject Immediately. Well, I'm telling the *story*, like I told you at the beginning I was going to do—try to do—and I'm not going to address the radioactive question of the Civilization of Dragons. There's a lot of ink spilled elsewhere/space wasted on the internet over this, and the truth is I'm not interested. As far as I'm concerned that's the story we're *still* telling, and I'm not sure we're out of the foreword yet. It wasn't so long ago when all the so-called scientists said that humans were intelligent and that animals weren't, humans were the solitary unchallenged masters of the globe and probably the universe and the only question was whether we were handling our mastery well. (No. Next question.)

But if you insist on knowing whether a dedicated latrine area is a sign of civilization, the answer is no; most den-living animals have something like it. Old Pete's caged dragons certainly had a dedicated latrine area, but then so does *chinensis*, for pity's sake, and nobody would mistake *chinensis* for being intelligent. And I couldn't have told you for sure that the trenches and the slope were dug rather than just found. You could at this point if this is all really getting up your nose (ha ha) also discount the mind stuff—I warn you you won't be able to for much longer, so enjoy it while you can—by saying it's merely the way dragons communicate, like dogs growl or whine or raise or flatten their ears and their tails and their hackles.

I could argue for a fire in a hearth, but I admit that dragons being central-Australian in origin and having their own unique relationship with fire including a built-in lighting mechanism confuses the issue—having a fire going at home for a dragon may be no more intellectual than a wild dog making a nest out of grass. I was myself more taken with the fact that Gulp pointed, but there are lemurs that point when they're making their "watch out" noise, and vervet monkeys have different warning calls—"watch out that's an eagle" or "watch out that's a snake," and everyone looks up and runs down or looks down and runs up. That's pretty good language, even if they can't discuss the meaning of life with it.

You know I'm really glad that they'd discovered the lichen on Mars before Lois and I got together. It's that lichen that really threw the barracuda in the guppy tank. It meant all the hardcore scientists were already off balance when the idea came up that there really was something even a little more special and unusual about dragons than that they were really, really big and vomited fire. After the Martian lichen, some of the scientists came quietly.

But that's another story. I'm getting ahead of myself again. It gets harder to tell it in order as I get nearer the end. Not the end, nothing like, but the place I am, writing this.

I'm back at the how-do-I-tell-it place again—where I started—and where I am now more or less permanently, ever since Gulp picked Lois and me up and flew away with us. Where there are no he-saids and she-saids—except for that gibbering chucklehead Jake. The where that is the why I didn't want to start, because I knew this was coming. What will it be like when we get an astronaut to Mars and he or she gets friendly with the lichen and is invited to sit in on one of their group sessions? Which they probably will, since the lichen seems to have been disappointed with the conversations they've/it's tried to have with all the probes. What will that be like? It'll be STRANGE. And I bet when the astronauts write up their reports they'll be using lots of phrases like "this is impossible to explain but . . ."

I don't know how long we—Lois and I—were in that cavern, except to go to the toilet, before they let us go anywhere else. I think, from the daylight through the latrine chimney, and how often they fed us (and how often we went to the latrine), it must have been about five days. But I kept falling asleep, or maybe I just kept passing out, either because I was very, very tired (which I was: weirdness and terror will do that to you) or because (because of the weirdness and the terror) I needed the escape. When I was asleep I could be somewhere *familiar* . . . which is pretty funny when it was so often a cave full of dragons. It's just it was a different cave: *ow*, that laughter hurts.

Lois stuck close to me all those first days; I don't know if she was pretty weirded out her own self or whether she knew I was in trouble—or whether she was picking up "trouble" from me or the dragons—but she seemed even to lose interest in Gulp for a while. I'd wake up out of one of my sudden naps and not immediately see her and think okay, that's fine, she's finally gone exploring, that's a *good* thing, trying not to feel utterly lonesome and forlorn, and then there'd be a swirly sort of commotion like looking down the top of a blender with the lid off after you've dumped something really challenging in, and there would be Lois surfacing from the bottom of the heap of dragon scales.

I also fell asleep a lot—although I think that *was* more like passing out—in the middle of my attempts-at-talking with the black dragon, who I started out calling Nero because I kept thinking about burning, but in the first place that only scared me worse, and in the second place it was pretty unfair under the circumstances. He never so much as showed me his teeth, let alone shot fire at me the way Gulp had, and he couldn't help being *big*. (I don't know who it was fired at me when Gulp first arrived with her passengers, but I'd stake Smokehill's ownership deeds that it wasn't him. He wouldn't have missed.)

And that sense of *waiting* he did so well—at first it rattled me too, but then *everything* rattled me—and never mind what a wuss I am, it would have rattled you too—and then I began to, I don't know, be kind of grateful, or to rely on it, or something, and then the waitingness seemed to be even a kind of serenity, even, almost, a kind of comfort (at this point I started worrying about what I knew about prisoners identifying with their captors and people in institutions forgetting how to live in the world, but at least worrying, even about very weird new things, made my brain feel sort of like it still belonged to me, that we hadn't totally parted company as a result of recent events), and by the time they let Lois and me out of the fire-cavern for the first time since we'd come in, I'd started calling him Buddha. Which became Bud, of course.

I think it was him who told Gulp to take us outside, although it may have been Gulp's idea. At first I think I—and probably Lois too because she was attached to me—were strictly Gulp and Bud's problem. After the initial brief outburst of semi-mayhem the other dragons sort of sat back and said "good luck" or "better you than me" or something (possibly "I hope you get over this dumb idea *soon*"). It took longer before I started getting any kind of an individual fix on any of the other dragons, although I was often aware of that barely-restrained-avalanche thinking—or "thinking"—from them, like a bunch of journalists being held back by the yellow tape at a crime scene on a TV cop show.

The thing is that as the hours, or the days, passed, I got more and more fixated on sunlight, sky, trees, fresh air, and less able to think, or try to think, about anything else. Some of that was just fear, of course. All there was in the cavern was stone and fire and darkness—and dragons, the smallest of which still made me look like a Yorkshire terrier standing next to a hippopotamus. There were no dragonlets that I ever saw, except Lois.

I don't think it was dark in there to the dragons, or maybe they just liked dark. But they moved easily among the shadows, winding their ways among the boulders and stone pillars, and there was this almost-motionless thing they did, where all you could see was the glow of their eyes (dragons don't blink nearly as often as humans do; mostly their eyes are either open or closed), and then you'd try to follow the rest of them and decide which of the hummocks were stone and which of them were dragon, and then every now and then a boulder would move. Occasionally the firelight fell on someone's side so you could see him or her breathing, but not very often. I think this probably made it worse, the *not* knowing, although being a Yorkshire terrier surrounded by hippos, how much detail did you need? You're alive because nobody's eaten you. Or sat on you.

But I got so that I couldn't think as far back as the Institute and other human beings—Dad, Billy, Martha—that was too hard. Even not remembering Eric or f.l.s or cleaning *odorata*'s cage, which you might think was a good thing, left a hole, made me less me. The dragons weren't being deliberately cruel—you know, something like, hey, his kind is responsible for all our problems! Let's make him suffer!—or even thoughtless. I was just too strange for *them*. (But presumably a lot less scary. At least as just me, all by myself. As the forward scout of the army at your gate, maybe scary enough.) And maybe Bud figured out that what he was increasingly picking up from me was misery.

On the fifth day, if it was the fifth day, Gulp moved forward from whatever shadows she'd been in—although mostly I could see her, like I could see Bud, near to Lois' and my corner, and the other dragons stayed farther away—anyway she unwound herself from some shadows and then carefully did her invitation-for-transport display, which is that she folded herself up as low as she'd go and then laid her neck and head flat on the ground in front of us . . . which I might still not have got except that suddenly there were some very queer-looking things in my head that were enough like trees, in my tree-deprived state, that I was willing to jump at anything that looked like a chance.

With us in our small-by-dragon-standards niche, and having her arm's length—*my* arm's length—away, her breath was like the blast from the biggest fan heater you ever imagined although I swear she was trying to breathe shallowly. Lois clambered up her head to the top of her skull at once, making a happy peep this time, but when Gulp didn't move, I, well, I didn't jump, couldn't she just have pointed to the door and I'd *walk*? But that didn't seem to be an option. She rolled her ginormous eye at me—and I've already told you that being glared at by a dragon is a powerful experience—and I took a *deep* breath—just taking a deep breath makes you feel extra paltry, by the way, in a cavern full of dragons. And I reluctantly followed Lois, although I went the long way up her shoulder. Even the thought of getting out of the cavern didn't make me like stepping on a dragon. And I wasn't even thinking about the throwing-up part of traveling that way.

But I also didn't really know that she might not be taking us farther in. The trees in my head really weren't very good trees—not as a human thinks about trees—not as a human who doesn't yet know how to *connect* thinks about trees—and I was afraid they were just an echo of my longing. Maybe the caves had sort of greenish geometric rocks farther in (although it was a geometry I didn't know and I wouldn't have wanted to say they were rocks either).

I had my eyes closed for a lot of it—rocky walls flashing past that close are *not* comfortable viewing—and there were a lot of lurches that if they were dragon stair steps were a lot too long for human legs. But I noticed that we were humping our way upward not down and I think it probably would have broken what remained of my sanity if it had turned out she wasn't going to take us out of the caves after all. But she was. I smelled it first—cool, moving air that didn't have burning in it—and then I opened my eyes and saw *daylight*. . . .

It was another sunny day outdoors. *Outdoors*. I had felt so far away, not just underground, which is intense enough to someone like me whose desk is always as close to the window as I can get it and who can't sit still more than a few hours without going outside, barring blizzards, and even then I'll probably go stand on the doorstep and look hopefully for any sign of it stopping till the flakes make my eyelashes stick together and I can't see any more. But in the whole crazy inexplicable business of trying to talk to Bud, it felt like years had passed in the flickery reddish windowless darkness—I was crazy enough by then to wonder if maybe years *had* passed, like in old tales of people who visit the fairies.

I slithered down Gulp's shoulder and fell on the ground—like the stories of the early ocean crossings, when sailors and passengers get out and kiss the ground when there's finally some ground to kiss after months at sea. But at least they'd had air and sky.

I *plastered* myself against the bit of ground I landed on, like it was my best friend, which it was. I even bit off some grass—well, it wasn't grass, but it was some kind of green thing. I suppose I might have poisoned myself, but I didn't. It had a bitter taste but it tasted *good*. It tasted of sunlight—of the world aboveground, of the world where humans existed—I don't know. I almost felt crazier from having got outside again—from having spent five days (or five hundred years) trying to adjust to being a light-deprived lab rat and being scared out of my small lab-rat mind about one of the dragons losing its temper. Bud may have been boss dragon but I knew without being able to talk to any of them about it that not everybody agreed with him about wasting time on me.

Bud had followed us out, and was lying down, trying to look small, I think, like Gulp tried, but he had his head raised—oh, a mere seven or eight feet off the ground—watching me. After I had crawled around on my hands and knees for a few minutes, just reminding myself of dirt and plants—I think I did some whimpering too—I stood up, staggering a little, although I'd been walking in the fire-cavern okay, and turned my face up to the sun, and did a crazy little dance—and Lois did it with me, cavorting and peeping.

One of the weirdest things about the fire-cavern was how *quiet* it was. Except for Lois and me nobody ever said anything—or growled or barked or whined or peeped or chirped or chortled or shouted. Mostly you heard nothing at all, except the sound of your own breathing—and a sort of low, eerily harmonic background *sssssssssh* that was presumably the dragons breathing, but you couldn't identify it. It sounded more like gremlins to me—some kind of cave spook whispering around in the dark. Occasionally you heard these great *big* creatures moving around, big soft echoey rustles, a few clicks and clatters of talons and wings; and occasionally they made one or another kind of rumble, like maybe a dragon cough or a dragon snort, but they didn't talk. Or hum. Not to hear anyway. (That came later, when the other dragons started deciding that Bud and Gulp's idea about me wasn't so awful after all. Or maybe it's just that dragons are good losers.) You did hear the fire a bit, but a dried-dragon-dung fire doesn't crackle like a wood fire does, as well as being too purple-blue.

And my human thing about talking had gone away too. You know how I kept talking at Westcamp after Gulp arrived. Not in the dragon cave. I hummed a little bit back at Lois but that was about all. It was almost like my mouth was pressed shut, by the weight of all that darkness and all those dragons.

But I had a little tiny epiphany then, that first time outdoors, with daylight on my skin and in my eyes. You know how deaf people are taught to talk, if they can learn it, because even though they can't hear, it makes it easier for them to communicate with hearing people, who are used to talking. And then hearing people who want to be able to talk to deaf people learn sign language, and then—sometimes—they talk at the same time as they use the sign language, to help the deaf people, lip-read, I suppose, or get used to the

way the mouth is always flapping in hearing people, or
something.

While I was still high with being outdoors again—with
being reconnected, even if only barely (where the hell was I,
in all of five million acres of Smokehill?), with my *life*—I
went over to Bud, stopping when I was still far enough away
not to get a crick in my neck by looking up to where he was
holding his head (which he probably had as low as he could
without getting a crick in *his* neck), and started *talking*. Out
loud. Like a normal human. Like I hadn't done for five days
in Bud's cave. I've always been a big hand-gestures person,
like Mom—Dad only waves his arms around when he's
mad—so I used hand gestures too. I tried to make pictures
in my mind while I was telling him the stories—like the
hearing person using sign language—but my words led the
pictures. Us humans, we lead with words. This is how *we* do
it. And—I think—they got it. Maybe they had a great big
dragon epiphany too.

It's been and still is all totally hard sweating diafreaking-
bolical work after that—in fact in a way it's been *worse* because that's when I started to believe in what we were doing,
Bud and me, talking to each other—here we go again, like
when I first began to realize what raising Lois was really
going to be like. But this time—this time I was going to let
myself know how hard it was going to be, and do it anyway.
I know how dumb this sounds, but I wanted to be a grown-up
for Bud. This was different from what had happened with
Lois. Duh.

But if you've hung on this long because you think I'm going to Explain Everything—stop now. Put this down, go
away, wash the car, look up the horoscope for your goldfish,
and I'm sorry I've wasted so much of your time. Give this
book to your library (if they want it). But it was a big thing,
that day, for me anyway. Back there in the dark Bud had
been patiently holding the dragon space for me—while I
mostly cowered in my niche. (Of course I couldn't cope, any
more than I could have coped with a dragonlet, which was

clearly impossible.) But out here in the light I could see that
that *is* what he had been doing—that it wasn't all just being
in the dark surrounded by dragons and making stuff up to
make myself feel better. It was happening in daylight too.
Bud was listening. Bud *wanted* to listen. To *me*.

I think the last few days had been pretty intense for the
dragons too. I may be unbelievably weeny in dragon terms
but that I was there was epoch making. And look what
trouble one *really* weeny new germ can do somewhere it's
never been before.

The point is that that was the first day it seemed to me
possible—a human talking to a dragon. That it wasn't just
craziness and desperation and darkness. The craziness and
desperation may have started it . . . but it had a future. Talking to each other had a *future*. There is pretty much no bigger *wow* than that.

So I told him—them—because Gulp had moved to lie
down by Bud and was obviously "listening" too—about
finding the dying mother dragon who'd only just given birth,
and how Lois was the only one of her dragonlets still alive.
How I'd tucked her down my shirt without thinking about it,
and run away. How I'd made myself doolally trying to keep
her alive, and without knowing *how* to keep her alive, and
my only excuse was that she'd survived. I told them about
the Institute—I can't begin to imagine what my pictures of
the inside of the Institute must have looked/felt/smelled/
something-else/whatever to them—and about the human
laws that made what I'd done so dangerous. That part didn't
go in pictures so well, but I tried. (So *you* try making a picture in your head of *laws*. All I could think of was that big
famous picture of the Constitution, with John Hancock's
signature taking up half the space. So, I skipped over the
law thing a little.)

I told them that the Institute existed only because they,
the dragons, existed, and that we were doing the best we
could and knew how and although that wasn't very good it
was the best we could, and that we were probably losing too,

and that if anyone ever found out about Lois that would probably be the end of the line because the people who were against the Institute kept imagining that we *were* doing something like Lois, although we never had before, and that if they did find out, and especially if they figured out who her mother was, they'd say that she was the daughter of a rogue killer dragon and genes will tell and she had to be destroyed twice, first because she was illegal anyway and second because of her mom.

What I didn't try to tell them about was the dragon dreams. And that's funny too, because I planned to, to the extent that any of this was planned. Once I was telling the story I would've told them about the dragon dreams, how I felt that especially at the beginning they were helping hold me together, like rope, or a straitjacket—and I sort of hesitated on the brink, with a tentative picture of Lois' mom as I saw her in my dreams, and there was almost this *pause* where I swear everyone understood everyone else, two dragons and one human—I don't suppose even Bud got even 10 percent of all the rest of it, the question was what fragments were he and Gulp fishing out of the nutso deluge and what were they doing with them??—and it was about this thing I knew was crazy, about Lois' mom, *this* is the place where we understood each other—and then while it was over in just long enough for it to have *been* a pause, it was like that was all that was necessary. I didn't have to tell them. Lois' mom in my head, keeping me together. Yes. Of course. Oh. . . .

I was losing it pretty bad with the pictures by now but they probably picked up the hysteria. I told them I didn't know why Lois had survived, and I sure as hell didn't know why I was able to talk to dragons, even the tiniest, tiniest, *tiniest* bit, or they to me, to the extent that I or they were talking, but we were, weren't we, communicating, even though it was kind of messy, and we were probably creating a new all-singing all-dancing Day-Glo definition of "blunderbotchandscrewup."

But I'd got it that Gulp was sending me trees, right? I

assumed it—the communication—that it was happening—had something to do with Lois—with Lois and me. Something to do with having to be so all-berserkingly involved with her to keep her alive—probably it was just standard op for a mother dragon and her dragonlets, but it was whopping-meganormous-vast, *incomprehensible* new ground for a dragonlet and a human. I wasn't even a grown-up, you know? Although maybe that meant I was like squishy enough to adapt, when a grown-up would have been all stiff and solid and filled up and couldn't. Maybe the success *of* the involvement though was why she survived—either that I didn't know that I instinctively knew what she could or couldn't eat, for example, or that the bonding to Mom—and any mom would do—is as important as what a dragonlet eats—or who the mom was.

So her side of the adaptation process was why she made so much noise—why she tried to talk like humans talk. I'd pretty much always secretly believed that she was, you know, intelligent, more like humans are intelligent than like dogs (or mynah birds) are intelligent, but I also knew I was loopy from the strain of the relationship that was keeping her alive. . . . But I also thought about Mom and Katie and I figured it's just part of momming that you think your kid's wonderful. Even if you're a human and your kid's a dragon.

So I'd kept a low profile about certain aspects of just *how* Lois might be wonderful. That she might be dorky-checklist-human-IQ-test-intelligent wonderful. Which would presumably mean that *dragons* were dorky-checklist-human-IQ-test intelligent. Which is way too scary, you know? Well, you do know, because a lot of people out there now are reacting like we've declared the earth is flat after all, or that being a heroin dealer is a life-affirming socially responsible career choice, by suggesting that dragons will talk back to us as soon as we get the common language problem sorted out better. My suspicion about Lois *could* just have been that I was suffering from momness, and maybe that would have been a good thing, or at least easier, simpler, and a whole lot less scary.

Till now. Till the last five days. Since Gulp had brought

us here. No, before that. Since Gulp had apologized for almost killing me. I'd known then, beyond any so-called rational doubt, but I hadn't taken it in. My taking-it-in faculty was fully occupied with the daily fact of Gulp's visits. And I was probably too used to *not* facing this with Lois, in case I was wrong. Or maybe in case I was right. Martian lichen or no Martian lichen—vervets with language or no vervets with language—philosophies of humanness and that Earth is a community, not a police state, or no philosophies of etc.—it was still too big, too strange, too far away from the way I was used to thinking. Too impossible. It wasn't just being underground with a cavern full of dragons that had freaked me out so badly, you know. At least the guys who found out about the lichen on Mars, it was happening on *Mars*. This was happening *here*.

And now comes the show-stopper, the super-jackpot question, the one if you get it right they don't just give you a huge ugly new house and an even huger uglier new car, you will also be expected to solve world hunger, kiss babies and walk on water, so think carefully before you answer: If dragons are intelligent like humans—or more like humans than like dogs or mynah birds or vervets—and just by the way, dragons are up to eighty feet long and can spout fire at will—why are dragons a dying race and humans dominate the planet in a sawing-off-the-tree-limb-you're-standing-on kind of way?

I still don't know the answer to why dragons are dying out, just to get that over with since it's usually the first thing that pro-dragon people ask me. (The anti-dragon people all still keep saying, How do you *know* they're intelligent?) I think I don't know because it isn't an answer like that there's something in the water that shouldn't be or isn't that should be, or like that. I don't think it's even the restriction of usable territory. They could've expanded a lot more than they have in Smokehill and while, no, okay, I *don't* know *how* intelligent they are (How intelligent are you? How intelligent am I? At what point does this become a dumb question?), I think they're quite intelligent enough to have been clandestine about it if they wanted to be. Okay, maybe they *have* been, and presently unknown underground mazes all over Smokehill are stuffed with dragons. But I don't believe it. (Or anyway not unless they've also bred a sheep that lives in the dark and eats rocks.)

Maybe their intelligence doesn't run that way. I think it probably doesn't. Because this is one of the things I think about dragons, when I try to think about the way they think: they didn't evolve to be paranoid the way we did. They didn't need to. They evolved to be huge and very difficult to kill. Yes, they're meat eaters, so their prey wouldn't be too fond of them, but prey tends to survive by running away (and by breeding like crazy), not attacking. And most other predators a dragon can just *laugh* at. Or whatever they do. They do have a sense of humor. I think. Lois' sense of humor could be just from hanging around me too much, but I don't think so.

(I think there's humor in the way Gulp *collapses* when she's inviting me to walk up her shoulder and up [and up and up and UP] her neck and sit behind her head. You know how a dog you're scolding may suddenly go all limp, when what they're saying is "Yes, yes, you're right, I'm sorry, you're the boss"? If it's a dog, the next thing it does is roll over on its back and offer you its tummy, which isn't practical in a dragon, with the spine plates. But I think Gulp is having a little dragon joke that goes, "Walk on me, master, I am as dirt beneath your feet." And she means it about as much as the dog means it, who is watching you closely and is going to start wagging its tail the moment your face starts to smile.)

Anyway. The point is, dragons never learned to take threats to their existence seriously, and it's too late now.

I also think, by the way, that because they live so long— I'm pretty sure Bud remembers Old Pete—and don't waste energy being paranoid, that their sense of time is a lot different from ours. I don't believe Bud kept us—me anyway— underground for five days to intimidate us—me—I think he thought we were just having a nice chat, *trying* to have a nice chat, here *finally* was the perfect opportunity for a nice chat, he was really interested in the chat, and it hadn't occurred to him till—maybe—he began to read/guess from all that "trees and sky and sunlight and despair" stuff in my head, that I wasn't finding it as interesting as he was, that I didn't have the attention span that he did. Maybe he was picking me up well enough to notice that my ability to make pictures in my head was starting to get worse, not better, and he figured I was getting like tired.

Meanwhile humans succeeded in the evolution game partly because they learned to be paranoid so successfully. To hit first before the other guy hits you. It worked with sabertooth tigers. Who's extinct? But who's bigger, meaner, faster, and has longer teeth? The tiger. Humans are soft little things. The only weapon they have is their brains.

Dragons are going under because they don't understand how to fight back. Maybe they could have evolved to be able to fight back, a long time ago, if they or some of their genes realized it was going to be necessary some day. But it's too late now. Sure, they'll fry the occasional human who tries to murder them, but they don't get it about *extermination* or *war*. As soon as the Aussies really organized to get rid of them, they didn't have a chance.

Okay, okay, enough with the cheezy philosophy, you want me to get to the famous story about Bud and the helicopters, right? My great moment? My great moment, crap, I was just totally, *totally* lucky that the major in charge was brighter than some career military types and didn't automatically believe that you shoot first and ask questions later. Maybe the kind of gunnery you can carry on a helicopter is limited, and they didn't want to blow *me* up—but even that's lucky, that they didn't decide the possible death of one civilian would be just an unfortunate friendly fire incident—an acceptable loss in a battlefield situation.

Because outside Smokehill, by the time I disappeared, the anti-dragon lobby was lashing the populace into a frenzy, and the Searles had just about won. Congress was about to pass legislation to kill all of Smokehill's dragons because they were *a danger to humanity*—and Smokehill had THOUSANDS of them! And each and every one of them was TEN MILES LONG!—which is what had been going on back at the Institute while Gulp and Lois and I were getting acquainted, and why Dad had lately found himself under something a lot like house arrest. All because of one crummy stinking little poacher who thought he was going to look like a big guy by, what, bringing home a dragon's eye? Selling slices of her adrenals for enough money to buy Hawaii (as long as he did it fast enough)? And who happened to have parents who were millionaires (so what did he need more money *for*?) and would much rather blame the dragon than the fact that their son was an evil creep.

The irony is that it was my disappearance that *almost* gave the final victory to the Searles. It's so *almost* an almost that of all the *almost* moments I've told you about, that's probably the almostest of all.

But the amazing thing was Bud. He'd got enough of my story to know that something had to be done. I think he'd been worrying about what was happening ever since Lois' mother died—what it meant besides the loss of six dragons. I understand worry. His worry engine cranked up a gear.

I'm not sure about this, but dragons just obviously don't breed very often, or there'd be more of them. I don't myself get it why you want a situation where there's only one mom who has a litter of babies instead of several moms with one or even two each, but hey, there's so much I don't get that sometimes I almost want to be put down someone else's shirt and let *them* take care of everything for a while. Like I wonder if Bud is in communication somehow with the dragons in Kenya and Australia—that they all know they're dying—dying out. And the humans are so clueless they just killed a *mom*?

Presumably everyone (everyone in Smokehill or even everyone everywhere) knew that Lois' mother was about to have her babies. This was an important event. Killing any dragon is going to upset the rest of them—just like murdering humans upsets us. But a mom and her dragonlets must be a community tragedy—and a major tragedy for a declining community. Which is probably why Gulp lost it when she saw Lois and me in the meadow. And maybe why Gulp's first appearance underground with me on board as well as Lois was not greeted with hallelujahs. Even dragons, under extreme stress and grief, can be a little crabby. And their sense of time is probably why it took them so long to react at all—by human time measurement.

Anyway. So the afternoon we heard the helicopters coming there were five of us outside—Bud, Gulp, Lois, me, and another grown dragon, because I seemed to be beginning to pick her up too, in my head I mean, I don't know how she got chosen or if she chose herself, but she seemed to be another one who remembered Old Pete.

(By then I was beginning to learn that dragon language has stuff in it that translates into sounds—like human language—more than into pictures, and that includes that they have names, and that their names are mostly soundy rather than picturey. Most of it's still pictures—at least most of what I can pick up is pictures—what dragon words I can "hear" are full of *brrrrrry* nonnoises that make your skull buzz, if you're human, which makes me wonder if maybe there's a lot of talking going on after all, just below a pitch I can hear. I named her Zenobia because that's a little like what her name really is. *Zzzzzzzzznnnnnnmmmm* is closer, but harder to say with a human mouth and throat. Once I'd started again I couldn't stop trying to talk. And, after all, if they were going to try to "talk" to more humans than me, they'd better get used to it.)

This was at least another week after the first time they'd brought me outdoors; I know, I'd make a rotten Robinson Crusoe or one of those people, I just didn't keep track. I meant to. But I didn't. And time felt so funny in the dragon caverns anyway that I was never sure it was the next day when they brought me up again, or how long we'd been below. Talking to Bud also seemed to make my own time sense go funny—more so as I got better at it, if you want to call it better, but let's say more so when I didn't keep falling asleep/passing out so often. Like when we made the connection—because it was a bit like that; it wasn't like you say a sentence and then shut up, it was more like going into the room with the person you're talking to so you can hear each other—when I went into the same "room" with Bud I moved into dragon time or something.

What I was definitely aware of was that I really had to get back to the Institute *soon*, that I should have gone back a long time ago already—if the dragons felt like letting me, which wasn't a question I'd asked yet. Or figured out how to ask. But I also knew that the more, um, dragon communication I'd learned by the time I went back, the more persuasive I'd be able to be (I hoped) about what I *had* learned and how important it was. One more reason I didn't know how much time passed is because the process of trying to stuff myself with Practical Demonstratable Dragonese was different above- and belowground. Belowground it was easier to pick up the pictures and the *brrrrr*s. Aboveground it was easier to make *sense* of the pictures I'd picked up. *Easier* is a relative concept though, because none of it was easy, and I was dizzy and headachy *all the time*. I wondered if Bud ever got a headache talking to me. But if he did, did he notice? Like that there's this eensy weensy alien pebble rolling around in the bottom of his tourist-bus-sized skull?

And have I mentioned recently that languages are *not* one of my talents?

But I think Bud was a lot clearer about one thing than I was. He'd got it that dragons were in danger, even if he hadn't got it about Congress. (About dragon government: I don't know, but I think maybe Bud *is* Congress.) Maybe the *dragons* have a long history of dragons failing to communicate with *humans*—surely they'd've tried when the Aussies first started wiping them out, for example? They wouldn't be so bewildered they wouldn't try to say "please stop, can we negotiate"? Or wouldn't they recognize humans as intelligent any more than we recognized them as intelligent? Maybe they only saw us as a plague they couldn't defeat—like a book or a movie about the planet being taken over by aliens or apes. Or germs. Or Yorkshire terriers. Maybe I was a big surprise to them too.

But—particularly if they'd thought about all this before—Bud would know that I wasn't going to be able to go back to the Institute and say, "Hey! Dragons can talk in their heads and in mine too (sort of)!" Because I was going to *prove* this—how? Everything I could have—and, of course, eventually did—tell anyone could be seen as raving. Which a lot of people *do* see it as. Still. But some of the important people believe me. And part of the reason why is because of Bud the day the helicopters came.

The dragons all heard them long before I did. Lois heard them too and when I was puzzled she sent me a picture of a wider-than-tall blob with something funny going on at the top and going *gup gup gup* which I didn't understand at all—although it was also yellow, and I've never seen a yellow helicopter—which may give you another tiny glimpse of how hard the learning process is, because a helicopter is something I know. (The dragon pictograph-with-nonsound for *dragon* doesn't look or sound anything like the human idea of a dragon either, even after you've plugged in, *and* it varies from dragon to dragon, like some of it's style, like some of them present Essential Dragon as wearing All Star high-tops and jeans, and some of them rhinestones and black velvet. Maybe Essential Helicopter is yellow?)

While I was still trying to figure it out, Zenobia and Gulp headed for the tunnel to the cavern. Gulp tried to take Lois, but she wouldn't go; she came and hid behind me. Hiding behind something the size of me away from something the size of Gulp is pretty funny, but Gulp would have realized that the only way she'd nab Lois was by force and I also think I picked up something between Bud and Gulp which I think was Bud saying, Let her stay. So Gulp and Zenobia left. And Lois and I . . . and Bud . . . stayed where we were.

I was already worried, before I heard the choppers too. Even when I can't pick up specifics I can sometimes pick up atmosphere—well, everybody (every human body) knows about that, it doesn't have to be something esoteric about dragons. You walk into a room where there's a perfectly ordinary conversation going on and your ears are telling you it's a perfectly ordinary conversation and the hairs on the back of your neck are telling you it isn't. There was some hairy atmosphere going on and *not* knowing was bad enough.

And then I heard it—*whompwhompwhomp*—and then I *really* panicked. I started shouting and waving my hands at Bud again—I got so crazy I actually grabbed one of the . . . the spiny wart-things on his front feet, like I could pull him toward the cavern door, like a dog on a lead. (I was pulling on a toe, you know, because that's what I could *reach*.) And for the second time since I'd met my first dragon I burst into tears, for reasons not too dissimilar from that first time, and if you want to despise me, feel free, I don't care. I didn't want to see another dead dragon. Another dragon stupidly killed by humans. And by then Bud was also my *friend*.

The choppers found us all right. Bud would be pretty hard to miss if you were even half looking. Most chopper flights don't see dragons only because dragons get out of the way as soon as they hear the chopper. I can imagine the guns trained on him and all that. But they saw me too, and they tried to get me out of the way first since I was (no doubt mysteriously) still alive. It was like something on a bad TV movie, the blast of the broadcast voice telling me to move slowly away from the dragon. It was almost funny. Like moving slowly away from something the size (and firepower) of a dragon meant anything.

I suppose really they were not being that stupid—they could always try to kill the other end of him, which was a long way away, but I was stubbornly sticking by the fire-breathing end, and remember that dragons can breathe a lot of fire *after* they're dead. I should say that Bud was now lying flat on the ground—he'd put his head down as soon as the choppers came into sight—the way Gulp had the day she met us, or when she was inviting us for transport—and all curled in on himself too, so maybe you couldn't see quite how many *miles* of him there were. Well, it makes perfectly good any-old-species sense, doesn't it? If you're trying to look nonthreatening you try to look small and weak. It's just very hard to do effectively if you're a dragon (but proves they have, you know, imagination).

And I think they didn't realize just how big Bud is. Or maybe Major Handley involuntarily found himself wondering what the hell he *was* seeing—because I was jumping up and down beside Bud's nose screaming idiotic things like *Don't shoot, Don't shoot! He's okay! We're all okay! Please don't shoot!* Although how, exactly, even a bright human at the head of a deliberate show of military force (to impress the *dragons*?) figured out that I wasn't begging to be rescued I'm not sure. Maybe he didn't know either and—since I'd survived this long—was waiting for clarification. The "extermination" order for our dragons hadn't come yet—there was still room for doubt. Or negotiation.

I tried to talk to him about this, later. He just looked at me and shook his head. He's still a career military guy and I'm still a bleeding heart dipstick. I'll be sending him birthday cards for the rest of his life to thank him though.

Anyway. Lois was jumping up and down with me and shrieking—I think I've mentioned she had a very piercing shriek—and the poor major wouldn't have known about her. Even if he thought Bud was not making any moves because he was dead, Lois was obviously alive, and big enough to do damage if she had the inclination. She even looked enough like a dragon by then that you might even guess she was one.

There were three of them, but it was the major's helicopter that sank down a little lower as if for a better view. As I say, I think they didn't really get how big Bud was. But there was a sudden, gentle picture in my mind not unlike a nudge with an elbow, and I turned around and *flung* myself up Bud's shoulder a lot more enthusiastically than I'd ever climbed Gulp's. But then I was even more desperate that day than when she'd flown us away from the first helicopter coming after me.

I *galloped* up all that neck, half bent over, scrabbling at the spinal plates with my hands—remember that dragons are slippery—but I didn't perch on his neck. I climbed the rest of the way, on to his head. I could brace my feet against the nobbles and hold on to the smaller, less sharp-edged spikes. Lois, for once, remained where she was, although she stopped shrieking to peep at me, and there was a gust of something through my mind that I'm pretty sure was envy.

And Bud slowly uncurled. First he raised his head and neck, and then he stood up, and then he stood on his back legs and *craned*. And I found myself staring into the major's helicopter at a lot of platter-sized eyes and wide-open mouths, and shouting over the helicopter din, *It's okay, see? He's okay. I'm okay. This is Bud. We can talk to each other. Sort of.*

CHAPTER TEN

The rest of the story everybody knows. The whole world knows. They ran that first TV news shot with a thirty-second delay because they weren't sure they weren't going to find themselves running live footage of a brainless seventeen-year-old boy being made into dragon canapes during prime time. The Searles actually did us a favor about this. They pulled all the stops out to get us off the air after that first live broadcast, and the head of NYN got so pissed off that he said nothing would prevent him running it—and ran it at the top of every hour as a news update on every one of his 1,000,000 local stations all that day, just to spite the Searles. It's possible that what he was really pissed off about was the amount of money he'd been spending on having several of his camera guys at the Institute waiting for something to happen, but when Carol Domanski started transmitting what she was watching out of Major Handley's helicopter all was forgiven in a really big way. (You probably know Carol later got a Pulitzer for what she's done on dragons, but she's actually done it well, so good for Carol. And the Pulitzer committee.)

If you saw it that first time, you know that it looks pretty bad—that's our fence tangling up the transmission—and the beginning is a big grainy blur. (The picture *would* cut in at the worst possible moment in terms of me looking like a dangerous lunatic.) But they cleaned it all up later, so that the Searles couldn't get anywhere claiming it was faked. Not that they didn't try.

I'm not sure they aren't still running all our live programs with a delay, in case of accidents. There haven't been any accidents and Gulp has got quite blasé about all the people and lights and wires and fuss that TV programs create—especially a lot of fuss, because of what our fence does to the equipment, and the Wilsonville garage isn't a plausible alternative if you want to film a dragon. Although even if you really *desperately* want to film a dragon and have the best fence-resistant gear going, you still have big problems because you have to *get it to the dragon. We* go to *them.*

Dad flatly refuses to let more road be cut into Smokehill—and some suggestion about motocross-type bikes or three-wheelers made him apoplectic. Noises have been made about pack ponies, which Dad would consider, but first they have to come up with a solution to the fact that every pony, horse, burro, donkey, and whatever else they've tried so far has instantly lost its training at the first whiff of *dragon.* (They haven't tried camels yet.) Sometimes they go nuts before they're even taken off the truck. Horse van drives through gate, sound of meltdown in back of van, van drives back *out* through gate. Meanwhile the sky would be black with helicopters—if Dad would allow that either, which he won't. Fortunately Smokehill's Friends tend to the eco-loony fringe, so Dad's got some help.

Gulp was our first star, more than Bud or even Lois, although Lois is a close second, and anybody who even half understands what all this has been about loves Lois best (I'm not partial, of course not)—but fifty feet (plus tail) of Gulp is *impressive.* Gulp, of all the big dragons, is the only one who really cooperates with being filmed, although there are snaps and crackles of several of the others. Gulp doesn't really get it, about people being fascinated by her. As far as she's concerned—at least this is how I read it—she's just doing her penance for almost frying me, that day we met. Want to imagine how fast a dragon holding a human baby would have got itself killed (supposing someone just happened to have a lightning rifle in his back pocket)? Especially if the kid's mom had recently been made into kabobs?

Lois, I swear, was *made* to go on TV though. She is interested in *everything*, and as long as I'm still somewhere relatively nearby, she is a shameless flirt with everything else human, or that's how it comes over. She figures that humans are her family, and she's just thrilled any time another of her strangely shaped relatives wants to meet her. For some reason people carrying blinding lights and trailing leads and yelling are included—even the ones whose first reaction, on seeing a great scaly lump on little bent legs lolloping briskly toward them while making extraordinary noises that allow a too-clear view of teeth several inches long, is to run away. Lois has a very generous heart as well as a lot of energy.

Anyway, Gulp didn't fry me that first day and she hasn't fried anyone since and she's not going to, but even I, who spends, and who has already spent, more intensive time with dragons than any other human ever has, I've still never got over how big they are, so I can hardly blame the TV crews—as well as what are now our rivers of visiting scientists—for being a little jumpy. Gulp, fortunately, doesn't *run* at people the way Lois does. I suspect even some of the TV people pick up her fatalistic stoicism, even if they don't know that's what they're picking up. They're probably just telling themselves that anything that large is kind of oppressive by definition.

Maybe that's why they usually end up liking Lois so much. She's still small, comparatively, and she seems to have the gene or the pheromone or something for being fetching. It can't be her big deep soft brown shining long-lashed eyes because she has small poppy greeny-reddy eyes increasingly surrounded by knobbly spikes and eyelashes like stilettos. There is just no *way* to make out a baby dragon as *cute*. Lois is cute anyway, and her energy level, if you don't have to live with her, is pretty appealing. You know how charming it is when some dog you've never met before comes rushing up to you like you're his long-lost best friend. The enthusiasm is contagious. For a few minutes you think maybe you *are* best friends. Then you begin to wonder what the dog must be like at home. I don't think most of the TV people ever get this far thinking about Lois because she is, you know, a dragon. I suppose I can't have it both ways, expecting people who've never met a dragon to get it about dragons and then feeling crabby (or superior) when they don't.

We don't have mere rivers of ordinary tourists, of course, we have oceans of them—galaxies—Avogadro's numbers of tourists. They still rarely see any dragons but it doesn't stop them coming, and we now have loops of some of Gulp's and Lois' finest video moments on big screens in the tourist center, as well as the one of me being spastic on Bud's head. I can't risk just going into the tourist center any more myself, it's like being a pop star or something, and don't laugh, because it's ghastly.

Lois and I hide out in this *fortress* a little beyond where the Rangers' cottages all are. When we first came back to the Institute we were guarded twenty-four hours a day by some of Major Handley's guys—from our new fans, sure, but also from the Searles and their goons, who were not good losers—and then the fortress got built. I didn't know anything could go up that fast—it was like watching time-lapse photography. It was amazing. It also must have cost a fortune. Dad is still pretty protective about me in some, sometimes weird, ways, and he seems to think it would blight me or something if I knew what it cost. With everything else that's happened I think this is pretty funny. Maybe it's just something he *can* protect me from.

And where's the fortune coming from, you're asking, or maybe you're not. After all, the galaxies of tourists not only buy tickets but they now *all* buy ye olde genuine Smokehill souvenirs by the *barrow*load—most of 'em stagger out of here now carrying shopping bags like they've just bought the week's groceries for a family of eight. It's mostly just the usual souvenir junk too, only with dragons on it, plus a few Smokehill specials, like real dragon scales, and the only place you can buy *our* dragons' scales is at our tourist center gift shop, and while a dragon scale is only sold as a dragon scale, I'm sure a lot of tourists go home telling themselves that really theirs is one of Gulp's or Bud's (Lois doesn't shed proper scales yet). This isn't necessarily tourists being blind and stupid either—dragon scales are all the same color after they've been off the dragon for a little while, whatever color they were on the dragon, so why not imagine yours is from your favorite dragon?

Everybody wants scales though, so it's a good thing we now have lots of dragons to provide them. I mean, we've always had lots of dragons, but after I collected a few bagfuls at Dragon Central and went through a really amazingly silly nonconversation with Bud about whether it was all right if I took them away, the dragons started collecting them for me. I don't think anyone has a clue what I want them for; it's just another of those inexplicable peculiarities of humans.

It's funny about the scales. Dad always said it was a bad idea, our Rangers have better things to do with their time than haul trash for tourists, tourists are just fine with coffee mugs and mouse mats that say GREETINGS FROM SMOKEHILL. And I remember the flap when Mom and Katie and the latest noise of consultants (okay, what's the collective noun for consultants—a fire sale of consultants? ha ha ha) brought him around, saying that it was something tangible about our *australiensis* that visitors could not only see but touch and take home with them. Not to mention scales being about the only things attached to dragons that don't disintegrate within a few months: Maybe it's something to do with the fact that scales don't actually stay on the dragon long. Dad did have to admit they made us money—and even a big bag of them doesn't weigh much, so they're not a burden to carry back to the Institute. Since Lois the sanctuaries in Kenya and Australia have started selling scales too, but all their scales are just from any old dragons, and they don't do anything like the business we do.

Then the postcard from that first TV documentary— filmed at the Westcamp meadow, so there is a lot of hushed, dopey voiceover narration of the *and this is where IT FIRST HAPPENED* variety—of Gulp prostrate at my feet sold like nearly enough for a down payment on Smokehill II. You can't see most of her, of course, just a bit of her neck and her head, with her face tipped down enough for her nearer eye to be looking straight at me, very much like the first afternoon, when she was apologizing. The panorama version—where you can see all of her—sold even better. And then there's our patent on Dragon Dolls. And Dragon Squadron was last Christmas' biggest seller—in both its computer *and* its board game formats—the sort of scene where parents were pulling each other's hair out in front of FAO Schwarz. They had to call in some kind of riot police in Denver, I think it was, when a shipment got hijacked to somewhere else.

And, okay, *yes* you can buy an *autographed* copy of the panorama postcard of Gulp and me, and Gulp doesn't sign autographs.

It's true that they built our fortress before the money really started rolling in, but maybe the bank manager Dad got the loan from could smell that it was going to. Or maybe he just had a sense of humor. Or maybe Dad made up the idea for Dragon Squadron on the spot (actually, it *was* Dad's idea—I didn't know he even knew what a game was, let alone a computer game) and promised him first editions for his kids.

And speaking of people who were born to go on TV (the spiny-ridged ones that peep and the two-legged ones that bellow), Eleanor also made a huge difference in how the whole story went over at the beginning, when a lot of the country was still mostly on the Searles' side and the Searles were trying to make out, oh, I don't know exactly, it all made me so angry I couldn't think about it, just like at the beginning when there was a dead dragon and a dead stupid evil jerk and Lois was a secret—the Searles tried to make it out there was some kind of child abuse going on with my dad sort of giving me to the dragons as a sacrifice or something, or like that famous psychologist who raised his kids in a box to keep out bad influences (and I think *my* dad is a control freak). Seems like poor Dad was always getting whacked for the way he raised me—last time it was for handing me over to the Rangers. (Nobody ever tried to argue that the dragons had handed Lois over. Duh.)

So some enterprising reporter started looking for other kids and there *are* only Martha and Eleanor and Eleanor took over immediately and said that they'd known about Lois from the beginning and like sue her, she's eleven years old. This took the wind out of a lot of political sails, especially when Eleanor told the story of how it was Martha who found out that Lois liked her tummy rubbed, you just had to wear gloves to do it. Hardened senior Republican senators watching on the video link were going "awwwww" and then trying to pretend they were coughing.

Then the Searles tried to make it out that someone had taught Eleanor what to say, but the same enterprising reporter managed to convince Katie to let Eleanor have what amounted to a press conference, with questions from the floor and stuff. By the time Eleanor, perfectly self-possessed and articulate, had explained that it maybe wasn't true that I was the only human who'd ever tried to mom a dragonlet—there were one or two old Australian folk tales about it (they're in one of Mom's books) but they were so bizarre that the white guys that translated them thought they were about taking too many drugs, the Searles had *lost*. And without the Searles goading them nobody wanted to look bad by trying to put me or Dad in jail. So it was Gulp and Lois and Smokehill to a landslide victory. Just like Eleanor's is going to be when she runs for president in forty years or so.

I've gotten ahead of myself again. But this is sort of the happy ending part—or at least the cautious if a trifle shaky happy beginning—and also I didn't think the story was going to go on this *long* and I'd like to get it over with. But there's some other stuff I want to tell you the real version of. Like the animal rights activists breaking into Smokehill and letting all the things in the zoo out and how one of them (the zoo critter, not the activist) tried to eat Eleanor. There's a lot that happened in those last few weeks, after Lois and I fled west and the Searle army closed in, but I can't be bothered sorting out most of it, and there are already millions of people writing magazine articles and thumping great books on everything to do with Lois and dragons and Smokehill now so you can read *them*. I'm mostly only writing this at all to make Dad and Martha happy, and a little bit to try to get in some of the stuff all the other great thumping books leave out, or get wrong. Like the animal activists—there *weren't* any, okay?—and anything even *trying* to eat Eleanor.

They'd started having regiments or units or whatever you call them of the National Guard (let me see, a noise of consultants, maybe a Saruman of National Guard?) moving in on Smokehill. The president hadn't quite declared a state of national emergency but I guess he'd allowed as how there was at least a clear and present danger of something or other. (All of those thousands of ten-mile-long dragons are *hungry*.) You remember a busload of tourists had actually seen a dragon flying about half a mile away— so just how much obviously threatening behavior are we going to put up with from this final handful of a nearly extinct creature, anyway? The Searles' spin doctors made it sound like it was like an armada of kamikaze bomber dragons and the tourists on that bus were all in the hospital being treated for Posttraumatic Stress Disorder. So the guys in camouflage with funny hats rolled a couple of helicopters in.

You remember that helicopters are the only things that can fly in here, and even they have instrument difficulty, and first you have to get 'em through the gate, but after one of our dramatic rescues about twenty years ago we got a little tiny extra driblet of congressional money to build a garage outside the gates where all the garages and the parking lot are, to hold a flatbed truck that would carry a helicopter with folded-up blades through the gate. We couldn't afford a helicopter but we had our very own flatbed helicopter-carrying truck, which I suppose at least saved transporting *it*, since it went about five mph and made our solar buses look sporty.

There wasn't any place to put everybody so at first the Guard and their helicopters were camped outside the gate, and there was a lot of shouting about that, because the gate was so (comparatively) small and if they had to "mobilize" quickly, there'd be a bottleneck. Also the tourists objected to their parking spaces being taken up by heavies in uniform, since Smokehill was still open for business. Eventually Dad got semi-overruled and most of the people still stayed outside the gate but the first two helicopters and three guys to look after them got brought through. Our new tourist attraction. Not. (But it freed up some of the parking lot.) Well, that made everybody in *our* party really nervous, because the last thing they wanted was any of this gang being able to move anywhere fast, so people began to think of creative ways to make sure this didn't happen.

Martha started chatting up one of the guard Guards— have I mentioned that she'd started getting really *cute* when she hit her teens?—and he showed her a lot more about his helicopter than he should have, but then she's just a dumb girl, isn't she? So when the order finally came that they were going to start Operation Dragon Vanquish (I am *not* kidding) by finding out what had happened to me, there was a flurry of people putting plans of action into action. I don't know exactly what Martha did to her helicopter (when I asked her she said demurely that she "disrupted the synchronization between the front rotor and the rear one." With a little help from a wrench. "Oh," I said) but that still left one. Now pay attention, because this is where it gets exciting.

Eric *opened one of the cage doors at the zoo.* Just think about that for a minute. Eric. Opened. One. Of. The. Cages. *Eric.* But we were looking at the possibility—no, the *likelihood*—of losing Smokehill, so last-ditch efforts were in order. I'm still really impressed. But this is the best part: If you're going to do something like let something out of its cage to make an uproar, you want to let the one that's going to cause the *most* uproar out, right? Like, you might say, the biggest stink. So guess who he let out. You get three guesses and the first two don't count.

So then he came screaming up to the Institute, which was by then buzzing with Guards doing moving-out things, and all these great horrible (Martha said) army super-jeeps and things were rolling through the gate like Grond at the siege of Gondor, and Eric had a tantrum of, I guess, epic proportions even for Eric (even Eleanor was almost impressed), and nearly brought the entire National Guard to its knees single-handed, between the tantrum itself and—well, you guessed it, right?—*odorata*, who was cavorting around having a high old time doing what *odorata* does.

It just happens that this was all going on during *odorata* mating season, so all the males would have been trying out their courting steps anyway, and while the young males had all been too crestfallen (so to speak) while they were all crammed in the same cage with the big guy, once they got let out they decided to have a stab at the show themselves, so we had mating-dance *odorata* pretty much all over the landscape—I'm sorry I missed it—and big strapping members of the National Guard passing out from the smell right and left (have I mentioned that *odorata* is especially smelly during mating season? Because the males are proving to the females that they can protect them) and Eric trying to kill anyone in a Guard uniform, claiming that some damned soldier had opened the cage door and that he was going to have the entire Guard court-martialed unless they brought the guy who did it forward and let Eric kill *him*. And, you know, one of the reasons Eric was so convincingly off his rocker was that he was worried sick about the possibility that *odorata* might get hurt. He'd decided that it was worth the risk, but he still hated doing it. And it made it really easy for him to *channel* that hatred at the guys who were making it necessary.

Dad had been on the phone at that point for about forty-eight hours straight, trying to get hold of somebody who could cancel the order to do this big search for my dead body—I mean, where's a nice little international incident when you need one? If there'd been any *real* news going on even all the Searles' money couldn't have turned our dragons into a civil war—because he knew that as soon as they found anything they could pretend was evidence that I or anyone else had come to some kind of harm, they'd start killing dragons. Don't ask me how they were managing to discount my twice-daily check-ins—that the dragons were holding a gun to my head and making me say I was okay?

I asked Dad about this when I was trying to write this part, and was sorry then, watching it in his face as he went back to that terrible time. Finally he said, "Nobody sounds too great on our two-ways and the one you were using was worse than usual. Somebody decided that maybe it wasn't really you. That I'd rigged it somehow. That's when they started . . . keeping a watchful eye on me." *Jesus.* If I knew who it was I'd . . . hang him out to *dry* and then give him to the dragons *for their fire.*

So everything had gone seriously wrong enough that Dad—and Eric—thought it was worth it to tell me to get out—the way the party politics were being driven, finding Lois would be even worse than finding me dead—gee, thanks—but whatever they were going to find (or whatever they were hoping to find) they were still going to start looking at Westcamp. Of course back at the Institute they didn't know about Gulp. Dad has said since—and I did *not* ask—that he got ten years older for every day after I disappeared and there was no news of me of any kind. . . .

Anyway. Even *odorata* couldn't make the second helicopter dematerialize, of course, although they were doing a very good job of razing troop strength and creating rampant chaos—and the big strapping guys keeling over weren't later on going to admit that it was just a bunch of smelly lizards, so that's where the violent, club-wielding animal activists got shoved into the story. Okay, there'd been some animal *rights* guys—way too low-key to call activists—hanging around, but they only wielded banners and they never made it through the gate. (Although they did spray-paint one or two of Saruman's jeeps.)

But meanwhile Eleanor was also on the case. While Eric and *odorata* were doing their various dances, Eleanor was hitting herself over the head with a shovel—you know how scalp wounds bleed—and staggering in to the Institute covered in blood and crying for Katie. (Martha says she really was crying and she really was staggering but Eleanor says she wasn't, that it was all planned. Martha says that it wouldn't have worked if she hadn't really been crying and staggering and that she was paying her a compliment so please relax but it was also the *stupidest* thing she'd ever heard of, and I say amen to that, also that she's amazingly brave and maybe that's all that counts, since it worked, aside from the fact that it was an utterly idiotic thing to have done and she's lucky she didn't give herself permanent brain damage.)

Katie understandably pretty much had a heart attack on the spot and gathered up her freely bleeding child and demanded the remaining helicopter to fly them out to the hospital *now*. Dad—who is very capable with needle, thread, sutures, staples, and those butterfly things, as most of us can vouch for—instantly backed her up, and so that's what happened. Martha says she couldn't be *sure* that the reason the helicopter crew volunteered so fast didn't have something to do with the rapidly-spreading *odorata* smell, but the point is that was two helicopters out of two (they never did figure out exactly what went wrong with the other one: ninja chipmunks maybe?), and it took another six hours to get more helicopters "mobilized" to Smokehill, and that's when they started hunting me. That last conversation with Dad was with the new helicopters rolling through the gate but he couldn't just *tell* me that with Saruman monitoring him and that last shout from Eric was only because even Saruman was a little leery of him after his *odorata* performance, and he'd managed to snitch a two-way.

But all of this had given Gulp and me a few more days to

make some kind of a relationship, and who's to say if I'd put my hand on her nose the day before or even six hours before and started thinking pictures at her, it would have worked?

The new helicopters flew directly to Westcamp, and found no me, of course, but all my gear—including all the stuff that would let me stay alive in Smokehill—was still there. *And* of course there were signs of some big animal having been around a lot and a lot of recently-shed dragon scales, if any of them were clever enough to recognize them, which, since it was Handley and his guys, they probably were.

(Dad certainly was, when they brought some of the scales back to the Institute. He says he kept telling himself that we'd all made the best decisions we could have right along from the beginning—from the moment I put Lois down my shirt the first time—and that if it was now all going horribly wrong we still couldn't have done anything else. But that's one of the worst things about this whole story, what those fifteen days I was missing did to Dad. It didn't do anything good for Martha and Billy and everybody else but Dad was, ultimately, responsible, and I was *his* son . . . and I really was the only family he had left. And even if you counted Lois—which I did—she was missing too.)

I don't know if they commented on the vomit but I do know that the glaring lack of blood and guts gave them some pause (nobody had told them dragons generally don't leave crumbs). My stuff had made them decide it was me that was missing after all, no impostors necessary, the lack of blood and guts made them willing to assume that I was still alive, and Dad's phone marathon had eventually put some brakes on the whole gone-bananas spectacle of Dragon Vanquish—but since they had all this hardware flying around already they decided while they were out there they might as well look for me. So they did. And they had some kind of fancy infrared dingledangle and some high-tech bozo to read it, so they could keep looking for human-shaped things of the right temperature, since there would only be one of them out there. Unless another poacher had got in, of course. And unless I was dead after all and the dingledangle wouldn't find me.

I wonder, now, if it was just accident that Bud took us outdoors the afternoon that the choppers were due to fly over that meadow. Because even infrared gizmos can't read dragons through rock. Let alone small human visitors.

And Eleanor has an interesting new scar under her hair, and Eric got *odorata* rounded up again—which wasn't as hard as it might have been because the local landscape doesn't really suit them and they were beginning to drift uncertainly back toward their cages like sozzled party-goers stumbling home at dawn—and there was a record-breaking number of *odorata* babies the following season, so much so that we had to negotiate with some other zoos to build *odorata* cages and take some of them off our hands. But by that time we were golden and any zoo lucky enough to have anything to do with us would do pretty much whatever we said.

I doubt Lois is ever going to get as big as she would have, if she'd stayed with her mom, if her mom hadn't died. And she's still a lot paler than any of the rest of the dragons I've met, although it's become a kind of pinky-coppery-tawny-iridescent pale and—okay, never mind everything I've said about how ugly she is—is really kind of pretty, although I don't know if any of the guy dragons are going to think so when she gets older, and I don't suppose chances are she'll be let (is "let" the right word?) breed, unless the dragons decide that the bond she and I have is the sort of thing that might get passed on somehow—or would be worth passing on. (No, I don't know if dragons have sex for fun too. And I probably wouldn't tell you if I knew.)

Sometimes thinking that I've ruined Lois' life really bothers me and sometimes it doesn't. I mean, she's alive, isn't she? And it's horrible that her mom died, and her brothers and sisters. But at the same time if all that hadn't happened the Institute would still be worrying about how to keep the government from readjusting our status so the oil drillers and the gold diggers and the country-getaway builders and all the other greedy villains could come in and ruin our dragon haven—the only dragon haven left on the *planet* where the dragons are thriving—and now certainly the only one where they hang out with humans.

And yet the millionaire parents of that utter total absolute piece of dog crap that killed Lois' mom nearly got their evil law blasted through Congress (with a little help from the oil drillers) to kill off *all* our dragons. And if they'd succeeded, I don't think the Kenya sanctuary would have lasted much longer, or the Australian park. I've told you, the dragons besides ours aren't doing too well, which in a weird way gives people the excuse to make them do *worse*. And they may not want to admit it, but some of them are glad of the excuse. (We're still waiting to see what effect what's happened here may have on the other two parks. We're waiting *hopefully*.)

Dragons make people very, very nervous. You think the panorama of Gulp and me sells so well because it's cute? It sells so well because it gives people a cold feeling in their throats and a flutter around their hearts. Dragons are, as everyone knows, so *big*. They make Caspian walruses look small. And they aren't safely in the ocean like whales, or Nessie in those lochs—you can't stay on the shore and keep away from them. Dragons belong on land. *And* they fly. *And* they breathe fire. And real dragons aren't beautiful, at least not like the paintings of Saint George. Those dragons may be dying on the point of some dumb hero's spear, but they're also gorgeous. The real ones are just BIG. And strange. And pouched, of course. And smelly. All the photo shoots and TV documentaries can't make them romantic. Just *real*. Which is a mixed blessing. And why, even though we're golden right now, we know we have to work at *staying* golden. Not to mention that the side effect of all this popularity is keeping me out of jail, which is good too.

I keep away from arguments on dragon intelligence. In the first place I can't be bothered, and in the second place I have a good line in being young and dumb myself. I didn't mean to, but you try waking up one morning to discover you're an overnight sensation—especially when you've been tired and scared half out of your remaining half a mind for most of the last two years—and see how well *you* come across in your first big national interviews. (I should have got Eleanor to write my lines.) The first big national interviews that are, as well, going to make the difference between whether your dad and your friends and your entire world gets prosecuted into oblivion or not, for something you did. Sure I agreed to be interviewed—I was desperate.

Well, we won. But most of it hasn't been much fun. Wildly exciting, some of the time, and fascinating, but rarely fun. There's been a lot of pressure on us from the beginning to go on tour, Lois and me. Gulp's too big and also too scary and also practically speaking impossible to transport. Just one kid sneaking back to watch Gulp take off from the Wal-Mart parking lot in East Styrofoam and getting a broken head from being caught in the backdraft would destroy all the good we'd done, not to mention the wear and tear on poor Gulp even if nothing went wrong. (It probably bothers me the most that she'd try to do it, if I figured out how to ask her.) And I won't risk it with Lois either—I wouldn't even when she was still small enough to squeeze in the back of a big station wagon, and the Searles still looked like they might win, and I was still desperate.

Dad backs me up, every time, when I say No tours. And he's still the head of the Institute, as well as my dad. Dad says that I'm the real expert, and he's right, of course, except that "expert" is *not* what I am, but it takes a really big person, it seems to me, to sit back and let your barely-eighteen-year-old son take the lead in your life's work, which is essentially what my dad has done. (Have I mentioned recently that he's the *real* hero? The *human* real hero.) And yet he's as happy as a puppy in a closet full of shoes, because he can finally study his beloved dragons up close—although he's still at the early "ow ow ow" stage of the Headache, which gets in the way. Turns out all humans get it—sometimes even some of the TV crews and they're not even trying to communicate anything except "please do something that will get me a bigger budget."

(And just by the way, Dad and I had the *worst* roaring and thundering argument of my entire life when he found out about *my* Headache. I know what it was, of course—he'd been feeling like a Bad Father all along, about everything, and especially about the eczema, even though I'd managed never to let him *see* it, which probably made him even more suspicious, and the truth is there are more bits of me that will never be beautiful because of Lois, and while Dad kept uneasily letting me make that decision, he didn't like it, and he was pretty sure I wasn't telling him the whole truth, which I wasn't. I never told *anyone* about the Headache. Because I didn't have to. And that pushed him over the edge. I kept yelling at him, "So, what were you going to do? Make me send her *back*?" Stupid of me maybe to tell him at all, but it was going to come out anyway as soon as he read about it here.)

I might as well be writing this as working on my dictionary because my dictionary is getting nowhere fast. Not that in some ways we aren't getting *somewhere*—or I hope we are. It's pretty funny watching Lois—often now with Martha—giving Gulp her talking lessons, for example. I've told you that dragons mostly don't seem to talk out loud—or anyway what we'd call words are only maybe a quarter of dragon language and it's a support quarter, not a leading quarter. It seems to me there's a fifth fifth or sixth sixth in there somewhere that I don't even know what it *is*, and I think there's some kind of layers action too. . . . But meanwhile Gulp is learning to burble. What we're going to do with the burble—or the cheep, chortle, peep and whatever else—I don't know yet. But you know, why do dragons have the vocal cords and the larynxes if they don't use them? Maybe they fell out of the habit of talking out loud as they got good at the head stuff. Or maybe they stopped talking out loud after the Australian "war" with chatty, deadly humans. So we're going to begin a *new* habit. I hope.

But the stuff that is the most translatable into human word facsimiles is surface stuff, like where the food is, and bees go back to the hive and tell each other that, you know? And nobody gets into screaming contests about how intelligent bees are. If you were only using your ears and eyes, a dragon sentence like "There is a valley north of that hill that you can see from here, and then west of the hill beyond that which you can't see from here, but you could if you flew up a few [tree lengths? Dragon lengths? I still don't have much grip on dragon measurement and yes this is another problem] which has a good spring at the bottom of it" would come out something like "There is beyond [something] and beyond [something else] [something] of [something] good [something]." And they don't "speak" in "sentence" shapes anyway. You see why I keep getting mixed up.

I'm guessing that Bud and Gulp are still the only ones on the dragon side who are working more or less from the same page (of the dictionary, ha ha) that I am—we're the ones who had our little/big epiphanies, that first day aboveground after Gulp had brought us to Dragon Central. We're the ones who thought "Right. Here's the starting line. . . . Uh, where's the *track*?" Gulp is learning to talk out loud. Bud watches over my shoulder a lot when I'm using my laptop, and he's seen that graphics program. Maybe it's just as well I don't know what a dragon laugh is. And speaking of intelligence, *I* think that the dragons, as we go on yattering and yammering at them (and squeezing our skulls and saying "ow ow ow"), are beginning to feel about us kind of the way we feel about dogs. (And when your dog goes "roooaaaaoooow" at you don't you sometimes go "roooaaaaoooow" at him back?) And we've been living with dogs for forty thousand years and are *still* arguing about how best to get our point across to them.

Dad, by the way, doesn't disagree when—usually I've

just come away from a particularly frustrating session with some member or members of the white coat brigade, which tends to put me in a ranting sort of mood anyway—when I say that dragons are *more* intelligent than humans. He says I'm prejudiced, but he doesn't disagree. He just says we don't know yet. He likes not knowing. He likes the process of finding out. It makes him happy. It's the first time since Mom died he's been happy.

And we're actually *talking* about her for the first time. Or not talking about her so much as just letting her be part of the conversation. Mom said this, Mom said that. (And I wish I had more of her humor when the white coats start sticking me with their specimen-impaling pins, which is what it feels like sometimes. The scientists who can't stand the head-aches but don't give up easily study *me*.) But it's like she's part of our family again. The door's been opened. It was like *nailed* shut for six years but it's open now. I knew something important had happened when I heard him call her Mad, one evening, at dinner with Billy and Grace. Up till then if he mentioned her at all he called her Madeline, which he'd never used when she was alive.

It makes both of us miss her more in some ways but . . . well, it's the way it is. Somebody you loved dying isn't something you get over, you know? You get used to it because you have to. You carry it around with you—because you have to. And even after I stopped scratching my cheeks and playing Annihilate all the time and became something more like normal again from the outside, missing Mom was still in there doing stuff to me.

Since Dad and I started talking about her again I've stopped dreaming about her. This is mostly a relief, but I miss it a little bit too. And since Lois has dragons to teach her how to be a dragon I don't dream about Lois' mom either. I miss those dreams a little too. I just don't like people *dying*, you know? And Snark would have been way jealous of Lois, but he'd've got over it. And at least Snark was old, for a dog. It wasn't exactly okay that he died, but it so *wasn't* okay in *any* way that my mom and Lois' mom died.

So the short answer to that question I asked way back at the beginning is . . . yes. If Mom had still been alive and I'd still been more or less, you know, sane, I probably wouldn't have noticed the dying dragon's eye, not the *momness* of it. I would have been horrified and sorry—and I'd've got on the two-way as soon as I got clear of the remains of the poacher, and called Billy, and the story would have been a lot different because there would have been no Lois. Even if I'd noticed that one of mom dragon's babies wasn't quite dead yet, that would have just been one of the horrible things, that it took a little while to die, that I had to watch the last one die while I waited for Billy. It would never have occurred to me to *do* anything about it—what could I possibly do? Eric's got incubators, but a fetal squodge wouldn't anything like make the journey back—and of course an incubator would never have worked on a dragonlet anyway.

Or back up a little farther yet—if I hadn't been a jerk about my first overnight alone in the park—if I hadn't been determined to make that twenty miles—I would never have seen the dying dragon in the first place. But why *was* I so determined? What *was* mom dragon putting out on the airwaves as she lay there dying—about being a mom and dying and leaving her babies behind? And why was it me that picked it up instead of another dragon? And I wouldn't want to bet against it that it was partly *frenzy* that helped keep Lois alive—that I COULDN'T BEAR her dying—because of what her and her mom reminded me of.

So is Lois, and just maybe the entire future of *Draco australiensis*, worth Mom's life? I don't have to answer that. It's what happened.

Anyway. I pick up some of the head stuff. Yeah. It's there, I'm not imagining it, and I'm not going to argue about it any more. But I think the only reason I pick up even as much as I do is because I'm picking up some of the *dragonness* of it, and I can do that because of Lois—and her mom. Which isn't something I can pass on to anybody else—yet. But the possibility that there's some kind of osmosis going on also gives me the best excuse to go on *living* with dragons, which I do, a lot of the time now, although even I have to take a break sometimes. Also the weather sometimes has something to say about where you are and where you stay in Smokehill.

There are fancy new premises (built by more Dragon Squadron money) out near where the dragon caves are—the dragon caves I stayed in, that is, since I (and Dad) aren't making any statements about whether they're the *only* dragon-inhabited caves in Smokehill or not—we're pretty sure not. It's still hard, counting dragons—and those caves go on and on and they *all* have spooky gremlin things-moving-around-in-the-dark noises. Now that we're meeting our dragons face-to-face it should get easier though, shouldn't it? Well, we still never see more than a few of them at a time, and I'm pretty sure I'm the only human who's ever seen more than the same half dozen that are the *human liaison committee* (sorry, little joke here—dragons do *not* do bureaucrat language).

I'm pretty sure now that Billy was worried that the caves up by the Institute we were going to open to the public had dragons in them somewhere, or were connected to caves that had dragons in them somewhere, or at least spooky gremlin noises in the dark. Although he's never said so. And part of that fear would be the suspicion he and Dad both had that we weren't going to go on stopping *australiensis* from going extinct for much longer, and what if the tiny little additional pressure of lopping off the tailest tail end of the Smokehill cave network was the tiny little additional pressure too far?

And somehow once the money started pouring in, the plans for the Institute caves changed. Only the first couple of caverns got opened to the public after all—and all the ways out of them have been very, very, very, very, very, very thoroughly sealed off—although it's like having won the main issue, there was a kind of hands-washing-of, *right okay now go ahead and do your worst* declaration and the pointy-head designer from Manhattan or Baltimore *did*, and those two caves, which are good big ones, are a kind of Madame

Tussaud's of dragons with a little Disneyland thrown in. I can't bear the place myself but tourists cram in there in their gazillions.

But it makes me wonder what the Arkholas know that they still aren't telling us. There were always a lot more of them and only one of Old Pete—and he's the only one who wrote anything down, and while he couldn't be bothered most of the time talking about humans, he did often write about how he couldn't have done what he did without Arkhola help, and how much he admired them. What the Arkholas do instead of keeping journals is make songs. There's one I think I haven't told you about, about dragons flying. And the most interesting thing about it is that it's really old—long before Old Pete brought any dragons here. I'm so horrible at learning languages. But I'm going to have to try to learn Arkhola. Billy says Whiteoak would teach me. Uh-oh.

Anyway. We've got these fancy new premises pretty near Dragon Central—that's Bud's caves—which we call Farcamp. We had some trouble deciding where to put it. I didn't want the dragons to feel that we were harrying them by getting too close to where they lived, but as Dad and Billy pointed out, us feeble little humans can't actually commute very far in a day, and we need to be somewhere close enough to get there and back, especially in less-than-optimal weather (in bad weather you don't go *anywhere*) since except me nobody's ever been invited to stay, if you want to call what Gulp did inviting. I said that if the dragons wanted to talk to us, *they* could do the commuting. We finally compromised on a place near a biggish opening aboveground of a series of caves not too far for feeble humans, which are some kind of wing of Dragon Central, but not dead close to where the helicopter found me standing on Bud's head and screaming.

There was a lot of grumbling when the plans for Farcamp were presented because of all the tactical problems (see: no more roads and limited helicopter usage *and* they still haven't got anywhere with the pack ponies, but we've now got college kids and off-season athletes doing two-legged bearer stuff which is a hoot, like something out of an ancient Stewart Granger movie about Darkest Africa) and then when they get there, there *still* aren't any dragons??, but Dad and Billy and our eco-loony Friends had worked up some heavy environmental impact stuff that made it necessary not to be any closer to Dragon Central, and since we were now the hottest topic around nobody grumbled too loudly for fear of not getting clearance to visit.

But the dragons *do* come, to us, to the Farcamp caves. There's always at least a couple of members of the human liaison committee waiting for us politely at the cave entrance—which I call Nearcamp, another of my feeble human jokes. Although the whole business of working this out really made me want to go "neener neener and who says dragons aren't *intelligent*?" I also saw the caves before the dragons started using them a lot, and I've seen them now that they do use them a lot, and I can tell you that they've put in a latrine. And I can't actually swear to this, but I think the rock is getting blacker and redder and shinier and silver-threadier too. And the gremlin noises get more *resonant.*

But I'm the only human who's got in that far—to see the latrine, or listen to the gremlins in the corridors. This makes more of the white coats nuts, but they can't do anything about it. In the first place, most of them, the headaches make 'em so sick they have to flee back to Farcamp, in the second place, it's in the new dragon-contact *rules* (and guess who helped write them), and in the third place, who is going to get around a dragon lying across the entrance of his or her cave? Even if you had the nerve to tiptoe up to one and maybe pretend you didn't want to disturb it and would just creep past, the moment it turns that *eye* on you, and it will. . . .

The human reception area at Dragon Nearcamp is still pretty minimal. This was my idea first, but not only my dad but also a few of the brighter ethologists and sociologists that the new, expanded Institute was already attracting were saying the same thing. When us humans want human stuff, we'd go back to Farcamp and decompress. But it's turned out to be totally practical as well as sensible because I'm still the only human so far who can hack the headaches for more than a few hours, although Dad and Martha are beginning to learn. Nobody but me has ever picked up a mental image they can use (although I wonder about Martha, with her empathy, which seems to me almost telepathic, but she says it never comes in anything you could call pictures), but they sure do get the headaches. Real howlers, sometimes, and with visual disturbances, sometimes really *graphic* hallucinations, and a good bit of vertigo and nausea thrown in.

I don't know if I put up with the headaches better because I'm getting something out of them, or because they're not as bad as what everybody else gets or because I sort of grew into them. If it's that they're not as bad, I'm *really* sorry. Maybe we'll get over this eventually, or find a way around it. We've only just started after all. I figure we have the time. I hope we have the time. I'm worried that some ruthless impatient human is going to decide that the only way—or the fastest way—would be to raise a dragonlet the way I raised Lois, which I can't believe any dragon mom would agree to. Would any *human* mom—? Exactly. But there's still a little problem sometimes convincing the rest of the human world that dragons aren't still *just animals*.

I've also tried to find out—mostly from Bud—if trying to talk to humans, well, not if it gives them headaches, exactly, because I wouldn't expect it to be the same thing, but if there are any *drawbacks* to trying to talk to humans— anything that goes wrong with the dragon because of talking to humans. I can manage to get the idea of pain across—I think—and I'm pretty sure Bud is blowing me off. I'm *such* a master at being blown off. My impression, for what it's worth, which is probably nothing, is that there is some kind of recoil, for dragons, but physical pain isn't it. This worries me too. But it might explain why there aren't too many of the human liaison committee, and why the rest of them tend to stay out of our way.

We've just been so **LUCKY** in a lot of ways. Major Handley was maybe our first piece of brilliant luck—at that black bleak moment when it looked like the Searles and their gang of crooked creeps were going to win. A career military guy capable of independent thought when his *orders* were to shoot first (as I found out, although not from him) and ask questions later. You don't get luckier than that. But a bright career military guy who obeys orders still had to stop and think about *how* to obey his order. I wasn't running away, you remember—I was running *toward* the big black scaly monster of all the Searles' bluster—and then Bud did his extension-ladder trick and the major looked at me standing on the top of Bud's head and waving and shouting and figured that while I looked pretty upset, I didn't look like it was the *dragon* that was upsetting me. And that moment, I think, is when our luck turned.

There are a few things that haven't gone according to plan. They still haven't repealed the law that makes my saving Lois' life a life-sentence felony. They've changed pretty much all the other bad laws about dragons but they can't seem to shift that one. Don't ask me why. The human world makes less and less sense to me. But that's one of the reasons we need to stay an internationally trendy soap opera with rare endangered animals. And me a pop star that no one dares prosecute.

Some of the other reasons are lying around me like medium-sized mountains as I write this, in the dragon Nearcamp. I'm the only human here tonight. Katie doesn't let Martha come as often as either of us would like—she thinks the headaches might stunt her growth or something. If they stunted mine, I'm *grateful*: being loomed over by dragons makes me really dislike looming over other humans—and there's a really nice ethologist from Illinois who's been here most of this week. She's done almost all her work with horses but she gets it about dragons, I think because she doesn't assume her horses are just dumber than humans. They're *horses*. But she had to go back to Farcamp because of the headaches—and in fact I had to lead her out of the cavern because she was seeing so many starbursts and whirligigs. What people see varies—she's a starbursts-and-whirligigs type. She'll probably be back in a day or two after she's had a lot of sleep and a large bottle of aspirin.

It's getting late and almost everybody here is asleep. Lois is the nearest to me—only a small hillock, maybe the size of a big pony—a rosy, bronzy hillock in the purply reddish firelight, snoring into my shoes. (Most dragons don't snore either.)

I don't *think* dragons have a written language—although I've started to wonder about some of the scratches on the walls here and at Central: I started out thinking they were geological, and then I thought they were about the dragons hollowing out their living quarters to suit them, but lately, hmmm—anyway I still don't *think* dragons have a written language, exactly, maybe they're just doing a dragony Lascaux thing. Maybe they make songs, like the Arkhola. Hmmm. . . . But Bud spends so much time (as now) watching over my shoulder when I'm using my laptop (he doesn't seem to have any trouble staying awake) that I'm not so sure about that any more either.

And then sometimes I think he's just doing some kind of experiment in communication when he knows I'm concentrating on something else, because when he's looking over my shoulder I usually have this really strange, low-down headache, almost a throat- or a chest- or a stomachache. . . . I admit I'd just as soon not wake up some morning and discover I'm growing scales and spinal plates. I mean, if it's necessary, okay, but I'd rather *not*.

You're trying to be as objective as you can when you take notes. Mom and Dad—Mom in particular—had this whole rant about There Is No Such Thing as True Objectivity—but then she was a *very* Bad Scientist—and for ordinary lock-the-lab-and-go-home-at-night scientists, maybe how they are is not so important, but in my dragon notes I almost always start out by mentioning what sort of a state *I'm* in—which is something I learned from Mom. If you've been up all night feeding orphans, it shows, next day, in your work (she said) and it's just arrogant of you not to make note of it. Pretty much everything I ever wrote in the first year of Lois' life starts SOS, which stands for Short of Sleep. How can it *not* be important to how reliable my notes are when I'm so tired I'm hallucinating dragons hiding behind the trees around Billy and Grace's house?

My notes now start with H, HH, HHH, or, occasionally, HHHH, which is about headache intensity. XH is the new Bud headache. This that I'm writing now is headed XH, and I'll look over all the H headings when I get back to Farcamp or the Institute and probably try to even them out a little. And I have an increasing series of symbols for moods and feelings and stuff, although that's partly because I think some of the moods are actually dragon-language-background-layer and not me at all.

I have trouble reading some of my early notes about Lois because I was still trying to make up a shorthand that wouldn't get me slapped in jail and Smokehill turned over to developer piranhas if anyone found one of my notebooks, or broke the password on my computer (I am *not* a computer genius). I can read most of them, but not all of them. But everything, up till I started this, was still all notes, daily fragments and questions with no answers and unconnected details and ravings (lots of these). Dad's the one who told me that how I felt about all of it is valid too. Maybe our first conversation about it, when he started really leaning on me about writing this, went like this: "Valid for *what?*" I said. "Who cares? Lois is who's important—and now all the other dragons."

Dad made scritchy noises running his fingers through his beard. (I don't think I'm just being whatever-my-old-man-is-I'm-not-going-to-be although maybe I am, since it's obvious that unless I'm kidnapped by aliens and even if I don't ever get any PhDs I'm going to be head of the Institute some day too, but I *shave*. Actually one of the reasons why I shave may be the scritchy noises Dad makes when he's thinking about something.)

"You're the human," said Dad finally. "Sure, it's about our dragons, but most humans are mostly interested in other humans. You're a way for the ones who aren't so interested in dragons to get it. By tuning into *you*. And I know you don't want to hear this, but it's your story too."

Actually this freaked me out. I can just about stand having Bud staring over my shoulder all the time and Lois glued to me (almost) all the time, but they're my *friends*. I don't want a lot of strange humans staring at *me* for a clue. Not me, boss.

But then I thought about what Dad had done, keeping the Institute going—have I reminded you recently that he's the real hero of this story?—and I thought about Eleanor on national TV . . . and then my mind did a sort of somersault and I thought about all those books I read when I was a kid about ordinary kids who lived in towns with streetlights and movie theaters, who went to school and played football and ate at McDonald's. The way I'd *sucked* them down, because I wanted to *know*. And okay, they were fiction, but they were real fiction, if you follow me, and how did the authors know how to make them up?

So then I thought about how I had felt about all of it. I thought about what had been going on behind the notes, as I reread my notes. And then I thought, okay, maybe I'll try it. And then I got the worst case of writer's block you can imagine, and I buried myself in dragons in the hopes that the Headache would hammer it all out of me. Either the writer's block or, preferably, this idea of Dad's (and, it turned out, Martha's too) about writing about how I *felt*.

And how I feel, here, in a cavern full of dragons, is that it's all so *interesting*. Which maybe you're thinking is an anticlimax, but in that case I feel sorry for you because that just means you don't really know about interesting. Interesting is as good as it gets—and no I'm not getting all *masculine* here, okay? I can say the word "love" and not throw up or turn blue. It if makes you happy, you can say that interesting is part of love—and if you'd like me to say I love my dragons, fine, here we go: *I love my dragons.*

But it's turned out to be so much more than *just* (!) raising one baby critter no human has (probably) ever raised before. I'm still scared to death too—not *of* the dragons any more (except in terms of the fact that they're still BIG and I wouldn't survive being stood on, however accidentally, and however sorry they were afterward), but *for* them. Every now and then I heave this huge sigh like my lungs are going to burst before I get enough oxygen in and out of them, and it's *all about everything.*

I have to kind of get up and give myself a shake every now and then, like a snoozing dog, or one of those cartoon characters rattling himself back into shape after a piano or a brontosaurus falls on him, if the dragons and I are in the caverns. But if we're outdoors and we've started early and it's a nice day, I'll suddenly wonder why it's getting dark and why I'm so hungry and I'll realize we've been at it for twelve hours or more. (Dragons eat about every third day, I think.) Part of this is the headaches—they're confusing— Martha calls it *fuzzying,* and she's right, it's like they rub up your brain till it looks like a sweater a cat's been clawing— it's not just that they hurt, although pain can make you stupid too, even if it's a pain you're used to. I wish I could figure out what Bud isn't telling me about not getting headaches.

And I guess I've grown up strange, probably as strange as Lois, in my own way. But I was already strange four years ago when I met her, when she wasn't quite as long as my hand. But—if you're asking—I wouldn't have any other life. (There. That's how I *feel.*) I wanted to work with dragons, and you can't get any more working with dragons than this. Some of the old lifers here are about the only people who still treat me like I'm normal—without thinking about it, I mean. Even a lot of the Rangers are a little, I don't know

how to put it, awkward. Wary maybe. I should be a fresh-
man at some college this year, hanging out at the student
union and drinking beer. I was too young to drink beer
much when I met Lois, and I can't now, because of the headaches. You could say that while Lois has finally got to return
to her people, my reward has been to leave mine. But it *is* a
reward, even if it's a little complicated.

Hey, it's late. The fire's dying and I think my battery is
too. Even Bud's eyes are almost closed: just a glint where the
lids meet in the middle. I'm going to shut up now and get
some sleep myself.

EPILOGUE

I wrote all that five years ago. (So, yeah. I've got all old and gross and legal-adult and everything. Deal with it.)

It's taken that long to get it through the Searles' lawyers. When I wrote it I hadn't even thought about the Searles'-lawyers aspect. I was only worried about trying to tell the story as well as I could without looking like any more of a moron than I had to—plus what people like Dad and Eric would think when they read about themselves. I wasn't trying to hurt anyone's feelings (although I admit hurting the Searles' feelings didn't bother me a lot) but where do you start, or where do you *stop*, telling the truth?

But it's the Searles that were the real problem. Somebody told me what I'd written was going to have to go through some legal stuff and I said "whatever" and went back to my dragons. Then it took months to hear any more—but I'd never been *happy* about trying to write the story of Lois' early life so I wasn't sorry that it went away for a while. Then we started getting legal letters. At first I thought, Drop dead, I'm not changing anything, and then I thought, Hey, great, it's not going to get published after all and go out into the world and be read by strangers . . . and then *Dragon Drivel* came out, or whatever dumb thing they finally called it, which is the "sensitive" version I mentioned on the first page, and it was even more gruesome than I'd expected. So then I thought, Well, okay, I'll have a try at changing what the Searles don't like—or I'll try to change some of it. Our lawyers had helpfully highlighted what they thought were the most controversial bits.

And I did try. But then I thought, I'm supposed to be nice about the Searles and their psychopath son when I'm not being nice about my own family? And if I start being nice about everybody all that's left is the me looking like a moron part. So then I went stubborn all over again and said "drop dead" officially, and our lawyers translated that into legal speak and . . .

So it's been five years. And I didn't change anything after all. Our Friends got involved and it was all going against the Searles—even I felt a little sorry for them—a little—they're stuck in their own reality warp which they have to make everyone else agree with, except almost nobody does any more, however much money they spend. But I suppose it's hard saying "yes okay our son was a rotten evil creep."

Rereading it now—now that we've finally got the go-ahead, which gives me the grisly opportunity to have a fresh attack of second, or two-hundred-and-sixty-fourth, thoughts about doing it—what I remember most was how OVERWHELMINGLY shut in and squashed and paranoid it was, Lois' first two years. Even "claustrophobic" sounds kind of loose and easy, compared to what it really was. I know, I said this at the beginning, I said I didn't want to go back there, back to that tiny cramped heavy scared space, I didn't want to have to live through it again to write about it. But it gets worse with time, not better. I can feel the walls leaning on my elbows and my head is suddenly the only thing keeping the ceiling up as I reread what I wrote. Even though mostly things *didn't* happen, you know? Mostly they were still just days . . . *and* oh-by-the-way the crazy, appalling obsessiveness of every one of those days. Necessary? Sure. Fascinating? You bet. A fun time? *No cheezing way.*

I also keep thinking about all the stuff I left out. Maybe I left the wrong things out, you know? Too late now. I can get back there even less now than I could five years ago, and I'm not going to try.

Which reminds me of the conversation I had with Eric after I'd given what I'd written to him to read. He didn't say anything immediately when he gave it back, although that

wasn't necessarily a good sign. Eric's got human lately, by
the way. He's got a boyfriend. Yup. Boyfriend. He says himself (I told you he'd got human) that it hadn't ever occurred
to him that he was *gay*. He knew he wasn't very interested in
girls and then just didn't think about it any more—maybe he
was just 100 percent animal oriented—and Smokehill or
any place where you're dealing with tourists all the time is
not going to improve your opinion of the human race. Then
one day Dan kissed him and (he says) it was like . . . oh.

He looked at me and I waited for the blast. It's not like
he's not Eric any more, although the expression on his face
was a lot more sardonic and a lot less toxic than it would
have been before Dan. I tried not to shuffle my feet.

"Yeah, okay," Eric said finally. "Fair's fair. I was pretty
much a bastard in those days and I was more of a bastard to
you than to most people. But you were . . . bless your little
pointed head, you were such a lightning rod for it.

"I don't deny anything you've said in here"—and he gave
my manuscript a flap—"but there is other stuff. Like that
your self-absorption was way beyond spectacular long before Lois." He brooded, continuing to give the big wodge of
manuscript little jerky flips. The middle pages were starting
to stick out from the rest. I probably wanted to be mesmer-
ized by this because I didn't want to listen to what he was
saying, but I did think about what was going to happen when
those middle pages finished slithering out and you know
how the harder you grab on to the outside the more of the
middle waterfalls out. Maybe Eric and I could bond some
more over putting them back in order. I don't think so.

"The best thing about you when you were a kid was that
dog," he said. "That was a really nice dog and you did a really good job with him. So there was that in your favor.
Outside of that . . . you were so convinced you were the center of the universe—and the worst thing was you were right.
You were the only child of the directors of the Institute, and
the directors of the Institute were the rulers of the only universe that mattered. You bled arrogance like a slug leaves a
slime trail."

Eric's way with words.

"Jake, stop staring at your manuscript and look at me," he said, testily. That sounded so much like the old Eric I had to smile. I also looked up. He smiled back, sort of, but it was a pretty steely smile. "I was the grown-up, so I admit it was my fault, and my responsibility, and I didn't do it very well. All right, I did it *lousy*. And it maybe needed someone like you, someone catastrophically self-absorbed, and someone furthermore who doesn't have a clue about anything but his own strange little world—have you ever had a McDonald's hamburger, for chrissake?"

"Once. I didn't like it."

Eric snorted one of his laughter-substitute snorts. "Well, come to that, I don't like McDonald's food either. But I was twenty-six when I applied for the job here. I'd spent twenty-six years living in cities. Where there are always people everywhere—their noise, their buildings, their garbage—even if you're out in what passes for the country there's a permanent light haze at night from the nearest city and you're still smelling car exhaust. And you can always hear a car on a road somewhere, or your neighbors' TV through the common wall—and your electricity comes on wires from the power station. It may have taken someone like you to raise Lois—to raise a Lois. Someone far enough out of what passes for normal experience to connect with a dragon. That didn't make you a joy to have around."

"A misfit," I said, half involuntarily. I didn't really want to encourage him to keep talking about this, but I couldn't help myself. "A mutant."

"Nothing wrong with your genes," he said, and I remembered that my father was his staunchest supporter and Mom had actually liked him. "But a misfit, if you like. Just as Lois is. And the *mis-fit* the two of you have made together is changing the world. And yes, I was jealous, when I got here, watching you. That's the part Martha's got right. If a fairy godmother had offered me the chance to be a misfit like you—to grow up in Smokehill, to know it as the only world there is—I'd have been all over her."

"I do—I don't—I read the news—" I started to say, I started to try to say with some kind of dignity.

"Oh, the *news*," Eric said, like you might say, Oh, the *cat* threw up, or Oh, that's *chewing gum* on the bottom of my shoe. He shook his head. "You've changed. Or I wouldn't be bothering to tell you any of this." He did his laugh-substitute again. "Hell, I admire you now—I wouldn't want to be Jake Mendoza, hero of the universe—anybody designed the logo for your cape yet? Only time I've ever seen anyone with his head that far up his ass just keep on going and come out into the sunlight after all. Wouldn't have said it was possible. All part of the new physics I guess. I'm just saying . . . you were a damned annoying little bastard."

Only half to change the subject, because I also really wanted to know, I said, "When did you figure it out—about Lois?"

Eric looked away—up, down, sideways, as if he was looking for an answer like a lost tool that he must have left around here somewhere. "I can't remember not knowing. But I can't remember some kind of blazing moment of *Eureka! It must be that Jake's raising a dragonlet!* either. It's such a long time ago. Thank god it's all a long time ago." He went silent and broody again, but this time he wasn't looking at my manuscript, but at me, and worse, he seemed to see what he was looking at. More not-shuffling-feet from Jake. "Do you find it hard to remember, now? To believe that it was as bad as it was?"

I nodded. "Yeah. And I *like* finding it hard to remember."

"Yeah. Worst for you—for you and for Frank, and maybe Billy. It still sucked for all the rest of us. First the dead dragon and the son of a bitch who'd killed her, and—that was enough. And all those assholes wandering around, with their cheap suits and cheaper attitudes, demanding to know *everything*, including a lot of stuff they wouldn't be able to get their heads around anyway, but especially not when they'd already decided we were guilty and couldn't prove ourselves innocent. You couldn't turn around without another asshole wanting to know what you were turning around for. And we were guilty of course—just not of what they thought they knew.

"Slowly we all realized we hadn't lost the plot, there *was* something else going on, besides trying to save Smokehill. It wasn't just we'd made something up because we wanted it so badly. We all knew by the time you went off to West-camp, I think. But saying it out loud might make it true somehow the assholes could catch us at. We saw it in each other's faces—and jerked our eyes away.

"It's funny now. But the thing—the *only* clue—that something was going on besides major damage control and the likelihood that we would lose Smokehill—the one thing anyone could actually point to, that didn't look like desperate wish-fulfillment—was the way you were behaving. You weren't even on the planet—which in your case, Jake, is saying a lot. There was this crazy wired intensity about you—but what could be more important than the havoc over the dead dragon, the havoc that might cost us Smokehill? And the way you'd always hated the poor damn lizards in the zoo and the poor stupid fools who wanted to believe they were dragons because at least they were *there* and you could look at them—jeez, chill out—and suddenly all that went away? What else could it be but that you had got yourself a real dragon? And if you could hide it in a Ranger's cabin, it had to be a very small dragon. Baby dragon. So the one that got killed was a mom dragon. Simple. Simple when we knew you."

I took a deep breath and said firmly, "Eric, I always thought *you* were pretty arrogant."

Eric really did smile at that, a long, slow, glinty-eyed smile, like nothing I'd ever seen on his face before. "Takes one to know one, kiddo," he said. "And I dare you to put that in your story."

So I have.

Eric still cleans *odorata*'s cage, if nobody volunteers. What head zookeeper cleans his own cages? Eric's even got staff now. Mind you, I don't think—Dan or no Dan—Eric's doing it to spare anyone. He just doesn't want anyone being mean to *odorata*. So I suppose I have to say he's not only *not* the kind of bully who likes to assign the worst jobs to the people he hates most, that he *let* me clean *odorata* means that even if he did think I was a pain in the ass, I was a responsible, conscientious pain in the ass. I suppose this should make me feel better.

But a tremendous lot has happened in these five years, besides most of us lifers being able to start to *forget*. And if you've got this far in my dragon adventures and have learned to survive (or skip over) my philosophical blather and general rant you might like to hear about some more of it. Help make up for the five years you've been waiting. Ha ha. And if you *have* been waiting, the first thing on your last-five-years list is the story about how Bud almost flew through the front gate—at least according to the mail we, especially me, gets, that's the first thing on your list. (I get a lot of lists. People seem to think I'm going to find them helpful.) But if this is all really a soap opera with dragons—as it is, according to the mail—you might want to hear some of the rest of it too.

Like how I asked Martha to marry me. At Dragon Central with Bud watching us. Not that he knew that I was asking her to marry me (although I never know what he knows really). *I* didn't know I was going to ask her to marry me. I was doing my famous dragon headache skull squeeze—I've got pretty good at this; I can temporarily ease about 75 percent of human dragon headaches in about 75 percent of humans who get them (which is to say *all* humans who spend any time at Nearcamp). Although unfortunately it seems more to do with my hands than with the squeeze, which means I haven't been able to teach anybody else to do it, which is bad news for at least two reasons, the first being the obvious one and the second being that this contributes to the Great Jake Myth and while five million acres is plenty to hide in most of the time there's no escape from the mailbags they bring every day *and* I've begun to wonder if I'd better never go out the gate again myself ever either. Just like the dragons. (I did finally learn to do TV, but only because the public was so weirdly eager to love me that they turned my deer-in-headlights mental and physical paralysis into becoming modesty, and after that it was like, oh, well, okay, if it's going to be that hard to do anything wrong I suppose I might as well relax and go with the flow.) At least we had our honeymoon in Paris.

So that evening at Dragon Central, it had kind of been in the back of my mind for a while, I'm a retro kind of guy in a lot of ways and I'd begun to feel I was getting (even) less normal with every arriving mailbag and/or TV interview and I wanted to do this *normal thing* of marrying my sweetheart, okay? I was kneeling behind her and she was half lying with her legs stretched out in front of her, but she'd leaned back so her forearms and elbows were braced on my thighs and her face tipped up toward me with her eyes closed and even upside down she was so beautiful, so *Martha*, that I heard my voice say, "If you married me, you could get this on demand."

Martha's eyes opened and she smiled an upside-down smile. "I can get it on demand now." She closed her eyes again, and probably my grip on her skull faltered a little, because she opened her eyes and said, "That doesn't mean I won't marry you."

"But does it mean you *will* marry me," I said, pathetically, and she pulled herself up and out of my hands and turned around and said, "Yes, of *course* I'll marry you, you silly man, and I won't even tease you about it being for your hands," and then she kissed my hands, one after the other, and then she kissed *me*.

Bud was lying there with us—or some of the end of his nose was (the loooong hot rising and falling gust of his breathing politely angled past us), the rest of him going on and on to Wyoming or so the way the rest of Bud always does—and his eyes were half open, watching us, although it's interesting, there's no voyeur thing about it when he watches us, which he does a lot, although I'm pretty sure he has a pretty good idea what kissing is about. So after this kiss had gone on for a while and I started to get it through to myself that I'd just asked Martha to marry me and she'd just said yes, I wanted to jump around and shout and the only person [sic] available was Bud so I said, "Let's tell Bud."

It's a good example of the Marthaness of Martha that she didn't say, "What do you mean, tell Bud? We've spent five years trying to learn to tell dragons *anything*, or they us, and even *you* can't do it." She just said, "Sure," and got up out of my lap and we both went the few steps to Bud's nose and touched it with our hands. One of the things we have learned is that the getting-something-through—and I'm not going to call it "telling" or "communication" because that's a lot more grand than it mostly is—usually works better if the human has a hand on the dragon's nose, slightly depending on what the message is. (There may be other bits of both dragon and human that would work as well, but they'd probably be more embarrassing.) I sort of instinctively guessed that, that day I "told" Gulp that the bad guys were coming for us, and she got Lois and me away—but you tend to grab the other party when you're really urgent about something, and the reflex remains even if it's a dragon's nose rather than a human arm or shoulder. (And for those of us addicted to hand gestures, you still have a hand left over for flapping around.)

The refinement Bud has come up with is that it works better yet if the dragon curls its lip very slightly so the human can put his or her hand on the softer skin there just inside the tough horny outside. It's just about not too hot to bear, although I've begun to suspect that Bud anyway has pretty good temperature control. The first time Bud curled his lip at me of course I thought I was going to die—but he could have eaten me any time for months by then so why now? And if I was going to do something so offensive to dragon culture that I'd get munched in some kind of involuntary reflex (I've told you dragons are amazingly pacific; I doubt they've got any execution laws about anything) I'd probably already done it and *hadn't* been munched, so this new lip-curling must be something else. I figured it out eventually.

So now Martha and I both put our hands (delicately) on the hot red lip-margin of Mr. Dragon Chief and tried to tell him our news. I was thinking pair-bond-life-[that'showhumansdoit]-children-starting-just-now-hooray, more or less—pictures are better, but how do you put any of *that* in pictures? and stuff with high emotional content usually gets across the best even if there aren't any pictures—and Martha, who knew what I'd been trying to do with my dictionary almost as well as I did, was thinking something similar because I could actually feel her like an echo, "talking" to Bud.

And Bud, without moving, opened his eyes all the way and gave a huge sort of held-back (don't want to blow your tiny friends a few hundred yards across the cavern accidentally and bang them into the wall by unrestrained breathing) *wooooooaaaaw*, I mean with sound in it, and I've told you dragons don't use larynx noises much, and it sure sounded like "congratulations" to me. Furthermore Bud's *wooaaw* had roused the other dragons and there were little soft (little and soft as dragons go) rumbly *wooaaw*s from the moving shadows, and one of the moving shadows slipped away—I'd also got pretty good at learning to hear the diminishing huge rustle of a dragon leaving the vicinity: You'd be surprised how confusing dragon noises are; makes most people dizzy (and nervous) till they get used to it, *if* they get used to it—and while Martha and I were still sort of giggling and saying inane things to each other like "I didn't think dragons would be such romantics" there was a coming-toward-us gentle gigantic rustle and there was Gulp. And about two minutes later Lois was there too and for the first time in a year or so she forgot that she wasn't little any more and knocked me down. So Dad and Katie and Eleanor and Billy and Grace and Kit were only the second people to hear that we were getting married. The dragons were first. (Whatever they actually *got* out of what we told them.)

Now if you haven't already, this is probably the point

where you talk about how it's creepy, me and Martha getting
married, we'd grown up together, we were the only boy and
girl either of us had ever really known (besides Eleanor, and
it's going to take a better man—or woman—than me to
tackle her), we should be like brother and sister, and at best
we should go out and *meet other people* first, before we decide on each other, the implication being that then we won't.
Well, in the first place, I don't ever remember feeling like
Martha was my sister, although never having had sisters
maybe I don't know how I'm supposed to feel about one. But
while you're sitting there pitying me for being so limited,
think about it this way, friend: What if you'd met the girl
who was going to be the love of your life when you were
four and a half and got to spend the rest of your life with
her? Is that the biggest piece of luck you could ever have or
not?

Growing up together had also made us able to communicate or anyway react to each other on levels that people who
don't get to know each other till they're adults I think probably never can. I'm not using the "t" word again here. But it
was like that sometimes—like what I just said about hearing
her like an echo when we were trying to tell Bud we were
getting married. Martha and I are in this together, and that's
a big help. It makes it realer, saner, less just *incredible.* Even
if it's more stuff that can't be taught. We'll figure out the
teaching later. I hope.

I think both Katie and Dad had had those "they should
meet other people first" thoughts but life at Smokehill had
got even stranger in the last few years and *no one* would
understand any of it except those of us who'd lived through
it. (Eleanor is going to use this to get elected president, of
course, so her priorities in a partner are going to be different. If she changes her mind she could always marry a really
tough Ranger.) And we'd waited till I was twenty-one and
Martha was nineteen which meant they couldn't really stop
us although we wouldn't have wanted them to try. And they
took it really well after all. I could see them both worrying
but I could see them both being glad too so that was okay.

We didn't tell anybody till it was all over—*and* we were back from our honeymoon. Dad's a JP so he could read the words, and *Eric* somehow got a license to do the blood test. Don't ask me how. Katie cried. Eleanor didn't. Eleanor said, "*Great*. I can have my room back." To Eleanor's tremendous credit, she'd let Martha and me drive her out of their cabin kind of a lot, so we could have the room—they shared a bedroom—a couple of hours in the afternoons sometimes, when Katie was on duty somewhere too so the house would be empty. It wasn't worth trying anywhere else at the Institute—and out at Farcamp and Nearcamp and Dragon Central privacy doesn't exist.

We had the wedding at Dragon Central. This was so great a piece of serendipity it made the whole wedding business even more . . . something. None of the adjectives will do here: great, wonderful, amazing, terrific. Maybe I should just say *wooooooaaw* like a dragon. But about twenty of us Smokehill lifers creeping off to do . . . *something*? No way somebody—some wrong body—wouldn't have noticed and maybe said something to some other wrong body and . . . but twenty of us lifers going to do some kind of private something at Dragon Central? Sure. Everyone goes all hushed and respectful and admiring and wishing they were a member of the magic circle too. It was . . . *great*. Plus having Bud and Gulp and Lois and some of the others there—watching the latest unintelligible human ritual.

I don't remember ever talking about a honeymoon in Paris. Martha's always wanted to go to Paris and I've never wanted to go anywhere (no dragons). So we were going to get married . . . and then we were going to go to Paris. It was simple. I'd thought fine, I'll survive Paris because I'm going to be there with Martha, and she really wants to go, and I'll catch it from her. But I fell for Paris myself—loved it almost as much as Martha did. I kept thinking about being a freak who's barely been out of Smokehill, who's never even been on a plane before (two freaks, only Martha's always known the rest of the world existed, and she's visited her grandparents in Wisconsin a couple of times), and how Paris might have been Mars to us, and if this is what Mars is going to be like, well, those astronauts are going to have a great time when they get there, and I hope the lichen puts on a good welcome.

Dad's wedding present included five nights at this amazing hotel . . . all he'd said was that he'd "take care of it" . . . and I mean *amazing*. Reception was nearly as big as the Institute tourist hall and a lot grander, and our room was nearly big enough for dragons. There was one afternoon I'd actually gone out alone because Martha had admired this ring in a jeweler's window and—when did I ever go anywhere, right?—I hadn't bought her a ring although Katie had bought us plain gold wedding rings at a jeweler's in Cheyenne because she said (mildly outraged) that we had to have wedding rings and we didn't have to wear them after if we didn't want to. Rings hadn't occurred to me so then I thought that I hadn't done it properly (after all I'm Jake the Clueless Wonder Boy) so I was watching Martha *fixedly* like a dog watching you palming a dog biscuit, for any sign of wanting anything I could buy her in Paris, although it didn't have to be a ring. And there *was* this ring . . . so I went out to buy it, I can't remember what I told Martha I was doing.

When I got back she was just getting out of the bath and came out of the bathroom wrapped up to the chin in these huge pink towels so you couldn't see anything of her but feet and face, and her hair tied up on the top of her head all wet and curly, and she said something like, You know, Jake, you're doing really well here in Paris pretending not to miss your dragons every minute and only me to keep your attention . . . and she dropped the towels. I will remember that sight of her—the long golden afternoon light through the window blinds streaming over her like golden ribbons with every curve and hollow highlighted, and the white light from the chandelier in the bathroom haloing her from behind—I'll remember the picture she made when I'm on my deathbed and die happy. Oh yes, and she liked the ring. She wears it all the time. I'm still wearing the ring Katie bought.

It's true I was really glad to see my dragons again. Even after Paris.

So we got back to Smokehill and then Dad released the news and everybody outside was pissed off that we hadn't let our wedding be turned into a circus, and we went off to Dragon Central till the uproar quieted down. And then we got a cabin of our own outside the Institute—a new one (and yes, our Rangers came and sang for us, and I sang, well "sang," a little bit too because Whiteoak *has* been teaching me some Arkhola), beyond the fortress, which has become office and official dragon-studying visitor space, although everyone calls it The Fortress—which was great, having our own *house*, although we still spent most of our time at Dragon Central and Nearcamp.

We pack in some human food and a change of clothing, but that's all. The dragon caves remain *dragon*. Which among other things means you have to be fit and strong enough to climb up and down the dragon "stairs." They're mostly okay at Nearcamp, but the ones at Dragon Central, while they aren't as bad as I'd thought when Gulp was transporting Lois and me, are still pretty hairy for us midgets, and at the foot of a few of the *cliffs* I still had to ask for some tactfully-placed boulders for scrambling. Once you get to the big main fireplace room there are always plenty of shed scales if you don't feel like sitting—or lying—on rock. And warm water in the sulfur pools.

And the answer to drafts in caverns full of dragons is to *lean against a dragon.* Of course you have to choose one who'll remember not to roll over on you—and you say "please" first. Bud will unfold a wing a little and let you—well, Martha and me—sleep under that, which is pretty amazing. A dragon wingtip is surprisingly light, but you can feel the hot blood *whoosh*ing through it. Like sleeping *under* a waterbed. The first time we got stranded by a blizzard it was maybe a little dark—I will never learn to love windowless underground caves and purple firelight—but we were plenty warm enough. And there was plenty of toasted sheep to go around.

Sleeping with dragons is useful too—you know your brain waves change when you're asleep. You pick up dragon stuff when you're asleep that you can't when you're awake—well, I knew that, from that first time I spent with Lois at Dragon Central with probably every dragon there except Bud and Gulp (and Lois) wanting me *somewhere else*. But the wanting-me-out-of-there, and the mortal terror, made the subtler stuff hard to recognize. Especially through the Headache. And then in the early days of Farcamp when I was spending every minute I could get with the dragons it sometimes got to be a little too much—well, I mentioned it five years ago, about not wanting to wake up some day and discover I'd started growing spinal plates. But with Martha with me it was suddenly okay—it was good. I stopped losing being human, you know? No matter how far into the dragon labyrinth I went.

And it also makes sense, about brain waves, in a way that a lot of stuff about dragons does not. But this doesn't mean we're going to start having a human dormitory at Nearcamp, so don't bother asking. You'd never sleep through the head-aches anyway.

Martha and I got married two and a half years ago. That's a really good time to remember. Back a little farther, to when I finished writing this book the last time, that isn't so good. Five years ago is about the start of the really rough year or so I had learning to let go of Lois—and her to let go of me. There's some of that starting to happen at the end of what I wrote back then.

It was sort of easier in a gruesomely traumatic sort of way than it might have been because as soon as the world found out about Lois—as soon as the tape loop with me prancing around on Bud's head started playing around the world—our lives changed so drastically that we didn't know which way was up and which way was down (although if I'd fallen off Bud's head ninety feet up I'm sure it would have hurt, ha ha). So I spent a lot of that first year after the World

Found Out feeling torn apart anyway and "losing" Lois was . . . it was, as I think about it now, not even the *most* shocking thing, which made it worse, if you follow me, how could anything be more shocking than *losing Lois*? Even if all that was happening was that she was growing up and that was good?

But what happened to Smokehill—all that attention and all that money, suddenly, after we'd been this goofy fringy theme-park kind of thing—the theme being our endangered invisible but smelly dragons—counting every penny, and yeah, okay, *paranoid* from the beginning, but we had cause, didn't we? Whatever Eric says about what growing up as the center of the Smokehill universe did to me, it did to me what it did to me because that's how it was. And then Smokehill changed. *Smokehill* changed. Lois and I were just the detonator for the Big Bang and the new universe. It was not so surprising that we lost each other in the process . . . even if we were going to have to lose each other anyway. So that Lois could have the life she should have. And I could have a life at all.

Well, you don't need to know a lot about that, and if Eric's right, then I don't really want to tell you about what even I know isn't me at my best, but it's one of those things I feel I should mention, because it's a *big* thing.

So by the time Martha and I got married Lois was spending most of her time at Dragon Central, which meant she was spending at least a major minority of her time without me, and she'd had a growth spurt about a year after we met Gulp so the idea of touring her died the death more easily than it might have if she'd stayed little longer (although a couple times a year we still get some enterprising head case who wants to provide the specially designed airplane to carry a dragon, and take us around to all the football fields in America, but Dad gives 'em short shrift). And then Martha and I *did* get married and after that it was a whole lot more okay that Lois had her own dragon family and her own life without me.

We still don't know where Lois actually fits in the family,

by the way. The weird thing is that as the new post-Big-Bang hierarchy settled down, Lois got kind of taken over by Gulp while Bud kind of took me over. Oh, Lois and I saw and see a lot of each other, a lot by anybody's standards but ours, and when I was with the dragons she turned up pretty fast and stuck pretty close, and sometimes at first she still came back to the human world with me for a little while.

Grace—and Eleanor—who rarely got out to Farcamp, were always really glad to see her, although "glad" is easier to identify with Grace. Eleanor tended to say things like, "The bigger you get the more you *smell*." Or, "Nobody's going to respect a pink dragon. I hope you're going to turn green or something soon." Although I think it wasn't only that I understood what the words meant that I was the one who got pissed off when Eleanor said stuff like this. Eleanor gets better at aggravating me as she gets older. And Lois isn't really pink anyway. Not *pink* pink. Also I tell myself that Eleanor is just developing useful skills by practicing on me and it'll all be worth it when she hits the campaign trail and makes hash of her opponents during the debates ("and furthermore you *smell*").

But Lois came back to the Institute less and less once she hit her growth spurt. By the end of her third year she wouldn't fit through ordinary doorways any more—and although she didn't have keeping-up problems with people on foot, she couldn't squeeze into the back of a jeep any more either, while her wings weren't anything like big enough yet for flying. She also began to lose interest in strange humans—every new human wasn't immediately her new best friend, the way she had been. She would still turn it on for a TV crew, but you—well, I—could begin to see that her heart wasn't in it. It was as if she was being *polite*. Where did she learn polite?

She was learning to be a dragon. Who are I swear genetically polite. Which was the thing I'd wanted most of all, Lois becoming a, you know, genuine, 100 percent dragon, and that did take a lot of the edge off the whole mom trauma.

What stopped me from getting too comfy about it though was that she was also obviously sweating learning "dragon language" almost as badly as I was. Like maybe there's a developmental window for learning language in dragons the way there is in humans, and if you miss it, you've had it. And that made me feel really, really, really bad.

But there are a couple more things I think I know now that I didn't then—three or four years ago. Now pay attention because I'm not going to tell you twice. I'm getting out into woo-woo territory and I don't much like it out here. Or rather, I like it fine, while I'm *out* there, with Bud, or occasionally some of the others, it's coming back to human ground level with what he or they have given me I find kind of bad, looking at it as a human and wondering what the hell I do with it and how to explain it in any way another human—any human but Martha—is going to believe—or be able to make sense of. Yeah, everybody gives me lots of slack—make that *lots* of slack—because of Lois, but old habits die hard and nobody outside space opera and unicorns likes the "t" word either. Maybe especially when the only stuff I bring back that isn't bits and pieces *is* all woo-woo and nothing I can shake down into words and put in my dictionary. So don't ask me any questions, okay? Just listen.

One of the big questions has always been what Lois' mom was doing having her dragonlets so far away from the rest of the dragons—from anywhere dragons ever go in Smokehill—and especially from her midwives. Okay, you think, maybe the dragons did it differently when they were in cages, and maybe what Old Pete saw wasn't like what they'd be doing on their own. But that's not it.

The reason it happened is because she had a . . . uh, I'm going to call it a vision . . . that told her to. That told her to go off by herself and have her babies alone. I can still hardly think about it, it's so awful—her going off like that, and what happened. And it might explain why Gulp was quite so, well, beside herself, when she first found Lois and me. They'd known Lois' mom died, of course (I think dragons feel it when one of them dies), but somehow they'd missed that one of her babies had survived.

Or then again maybe they didn't miss it. I'm pretty sure I got what Bud is telling me about Lois' mom, but I'm not sure about this. It wasn't till two years later that we started getting those dragon sightings away from the usual dragon stomping grounds. But maybe a dragonlet has to be two years old before it starts showing up on dragon radar. Or maybe Lois didn't show up on dragon radar because her radar was crippled by being raised by humans. Or maybe part of the original vision included that the dragons should go looking for some kind of sign two years after Lois' mom died. (Okay, she did have her own name. It's something like *Hhhhhlllllllssssssssn*. So I call her Halcyon.) I like that version myself—that they didn't know what the sign was they were looking for. Which really does explain why Gulp briefly lost her mind.

It's obvious that all those dragon headaches I was having before there were any dragons around but Lois, weren't Lois herself, but Halcyon, or Halcyon's ghost, if you like, although you probably don't like. Why *did* Lois survive? There is NO WAY that poor globby fetus had a prayer of surviving, stuck down some strange species' shirtfront and fed alien liquids. But she did. She did at least partly because . . . because Halcyon's ghost was making me have Mom Dragon Vibes? (Was Halcyon's vibes coming off a grotesque human dwarf like me what sent Gulp—briefly—mad?) I don't know. But a big piece of the answer about Lois is there somewhere.

Here's the, uh, controversial bit. So far this was just the *easy* bit, okay? I mean I've told you a lot about Halcyon already, but I'm guessing you've been finding it a little hard to believe—you weren't there having the brain version of the hamster running up the inside of your pantleg, and I was, and I still tried really hard to make out that it was just dreams and shock and native goofiness. So I keep trying to make being haunted by a dragon ghost sound more convincing—or maybe I'm just hoping if I mention it often enough you'll start accepting it just because it's *there* all the time like a tree or a house or that tub of yogurt in the back of the fridge that turned green months ago. Familiarity breeds getting to used to the idea. My master plan.

Okay, here we go. Bud believes that what's happened to Lois and me is not only the thing that's going to make it possible for dragons and humans to learn to talk to each other—but that it pretty much wouldn't have happened any other way. Some poor dragon mom was going to have to die all by herself and all but one of her babies die with her and that one remaining baby get picked up by a human just in time for the dying mom to somehow kind of *zap* herself into her surrogate. And the human had to have been young enough and/or weird enough—like maybe dragon-as-center-of-universe weird—for the zap to take. I don't want to even think *about* thinking about the odds . . . or what that might mean about how stuff gets, you know, arranged . . . is it worse to be scared to death by the odds or to consider the possibility that it *was* what-I'm-calling arranged? Brrrrr. Whatever you do with this idea, it makes *me* colder than a cavern without a dragon to lean on.

But if Bud believes it I believe it. Some of the other dragons don't. But there are probably stick-in-the-mud dragons like there are stick-in-the-mud humans, who don't want to believe anything too new and strange and world-detonating, and personally I'd be happy to entertain a better (i.e., less scary) hypothesis if you've got one but I did say *better.*

One thing that makes me think Bud is right, besides the fact that he's Bud, is that while Lois is sweating learning dragon language almost as hard as I am, we talk to each other better than we talk to anydragonbody else, most of the time, Lois and me. Maybe it's not really all that much *better.* But there's a kind of ease or fit to it that I don't have with any of the other dragons, even Bud. For example we have a, uh, let's call it a glyph, although it's maybe more a kind of spasm (maybe helps to explain the headaches, and the *wigglyness* of the dragon alphabet—or alphabets—or that *moods and layers* thing, thinking of a, uh, unit or module or something of it as a spasm) for "frustration" which we made up together out of how we felt about trying to learn to talk to (other) dragons. But when I used it on Bud he knew instantly what I was "talking" about, so Lois and I get gold stars and pats on the head for that piece of initiative-taking homework.

You don't have the smiling, nodding, pointing to your chest and saying your name option with dragons. Nor can you point to another object and say "rock" and wait to see what they say. They won't say anything. If you've been pointing at a rock and saying "rock" for the last six months, however, if you've been working at it really hard, you may have begun to wonder why after you say "rock" you very often get a kind of heavy sensation in the palms of your hands and the soles of your feet (and furthermore it seems a bit *diagonal*. Right hand, left foot. Left hand, right foot). Although the first elation (supposing you manage to be elated through the confusion) drains away real fast as you start to wonder if they're talking about a kind of rock, a size of rock, a shape of rock, a color of rock, weight of rock, age of rock, even a hardness of rock, or a kind/size/shape/color/weight/age/hardness of anything, or maybe it's about something else entirely (Where it came from? How it was created? Or if it's a big rock, which way its shadow falls as the sun rises up over it and goes down the other side, and no I am *not* joking) and maybe it's not "rock" at all, but "thing pointed at" or "humans sure are into rocks, I wonder what that's about?" "Hello" in dragon is a sort of short, stylized flash of . . . something like my first look into Halcyon's dying eye, and it'll knock you over if you're not ready for it.

And there's not a lot you can do about the Headache but try to wait it out. See if you're going to be one of the lucky ones, and that it won't just go on swamping you (flounder flounder squelch squelch), that you'll be able to kind of go with the flow after a while. And that's already supposing that you're one of the (lucky) ones that don't just dissolve into a quaking, gibbering mess the first time you get within hailing (so to speak) distance of a dragon, and, more to the point, don't *stay* dissolved (and gibbering). Almost everybody gets a little melty around the edges on first introduction. But some people can't learn to cope. And you can't blame them—well I can't, anyway. It's the size of three or four Tyrannosaurus rexes, *and* it breathes fire, you know? What's not to be brain-burstingly afraid of?

But despite all the up-against-itnesses, see above, I'd much rather be at Farcamp and Dragon Central because when I'm at the Institute I start to lose faith in my dictionary—and the dictionary has to be what I'm *for*. Maybe I can figure out a way to break the idea of "dictionary" out of words on a page . . . but even the Son of the Son of the Son of the (okay, Daughter of the) Best Graphics Package in the Human Multiverse—I mean the latest update of the one I was using at the beginning—hasn't shown me a way to do it yet. Maybe because all the graphics packages are designed by humans. I need some kind of three- (or four-, or five-) dimensional Senssurround thingummy. Any major computer whizzes out there who want a *real* challenge?

Us humans, we still think word = word, mostly. I'm still best with Lois partly I think because we're kind of on the same level—young and stupid, and, you know, disadvantaged—we didn't get raised right, in our different ways. I'm second-best with Bud but I think the second- part is because *Bud* is so far beyond me.

Here's another thing you're not going to want to hear: Okay, so, maybe it's because they're so much bigger, maybe their brainwaves are bigger somehow or something, and they can't fit in our tiny skulls (that's aside from the three-or-four Tyrannosauruses **eeeeek** brain-melt aspect). But (you sneer: I can hear you sneering) if dragons are so bright, why are they living in caves instead of out conquering the galaxy and living in penthouses and eating their toasted sheep off jewel-encrusted platinum platters?

Now you just sit there and think that back at yourself for a minute. Why do dragons live quietly in caves and human beings have invented global warming and strip mining and biological warfare and genocide? Who's the real winner here in the superior species competition? What dragons do is *think*. That's what they're really good at. Like it or lump it. And that's why when I get out there in the dragon space, it's okay . . . except I'm only a stupid human and I can't go very far, and even as far as I can go it's farther than I can bring back with me to all the other humans, who even when they don't want to kill something or pave something over, still tend to think in terms of x = y and only if x and y both take up normal space in three dimensions and can be measured and checked off a list.

Yeah. I'm prejudiced. Sue me. Or take this book back to the bookseller and demand your money back because you don't like my politics. But all right, enough of the woo-woo and the politics. I'm still human, no spinal plates yet, and I guess I kind of need to spend some time at the Institute . . . and at least that means Martha and I get to sleep in a bed in a house sometimes and the house is *ours* and we can *close the door*. So you can relax now. I'm going to tell you the story you want to hear, about Bud. I'm going to tell you about something that everyone knows happened out here in the human-approved three-dimensional world. Well, let's say something that made the news, which isn't the same thing, but it'll do in this case. And I'm finally going to tell you *why* it happened.

This was about twenty months ago as I'm writing now. I was back at the Institute, stoically showing myself to hordes of tourists (we've got a new amphitheater that'll seat one thousand and when I'm scheduled to do the Q&A it gets booked out way in advance) and grinding away at my dictionary. I do the dragon side of the dictionary better at Farcamp, and I do the human side of the dictionary better at the Institute. Caught between two worlds and don't belong to either? You bet.

I knew Martha wanted kids—although I can't remember ever especially hearing her say she wanted kids, it's just always been there, like Paris, since she was seven or so, and yes, when I was trying to explain "marriage" to Bud kids came into it. But she hadn't started talking about babies like maybe *now* till she was pretty sure I was mostly out of my bereft-mom phase. It has to be a little bit strange to have to deal with a twenty-two-year-old husband who's already been through the full pulverizing parental experience, in an all-new Short Intense Variant of the usual scheme, and is kind of off the wall. But Martha took it in her stride. I guess I'd also got over my earlier decision that nothing on Earth or in the outer reaches of the solar system would ever make me have human children if Lois and I lived through our little adventure, although that had something to do with the idea that these human children would be *Martha*'s babies.

Besides, there were babies in the atmosphere. Because I was pretty sure Gulp was pregnant. I don't know how I knew it, other than I'd got it off Bud, Lois and Gulp herself. (Although Gulp's thoughts/telling/sending/being were significantly different from Lois and Bud's, that made it kind of more likely to be what I was guessing somehow, sort of like how some languages you speak slightly differently if you're a man or a woman or a child. You speak pregnancy differently if you're the one who's pregnant, if you're a dragon.)

I hadn't told anyone but Martha because I didn't want to answer any of the 1,000,000 questions that would follow, or waste more time turning down the 1,000,000,000,000 study proposals the news would produce—although to be fair, poor Dad would have to do most of that part. We had a lot more help than we used to (Eric had *four* assistant keepers, for example, which is how he got to spend time at Farcamp, in spite of the renovated and expanded zoo) and Dad had as many graduate students as he wanted—in fact he had to keep turning them away—but no matter how much he delegated, pushy people were still always trying to go over everybody else's heads and talk to the big chief boss of the Institute, which was still Dad. Some things don't change.

Anyway Martha and I had cleared a little time one day to have a Paris morning, which meant we slept in, which is pretty much an alien concept at Smokehill. And we were talking about babies. Again. There's another reason I'd come around to the idea of human children (so long as they were Martha's). Are you with me here? Okay, so *you* get a gold star and a pat on the head: Maybe the next thing was to try to raise some dragon babies and some human babies *together*. Maybe the reason my headaches had been so bad from the beginning was because I was already fourteen and three-quarters and like my fontanelles had closed years ago. I had no idea how long dragon gestation was, and my experience with Lois wasn't much to go on about normal dragonlet development, but if there was a human baby around about a year after some dragonlets were born which was maybe when normal dragonlets start spending serious time outside mom's pouch. . . .

So not like we knew what our time frame was or anything, including how long it might take for us to provide the human side of our new equation, but it probably wouldn't hurt to start trying. . . .

It should have been a lovely warm romantic morning— we'd had a few Paris mornings before and they'd been a huge success—but it wasn't, this time. It wasn't, because every time this idea of *children* touched me it was like being shot or hit by lightning. It got worse till I was literally jerking with the jolt of contact. I was too confused and (increasingly) upset to think about what might be causing it (aside from brain tumor redux of course) and it was Martha who said, "Someone's trying to get through to you. One of the dragons. Bud. It has to be Bud."

And suddenly she was right—or rather as a result of what she'd said I was slowly orienting in the right direction like tuning your aerial, and I could start picking it up. First time, mind you, that anything of the sort had ever happened, long distance messages between us and our dragons, and I was finding it horribly uncomfortable and, you know, *deranging*. We both got out of bed and Martha made coffee, but I kept spilling it, and when I tried to get dressed she had to help me. It took about another hour of shivering and twitching before I could begin to hear it or read it or have a clue about it besides *urg* or whatever you say when someone keeps poking you and the poked place is getting sore. And what it said was: *Coming for you. Be ready.*

Coming for me at the *Institute*? Have I mentioned lately that Bud is eighty feet long (plus tail) and his wingspread is easily three times that? And I may not have impressed on you enough that the Institute is pretty much buried among its trees. The only conceivable place for even a medium-sized dragon to touch down is just inside the gate, and even at that he's going to have to be one hell of a tricky flyer—and Bud isn't medium-sized. But if anybody was going to be a tricky flyer it *would* be Bud. Which was okay as far as it goes. Which wasn't far enough.

I did think briefly about some of the more open spaces on the far side of the gate, but I didn't think of them long. In the first place there aren't any wide-open spaces on the other side of the gate for at least a couple of miles—sure there's a lot of parking lot but it's full of streetlight stanchions (yes, at our front door—but they're really dim and the fence blocks the light) and the row of garages runs down kind of the middle of it, and beyond that was the first (or last) of the motels and the gas stations.

And "letting the genie out of the bottle" didn't begin to cover what letting one of our dragons fly out through the gate would do to our lovely user-friendly new reputation, no matter how good the excuse turned out to be. And while I was sure *I* would see it as the perfect, ultimate, unchallengeable excuse, I couldn't be sure it would translate that way to all the people who only knew anything about Smokehill from reading about it over their coffee in an apartment building where they have to walk three blocks to see a tree, and their idea of "animals" is the Pekingese next door or the goldfish across the hall. And what had happened once could happen again, which had been the only point worth making about the poacher. So it was going to have to be the little squeezy-by-dragon-standards space inside the front gate.

The best thing I could think of to do was tell Dad. He

was, as I keep saying, still the big boss of the Institute. If he said "we have a dragon flying in and we need the space inside the gates *clear*" people had to listen. And he did and they did but it was still a messy business—the first thing tourists do when you tell them it's an emergency is *complain*. Cooperate is way far down on the tourist-response list. You'd think the idea of seeing a flying dragon up close would appeal to them, but their first reaction was that they'd paid their entrance fee and they were going to stay *entered*. Then Dad applied me to the problem like a tourniquet to a wound—or maybe more like a gag—anyway having made the announcement and got the Rangers on shepherding duty (a lot of tourists all moaning together doesn't sound so *unlike* a bunch of baaing sheep) I played the Pied Piper out through the gate and then hung around answering questions while the Rangers rounded up the stragglers.

"Answering questions" is a euphemism for saying "I don't know" a lot punctuated by trying to waffle gracefully. ("Do you really talk to dragons?" for example. You know I *am* going to chicken out of turning this over to a publisher at the last minute.) But the new post-Lois breed of dragon fanatic calms down immediately when I show up, like a chick under a heat lamp, which is useful. So then after I *didn't* answer questions for a while ("*Why* is there a dragon flying in?" "We're just clearing space for everyone's safety") I signed about a million autographs which always makes me feel like such a jerk.

It still took an awful lot of time to get everybody out through the gate. As *would* happen, we had a couple of world-champion whiners that day, as well as an unusually frisky assortment of demon children. It was really tempting to say, "Right, on your buses, you're out of here." But we'd let them back in when Bud had done whatever he was doing (I'd been trying *not* to imagine this) so meanwhile why not let them have the chance of most people's lifetime and see a real live dragon up close and personal? Although the Rangers were ready to deflect any rebel faction. Also, the grumps were right, they *had* paid their entrance fees.

Or you could call it a calculated risk. It's not uncommon for a busload of tourists to see a flying dragon any more, but it's nothing you can count on. But it brings 'em back, hoping to see one, or even hoping to see one again. No matter how hard you're hoping for a puppy for your birthday you don't *know* till that morning and the wobbly box with air holes and ribbons around it going "mmph mmph ooooo" that it's happened. Seeing Bud should be the puppy *and* the triple-chocolate six-layer birthday cake of longed-for surprises. With any luck every one of the tourists standing around in the parking lot would rush back through the gates after and sign up to be life members of our Friends. Including the grumps. Converts are always welcome. We still need as many people to love us as we can get. Dragons are still fashionable right now, but fashions change.

This is also a good example of how we think about our dragons. We weren't worried about how the *dragon* would behave. Especially not after I told Dad it was Bud.

When the last of our solar park buses came out through the gates (they were still slow even now we had money to keep them running properly), I went back inside again and waited on the, er, landing pad, and tried not to chew my fingernails. I've never been a fingernail chewer but it felt like a moment when a brand-new bad habit might be in order. Martha came out to wait with me—tucking her hand under my arm and keeping me from fidgeting myself to pieces—and Dad, and a few of the Rangers, and Eric. The tension level was so high even the premium-class grumblers shut up. Maybe it was sinking in that they were going to *see a dragon.*

I've told you that our fence does weird things to your eyes (this includes standing outside the gates looking in). One of the things it does is make a low heavy cloud cover even lower and heavier. It was cloudy that day. I began to *feel* Bud getting close—feel the *urgency* of him—before anybody could see him. And then when he finally did break through the clouds he seemed already right on top of us. The tourists gasped and one or two of them screamed. Well, think about it: eighty feet is a tennis court plus some extra feet of tail or three tourist buses end to end and now here it is *flying* at you, and among other things, however much we're beginning to learn or guess about the way dragon bones are made so that dragons aren't as heavy as they look, they're still *waaay* too big and heavy to fly—any sane person looking at one could tell you that. Okay, planes fly, and they're even way-er too big, but we all learned about how those stiff wings are built so the air rolls over and under 'em and gives 'em lift. Dragons' wings flap like birds' or bats' wings flap—like the biggest bird (or bat) out of your worst nightmare's wings flap. And the dragon smell comes at you like a spear—I don't know why a *smell* is scary, but it is. So when a dragon is directly over you, well, even if you're me and you're kind of used to it, your medulla oblongata is still telling you "the sky is falling, you're about to die, run like hell."

Bud looked blacker than ever against the blurry, swirly gray background, and the red eyes and threads of red that flicker over some of his scales I'm afraid make him look a little like some evil dragon out of a fairy tale, the kind that eats princesses—and he is a *lot* bigger even than Gulp, and while every one of those tourists may have had a copy of that panorama postcard of Gulp and me clutched in their hot little hands, here it is not only enormously live but EVEN BIGGER. I'm impressed there wasn't more screaming.

And speaking of eating princesses, as he swooped the last little way toward us, he kept turning his head back and forth like he was choosing which princess-substitute he was going to snatch first. For anyone whose brain was still working it probably looked like he was looking for me—the announcement had been that Bud was coming for me, and there I was; maybe the tourists were expecting me to wave—but I knew better. He knew exactly where I was. I wasn't the problem. He was trying to figure out where and how to land. I've said this was the only possible place for him to land—I didn't promise it was *going* to be possible. And when I saw all of him overhead like that ("The sky is falling! You're dead meat!") I thought, "He'll never make it. What do we do now?"—because by now I felt as urgent as he did—I'd sucked up enough of his urgency that I felt all squeaky-stretched like an overinflated balloon, and whatever it was he wanted, I *had* to do it, even if it meant sprouting (smaller) wings myself and flying after him.

I've never seen anything like the way Bud landed. There was *so* not enough room for him. It looked for a minute like he was going to fly straight through the open gate after all—fortunately the tourists were all paralyzed for that minute—and then at the last possible instant, or maybe slightly after that, he reared up, not unlike the super humongous, four-legged version of a bird stalling to land on a branch—and the wind from his wings was *terrific*, and he had all four of those legs thrown out in front of him and you could see the dagger tips of those demolition-grappling-gear claws sparkling in the murky, oppressive light—and as he landed, he *threw* himself backward, just to stay in place, and it was like a tornado and an earthquake all at once, plus the massive *boom* of those wings, which he *whipped* together with a noise like thunder: and even so he was all kind of piled up on himself because there wasn't ROOM.

I felt Martha kiss my cheek and her hand briefly in the small of my back as I bolted away from her, into the hurricane and the thunder and the earthquake and the claws, because Bud was saying *now now NOW NOW* and he hadn't actually finished landing, or perching, or settling on his tail like an old-fashioned rocketship, and he curled his neck down toward me as I ran as fast as my little short human legs could carry me toward him. He curled his lip at me and I just about got the message so that when he opened his mouth just wide enough I already had a foot on his lip and was groping for purchase with one hand—I've said that dragon teeth are wide-spaced. Well, I have to say they're not quite wide-spaced *enough* when you're throwing yourself between them, and it was *not* at all comfortable as I belly flopped into his mouth—what do you call it when you don't impale yourself on the points but get stuck *between* the uprights, like someone falling into a spiked fence? That's what happened to me. I had aimed toward the front as his mouth opened, simply because that was the end nearest the ground, but since he then promptly closed his jaws *over* me I was just as glad that I wasn't back nearer the hinge where he'd have to concentrate more not to squash me.

It must have looked pretty, uh, peculiar. I knew Dad and Martha and our lot wouldn't be worried—a little taken aback maybe, but not really worried—Martha told me later there was a lot more screaming at that point (even if I wasn't a princess or a virgin and furthermore had obviously gone willingly, which your average evil villain dragon type presumably wouldn't have found nearly so much fun) but that may have been Bud's takeoff: I couldn't see it, obviously, but I could *feel* it. I imagine the laws of physics would tell me that he'd've lost all his momentum even by landing long enough to pick me up, which probably took about a minute, but from where I was lying, he sprang back into the air again because he *hadn't* lost all that momentum. He flung his head back—so it's a good thing he had closed his mouth again— gently—although some of his side teeth had little low crags on the inside like vestigial premolars or something, and I could get a grip on these with my hands.

And I felt—facedown in the dark of his hot resiny-organic-fire-smelling mouth—every muscle in his body slamming down against the earth while his wings unfurled and unfurled and *unfurled* till I imagined them stretching across all of Smokehill to the Bonelands and then clapped forward to scoop the air violently out of the way so we could just *dive* upward—you know all those stories about all the mega-Gs pressing the fearless astronauts into their padded flight seats on takeoff, speaking of old-fashioned rockets that sit upright on their tails . . . well, I swear I had all those Gs and I can sure swear I didn't have a padded flight seat. I felt like all my brains were about to be shoved out through my face, and my heart would punch a hole through my breastbone in a few seconds. The middle of me was pretty well held together by large teeth, but then there were my legs, that were simply going to come off and get left behind.

And then we were airborne. I felt him level off and he parted his jaws again ever so slightly, and I, trying not to be any more absolutely clumsy than I had to be under the rather awkward circumstances, dragged my heavy, stiff, semi-detached legs the rest of the way into his mouth. This was not a hugely fun process. Bud, big as he is, still had to counter-balance my heavings and floppings and I was way too aware of how far down the ground was as Bud twitched his head and sideslipped. It's not at all drooly, a dragon's mouth. A bit damp, but it's more like what you might call humid, because it's so hot. A sort of jungle experience, only without the vines and the monkeys (and the poisonous snakes and spiders and whatever). I managed to lay myself down along one side, be-tween teeth and jawbone, like an extra-large plug of chewing tobacco, and I won't say it was comfortable including for Bud (chewing tobacco doesn't kick and thrash), but it could have been worse.

It was a long flight. He set down only once, after only about half an hour or so, near a stream where we could both have a drink; and then I climbed up his shoulder and neck and lay down in that hollow at the base of the skull, and the space there on Bud was a lot more comfortable for me at my runty but inconvenient human size than the space on Gulp was, I don't know if it was from being bigger or being male, or maybe I was just more used to riding dragons by then (al-though in fact I *don't* ride dragons, barring emergency) but I half curled up and half went to sleep. I didn't even get cold, although it was cold, and the breath from Bud's nostrils was steaming like a (very large) teakettle.

But even though I was dozing I was aware that we just kept going on and on and on—the sky cleared in time to see the sun finish setting and then the moon rose, a blazing big full moon, and then it rose up farther and over us, and the stars wheeled along with it, and still Bud was flying, no *rac-ing*, over the landscape. Whatever I've pretended to under-stand about the laws of physics, I doubt that they're all suspended for the flight of dragons, and I imagine something Bud's size, to keep flying at all, has to fly at some speed. But it was more than that. Bud was pouring it on. The thrust—the *bang*—forward of each downbeat of those enormous wings had an almost audible *THUNK* about it, like feet hitting pavement; when I peered ahead the wind clawed at my eyes. We were on our way to whatever we were on our way toward as fast as Bud could take us. Which is why, I imagine, it was Bud himself who came for me. Although I would have had trouble throwing myself into the mouth of almost any other dragon.

When I raised my head and looked forward (eyes watering in the gale) I could just see Bud's head, an outline of a craggy red-flecked moving blackness in the surrounding smooth moonlit gray. We were out over the Bonelands by now—pretty well nothing as far as you could see in any direction except rock and shadows. Bud's blistering urgency, which had settled to a kind of intense dull roar once we'd started, came back again, like spikes of flame surging up out of banked embers. The moon was getting low and dawn wasn't too far off—and I picked up that we had to get there, wherever there was, before the moon set, and it was like suddenly Bud kicked into some final burst of overdrive and my scalp was getting peeled off, the seams on my clothes were going to part any minute, and I wasn't just curled up and dozing any more, I was hanging on for dear life.

At last we slowed and banked and began to come down. I couldn't see what we were coming to, and for a moment I didn't care, because I'd been wondering just how much this flight had taken out of Bud, and as he tried to organize himself for landing in a space that had plenty of room even for an eighty-plus-foot dragon, I realized just how exhausted he was. His wings would barely hold him—us—and he juddered and jerked like a plane running out of fuel, and when he landed he landed like a wrecking ball, and the Boneland dust whirlpooled up around us. I'd been pretty well dug in where I was, and I bounced, and my neck was probably going to hurt a lot pretty soon, but I was still clinging on.

Bud—? I said, frightened.

Go, he said. *Go.* There was more to it—I assume it was something about "I'm okay don't worry about me," and his voice, or his signal, or his space, still sounded like Bud, and if this urgency to get me here was something he was willing to half kill himself to make happen, the least I could do was whatever he'd brought me here for.

I climbed down, and a dragon I knew slightly, Opal (Ooooo*aaaaaa*llllll), was right there, fairly dancing with impatience, and I looked at her, and looked at Bud, and they both pointed their noses in the same direction, so I went thataway. Thataway was a lump of black rock sticking up out of the desert flatness of the Bonelands; the kind of lump of rock that makes you think "caves," which the Bonelands are, by reputation, full of, although us humans don't know much about them, bar the little that a few fool-hardy speleologists have mapped. I could feel that I was going toward dragons before I could see them . . . and then I could feel Gulp . . . and then Lois . . . and there were at least three more, dragons I didn't know so well, like I didn't know Opal.

Lois came running out toward me, silvery-coppery in the moonlight, and I was getting off her something I'd never had before, and if I'd been able to make sense out of any dragon it should have been her, but again, all I could pick out of it was URGENT URGENT URGENT NOW NOW NOW. She chased after me like a sheepdog, but I was half walking and half trotting as fast as I could, and all my bones ached. It had been a lot harder on Bud, but I was near the end of my pathetic human strength too, stiff and bruised with it, and half stunned with sleeplessness.

When Gulp raised her head I could finally make her out from among the weird shadows. Some of my slowness to take it all in was just how tired I was. There was enough moonlight, now that I *saw* what I was looking at, to see that she was . . . orange and maroon and crimson. And I at last realized, although they must all have been trying to tell me, that I'd been brought to witness Gulp's babies being born: and

I broke into a shambling run. I didn't know anything about moonset, I didn't know anything about anything, but I finally had a clue. . . .

A whole lot of sad and overwhelming stuff spilled out of me from the last time I'd seen a mom dragon and her babies, and as it went a whole lot of lovely warm *live* dragon stuff came pouring in . . . like that what I'd been guessing about the "midwives" wasn't quite right: Mom knows how many babies she's got, and chooses an escort for each one— almost like a godparent sort of thing—to help each tiny little dragon droplet from her womb to her pouch. Usually the escorts are all female, although sometimes Dad is invited to be the last one. Dad had been invited. That was Bud. And Bud said, I think it should be Jake. And Gulp said, Great, I thought of that, but it seemed a little way out there, even for us, but it's the next step, isn't it? And Bud said yes—or something like that, I don't know what they *said*.

Lois was there because *she* was an escort.

Gulp had six dragonlets—and I could *feel* these tiny soft glowing blobs in my—I have no idea my what—somewhere. Somehow. Faint and fragile but *there*. They were a kind of orangy maroony themselves. They were . . . like coming from somewhere and going to somewhere, and I'm not sure I just mean from one piece of Mom to another. But it was almost like someone—Gulp?—had me by the elbow (the dragon-head-space elbow equivalent) and was saying, Here, look right *here*. Otherwise it would have been kind of a huge stupendous glittery fireworks display and I'd've just kind of stood there going, Uh, wow.

Five of the dragonlets were already in her pouch.

The moon, I swear, paused and *hovered* while for the second time in my life I picked up a smudgy, wet, blobby, just-born dragonlet, and felt its little stumpy legs moving vaguely against my hand . . . but I knew the difference at once, and grieved all over again for Lois and her mom and her dead siblings, because this one wasn't confused or bewildered or terrified, it was just waiting for the next thing to happen; it was borne up comfortably by what was supposed to happen, even if it was happening a little slower than it was expecting, and I imagine my hands didn't feel a whole lot like whatever a *dragon* dragon escort does. I don't know if *I* was being borne up too—like someone helping me "see" the six dragonlets—or whether any fool, having got that far, could see what to do, but the slit in Gulp's belly that was the opening to her pouch was perfectly obvious, and Gulp had curled herself around and stretched out a foreleg so her last, pygmy dragonlet-escort could scramble up it (cradling a sticky dragonlet against his own permanently-scarred-from-previous-dragonlet-experience belly) and reach far enough.

The dragonlet—*my* dragonlet—was a very specific orange and maroon blob in my mind's eye/somewhere/whatever even though the little thing in my hand was only a bulky shadow—surprisingly heavy for its size the way almost all baby things are—could I just see an edge of that bruise-purple color that poor Lois had been? Or did dragonlets only turn that color if they were living down someone's shirtfront and eating deer broth?

It was already hot. So if this was the time when baby fire-stomachs get lit up, at least the escort isn't expected to do it. Not this escort anyway.

I put the blob at the lip of the pouch and made sure it got in it, and then stumbled down the foreleg and leaned against Gulp—and watched a lot of shards of memory and grief and fear toppling and tumbling over one another, some of them bursting like sparklers and spinning like Catherine wheels. Lois came and pressed herself against me like she was remembering too.

And—snicker if you want, I don't care—I talked to Lois' mom, *talked* to her, to Halcyon—and she told me that yes there had been some doubt about the keeping-the-human-up-there part of the Lois-and-Jake high-wire act (let's try a parasol for balance but I don't think he's ever going to be ready for the unicycle): I hadn't been so far wrong, guessing that being only fourteen when it happened and still a bit squishy myself was part of what made it possible, and even so it was only *just maybe* possible. Halcyon had like watched my brain *shimmy* with the headaches—but the, um, markers she'd left (remember "shouldering aside your gray matter and putting up signposts for other travelers, *eeeeek*") had given Bud somewhere to start—and some warning about human fragility. She'd worried about the burns too; even young healthy fourteen-year-old human skin is eventually going to get tired of being reburned all the time and refuse to heal. It was maybe true, what I'd said to Eleanor, that you get used to it. But some of it was Halcyon, who was unhappy she hadn't been able to do it better, that I still had headaches, that the "eczema" had left scars. I could feel her worry and her care, and hey, moms are moms, however many pairs of limbs they have. And she'd been all alone, really alone, much more alone than I'd been.

All this so that there would be some future for dragons after all, and there *was* some future, because Lois and I— and Halcyon—and Gulp and Bud and Dad and Martha and the rest of us on both sides—were *making* it.

Halcyon was talking to Lois too—I could feel *that*—but I don't know what she said. Some of what she said was the same as what she'd said to me, I guess, but she'd've been saying it differently. What I could feel was Lois shivering like a frightened puppy—Lois had never shivered in her life that I knew of—and I put my arms around her neck (although I couldn't reach the whole way around any more), thinking, Halcyon had a choice. It was a horrible choice— she's the one who died, who knew she was going to die—but she did make it. She was a grown-up, and she *decided*. I was only fourteen, but I'd had the life I'd had, including that if there was a live baby orphan anything I *had* to try to keep it alive (and that I was nuts in this case enough *to* try)—but I was still old enough to make a choice, and I made *that* choice—that impossible choice—and while I've already moaned and whimpered about how the loss of my own mom had kind of removed the "choice" part of my choice—I was still, you know, *responsible*, and I still made it.

But poor Lois had never had any choice at all. Or not much of one. She'd chosen to stay alive. She'd fought like anything to stay alive—and her mom and me may have been helping her as much as we could—but she was sure in there herself, struggling like gosh-damn-and-wow to keep breathing. And then again . . . if you're going to believe me about Halcyon, then maybe it's not such an enormous leap of credibility or imagination or hope or what you like, to think that maybe Lois did have a choice. When the souls were all lined up that day in the recycling center, the head angel came in and rapped on the desk to make everybody pay attention and said, Okay, gang, we need a volunteer, and explained what the volunteer was going to have to do. There'd have been dead silence for a minute, maybe, and then the Lois-soul put its hand-equivalent up and said, Yeah, okay, me, I'll do it. . . .

I hope Lois' siblings all got a good go next time round. A real life. An adventure or two. True love. Whatever.

Whatever else a dragonlet escort is maybe supposed to do, I hope some of it got sucked out of my strangely shaped wrong species (and as you might say nontraditional gender) self because after the sixth blob went to join its brothers and sisters in Gulp's pouch and Lois and I had our "conversation" with Halcyon I literally fell down where I stood and slept. (And felt ninety years old and *arthritic* when I woke up.) But Bud and Gulp must've been braced for Jake getting most things wrong when they decided to have me there.

I've told you that you pick up dragon stuff when you're sleeping that you can't when you're awake. I probably soaked up more in that one short sleep than I had in all the years before, and while I damned *forgot* most of it again when I woke up, like you forget most of your dreams, still, something changed. I don't pick up "words" any better than I ever did—nothing I can revolutionize my dictionary with, unfortunately—but my brain has learned how to handle dragon space!!! It's like there's a whole new lobe grown on my brain: the dragon lobe. It CAN be done! *Even the headaches are better!!!* Wow. I mean, *wow.* I hadn't even realized how gruesomely awful the headaches—the Headaches—have been the last seven years—*seven years*—almost EIGHT—till they lightened up. They're still there. But they're easier. Martha says she doesn't feel like she needs to use a hammer when she tries to rub the tension out of my neck and shoulders any more.

I think Gulp's babies were early. Even as unborn pre-blobs they're already countable individuals to their mom—but neither mom nor blobs, I think, have a reliable sense of when they're going to be born, any more than human moms do. And so I think that's why they didn't have me on tap, so to speak, at Dragon Central, where it would have been a comparatively short hop for a flying dragon to take me to the birth place in the Bonelands. Mind you, I have no idea how they would have convinced me to stick around—I guarantee I would *not* have understood "Hey, Jake, wanna be escort to one of Gulp's babies?"—but they'd've thought of something. They could always have just got in the way. What would I have done? Forced past them? Playing tag with a dragon just doesn't appeal much.

I'd wanted to walk back, that morning in the Bonelands after I woke up, but I was staggering and kind of crazy, and still full of the dreams I was half forgetting and that were half turning into a new part of me, which is maybe why I was staggering and kind of crazy. (Kind of crazy includes that I was two or three hours of a big dragon flying full pelt *into* the Bonelands and the nearest good water supply was back *out* of them again, and I wanted to *walk*.) Anyway the dragons wouldn't let me walk anywhere. They'd brought Bud like six sheep to help him recuperate, and he'd specially char-grilled a piece for me, and we lay around like we were on holiday for a couple of days—all eight of us (fourteen if you count the tucked-away blobs)—and then he flew me back to Dragon Central. We all went together in little hops, because Lois couldn't fly very far yet. Let me tell you flying in a *troop* of dragons (a squadron, just like the game) is even more amazing than *anything.* Life. The universe. Everything. And Gulp looked . . . I don't know how to describe it. Transcendent.

But I had had a look at the front part of the caves—where we all went as soon as the sun got high—and with my new dragon-sense I got a promise (which is like putting your hand into your empty pocket and finding that someone has slipped you something, money or chocolate or a magic ring) that I'd be brought back to the birth place in the Bonelands from Dragon Central some time. Because I think that is *the* Birth Place—and you remember what I said about the Dragon Central caves, how it's like the rock itself had become *dragony*—it's like that only way more so at the birth place. At the birth place you *know* the stones can talk to you. Now if only I could learn the language.

I'm also no longer sure about *mom* and *dad* in dragon terms. I'm not sure but what it's some kind of marsupial kibbutz, in those pouches, and that while maybe Gulp and Bud contributed some of the eggs and sperm—assuming it's even an egg-and-sperm deal, which I don't know either—they may not have contributed all of them. Put it on the list of stuff to try and find out. Including whether the kibbutz thing might have something to do with getting 'em started on how dragon communication works. Maybe the birth place will tell me.

One more thing that I did learn is that having your dragonlets born during a full moon is maybe the best good luck omen there is. Dragon moms start doing whatever the dragon equivalent is of "star light star bright first star I've seen tonight" as moons get full toward the ends of their pregnancies. Are dragons superstitious? Beats me. Do dragons actually have an oar in the ethereal what-have-you so that wishing on stars (or whatever) actually has an influence? Beats me too. But it won't surprise you if I tell you I think dragons are capable of almost *anything*. And if you want to think that I say "good luck omen" because *I'm* superstitious and that's not what the dragons were telling me at all, that's your privilege. But my version is that it would have been a very bad omen if Gulp's last baby had missed—had got into the pouch after moonset, when the only thing touching its gummy little hide was darkness and clueless human hands.

So at least Lois had had something going for her.

Oh yes, and what did we say when everyone wanted to know why the big black dragon had come booming in for Jake? What was that all about? We *waffled*. Oh, my, how we waffled. Now that we've been kind of winning for a while (and there's even money in the bank, we've NEVER had money in the bank before) Dad's developed quite a flair for waffling. (I'm still a lousy waffler, so I just disappeared.) Katie's really good at it too—she's always been a gift to the business admin side, and she's done more and more of the Interface with Outsiders stuff since Mom died—and she got him started on waffling as a fine art (as opposed to his natural style of thumping and roaring). Katie's weakness is being too nice, which has never been one of Dad's problems.

So you're reading it here for the first time, about Gulp's babies. The publisher who thinks they're going to get this—although they haven't actually read it yet, so who knows—have already been sworn to ninety-six jillion kinds of secrecy, with sub clauses about underlings being chained to their desks with no internet access till pub date, etc. And even if it does get out, it doesn't really matter. I hope. Our security nowadays makes your average bank vault look like a wet paper bag, and a lot of the Dragon Squadron money has gone on the fence—which at this point probably would hold up against a bomb or two. I wish I knew whether I should be glad about that or not.

It was about two months after this, after Gulp's babies were born, that Martha told me *she* was pregnant.

There should be a very large white space here on the page . . . because I don't care how much else has happened to you in your life and how many unique things you've been a part of and how many endangered species you've rescued and how many laws of science and biology you've personally exploded . . . there's *nothing like* the prospect of your own first child for making your life turn over and start becoming something else.

. . . And it got worse fast. First Martha said that she was going to spend as much time at Nearcamp and Dragon Central as she could—which is to say as much of the headaches as she could stand—which I understood but didn't want her torturing herself *and* who knew if this would mean the baby was busy adapting and wouldn't have to have dragon headaches or whether it would just start having the headache before it was born, which seemed pretty rough. Martha said no, she'd be able to tell if the baby was unhappy. I'd've (nervously) said okay to that one . . . till she said she wanted to *have* it at Dragon Central, I mean, *born* there. She said that if she had a totally free hand she'd have it at the birth place in the Bonelands, if the dragons would allow it—and when I started bouncing up to the ceiling and making holes in it with my head she said, Jake, calm *down*, Dragon Central was good enough.

And I said something like GOOD ENOUGH??? And the conversation went on like that for a while. Her point was that birth *was* a big deal (. . . duh . . .), and that Gulp's dragonlets' birth that I'd been able to be a part of had changed me profoundly and made my connection to the/my dragons so much stronger and the least we could do was try to return the favor. And I was damned out of my own mouth because I'd told her about this. And I could see her point but I couldn't stop gobbling about "safety" and "if something went wrong" and so on.

We were still arguing and in fact we had *so* not come to any conclusions or even any working hypotheses that we hadn't told anybody, not even Dad and Katie, yet, when Dad and Katie came to *us* and said that, uh, well, they'd decided to get married.

"Oh, that's *great*! That's *wonderful*!" Martha said, and grabbed her mother and swung her around in an impromptu tango. And I hugged my dad, and he hugged me back, which is absolutely the dragons' fault, all that sticking my hand (or more) in dragons' mouths and learning to see/hear/read the atmosphere and all that group-bond stuff with dragons and so on, I've got so touchy-feely with my human friends it's probably pretty repulsive, but they put up with it, probably partly because to the extent that they hang out with dragons it's happening to them too, which certainly includes my dad. So we actually hugged each other pretty well.

It's been this hilariously open secret that Dad and Katie have been together for, I don't know, *years* now. Eleanor, before she went off to boarding school last year (she's got accepted on some kind of Eleanor-invented fast track and is going to be a lawyer by the time she's seventeen or something: it may not take till she's fifty to become president), asked them why they didn't just get married and get it over with? Or at least move in together. Poor Eleanor—if "poor" and "Eleanor" can ever be combined—had the worst of it. She'd got Martha and me out of her hair but here was her mom still hopelessly soppy and silly with my dad—and pretending it didn't *show*.

"They just told me that it was their business and not mine," she said disgustedly to Martha and me. "*You* see if you can do anything with them while I'm gone. I don't get it—all those secrets when Lois was a baby, you'd think they'd be glad *not* to have a secret that they don't, you know, *have* to have." (I'm hoping Eleanor will keep this attitude. Think of it: a president whose default position is *not* "whatever we do we don't tell the voters." Can the country stand it? Stay tuned.)

So this was terrific news. We were still celebrating, and Martha had got out the cranberry juice to put in the champagne glasses because she wasn't drinking because of the baby, but since it was the middle of the afternoon we thought maybe no one would think about it being cranberry juice, and it's not like we had a bottle of champagne in the refrigerator waiting for a major announcement either. But we'd just made the first toast when Martha said, "So, okay, is there a reason you've finally decided to get married now and not two or three years ago?"

And the two of them looked at each other as guiltily and sheepishly as, well, teenagers, and then Dad said, "Well—Katie—"

And Katie said, "I'm pregnant," at exactly the same moment as Martha said, *"You're pregnant,"* and then Martha and I started laughing and couldn't stop, and Dad and Katie were obviously relieved, but they were also a bit puzzled till Martha finally gasped out, "So am I!"

So then the fun really began because Martha told Katie about her idea about the birth at Dragon Central and Katie thought it was a *great* idea and wanted to do the same, and then Dad started behaving in a way that made the way I'd been behaving look *restrained*, which isn't entirely surprising because while Katie was completely healthy and had popped out her two previous daughters with no particular effort and from what she said less drama than most women have to put in, she was now forty-six and so automatically on all the high-risk lists, and Dad *wasn't having any*. She'd have that baby in a hospital like a normal twenty-first-century first-world woman, and *there was no argument*.

Oh yes there was an argument. Martha and I were so fascinated we almost forgot to keep arguing ourselves. So pretty much within a day or two all of Smokehill knew that (a) Dad and Katie were getting married, (b) Katie was pregnant, (c) Martha was pregnant, (d) Katie and Martha wanted to have their babies at Dragon Central, (e) and the dads concerned were AGAINST this. Soap opera with dragons? You never saw anything like it.

I don't know how Dad really felt—we didn't dare talk about it, we might implode and there'd be a black sucking hole into a parallel universe where two generations of Mendoza men used to be—but he never said *This is all YOUR fault* although he must have thought it. *I* thought it. I could almost have done the black hole thing alone. *Of course* our baby should be born with dragons around. It was the obvious *right* thing to happen. And it was mean and horrible and two-faced and disloyal and *treacherous* of me to be trying to make something else happen instead.

But how could we risk it? (What had Gulp been risking? Was the sixth blob—was *my* dragonlet dangerously tainted or weakened by its contact with me?) And Katie was part of my family no matter whose sibling her new kid was going to be. But the dragons were a part of my family too, and the ties were . . . they weren't even unbreakable. They weren't even *ties*. They were a part of ME like my ear or my pancreas was a part of me. Like Martha was a part of me. The way the question kept presenting itself to me was, *Who was I going to betray?*

It was nearly getting to the point that the newlyweds and the almost-newlyweds weren't on speaking terms which would have been funny if it hadn't been us. And then Grace said softly into one of those dinner conversations that were only not getting loud and nasty through *violent* self-control of parties concerned, "Jamie married a midwife, you know."

Dead silence.

"Sadie's a midwife?" I said finally.

"You could see what she says—ask her advice."

What she said, of course, was "You're all *nuts*." But she still agreed to fly out and talk to us in person. Which was amazingly nice of her. Although I had the impression she hadn't decided whether to laugh or to bring a cattle prod to keep us at a safe distance. Maybe both. She'd only ever met any of us once, four years ago, on their way from Boston where they got married to their honeymoon in Hawaii—and they'd stayed here in Jamie's old bedroom, which was still a bit redolent of Lois despite a fresh paint job in the bride's honor. So she had a *little* idea of what she was getting into, and she came anyway.

It was my idea to take her straight out to Farcamp and Dragon Central and let her meet, uh, some dragons. Everyone else was still saying "hello." I was like at the end of my tether and starting to get rope burns.

She looked from face to face and said hesitantly, "Farcamp?"

I said, "Farcamp is where the humans stay when we want

to spend time with the dragons. Dragon—er—Central is—
er—next door."

She blinked maybe twice and said, "Okay."

But I knew that as soon as we all went to Dragon Central
and I actually tried to tell *my* dragons what was going on, or
at least finally let them pick up what I'd been trying to hide,
they'd have to know how much I both did and *didn't*
want. . . . My stomach hurt. The old scars throbbed, and the
inside felt like someone had tried to light me up, mistaking
me for a dragonlet with an *igniventator.*

Sadie didn't disintegrate nearly as much as most people
and she pulled herself together really fast. Maybe it's the
midwife training. Which isn't to say she didn't have a rough
time. Everyone does. She shook like a leaf and Martha had
to hold her up when she saw her first dragon—lying just
outside the cave mouth of Dragon Central. She—Valerie
(Vhaaaaaahhhh r*eeeeee*)—recognized Sadie as a new human and raised her head only a very little and very slowly,
and didn't move the rest of herself at all, at first, till Sadie
stopped clinging to Martha and at least half stood on her
own feet again. And then Valerie unwound that long neck,
which is one of the things dragons do, you're even *used* to
how big they are, and then it's like that day Bud came to
fetch me when his wings seemed to unfurl hundreds of
miles: when they stretch their necks out toward you the neck
goes on and on and *on* like the yellow brick road and however many times you've seen it you're briefly not sure if
there's maybe a wicked witch involved this time after all.

Valerie brought her head about ten feet from us and Sadie
gallantly held her ground. I went up to human-arm's length
of her—it's no wonder I'm always surprised how big I am
with other humans because I'm so used to being bug-sized
next to a dragon—and she lifted her lip in what was now
standard-dragon invitation to known-human-friend for a
chat, and I put my hand there and she said something like,
Hmmmm? which meant, more or less, *A new one, huh?* and
I said yes, and Valerie said something like, *And there's a*

purpose to this one, a different purpose, a new purpose? and I rubbed my hand over my face in the basic human "arrrgh" gesture and said something like zlk09&dflj;kgo*&^vx +iueaiiiimmbjdcudpf!!!! because this was so way beyond my powers of communication, and Valerie "laughed" and said, *You'd better talk to Bud.* (I don't know how the dragons managed to pick up what I call him, but I knew the dragon "word"—the tiny mind-spasm—they used to name him to me wasn't his dragon name, and it *felt* like Bud . . . but that's more stuff I can't explain. They call Gulp Gulp to me too, and Lois I think *is* Lois, even in Dragonese.)

The two of us other humans each had a hand under one of poor Sadie's arms and we were both saying, Look, are you sure you're okay, you don't have to do this, you don't have to stay. It's hard on us old-timers too, watching a newbie go through the initiation hazing and of course in this case we felt guilty because it wasn't her idea, we'd asked her to come. But she was saying, No, this is fascinating, this is amazing, don't you dare take me away, wow, I never imagined. . . .

We got her down the long first tunnel and into the hearth-room, and she met Bud and Gulp and Lois. She had to sit down—there are a couple of decent human-chair-sized rocks near the hearth, with hollows where your bottom goes, full of shed scales: I had a furniture-moving party with a couple of dragons a while back—but even though she was a little floppy her eyes were obviously focusing as she looked around, and she didn't throw up or pass out or anything, which, trust me, is *very good* for a first timer. Martha did the out-loud version of why we were there with the hand gestures, which was as much for Sadie's benefit (yes we *do* talk to them, the rumors are true) and then I put my hand inside Bud's lip and tried not to *shriek* at him, and he did the dragon equivalent of murmuring "there, there" and the funny thing is I actually *did* feel a little comforted.

It sort of seeped in, the "there, there"—like the answer-feeling, like trying to find out the dragon word for "rock." It was like the misery was a specific quantity, like forty bales of hay, and someone had coolly backed in with a large truck and smuggled thirty of them away. When I looked at Martha she was wearing the same fragile haven't-smiled-in-a-long-time smile that I could feel on my face.

Sadie went really quiet when we got back to Farcamp though and I made coffee and offered the aspirin and thought about feeling better, and Martha held Sadie's hands like you might a lost little girl's (while the person at the info booth puts out an all-points for Mom and Dad over the loud-speaker). You could see Sadie kind of coming back to her-self but the first thing she said was, "Light. We're going to have to do something about having enough *light*." And the second thing she said was, "You're going to have to give me a job, you know, if this gets out, they'll have my license off me so fast it'll leave tread marks."

Martha managed *not* to look at me triumphantly, but I said, or rather squeaked, "What if something goes wrong?" Sadie barely glanced at me—she was deep in thoughts of practical planning—and said, "Have a helicopter standing by, of course. You don't have to tell it what it's standing by for, do you?" Which in the new Smokehill was true, we didn't have to. We hadn't told the pilot why we were taking Sadie out here, for example. Mostly we still make every-body go the old slow route, including ourselves. But as soon as Martha got too big to make the hike she'd need the helicopter to get out here anyway. Anyone not on the Smoke-hill grapevine would assume it would whisk her *away* if she went into labor. Avoiding the question of why she'd want to be joggling around in a chopper going to Farcamp at all.

"It's still a long flight to the Wilsonville hospital—longer to Cheyenne," I said, failing to be reassured.

Sadie came back from wherever she was, and paid atten-tion when she looked at me. "Yes. But I can minimize the risks as much as anyone outside a big hospital and all its equipment can. And after that, Jake, I'm sorry, but you have to make the choice."

I looked at Martha, but I already knew I'd lost. I didn't

like it but in the end I believed Martha's vote counted more than mine.

So that was that. But do I think Bud . . . yeah, yeah, I *would* think Bud did something. But . . . once you're kind of used to answer-feelings, to getting your answer as a kind of slow leak . . . once the headaches have softened you up and made you spongy, so you can soak up all kinds of stuff, like pancakes in maple syrup (which is the *nicest* image I can think of, since spongy doesn't sound too great), I don't know . . . but I don't know how I let it go, even if I did think Martha's vote counted more. Justice and fairness don't mean *shit* when you're in love and scared to death. And I knew Martha wasn't dumb enough not to be worried. But I've told you why I named Bud Bud in the first place. He does kind of have that effect. Maybe Martha and I should have gone out there first thing and told him all about it at the beginning.

And once Martha had won there was no stopping Katie. Bud *has* to have done something to Dad. Dad *never* gives up, once he's made up his mind.

And then, about five weeks before Martha was due and nine weeks before Katie was, Gulp's babies made their first public appearances. I'd walked past Zenobia on door duty at Dragon Central and even my stupid thick human radar could pick up the excitement, but I didn't know what it was about till I rounded the corner into the big hearth-space and there were six small greenish and blackish blobs making slow lurching forays over the more-or-less level floor to one side of the fire—they're so (comparatively) small still at that age that it takes a lot of dragons staring at them to make you realize they're not just odd fire shadows, which is your first thought, but in that case why are all the dragons staring—? *Oh.* . . . Gulp had made herself into a half-crescent and the open side was toward me. Lois was a rusty-pink gleam beside her, and I realized one of the blobs was sitting between her forefeet. Which is when I figured out what they were.

I stopped dead when I first caught sight of the whole

scene, and then really couldn't move a second later when I realized what it was I was seeing. At about the time that I was going to sit down on the ground and make dopey chirping noises at them the way you might a litter of puppies, one of them peeled off and came straight up to me. I'm embarrassed to say that I no longer knew which blob it was I'd picked up at the end of that long bumpy weary terrifyingly thrilling windblown night, but he sure knew who it was had done the picking up of *him*. I did know he was a he, the way I'd known Lois was a she, and I knew why he'd come up to me once he had . . . well, because I knew.

As I started to kneel down to him it was like I could see the setting moon in his little red eyes, and for a moment I wasn't standing in the hearth-space of Dragon Central, but outdoors in the Bonelands, and there was a cold gritty wind blowing, and then I wasn't there either but standing by a dying dragon near Pine Tor. . . . If I learn a word for that knowing, I'll put it in the dictionary. And with what he's going to grow up to add to the conversation between dragons and humans, that dictionary may eventually be really worth having after all. Then I sat down and he hoicked into my lap, *so* like the way Lois used to, and I could feel the new little blob in my head that was *this* dragon, this dragonlet. And he said *Rrrrrrrr*eeep. I mean, he said it, out loud, the way Lois used to. Dictionary here we come.

We're going to *do* this, you know? This cross-species communication thing. We really are.

Well, you've had the baby dragons, and now I'll give you the baby humans, and then I'm out of here. But like I said at the beginning—the real beginning, not just this epilogue—there's some stuff I'm just not going to tell you. No way. Watching Martha's and my baby get born is one of those things. No, there weren't any complications, and Martha was in labor only about six hours, which everybody keeps telling me is short, but it didn't feel short at the time. Sadie was brilliant. The dragons were brilliant. Martha was the most brilliant of all. And it happened all over again for Katie, and the look on Dad's face. . . . And we're all really happy, okay? This *is* the happy-ending part—I just hope it continues, like through the next book, since I think I'm going to have to write another one, and maybe a next one after that. . . . But life is just so *amazing*, and when you think it can't get any more amazing it does, like when you hold your own baby for the first time, the world just stops, and you hang there in the very absolute center of the universe, and never mind Galileo and Newton and all those spoilsport *scientists*, you and your baby *are the center of the universe* for just that moment. And everything changes. And that's the way it's supposed to be, or it wouldn't be that way.

Us humans have sure messed up a lot of stuff but we haven't quite finished the job so maybe we can still *un*mess it a little. Maybe with some help from dragons. And Eleanor as president. Maybe in time for our babies to grow up into a slightly less comprehensively messed-up world. And, forgive my Latin, I can't help myself, but I hope I've got the subjunctive right:

Madeline Sophia Mendoza
born 11 April, 4:25 A.M.
at Dragon Central
seven pounds six ounces

Donato Francis Mendoza
born 6 May, 5:10 P.M.
at Dragon Central
eight pounds nine ounces

Arcadiae vias peregrinentur

ROBIN MCKINLEY has won many awards, including the Newbery Medal for *The Hero and the Crown*, a Newbery Honor for *The Blue Sword*, and the Mythopoeic Award for Adult Literature for *Sunshine*. She lives in England with her husband, author Peter Dickinson, two hellhounds, an 1897 Steinway upright, increasing numbers of rose bushes, and a stone's throw from her change-ringing bell tower.

Her blog is http://robinmckinleysblog.com and her website is http://robinmckinley.com.

BEAUTY CAN TRANSFORM ANYTHING—
EVEN THE HEART OF A BEAST...

ROSE DAUGHTER

by
Robin McKinley

National Bestselling Author of *Sunshine*
and *The Blue Sword*

"A beautiful retelling of *Beauty and the Beast*...
The language is compelling."

—Rambles.net

"Every sentence and every occurrence
seems infused by magic."

—*Fantasy & Science Fiction*

penguin.com

THE ULTIMATE IN FANTASY!

From magical tales of distant worlds to stories of those with abilities beyond the ordinary, Ace and Roc have everything you need to stretch your imagination to its limits.

Marion Zimmer Bradley/Diana L. Paxson

Guy Gavriel Kay

Dennis L. McKiernan

Patricia A. McKillip

Robin McKinley

Sharon Shinn

Katherine Kurtz

Barb and J. C. Hendee

Elizabeth Bear

T. A. Barron

Brian Jacques

Robert Asprin

penguin.com